STRAN...

Flinx found himself suddenly staring into near darkness with only the light of one of Alaspin's two moons casting shadows through the room. After a while he could see shapes moving against the far wall. A figure bent low over Clarity's bed, extending a canister before it. Abruptly it halted as something appeared between it and the sleeping woman. Something small, superfast, and hissing.

The man let out a startled oath and stumbled backward. It was enough to stir Clarity. One of the figures spoke quickly and intently.

"Stun the animal and then her. Now!"

The figure holding the cannister raised it and moved a thumb over the firing stud, which he never had time to press.

The minidrag's poison hit the intruder squarely in the eyes.

By Alan Dean Foster
Published by Ballantine Books:

THE BLACK HOLE
CACHALOT
DARK STAR
THE METROGNOME and Other Stories
MIDWORLD
NOR CRYSTAL TEARS
SENTENCED TO PRISM
SPLINTER OF THE MIND'S EYE
STAR TREK® LOGS ONE–TEN
VOYAGE TO THE CITY OF THE DEAD
...WHO NEEDS ENEMIES?
WITH FRIENDS LIKE THESE...

The Icerigger Trilogy:
ICERIGGER
MISSION TO MOULOKIN
THE DELUGE DRIVERS

The Adventures of Flinx of the Commonwealth:
FOR LOVE OF MOTHER-NOT
THE TAR-AIYM KRANG
ORPHAN STAR
THE END OF THE MATTER
BLOODHYPE
FLINX IN FLUX
MID-FLINX

The Damned:
Book One: A CALL TO ARMS
Book Two: THE FALSE MIRROR
Book Three: THE SPOILS OF WAR

Books published by The Ballantine Publishing Group
are available at quantity discounts on bulk purchases
for premium, educational, fund-raising, and special
sales use. For details, please call 1-800-733-3000.

FLINX IN FLUX

Alan Dean Foster

A Del Rey® Book
BALLANTINE BOOKS • NEW YORK

A Del Rey® Book
Published by Ballantine Books

Copyright © 1988 by Alan Dean Foster

Map by Michael C. Goodwin

Cover art by Darrell K. Sweet

Library of Congress Catalog Card Number: 87-91887

ISBN 0-345-34363-8

Manufactured in the United States of America

First Edition: July 1988

20 19 18 17 16 15 14 13 12

For all the readers who've stuck with Flinx and Pip since 1972, and wanted them back. And most especially for Betty Ballantine, who first saw potential in them and me, and who helped bring the three of us to life.

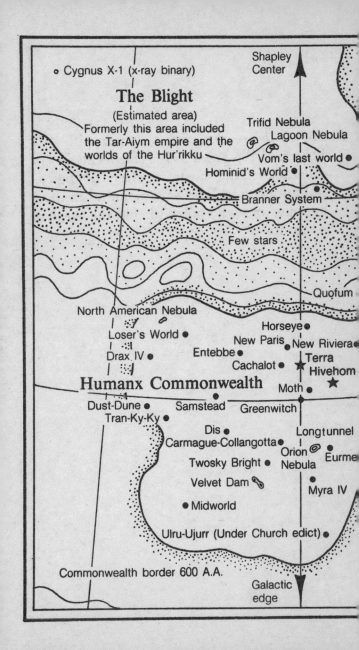

Chapter One

The man at the end of the table wore his attitude like a mask. In another place and time the intensity of his speech and gestures might have seemed unnatural, but they were perfectly appropriate for his present surroundings. He was a roly-poly sort of fellow topped by a short brush of inspired hair that crawled down to his shirt collar. Unlike his diatribe, his attire was simple and neat. With his mouth shut he looked quite ordinary. So did his five companions, save one. With that single exception, none was especially tall or muscular. They differed in coloring, though there was nothing unusual about that. They were of different ages. They came from different backgrounds and different worlds.

What had brought them together in this small room at this particular time was a burning fanaticism, a bond stronger than epoxene or duralloy cable—a cause each was willing to die for. They were true believers, and they knew without a shadow of a doubt that their cause was just.

When discussing it they were transformed. At such

times they sloughed off their daily personas and lives as
easily as a lizard sheds old skin. They sat before one
another fresh and gleaming, like the holy crusaders they
knew they were. Each brought something different to the
cause. The man who was speaking contributed money.
Another brought strength and physical skills. The man
seated beside her was naturally cunning. The six com-
plemented one another even as they shared the same passion.

They were the leaders of a growing band, having been
chosen by their associates to make the hard decisions, to
determine targets and courses of action.

The man who was speaking was known to his compatriots as Spider. It was an accurate description of his
mind, not of his physique. When he spoke of the Cause,
he no longer looked so genial. His eyes seemed to bulge
from his face, and his mouth contorted in a humorless
grimace.

None of them knew each other's real names. It was
safer that way. The others had adopted names such as
Flora and Lizard and Ormega—identification borrowed
from the natural world that they were dedicated to preserving. Ecology was their creed, worshiped without
question or hesitation. They had created unnatural relationships in order to better maintain the natural ones between species. Relationships that the civilization of the
Commonwealth was dedicated to destroying. Such was
their perception.

They were not alone in these beliefs, but they were
alone in their methods. They had moved beyond reason
into the realm of religion, a place where nonbelievers
were heretics to be stopped by whatever means necessary. For years they had been biding time, gathering
strength, testing the limits of their organization with subtle probes here, tiny strikes elsewhere. A chemical plant
sabotaged, construction of a shuttleport abruptly de-
layed, a few crucial votes influenced by money, persuasion, or occasional blackmail: all in the name of the

Cause. With each new success, each achievement, their confidence blossomed and new recruits were gleaned.

Until recently. The organization had grown beyond being a nuisance. It was now officially classified as a Problem, albeit still a minor one. Higher visibility meant more scrutiny by the authorities, more difficulty in soliciting adherents. They were no longer preaching to the already converted. The organization had reached a plateau. They could collapse in upon themselves, stagnate, or take the great leap forward. It was time to metamorphose from a cause into a movement.

Making that transition meant announcing themselves to the Commonwealth at large. It meant making a statement that could not be ignored, showing how far they were willing to go to support their beliefs. It was time at last for a major effort, for a spectacular display that would bring them the kind of universal recognition they had heretofore shunned but now demanded. Time for a demonstration on a scale sufficient to bring double, triple the usual number of doubters flocking to their banner.

Time to show the forces of destruction that they were a power to be reckoned with.

So it was that the six had gathered in this cramped and stuffy chamber, under the assumed names that they had come to regard as their only important ones, to decide the where and when and how of the announcement they were going to make. Though they had no official leader, Spider spoke first and longest because he was the most articulate among them.

When burning with the Cause, Spider could be spellbinding. His body was a mistake of familial genetics. Within that rotund, jovial shape dwelt the soul of a tall, sepulchral figure whose spiritual ancestors had once stalked the torture chambers of earlier inquisitions. He never hesitated, never second-guessed himself. Because he *knew*. Knew what was right, what was just, what had to be done. His companions listened with respect. All felt as he did but could not put their emotions into words as facilely.

It was dangerous for them to gather together in one place these days. As a result of recent activities, the organization had suffered injuries, though no deaths. But those activities had sparked more than the usual casual interest on the part of the authorities, enough interest so that the six had had to take circuitous paths to reach this meeting place in safety. Each was certain he or she had made it unobserved. Extreme caution was their shield, anonymity their protection. No one knew which worlds the organization had cells upon. The government was persistent but clumsy, easy to fool.

Soon it would not matter. In one blinding strike for Mother Nature they would voluntarily cast off their cloak of secrecy and announce themselves to a dazed Commonwealth. Every newsfax, every tridee would declare their name and purpose. Their purifying gesture would beget an avalanche of support that would shake the foul industrialists to their knees, and a new era of respect and love would dawn across this portion of the galaxy.

It would not be a random act, of course. They were as intelligent as they were dedicated. Even an act mounted for publicity must have behind it a legitimate purpose.

Given the extent of the cancer, they had no lack of targets to chose from. There was so much to be done and so little time in which to do it. Now, at last, after so many years of planning and building and laboring in secret, they could begin the real work. From now on the government and big corporations and ravening exploiters would have to deal with the avenging angel of the emergent organization.

And if some of them should die in the process? All had agreed long ago that the righteousness of their cause was well worth dying for. What mattered an individual life here and there when the sanctity of whole worlds was at stake?

Spider concluded his presentation with a brief recapitulation of the current situation before nodding to the woman seated to his right. She called herself Flora. Her eyes were blue, and her hair was the hue of spun gold. She was taller than any of the men except Stick, who sat quietly on the opposite side of the table. Her body was like desert heat. Gazing at it caused men to hallucinate. Stardom and fame could have been hers via the tridee networks, but such superficialities did not interest her. She had much more in common with Spider and Stick and the others seated at the table. The Cause excited her in a way no man ever had.

She was a biologist, not a starlet. When she spoke, the natural seductiveness of her voice masked the intensity of her devotion to the Cause. Her dedication and early military training had overcome the organization's initial resistance to her beauty. Now she was looked upon as merely another soldier. By herself she had induced two governments to alter their positions on issues important to her colleagues: one by persuasion, one by blackmail.

Now she held up what looked like a fragment of fabric half a meter square and five centimeters thick.

"Do you all know what this is? It's a new product and currently only available in limited quantities on the luxury market." The perfect slash of her mouth twisted, accomplishing the seemingly impossible by muting her beauty. "I'll tell you what it is: the latest and greatest perversion of the natural order for profit."

"Verdidion Weave, isn't it?" Ormega opted as she leaned forward for a better look.

Flora nodded brusquely. "A previously untouched organism from a previously unspoiled world. It's been genetically altered to enhance the comfort of a wealthy few, though there are plans afoot to lower the cost by increasing production." She made it sound like an oath framed in flaming quotation marks. "In other words, the bastards responsible for this plan on expanding their operation throughout the planet of origin."

Spider folded his hands in front of his belly. "A per-

fect world for our first major public operation. There are
no mitigating circumstances involved. It's not as if these
slime are altering grains to feed additional mouths. This
is a deliberate attempt to manipulate a natural environment purely for profit. We're going to stamp it out, shut
it down so thoroughly that every other company in the
business will think three times before trying anything
similar on any other virgin world.

"As you all know, our operations until now have been
limited to saving a single species here, a lifeform there.
This time, my friends, an entire world will be looking to
us for its salvation. We have before us the opportunity to
ensure the future tranquillity of a complete ecological
system. We're going in with a sword this time instead of
a scalpel!

"It's going to be expensive and dangerous. Anyone
who wants out can stay behind, and they won't be thought
the worse of for their decision. If our preliminary sortie
brings us the information we need, our chances of success will be greatly enhanced."

"I guess I'm not as familiar with this Verdidion Weave
and its background as some of you." Ormega was the
only other woman in the council of six. She was small
and dark and a lot older than Flora, but there was a powerful bond between them. They were bishops in the same
church. Ormega did not envy Flora her youth and beauty,
and Flora respected the other woman's experience and
knowledge.

"It's a complex and highly adaptable organism, as is
much of the life thus far cataloged on this frontier
world," Flora explained as she laid her sample on the
table. "Structurally it resembles the mosses, though it's
far more advanced than its relatives on Earth or Hivehom
or any of the other damp planets. Initially it was believed
that its reactions were purely piezoelectric in nature, but
further research by the exploiters indicates it's more complicated than that." She smiled wolfishly. "We've been

intercepting their confidential corporate transmissions for some time now.

"In its natural state it does not respond usefully, but these soulless people have been playing with its DNA."

"What's it been modified for?" Lizard asked.

"Carpet." Flora spit the word. "Just carpet."

"You mean people walk on it?" Ormega murmured. "A living creature?"

"It can support considerable weight. Stepping on it doesn't appear to cause any injury. Watch."

Flora placed the square of living material on the floor. Everyone rose or turned his or her chair for a better view. As they looked on, Flora stepped in the center of the dense growth. The green-and-rust-colored tendrils responded by rippling toward her feet to offer additional support.

"If you lean one way or the other," Flora explained, "the carpet actually shifts to ease you in the direction you want to go." Her companions could see that the glistening substance was moving her slightly to her left, like a tightly-packed column of ants.

Gingerly she stepped off the section of living carpet. The tendrils stopped moving. "It's a communal organism that can be grown in much larger sections. Or sections can be shaped and bound together to fit any room. It draws necessary moisture from the air and is nonphotosynthetic, so it requires no light. Walking on it is like walking on air, and it even exudes a faint hibiscuslike odor." Her exquisite blue eyes blazed, and her voice grew taut. "But it was *not* created to serve as a floor covering for privileged mankind!"

"In its natural state," Spider told them, "the Weave reacts by pulling away from pressure, not moving to support it. A much more natural and reasonable reaction. This"—He nodded toward the altered growth.—"is an abomination. It should not exist."

Flora removed a tiny perfume flask from the curved upper pocket of her jumpsuit and dumped the contents in the middle of the square of Verdidion Weave. Spider tossed a small incendiary capsule on top. The six watched silently as the mutated moss burned itself to a charred crisp.

It did not occur to any of them to think that the object of their loathing might feel more pain from being incinerated than from being walked upon, but that did not matter. It was not a natural growth but rather the product of perverse experimentation. It should not exist. Thus, they wasted no more thought on its destruction than they would on the destruction of those responsible for such a biological outrage. The Weave, like those who were responsible for its existence, was not worthy of sympathy or understanding. It continued to smoke pungently for several minutes following the cremation of the last cell.

Before the last of the smoke had faded away, the man who called himself Lizard was on his feet and speaking. He was slim without being sleek, neither was he gaunt of face like Stick. He was, in fact, exactly ordinary in appearance, of average height and build and younger than most of his colleagues. In many ways his very ordinariness made him the most dangerous member of the group. It allowed him to move unobserved in a crowd, to peer over people's shoulders without drawing attention to himself, to wear the garb of harmlessness.

His profession was equally innocuous. So was his private life. Not even his wife suspected his membership in the organization. She would have been startled to learn that he was one of the six ranking officials of what she thought was a harmless fraternal business society.

Yet whenever Lizard discussed matters dear to the heart of the organization, a sudden change came over him. His expression would tighten, and a nervous tic would begin in his left eye, increasing or lessening in intensity according to the passion of his speech.

At the moment he was in complete control of his emotions. Cool heads were needed now that they had decided to announce themselves to a corrupt civilization. Cool heads would be needed to carry out their mission successfully. Lizard had acted as the organization's point man on more than one occasion.

He was also responsible for the oversized image that now flashed on the wall opposite Spider's seat. Neither the table nor the walls nor the floor appeared to conceal anything as sophisticated as a holographic projector, which was a tribute to Lizard's abilities. He could make machinery blend into ordinary surroundings with the same ease with which he blended into a crowd. Homogenizing technology, he called it.

The hologram showed a small portion of the galaxy. As the six looked on, it shrank until only the stars of the Commonwealth were visible. The view narrowed further until they were looking at an unspectacular star orbited by only five planets.

When the view reached the third planet out, it halted and the image of a world began to pirouette before them like a dancer on a stage. Lizard resumed his talk, statistics spilling from his mouth. His colleagues showed only passing interest in information about gravity and diameter. What interested them was the world's unique and heretofore undisturbed ecology.

"Longtunnel," Lizard was saying. "Only a minuscule portion's been explored so far, but enough to hint at the natural marvels the place contains. Though the atmosphere's quite breathable, the climate's inhospitable in the extreme. A tough place to move around on."

"Thanks for small blessings," Ormega whispered.

"Too small, sadly." Lizard's left eyebrow began to twitch. "You know what the enemy's like. If they see a profit, the weather's not going to be enough to stop them." He returned his attention to the holo.

"Only one settlement so far. Little more than a scientific outpost." He gestured with a finger. Responding to his directional body heat, the image reacted by becoming a slightly curved section of planetary surface. Complex cloud patterns boiled above it.

"The one company we're particularly concerned about isn't a branch of a major Trading House." His eyes glittered, and vitriol stained his voice. "Their small size, however, has not minimized the amount of damage they've been able to do in a short time. The speed with which they brought that pitiful Verdidion Weave onto the market is proof of that."

Murmurs rose from his companions as he lowered his controlling finger. "Right now the scale of commercial development is limited. Unfortunately, there's nothing else on the market like the Weave. Demand for it is soaring as its properties become known. Those who order it know nothing and care nothing for the fact that its development is a crime against nature.

"We would not be assembled here if we were discussing the harvesting of a normal growth, but the Weave is the product of the worst kind of unregulated genetic manipulation. And the company that produced it is hard at work trying to bend many other lifeforms to their will." His voice was rising and the tic of his eye accelerating.

"Verdidion Weave is the forerunner of a panoply of abominations. The defenseless lifeforms of Longtunnel are particularly amenable to genetic alteration. To those for whom exploitation of the innocent is a middle name, the world is a biological gold mine!" Aware that he was shouting, he strove to moderate his tone.

"I have seen some of their proposals for additional bioengineered products, to be produced by manipulating Longtunnel's indigenous lifeforms. Most are the product of a single brilliant but morally bankrupt mind, that of the head of this firm's bioengineering division. This individual is the one cog in the company's machine which I do not think they can easily replace. Skill at bioengineering is cheap. Intuition is priceless."

"This individual was responsible for the development of the Weave?" Stick wanted to know.

Lizard nodded.

"Then I think our course of action has been determined for us." Flora's exquisite face was less than pleasant to look upon. "By excising this particular person we will at one stroke learn what we need to know to successfully conclude our mission as well as eliminate a possible future blemish on the natural order."

"That was my intent." Spider clasped his hands over his belly as he leaned back in his chair. "Longtunnel is both a suitable and an appropriate place for us to have our little coming-out party. The crimes being committed against nature there are of the worst sort, yet the firm which is behind them is neither too large nor too dangerous for us to deal with efficiently. Furthermore, they have opened only a single wound on this otherwise pristine planet. A wound, my friends, which we will suture and heal. We will simultaneously announce ourselves, serve warning upon our enemies, and cure a cancer before it can spread. It is agreed, then?"

There was no need for a show of hands, no need even for words, though several of them did nod approvingly.

Spider turned to Lizard. The two men were individual components of a greater whole, each like one leg of an insect working to carry the body to a chosen destination.

"I take it your people are ready to move?"

Lizard nodded briskly. "Ready and anxious. They've been practicing for a long time. They're eager for the chance to finally do something."

"They'll have their chance. We'll all have our chance." Spider's brooding gaze swept around the table. "No more clinging to shadows. No more limiting ourselves to issuing manifestos and inserting tracts in obscure faxes. No more begging for public service time on the major tridee services. After Longtunnel our name will be on everyone's lips. The entire Commonwealth will know what we stand for. The undecided will rally to our cause. Then we can begin in earnest to reverse the tide of exploitation which has dominated government policy for far too long!''

They would have raised a toast to their decision and to themselves save for the fact that none of them consumed alcohol or indulged in other narcotic substances. How could you preach the purity of the natural world if you could not keep your own body clean? They got high on one thing only: the passion for the Cause. The true Cause, the holy war against the rapacious despoilers of multiple environments, against the polluters and DNAnarchists.

There were other organizations that professed to work for that end, but the six knew them for what they were: weak, feeble, and uncommitted. Only those around the table were the true shock troops of the coming ecological jihad.

Lizard did something, and the holo vanished as though it had never been. They rose from their seats and began to leave the meeting room, whispering among themselves, excited but under control. Everyone knew what he or she had to do to make the operation a success. And it *had* to be a success. The robber barons and their Frankensteinian servants had been given a free hand too long. Now it was time to amputate.

They kept their voices down and dispersed rapidly. Time had taught them patience; experience had taught them caution. As they filed out of the nondescript structure into waiting vehicles or walked to the nearest public transport, they were already rehearsing their next moves, each concentrating on his or her assigned duty.

They certainly did not look much like the members of the ruling clique of a burgeoning terrorist organization.

Chapter Two

While Alaspin attracted its share of visitors, few of them were tourists. The majority were scientists for whom an unpleasant climate was merely a minor impediment to research. Here, at least, it was a consistent impediment. The weather in the broad, high-grassed savannas and the dense jungle that bordered them changed little from month to month. There were only two seasons: wet and not so wet.

The scientists came to study the thousands of temples and ruins left by an advanced civilization too shy even to name itself, which was thus called Alaspinian by default. They had left extensive records of their travels throughout this portion of space, but practically nothing about themselves. Yet they had chosen to live and work in primitive structures of stone and wood. Nothing was known of their disappearance, though the theory of racial suicide had numerous adherents. It was almost as if, embarrassed by their achievements, they had simply disappeared some seventy thousand years ago. Moved away somehow, others said. For if they had committed racial suicide, where were the remains?

Fragile bodies, the suicide supporters insisted. Or cremation in the jungle. These were theories upon theories that brought mild-tempered xenoarcheologists to blows, all impossible to prove because among the millions of carvings and records that had been left behind on small cubes of micronically etched metal, there was not one picture of an Alaspinian. There were endless images of plants and animals and landscapes and structures, but of the people who had recorded them, nothing.

It was one of those worlds where the thranx were more at ease than their human compatriots. The hot, humid climate was like a breath of fresh steamed air from home to them. The larger permanent research installations were all staffed by thranx, while their human counterparts came and went rapidly, gleaning bits and fragments of knowledge suitable for a paper or thesis before fleeing for cooler, drier worlds.

Prospectors outnumbered scientists in the frontier regions. Alaspin was rich in valuable minerals. Many of those who called themselves prospectors, however, avoided the rich alluvial plains of the savannas in favor of mining the limitless ruins, where the digging was easier and the ''ores'' more highly concentrated; already refined, in fact. A perpetual state of limited war existed between prospectors and scientists.

To those engaged in research, the prospectors were despoilers of tombs and destroyers of a still poorly understood alien heritage. Some of the more reckless and less caring explorers would not hesitate to tear apart a newly uncovered structure in search of a single marketable artifact, thereby rendering the entire site useless for scientific study.

Meanwhile, the poor prospectors, unsupported by fat research grants and surviving largely by their wits in a hostile environment, complained that the authorities always sided with the big institutes, while they already had located more sites and ruins than could be studied in a thousand years. They argued that every additional site they discovered only added to, instead of subtracting from, the sum of scientific knowledge.

In between drifted a small group of hybrids acknowledged by both sides, solitary individuals who were both prospector and scientist, travelers in whom the desire to learn warred constantly with greed.

Standing apart and aloof from the combatants and their eternal bickering were those who had come to Alaspin to make their fortune by other means. They came to serve the needs of prospector and scientist alike. For money, since no one came to Alaspin for his health. The climate was rotten, and the native lifeforms inimical.

Not every scientist was supported by a recognized institute. Not every prospector was grubstaked by a large company or criminal consortium. So stores were needed, and entertainments sufficiently simple and garish, and servicing facilities. The people who ran those businesses were the only ones who could really call themselves citizens of Alaspin. They depended on the planet for their livelihood. They were there for the long haul, unlike the scientists who dreamed of making the Great Discovery or the prospectors who pondered the one Big Strike that lay in the next vine-cloaked temple, the next virgin stream.

Lastly there was Flinx.

He belonged to none of the recognized classes that flitted across Alaspin's humid surface. He was not there to prospect and he was not there to do research, though he studied hard everything he encountered. Solitude was his primary backer.

The scientists thought him a peculiar student working on a thesis. The prospectors recognized a loner when they saw one and considered him one of their own. Who else but a prospector would have an Alaspinian flying snake, or minidrag, constantly riding his shoulder? Who else would discourage casual friendships and conversation? Not that the young man had to discourage actively. The presence of his horridly lethal pet kept the curious well away.

To those who were bold enough or ignorant enough to sidle up next to him on the street or in the dining room of the small hotel, he was always polite. No, he was not a student. Nor a prospector either. Nor did he work for one of the planetary service corporations. He was on Alaspin, he freely admitted, to perpetrate a homecoming. On hearing this, his questioners invariably departed more puzzled than they had been before accosting him.

Flinx treasured everyone he encountered, both those who questioned him and those who recognized Pip's distinctive blue and pink diamondback coloring and hurriedly crossed to the other side of the street when they saw him coming. The older he grew, the more fascinating he found mankind. Until recently his immaturity had prevented him from truly appreciating the uniquely diverse organism that was the human race.

As for the thranx, they were equally interesting in their own way. Their social system was very different from mankind's. For all that the two species got on supremely well, they had different individual priorities and beliefs. Yes, he was becoming quite a student of people, regardless of their size and shape and where they happened to wear their skeletons. Part of it was that he kept looking for another as unique as himself. So far he had not found one.

As he pondered, he wielded a machete. It was an extraordinary primitive instrument, no more than a large chunk of sharpened metal. Cheap laser cutters were available for sale in every outfitter's shop in Mimmisompo, but he had chosen the antique instead. Aiming a cutter and pulling the trigger did not convey the same sense of satisfaction that swinging the heavy blade did. A cutter worked neatly and soundlessly. With the machete you could smell your progress as you chopped your way through green and purple stems and striated leaves.

The destruction did not trouble him because he knew
how temporary it was. Within a week the trail he was
cutting would be gone as new growth swamped it, de-
vouring the sunlight it admitted to the jungle floor.

Tall trees rose all around him. He was fascinated by
one that was all buttressing roots and little trunk. It was
festooned with epiphytes ablaze with bright crimson
flowers. Swarms of tiny blue-black insects crowded
around blossoms shaped like miniature trumpets. Four-
winged relatives of Terran lepidoptera pushed and shoved
for their turn at the nectar.

Less decorative creatures tried to bite through his
boots, which sank three centimeters and more into the
gray mud through which he was traipsing. They smelled
blood. The high-frequency repeller clipped to his belt
kept most of the winged vampires away. His long-sleeved
shirt and his pants were impregnated with powerful an-
tipheromones, as was his wide-brimmed hat. So far his
sound and stink had maintained him unpunctured.

Though he did not know it, his appearance was little
different from that of jungle explorers from ancient times.
Such men would have killed for the chemistry and electronics that kept the worst Alaspin could offer at a safe
distance. The thranx, bless 'em, didn't need elaborate
protection. Few bugs could bite through their chitons.
Nor did they need the refrigeration unit that lined his
pants, keeping him cool by recycling his own sweat. Not
necessary, but a luxurious antidote to misery.

Also expensive, but money was something Flinx did
not worry about. While not dominatingly wealthy, he had
made himself financially independent.

A multiple humming filled his ears. He had felt their
presence long before he heard them. Pip uncoiled from
his shoulders and took to the air. There they were again,
in the trees off to his right.

Each was larger than the most massive hummingbird.
They darted toward him in formation and danced around
his head. He smiled fondly at them, then turned and con-

tinued toward the lake he had found on the aerial map.
It had struck him as an appropriate place to make final
farewells.

The reality was more lovely than the picture, he thought
as he broke through the last of the undergrowth and stood
there on the steeply banked shore. It was still quite early.
A fog was rising from the mirror-smooth surface of the
lake, softening the outlines of the trees and lianas that
lined the far shore. They were dream-shapes limned in
gold, glowing cutouts rising as if in offering to the mist-
shrouded sun.

The broad expanse inspired his fellow travelers. They
rocketed out over the water, swirling gaily around Pip.
She was the star to which they anchored their constella-
tion.

Until today. The time was near, and he knew it. He
knew because he could feel it in his pet's mind. Pip was
an empathic telepath, able to both transmit and receive
emotions to and from her master. The half dozen offspring that flew dizzying circles around her now were
equally talented.

They had been conceived during a visit to this, their
home world, and to this place Flinx had returned them
for weaning, though that was a term not literally appli-
cable to flying snakes. He had felt it was the right thing
to do, though how much of that feeling had originated
with him and how much of it had been imparted by Pip
he could not have said. Now he knew he had done right.
He had enjoyed the yearlings' company, but they were
growing fast. Seven meter-long, highly poisonous empathic minidrags were more than any one person could
be expected to cope with, so he had returned the prodi-
gals.

They were snakes in name alone, because that was
what they most nearly resembled. Even the xenotaxono-
mists called them miniature dragons, though they were
actually more closely related to the extinct Terran dino-
saurs, particularly the coelurosaurs. He could sense their

confusion as he stood there on the bank, the machete dangling from his right fist.

Waves of maternal repulsion were spreading outward from Pip like ripples in a disturbed pond. They washed over her offspring, battering them, driving them away. Gradually instinct took over where understanding was lacking. As they flew wider and wider circles around her, Flinx could feel the bonds between mother and offspring weakening. They did not break but became steadily less intense. It was at once beautiful and painful to watch, and it filled him with a righteous peace.

He no longer wondered if he had done the right thing in bringing them here. The dance of the minidrags continued, their incredibly agile shapes darting and spinning, iridescent scales catching the rising sun. Eventually they broke away one at a time, like children taking turns at the end of crack-the-whip, to vanish into the trees on the far side of the lake. Now they had truly returned to the world that had given them birth. Flinx inhaled deeply.

"Well and done," he said aloud, knowing that the words would not be understood but that Pip would perfectly comprehend what he was feeling. "That's that, old girl. Time you and I got back. It's warming up out."

Pip came shooting back to him, stopping instantly to hover a meter before his face. The long pointed tongue flashed at his nose and eyelids before she pivoted to settle comfortably on his neck and shoulders.

He allowed himself a final look at the lake, its surface still as glass. Then he turned to retrace the route he had chopped through the jungle. If Pip was sorry to see her offspring go, she gave no sign of it. If he sensed anything in her, it was a vast contentment.

Of course, he had no way of telling if he was actually feeling what she was feeling or if it was no more than a reflection of his own emotions. His peculiar sensibilities were as much of a mystery to him as ever, though each passing year seemed to bring him a little closer to coming to grips with them. It was like trying to strangle fog. One instant the talent was as solid and real as steel, and the next he would try to use it and there would be nothing there, nothing at all.

He worked hard trying to understand the mystery of himself. As he trudged through the mud, he tried to avoid brushing against the surrounding vegetation. In the jungle every leaf seemed to shelter something toothy or toxic. He was beginning to respect his talents instead of fearing and hating them. If only they were more predictable! Hard to build a fence when something kept taking away your hammer the instant before it struck each nail. So far his abilities had served to cause him trouble more than anything else. Unfortunately, he would have to learn to live with them. He could no more disown them than he could engage in self-mutilation.

Pip stirred against him even as the surge of emotion roared through him. He stopped and turned as he heard the humming.

A single adolescent minidrag hovered noisily before him. When he had turned on it, the yearling had backed wind, retreating until it was two meters away. There it remained, staring back intently.

Flinx knew he was not the first human being to establish a tight emotional bond with an Alaspinian minidrag. There were tales of other prospectors who had done so. He had met one such individual himself little more than a year ago. That man's minidrag, Balthazaar, had mated with Pip. But he had never heard of anyone bonding with more than one flying snake. One human, one minidrag. That was the rule. The yearling had to go.

"Go on! Beat it, scram!" He jumped toward it, waving his arms and machete. The little creature retreated another meter. "Fly away, get lost! Your home's not with me and your mother anymore. This is good-bye time." He rushed the minidrag. It darted back two meters and stopped, hovering half behind the protective bulk of a tree with blue bark.

Turning decisively, he resumed his march. He had

covered another twenty meters when he heard the humming again. As he spun in exasperation, the yearling quickly landed on a convenient branch, folding its pleated wings tightly against its narrow body and curling its tail around the wood.

"What's the matter with you?" He glanced down at Pip, who was staring silently at her recalcitrant offspring. "You've got a kid who doesn't want to leave the nest. What are you going to do about it?"

Flinx was constantly amazed at the complexity of thoughts that could be conveyed by emotions. Pip understood not a word he had said, but the feeling was clear enough. She uncoiled herself, spread her wings, and shot toward the adolescent.

The yearling nearly fell out of the tree trying to avoid her attack. Flinx watched as the two minidrags went around trunks and through branches, panicking the concealed native life and scattering it in all directions.

Finally Pip returned, breathing hard, and settled back on his shoulder. This time he simply stood and waited. A minute passed, two, before he heard the expected hum. The yearling hovered in the crook of two great branches, obviously exhausted and equally obviously unwilling to be driven away. Feeling Pip stir on his shoulder, he put a hand on her neck to calm her down.

"Easy." She felt without understanding. Her breathing slowed. "It's all right."

Her offspring picked up the same feeling and started toward him. He watched while it coiled itself around his left wrist.

"No, you can't stay. Understand?" He raised his hand and snapped it outward, tossing the flying snake into the air. As soon as he let it fall, the minidrag was back clinging to his arm, a brightly colored bracelet with flashing red eyes.

He flung it away several times. Each time it resumed its grip on his wrist or lower arm. "What the devil am I supposed to do with you?" If a flying snake could cringe, this yearling was doing exactly that. It buried its head beneath one wing.

Cute, damn it, he thought. All of Pip's offspring had been cute, dainty little leathery sculptures. Each of them carried enough neurotoxin in its poison sacs to kill a dozen grown men in as many minutes. Not so cute.

The minidrag's emanations were weak and indistinct, like its mother's. Affection, confusion, loneliness, fear, puzzlement, all mixed up together. Since the flying snake's intelligence level was far below that of a human being, he could never be sure exactly what it was feeling.

This one was very small, even for a year-old minidrag. Pip was clearly hesitating, trying to divide her attention between her master and her offspring. He wondered how she would react if he became violent with the adolescent. If he directed sufficient anger at it, he had no doubt she would somehow manage to drive it away, even if forced to injure it in the process.

Small as it was, it had probably been the last hatchling, so it was correspondingly reluctant to be weaned. But he had no intention of staying on Alaspin one day longer than absolutely necessary, certainly not to accommodate the feelings of a reluctant adolescent minidrag. There was nothing on this world he wanted to do, nothing he needed to see. All he wanted was to be on his way, wherever that was. He did not need an extra lifeform cluttering up his ship. He sighed aloud. He had been doing that a lot lately, he realized.

"Isn't much to you, is there?" A tiny, brilliantly colored triangular-shaped head peered out at him from beneath a concealing wing. "It doesn't work this way. One minidrag, one human. You can't have a three-way empathic relationship." The minidrag did not answer.

Perhaps he was not sufficiently mature. Certainly he was the runt of the litter. Flinx raised his left arm so they were eye to eye.

"I suppose if you're going to hang around, you're going to have to have a name. What's smaller than a Pip? A nubbin? No, you're a throwaway, so I guess we'll have to call you Scrap.''

Not flattering, he supposed, but appropriate. The small loop of muscle tightened around his arm, though whether in reaction to being named or merely to secure its perch, Flinx had no way of knowing. He would not take up much space, Flinx told himself. Pip could keep her eye on him on board the *Teacher*, which was stuffed with scraps of another kind. It would feel quite at home.

The big minidrag had relaxed against his neck now that her master's animosity toward her offspring had vanished. She paid no attention to the yearling. Obviously she felt she had done her best to discharge her maternal duties. If her master no longer rejected the adolescent, she did not feel compelled to, either.

He thought no more about his new companion as he retraced his steps. Alaspin was not a benign world. It was home to an impressive assortment of carnivores and poisonous lifeforms that did not discriminate in their eating habits between local and offworld prey. As Flinx had learned on his previous visit, this was no place to take chances, no country in which to relax and sightsee. So he did not think about either Pip or Scrap as he watched where he was putting his feet, trying to step in the muddy depressions he had made when cutting his trail to the lake. Leaves and vines teased his face, and he winced instinctively at each contact.

Although there were jungles more hostile that those of Alaspin, this one was threatening enough for him. He had never had a desire to join the Scouts, those half-mad men and women and thranx who were first to set down on a new world. Not even Pip could protect him against parasites and tiny bloodsuckers. He held tight to his antique machete. At least, he thought, the ancients had had enough sense to make them of titanium. Anything else would be too heavy to wield efficiently.

Another thirty meters brought him into the small clearing where his crawler waited. This was as far as he had been able to bash with it. The machine traveled smoothly over water and through most jungle, but dense thick trees defeated it. Thus he had been forced to leave it here and travel the rest of the way to the lake on foot.

It looked like an oversize chrome canoe on wheels, roofed in plexalloy and articulated in the middle. The highly polished sides reflected much of the burning sunlight, not critical here beneath the trees but vitally important for cooling purposes when out on lake or river. Armored grillwork shielded the underside, protecting sensitive machinery. It was not much wider than the driver's seat, which enabled it to pass between those trees it was incapable of knocking over. What it really was, was a giant, mobile heat exchanger, able to convey its passengers in relative comfort across Alaspin's humid, hot countryside.

Flinx had rented it in Mimmisompo, paying with a credcard whose rating, while not astronomical, had lifted the eyebrows of the merchant doing the leasing.

The crawler traveled on double treads, one fore and the other aft. It could carry three passengers seated single file behind the driver. There were no other passengers except Pip, and he really did not need such a large vehicle, but it was the smallest he could find on short notice. So he had shrugged and overpaid. It made even better time on the river than it did on land. An aircar would have been faster, but there were none for rent in Mimmisompo. The prospectors and scientists kept them busy ferrying friends and supplies. Flinx had come with money but no pull. In a small frontier city the latter was often the more important medium of exchange. So he had been forced to settle for the crawler.

No matter. He was only a few days out of town and on his way back. Having established a trail on his way in, it would take him a quarter of the time to return to the river, carefully dodging the leafy emergents the crawler had been unable to push over. Once back on the river, he would be traveling downstream instead of fighting the current. He was looking forward to spending one more night in a hotel instead of the crawler's cramped quarters.

Mimmisompo sat on the edge of an immense sandy beach, high and dry in the clear season and sopping in the wet. The shuttleport lay farther inland. It occupied one of the few high bits of land in the region, immune to seasonal flooding. Not the sort of place one would choose for a relaxing vacation, but he was anxious to return to it now.

At the top of the ladder built into the side of the crawler he paused to run a magnetic field key over the lock, and heard it click open in response. A blast of cool air struck him as he climbed inside, settled into his seat, and nudged a switch to close the door behind him. Probably no need to lock the vehicle out here in the middle of nowhere, but he had learned early on that the middle of nowhere was a country often frequented by unsavory types, and while the odds of anyone stumbling across the crawler were small, he felt more comfortable when they were entirely in his favor. The sight of an expensive vehicle sitting open and unguarded might be too tempting for even an honest prospector to ignore.

The mental flavor of the five departed young minidrags no longer lingered in his mind, but the crawler's cabin was still pungent with their odor. It was musky but not unpleasant. The recycler would soon have it cleared out. Curved metal ribs supported the otherwise transparent plexalloy walls and domed roof. After a quick survey of his immediate surroundings he began switching on instruments. Yellow standby lights gave way to green readies.

Like any modern piece of machinery, the crawler took only a moment to run a self-check and declare itself healthy. That done, Flinx turned up the recycler a notch and dug out a towel to wipe his face. You had to be careful when changing environments. While the air-conditioning unit he wore had kept his body comfortable, his face had been exposed to the air. Perspiration poured from his forehead and cheeks, ran down his neck under his shirt collar. The combination of sweat and air-conditioning could bring on a cold faster than anything else known to man.

It was a matter of choice. He could have worn a helmet and insulated himself completely from the local climate, but somehow that seemed the wrong thing to do at the minidrags' leave-taking. So he had left the helmet in the crawler and had tolerated the heat and humidity for the short hike through the jungle.

Putting the soaked towel aside, he downed a long swig of chilled fruit juice from the driver's feedline before starting the engine. The electric drive hummed smoothly beneath him. Pip slid off his shoulder to coil around an equipment rack next to the seat behind him. If she felt sad or melancholy at the loss of her five offspring, she gave no sign of it.

Scrap was less willing to find a seat. Despite Flinx's persistent efforts to dislodge it, the young minidrag insisted on clinging to his wrist. Finally Flinx gave up and put the crawler in motion. The adolescent was not heavy, and before long he would get bored and move off by himself.

The path he had bulldozed in from the river was easy to follow. Fast-sprouting jungle plants were already fighting for their share of the newly esposed route to the sky. He turned a tight curve, bending the crawler in the middle, to work his way around a tree three meters thick. The vehicle articulated vertically when he followed that maneuver by driving down and through a dry streambed.

Now that he had accomplished what he had come to Alaspin for, he was forced to contemplate what he was going to do next. Life was no longer simple. Once it had been, back on Moth, when all he had had to worry about was keeping dry and getting enough to eat and maybe swiping a few luxuries now and then to help out Mother Mastiff when business was slow. The past four years had complicated his life incredibly. He had seen and experienced more than most men saw and experienced in a lifetime, let alone adolescent boys.

Not that he was a boy anymore, he reminded himself. He had grown physically as well as mentally. Nearly nine centimeters, in fact. Decisions were no longer easy to make, choices no longer straightforward. Being nineteen carried with it a lot of responsibility, for him more than for most. Not to mention the emotional baggage that automatically went with it without right of refusal.

The only problem with seeing a lot, he mused as he guided the crawler through the Ingre jungle, was that he was not happy with most of what he had seen. In general, both man and thranx had been a disappointment to him. Too many individuals were ready and willing to sell out their principles and friends for the right price. Even basically good people like the merchant Maxim Malaika were essentially looking out for their own best interests. Mother Mastiff was no different, but at least she did not have a hypocritical bone in her body. She delighted in being a greedy, money-grabbing lowlife. He reveled in her honesty. She was the best human being she could be, given the sad circumstances of her life.

And what was to become of him? A universe of possibilities lay open to him. Too many, perhaps. He had not the slightest idea which to reach for.

Nor were weighty questions of philosophy and morality all that obsessed him right now. There was also, for example, the increasingly fascinating and complex matter of the opposite sex. As he had spent most of the past four years just surviving, women remained largely an intriguing mystery to him.

There had been some. The beautiful and compassionate Lauren Walder, many years ago back on his home world of Moth. Atha Moon, Maxim Malaika's personal pilot. A few others, younger and less memorable, who had flashed like brief blue flames through his life, leaving memories that burned as well as confused him. He found himself wondering if Lauren would remember him, if she was still working happily at her obscure fishing lodge or if she had moved away, perhaps offplanet. If she would still think of him as a "city boy."

He straightened in his seat. He had been little more than a child then, and shy at that. Maybe he was still something of a boy, but he was no longer nearly as shy. Nor did he look half so boyish. That troubled him. Any change troubled him because he could never be certain if it was the result of natural growth processes or his unnatural origin.

Take the matter of his height. He had learned that it was normal for most young men to attain their full growth by age seventeen or eighteen. Yet he had reached his full adolescent height by the time he was fifteen and then stopped cold. Now he had suddenly and inexplicably grown another nine centimeters in twelve months and showed no sign of slowing. He had gone abruptly from slightly below average male height to slightly above it. Height changed one's perspective on life as well as the way others perceived one.

The drawback was that it became harder to remain inconspicuous. It made him feel less of a boy and more of a man, though when a boy became a man, wasn't he supposed to be certain about things? Flinx found he was more confused now than he had been at sixteen, and not only about women.

If anyone had a right to feel confused, it was Philip Lynx, né Flinx. His was not a normal mind in a normal body. Better to be confused all the time than frightened. He managed to keep the fear in the background, out of the way, locked in the dark cul-de-sacs of his mind. It did not occur to him that it was his fear and confusion that prevented him from making further contact with members of the opposite sex. He knew only that he was wary.

If only Bran Tse-Mallory or Truzenzuzex were around to advise him. He missed them deeply, wondered where they were and what they might be up to, what mysteries they might be probing with their singularly penetrating minds. For all he knew, he realized with a cold chill, they might be dead.

No, impossible. Those two were immortal. Monuments both of them, spirit and intelligence molded in material everlasting, both parts combining to form a much greater whole. They had their own lives to live, he told himself for the thousandth time, their own destinies to fulfill. They could not be expected to spare the time to tutor one odd young man, no matter how interesting he might be.

Having always managed on his own as a boy, he could certainly do so as an adult. He would damn well have to find out things for himself instead of expecting another to do it for him. Why shouldn't he manage? He could do certain things that so far as he knew no one else could do.

They designed me well, he thought bitterly. My prenatal physicians. The rogue men and women who had employed his DNA for their plaything. What had they really hoped to achieve with him and his fellow fetal experimentees? Would they be proud of him today or disappointed, as they had apparently been in all the others? Or would they simply be curious, utterly distant and uninvolved? It could be no more than a matter for speculation, since all of them were dead or mindwiped.

Well, their subject was preparing to build a life of his own, independent and unobserved. Already he had crisscrossed a fair portion of the Commonwealth trying to locate his natural parents, only to discover that his mother was dead and his father's identity a mystery lost in the mists and rumors that were his heritage.

That desire to know had driven him for several years. Now he was beyond that. If he was ever to learn the truth of his genealogy, he would have to pry it out of some computer storage chip hidden somewhere beneath human ken. Time to put history behind him and look to his future, which would probably prove as complicated as his past.

Still, he considered himself fortunate. While his unpredictable talents had often placed him in trouble, they had also helped to extricate him from it. He'd had the chance to meet some unique individuals: Bran Tse-Mallory and Truzenzuzex, Lauren Walder, and others not nearly so pleasant. And then there were the Ujurrians. He found himself wondering how their tunnel digging was progressing. The AAnn, too, of course, scheming and plotting against humanxkind, always searching for a weakness, probing for an opening, watching and waiting to expand whenever the Commonwealth seemed weak or indecisive.

His thoughts were rambling, but he could not help himself. The crawler largely drove itself, and now that he had done what he had come to do, he was relaxed and at ease. He could easily see himself becoming a reclusive mystic, the old hermit of the trade vectors, cruising back and forth through the Commonwealth and even skirting its outermost boundaries in the wonderful ship the Ujurrians had fashioned for him. The *Teacher*. That was what they called him. A paradox, since the more he learned, the more ignorant he felt.

Truzenzuzex would have called that a sign of increasing maturity. He was a student, not a teacher, intensely interested in everything around him: people and places, civilizations and individuals. He had been exposed to bits and pieces of great mysteries. Abalamahalamatandra, who had been not a survivor of some ancient race but instead a biomechanical key for triggering a terrible device. The Krang, the ultimate weapon of the long-vanished Tar-Aiym, whose strange mechomental perturbations still echoed through his brain after all these years. So many things seen, so many places yet to go. So much to try to comprehend.

Intelligence was a terrible burden.

He halted abruptly, the crawler coming to a stop as he

released the accelerator. Pip's head rose sharply from the seat where she lay curled about herself, and Scrap's miniature wings fluttered nervously as Flinx clasped both hands to his head. The headaches were growing worse. He had always had them, but this past year they had become a constant companion, averaging several or more a month.

One more reason for abjuring permanent relationships. It was entirely possible, he had considered in the darker moments, that he was one more eventual dead-end experiment, and he had no desire to drag anyone else down with him. He had simply managed to last a little longer than the rest of their spectacular failures. What was truly frightening was that in the medical texts the difference between headache and stroke was little more than a matter of degree.

The painful lights began to fade from the inside of his retinas. He took a long, shuddering breath, then sat up straight. Something was happening to him. Something was changing inside his head, and he had no more control over it than a spaceport control tower had over a runaway shuttle. More changes. Piss on his progenitors, the sons of bitches who had arrogated unto themselves the right to toy with the unborn.

There was nothing to be done about it. He could hardly walk into a major medical facility and calmly request a full-scale examination on the strength of being the bastard product of an illegal and universally abhorred society of renegade eugenicists. On the other hand, he told himself, feeling better as the pain in his head went away, it might simply be that he was prone to headaches. He managed a grin. It would be amusing if all his fears and worries were groundless, and the only thing he was suffering from was the normal trauma of moving from adolescence into adulthood. It would also be wonderful.

It would also be unlikely.

The headaches were usually accompanied by a severe emotional twitch from another person, but there was no one else in the vicinity. Maybe a real headache, then. He would not mind the pain if that was the case. Sometimes even pain could be reassuring.

The fact that he could still suffer wrenching emotional dislocation here in the middle of the jungle was further proof of the erratic nature of his abilities, not that he needed additional confirmation. The fact that he had come to grips with his peculiarities intellectually did nothing to assuage their effects on him. They were a constant reminder of his abnormality, of the fact that whatever else he did, he would never be able to lead anything resembling a normal life.

If only he could learn to channel, to control his talents, to turn them on and off like water from a faucet. "If only," he mumbled angrily to himself, "I were normal. But I'm neither normal nor in control of what I am."

A light weight landed on his right shoulder. A glance revealed the scaly yet somehow understanding face of Scrap. He smiled.

"What am I going to do with you? You aren't going to find any bonders out there, anyone to share with. You'll be living in an emotional void, existing on overflow from Pip and me, all receive and no amplify."

What did minidrags do in the wild? he wondered. Could they feed empathically off each other? Certainly they could not act as a telepathic lens the way Pip did for him. He wondered sometimes what the flying snakes derived from their select relationships with certain humans besides physical companionship.

Just what I need, he thought, though not unkindly. Another oddball in the fold. Yet what better company for a self-declared outcast than another self-anointed outcast like himself? He was feeling much better.

What he would do was take his marvelous ship and explore the Commonwealth for as long as time and health allowed. Legends would grow up around him, the wanderer with the flying snake who touched briefly at this world and then that, only to move on quietly, leaving behind neither name nor place of origin nor knowledge of purpose. The Hermit of the Commonwealth. That had a solid ring to it. Stoic and aesthetic. There was only one problem with the noble life he had set out for himself.

It was a terrible way to meet girls.

Whoever messed with my brain, he thought glumly, and stirred up my genetic code the way a bartender would stir ice with a swizzle stick, left my hormones untouched. Determination of purpose and a burgeoning sex drive, he decided, did not go well together. It was a problem that had been at the core of many of man's troubles since the beginning of time.

With time and patience and study maybe he could one day locate a sympathetic surgeon skilled enough to rid him of his headaches, if not his inheritance. Maybe he could find a way to exert some control over his life. He had seen and done enough of the extraordinary. All he wanted for himself from now on was peace and quiet and a chance to learn.

Even as he was concluding the thought, he felt the familiar, damnable prickling in his mind. No headache this time, merely a mental tickle. But in its own way, because he could not shut it out, it was equally unsettling. It was a sensation easy to identify because he had encountered it too many times previously. Somewhere, someone was in trouble.

Pip and Scrap felt it also, Scrap darting in front of his face to batter at the plexalloy like a berserk bumblebee. The minidrag blocked his view.

"Beat it, get out of the way!" He swept the flying snake aside with the back of a hand, not pausing to think that were it so inclined, the yearling minidrag could have killed him in an instant.

Leaning forward, he tried to see between the trees. Cooled air circulating between the double layer of plexalloy kept condensation from forming on the inside. Nothing ahead but green jungle, and moments later, not even that.

There was the beach fronting the river. A hundred meters of clean, packed gray sand. In the rainy season it
disappeared. Now it lay as exposed as the finest bathing
beach on New Riviera.

No one on Alaspin would think of relaxing on such a
beach, however. There were thousands of similar retreats
lining the banks of dozens of major rivers, and a hundred
could be bought for a pittance—the bloodsuckers and the
insects would drain a body like a sponge set out for their
amusement if anyone tried to sunbathe on any jungle
beach without complete body protection.

The beach was spotless; empty. There was no cover
except what a man could bring with him. The crawler
chewed up sand as Flinx retraced the tracks he had laid
down earlier. His thoughts had eased considerably, and
he was already planning the hop from Mimmisompo back
to Alaspinport, where his shuttle waited to carry him
back to the *Teacher*, high in synchronous orbit.

Pip's wings ruffled his hair from behind. The flying
snake was up and anxious.

"Now what?"

Then he was wrenching viciously on the crawler's control bar, the front treads spitting sand to the left as he
turned it sharply.

Chapter Three

The figure lying in front of the crawler was as motionless as the huge pieces of driftwood the river cast up during the rainy season. Scrap continued to bump anxiously against the front window as Flinx set the engine to idle. Pip rose from her seat to settle on his shoulder.

He cracked the dome, letting the hot, humid air swirl around him for a moment before climbing down to the beach. A narrow track such as a turtle might make returning to the sea had been gouged in the sand. It led from the river's edge to the prone figure's feet, showing the route the refugee had taken from water to dry land. His eyes flicked over the slow-moving stream. There was no sign of a boat, nor did he expect to see one.

Reaching the body, he rolled it over on to its back and unexpectedly found himself recalling the line *"Diese ist kein Mann"* from the ancient Wagnerian tridee. She was no Brunhilde, however, and he was certainly no Siegfried. Beneath the dirt, scratches, bruises, and millimite

35

bug bites lay the battered shell of a very attractive woman.

She was still alive. If she had not been, his mind would not have reacted as it had. Her demise might have saved him a headache, but for the moment at least he did not mind having endured the brief pain. Her pulse was weak but not dangerously so—clearly she was in the last stages of exhaustion. The trail leading back to the river indicated she had made it this far on hands and belly. She only looked dead.

What he could not fathom were the shorts and short-sleeved shirt. Nice attire for a sealed hotel, but potentially fatal anywhere else on Alaspin. Her arms and legs were striped with millimite bug trails, and deep red splotches showed where drill beetles had been mining. They were bad enough, but he could understand them. The bruises were more cryptic. They did not look like the kind a drifting log would make, and there were no rapids anywhere along this stretch of river.

Her blond hair was cut short on top, sides, and front save for a single tail that trailed six centimeters from behind her right ear and ended in a soggy knot. A star had been shaved above each ear. He did not recognize the style, but then, style was not something he usually concerned himself with.

He felt her clothing. Thin, lightweight. Cool and utterly useless against Alaspin's rapacious insect life. You wore either jungle drill or two sets of something else. How the hell had she ended up here like this?

A dumb tourist determined to see the backcountry on her own, most likely. Tried to walk or float out when her vehicle broke down instead of staying with it and waiting for help. An infrequent bit of stupidity, but not unheard of. Birding or snake watching or taking tridee chips.

Then he reminded himself she might have come up-river in an enclosed boat. If it had sunk she would have had no choice but to swim or walk. That scenario made some sense. The water would also mute any emergency beacon signal. Maybe she was more unlucky than dumb.

He had no trouble picking her up and carrying her back to the crawler. Getting her inside was another matter. She was not that heavy, but he had to rig a lift with some rope and haul her up hand over hand. If not for the added muscle he had put on this past year, he could not have done it. Pip kept clear, watching, while Scrap darted anxiously around the limp body, no doubt curious as to why a living human being should be devoid of emotion.

The four passenger seats could be folded flat, making beds for two riders. He put her in the back of the crawler, then punched up the location of the first-aid kit.

As would be expected for a rental vehicle, the instructions on the self-injecting ampoules in the kit were simple and self-explanatory. Some looked pretty old, but none had reached their official expiration dates. The bites were easy enough to treat. Salve for the millimite scars, iofluorodene to kill the eggs the drill bugs had laid in her muscles. He also pumped her full of general antiseptic and fungicide. None of the ampoules lit up during injection, so she was not allergic to the stuff he was dumping into her system. He applied intravenous antibiotic and a spray over the bruises and cuts, then sat back and surveyed his handiwork. The crawler's air-conditioning had replaced the hot air with a fresh soothing coolness.

The bruises on her face and body troubled him, but there was nothing he could do for her appearance. The crawler's medkit was designed to keep people alive, not repair them cosmetically. Well, it would not bother her as long as she was unconscious. The best thing would be to get her to the hospital at Alaspinport.

She had a slight fever and was badly dehydrated despite the fact that she had obviously spent some time in the river. Either she had been afraid to drink the perfectly potable water or she had been unable to. He had no idea when she had last eaten, but her stomach and intestines felt anything but full.

After waiting an hour for the medication to settle in and take hold, he gave her two ampoules of multipurpose nutrients and vitamins in a sodium solution. The injected broth would give her strength and allow her system to begin some serious repair work.

An hour later his efforts were rewarded. She turned her head to her right and moved one arm several centimeters. Her neuromuscular system was functioning, then. The portable emergency scanner had not revealed any internal injuries, the light staying in the healthy pink range as he had run the pickup over her body. It had beeped a couple of times when he had passed it over the severest bruises. If it had gone over into the red or purple, that would have been an indication of broken bones or worse.

Giving her a last glance, he returned to the driver's seat. Back in Mimmisompo someone would be worrying about her, be it relative, traveling companion, or research society. He would find out and turn her over to them.

She really was quite pretty, he thought as he put the crawler in drive. The longer he studied her injuries, the more convinced he became that they were not the result of an accident. Her attire was proof enough that she was no backcountry veteran. He could see her offering a ride to some traveler in distress, only to end up mugged, beaten, and left for dead in the middle of the river. An unpleasant picture with the smell of truth about it. If she had met with foul play of some kind, it would explain everything.

Except why even a thief would want to beat her half to death. A pro would have simply knocked her out, tossed her overboard, and taken her goods, leaving it to the river and the jungle to clean up after him. Not that he was any judge of criminal ethics. His own criminal ethics, when he had been engaged in petty thievery as a youngster, had been radically different from most. He studied her in the rearview. Her bruises were not distributed at random. They suggested professional work of an unsavory nature.

He grunted. What did he know about it? It could have been anything from a simple slip on a railing to a lovers' quarrel. He was hypothesizing on air.

The crawler slid into the river, the buoyancy compensators humming to life as the treads expanded to function as paddles. He had opted for the durability and longevity of the crawler, but as he studied his damaged passenger, he found himself wishing he had rented a skimmer despite the delay it would have entailed.

It took three days of traveling with the current before the river bent to reveal the floating docks of Mimmisompo. Not once had his passenger opened her eyes, though she had moaned in her sleep. It did not make him uncomfortable to listen to her disjointed mumbling, because he was concentrating on her emotional subconscious. As expected, it was an incoherent jumble, alternating between pleasure and pain depending largely on how recently he had dosed her. The ampoules were keeping her alive, though, and her body was slowing repairing itself.

When he docked in Mimmisompo, he turned in the crawler and called for a robocab. It delivered them to the modest hotel where he had stayed on arrival two weeks ago. The manager coded his room without questions. He was glued to the tridee and did not even look up when Flinx returned with the limp woman in his arms. In Mimmisompo plenty of people came and went from their rooms in that state.

The lift carried them to the third and top floor of the hotel. Flinx passed the charged bar across the center of the door, then waited while it read the code and clicked open. Pip and Scrap entered first, Flinx following. He kicked the door shut behind him.

Marveling at her litheness, he placed her gently on one

of the two beds. After checking her vital signs, he treated himself to his first shower in days. When he reentered the bedroom, it was to find her sleeping as soundly as she had in the crawler.

This morning he had used the last of the crawler's emergency supplies. Tomorrow he would find her friends or, failing that, a physician. She lay still on the bed, barely illuminated by the moonlight pouring through the single large window on her left. Above her headboard the electronic bug repeller glowed emerald, ready to dissuade any intruder that managed to make it past the hotel's exterior defenses.

Flinx checked his own before tossing his towel aside and sliding gratefully beneath clean, cool sheets. The room was Spartan but spacious, dry, and insect-free. Outside the capital city of Alaspinport you could not expect more than that.

She was breathing easily, and he rolled over to stare at her. Pip assumed her familiar position at his feet while Scrap settled close by.

If others were searching frantically for her, they would have to wait until he had had a decent night's sleep, he reflected. He had earned it. Another day would make no difference to her or her colleagues, assuming she had any in Mimmisompo. He did not worry about other unlikely possibilities. Not with Pip resting alertly at his feet.

At least, he thought lazily as he drifted off to sleep, this was one time he had managed to do a good deed without involving himself deeply in someone else's problems.

Morning proved it was not going to be that easy. Somehow it never was. She was still resting peacefully when he awoke, rose soundlessly, and prepared to go out.

As he dressed, he could not help glancing in her direction. She was lying on her side, and the sheets had draped themselves provocatively over her body. In the light she was not merely attractive, she was beautiful.

He kept telling himself as he studied the rise and fall of her chest that he was only checking the regularity of her breathing. It was impossible for him to lie to himself, however. Pip's reactions always truthfully mirrored what he was feeling.

He left hurriedly, sealing his jumpsuit on the way out. She was not hurting, he was sure of that. Not with all the antibios, specifics, and endorphine analogs he had pumped into her. If anything, she ought to be floating half a meter above the bed. A last pass with the scanner was accomplished without a beep. She was healing rapidly, as much a credit to her own constitution as to his amateur treatment of her injuries.

Tough little lady, he mused. All the more reason to try to find out how she had come to be beaten up and dumped in the middle of the Ingre.

This was only his second visit to Mimmisompo, and he did not know the town that well, but he had learned long ago that information was often available in such places in inverse proportion to the actual population. Furthermore, it was not necessary to scour the entire community to find the answers he needed. There were always logical places to make inquiries. The official information booths were at the bottom of any such list.

Because of her wholly inadequate attire, Flinx went on the assumption that she was a recent arrival to the Ingre region. No half-experienced prospector or scientist would have been caught dead in the kind of clothing she had been wearing when he had found her, not even if traveling in a vehicle as secure as the crawler. You never knew when you might have to go outside. At the minimum she should have been wearing boots, a long-sleeved shirt, long-legged pants, repellers, and cooling threads.

Her assailants had known their business. You could not walk out of the Ingre. By the time a body could be located, the local fauna would have made identification difficult, determination of cause of death impossible.

What kept nagging at him was the apparent profes-

sionalism with which the beating had been administered.
Her bruises had been evenly dispersed across her body,
suggesting that whoever had handed them out had taken
care to prolong her consciousness for as long as possible.
It smacked of sadism, questioning, or both. He worried
about it all the way to Quayside.

The entertainment center was not crowded. It was too
early. There were drivers and cargo lifters, alluvial min-
ers, and one independent rarewood logger whom Flinx
recognized by the specialized trimming equipment dangling from his belt. Half a dozen men, nearly as many
women.

There were also two thranx, looking a lot more at ease
than their human compatriots. Each was chatting with a
human instead of with each other. It was rumored that
the thranx preferred the company of human beings to
their own kind. Flinx knew that was talked up by thranx
psychologists. Even now, hundreds of years after the
Amalgamation, there were still humans whose insecto-
phobia required attention and treatment.

He did not look at them twice. Man and thranx had
been so close for so long that they were no longer thought
of as aliens. More like short people in shiny suits.

The people in the entertainment center showed little
interest in the games and other diversions Quayside offered. Two men were idly toying with a quick-draw
shooting game near the back. No one else paid any attention to the horrific and extraordinarily lifelike monsters
that leapt from behind rocks or jumped from vines or
erupted from the ground to attack the two competitors.
The illusions had to be shot in the right spot the correct
number of times for a score to register. Their simulated
death throes were exuberantly noisy and dramatic. It was
the nature of the game.

The fact that each holoed creature actually existed, either on Alaspin or on another world, added to the game's
attraction, though Flinx was not sure a teacher would
have thought of it as educational. He never indulged in

the electronic entertainments. Once he had played one out of deference to a companion. It had left him cold. Though he was astonishingly proficient, there was no challenge to it. He credited his skill to good reflexes and never thought there was any more to it than that.

At the conclusion of the game some joker had repositioned the halo projector so that a large, carnivorous reptile had dropped down on Flinx from the direction of the ceiling. The result was just what the practical joker had been hoping for. Flinx had been startled and frightened.

Unfortunately, that had caused Pip to react defensively. Her highly caustic venom had burned right through the holo projector's lens, at considerable cost to the establishment's owner. With Pip hovering nearby, the chastened pranksters had paid the full cost of the damage.

He angled toward the only crowded table. The man seated facing him boasted a handlebar mustache that tapered to waxed, glistening points. They quivered like the needles on a praxiloscope when he laughed. His name was Jebcoat, and he hailed from Hivehom, a human born and raised on the thranx capital world. He was no stranger to heat and humidity. As near as Flinx had been able to tell from their initial brief contact weeks ago, when he had first arrived in Mimmisompo, Jebcoat had done a little of everything. If you asked him a question there was a fifty-fifty chance you would get an answer. The odds on truth were lower.

Flinx did not recognize his female friends. Jebcoat saw him approaching and broke off his conversation with the ladies to give the young man a broad smile. One of the women turned curiously to inspect the newcomer. She was a shade under two meters tall and wore implants that gave her pupils a silvery cast.

"This kid a friend of yours?" she asked Jebcoat without taking her eyes off Flinx.

He stiffened momentarily until he realized she was trying to provoke him. That was one way of taking the measure of a stranger on a world like Alaspin.

"He's no kid." Jebcoat chuckled softly. "I ain't sayin' he's a man, either. Frankly I don't know what he is, but you'd best watch your word footing around 'im. He wears death for a play-pretty."

As if on cue, Pip stuck her head out from beneath Flinx's collar and Scrap stirred on his wrist. The woman's eyes flicked from mature minidrag to adolescent. Flinx sensed no fear in her, which might mean either that she was as bold and confident as she appeared, or simply that his damnable talents weren't functioning at that moment.

The other woman was tall, but no giantess like her companion. "Go easy on him, Lundameilla. He's kinda cute, though a bit on the skinny side." She laughed, a short jittery sound that would make anyone in the vicinity grin. "You and him going together sideways wouldn't fill up a decent doorway. Care to join us?"

Flinx shook his head. "Just a question or two. I've been out in the Ingre, and I need to find out about somebody I ran into out there." The giantess's eyebrows rose.

"Find anything while you were out there?" Jebcoat eyed him speculatively.

"What I was looking for." Flinx saw that his approval rating had risen another notch. It was not considered impolite to ask questions of a stranger on Alaspin, but it was considered foolish to reply straightforwardly. Sometimes it was worse than foolish.

"Found something I wasn't looking for, too. About a hundred centimeters, slim, female, twenty-two to -five, pale blond with a weird haircut, and blue eyes, though they might've been dyed recently. Very nice."

"How nice?" the other man at the table asked, speaking for the first time. He was broad and burly and had not depilated in days.

"Extremely. She was wearing shorts and a thin shirt, one only."

"In the Ingre?" The giantess made a face.

"Millimite and drill bug bites everywhere." Flinx eyed the other man. "Also somebody had worked her over real careful and professional-like."

The heavyweight's smile disappeared, and he sat back in his chair. "Deity, what a world!" He turned to Jebcoat. "Spark any circuits?"

Jebcoat considered, the mustache temporarily stilled. Finally he shook his head. "I don't know a soul who'd be caught dead outside in the shorts, much less the shirt. How's her condition?"

"Improving. I emptied my crawler's first-aid kit into her. It was full when I started."

"Damn well better have been, or you could sue the renter." He glanced at the giantess. "Call up any memories for you, Lundy?" The tall woman shook her head.

"I don't know anybody that pretty or that stupid."

"What about ID?" he asked Flinx.

"Nothing. I looked." He eyed the other man, but that worthy was properly subdued. The situation was not amusing anymore.

"We'll ask around. Won't we, Blade?" The giantess's companion nodded agreeably.

"So will I," said Jebcoat, "but I haven't heard tell of anyone missin' local, and you know how fast that kind of news travels hereabouts."

"Nope, nobody missing," the other man muttered. "Nobody. Would've heard. When'd you find her?"

"Few days ago," Flinx told him.

"Then everybody'd know by now if she was known around here. Must be a newcomer," Jebcoat suggested.

"That's the way I see it."

"I know the agent at Alaspinport. If you like, I'll give 'im a call, take a copy of the last couple of shuttle passenger manifests, tridee the ID. We can run 'em through my processor."

"That might give us something," Flinx said gratefully.

"Not if she was brought in by private shuttle," Blade pointed out.

"Unlikely," Jebcoat said.

"Unlikely, yeah, but not impossible. If that's the case—" She eyed Flinx evenly. "—there'll be no record of her arrival."

"Maybe," Flinx said softly, "that's what the people who beat her up had in mind."

The woman stared back at him, then turned to Jebcoat. "You're right; he's no kid. You been around, boy," she told Flinx.

"That I have—girl." He braced himself, but all she did was smile approvingly.

"Come on, Lundy." The two women rose to depart. Lundameilla towered over every man in the room. Both drew appreciative stares. "We'll ask around for you, like I said. Meantime we got to get back and check on our dredge. Lundy and me, we got a claim up in the Samberlin district." As she came around the table, she bent quickly to whisper in Flinx's ear.

"You ever get up that way, stop by and say hello. Maybe we'll show you how we operate together, Lundy and I. You might say we could show you the long and the short of it."

"Leave the guy alone, Blade." Jebcoat was grinning hugely beneath the mustache. "Can't you see he's blushing?"

"I am not blushing," Flinx insisted. "Redheads' skin is naturally flush."

"Okay, okay."

As Lundy strolled past, Flinx felt a distinct sharp pinch on his left buttock. The giantess left him with that and a wink as she followed her companion out. He made a face at Pip.

"I'm attacked and you do nothing."

The flying snake stared back blankly. Not for the first time Flinx found himself wondering exactly what the minidrag's intelligence level was.

Jebcoat put both hands flat on the table. "Let me make one quick call."

He did not have to leave the table to do so. Flinx watched him work the communicator that was built into the table. Thousands of fine hardwoods filled the jungle surrounding them, and someone had gone to the expense of importing a plastic table made to look like wood. No wonder the thranx found their human friends a constant source of amusement.

Jebcoat chattered away at the pickup. Finally he shrugged and let the headphone snap back in place. "I tried the obvious: local cops, immigration records, a couple of friends. No one matching your description has arrived on Alaspin in the past two months, much less been reported missing. We still have to check Alaspin-port records, of course, but I ain't optimistic."

"What do you suggest?"

"Lemme get ahold of my buddy at the port. Lundy and Blade will spread it around the backcountry. But right now, as far as the authorities are concerned, your battered acquaintance don't exist. Since she's in your room, she's your responsibility."

"*All* yours," the other man said cheerfully.

"But I'm just on my way out."

"Offworld again?" Jebcoat was still trying to figure his young friend. "For somebody your age with no visible means of support, you manage to get around pretty easy."

"I have an inheritance," Flinx explained. Though not the kind of inheritance you're thinking of, he added silently. "I can't take her with me, and I don't want to just abandon her in the room. She's got no credcard, either."

"So?" Jebcoat asked. "The hotel owner would be delighted to put a claim on her."

"Hell," the other man said, "if she's as pretty as you say she is, I'll take her off your hands myself."

"Ain't you forgettin' something, Howie?"

"What's that?"

"You're married."

A cloud shadowed Howie's face. "Oh, yeah. I'd kinda forgot."

Jebcoat eyed him mercilessly. "With kids."

"Kids. Yeah," Howie muttered disconsolately.

Jebcoat smiled back at Flinx. "Howie here's been out in the Ingre too long. No, she's yours, my friend. You can do what you want with her. Wait till she gets well, take her with you, or just scram. But it's your decision. I don't want anything to do with it." He indicated the resting minidrags. "I don't have a couple of lethal empaths to keep an eye on me. Now, if you'll excuse me, I've other business to attend to. I'll get back to you if I find out anything about your mystery lady. Howie and I are discussing the price of a theoretical load of Sangretibark extract."

Flinx said nothing. It was illegal to export Sangretibark. For some it worked as a powerful aphrodisiac. In others it had unwanted side effects—such as cardiac arrest. But then, it was none of his business. Jebcoat was a friend so long as you treated him with respect. He would make a bad enemy.

He tried a couple of other contacts, with equal lack of success. No one knew anything about the woman he described. Once his query was met with an openly hostile response, but only verbally. Pip's presence prevented anyone from dealing Flinx anything stronger than a harsh word.

That afternoon he wandered back to the hotel, discouraged and puzzled. The woman lay where he had left her. At the moment she was lying on her back. As he eyed her, it occurred to him that while he had done wonders for her wounds, her appearance remained unchanged. She still wore plenty of dirt and grime.

He spent an hour cleaning her face, shoulders, arms, and legs with a washcloth. Thin red streaks had replaced the weals on her legs where the millimite bugs had dug, and the drill bug holes were already closing. The worst of her bruises were almost gone.

He lay down for a short nap, exhausted from the journey out of the Ingre and his efforts on her behalf. He might have slept through the night if the screaming had not awakened him.

Chapter Four

Instantly he was up and searching. Looking every bit as beautiful awake as she had while asleep, his guest stood across the room. In her right hand she clutched a small but wicked little knife. Her eyes were wild.

Pip hovered before her, little more than a couple of meters from her face and well within attack range. Scrap flew nervous circles around his mother. The young minidrag's constant movement was unsettling the woman more than Pip's hovering.

Flinx took it all in in a second and wondered what the hell was going on. The knife did not make any sense. Neither did Pip's threatening posture, unless you assumed the knife had been aimed at her master. But why would she want to threaten him while he slept?

That was when she noticed him sitting up on the bed. Her eyes barely flicked away from the flying snake. "Call them off, damn you, call them off!"

Flinx did so with a casual thought. Pip darted back to the bed.

The woman's breathing slowed, and the arm holding the knife dropped. "How did you do that?"

"All Alaspinian minidrags are emotional telepaths. Sometimes they'll bond with a person. Pip is mine—she's the adult. The adolescent's name is Scrap."

"Cute," she said tensely, "real cute." Then she shuddered and lowered her head. "I don't know how you found me. What now? Are you going to beat me up again? Why don't you just kill me and get it over with? I've answered all your questions."

Flinx's gaze narrowed. "I didn't beat you up, and I have no intention of killing you. If I held any malign intentions toward you, d'you think I'd have fixed you up?"

Her head came up quickly. She studied him for a long moment. "You aren't one of them?" she asked hesitantly.

"No I'm not, whoever 'them' are."

"Deity." She let out a long sigh, at which point her legs turned to rubber and she had to lean against the wall for support. The knife clattered silently on the hardwood floor.

Flinx slid off the bed and started toward her, halting when she stiffened. She still did not trust him, and after what she had been through, he could hardly blame her.

"I'm not here to hurt you." He spoke slowly, soothingly. "I'll help if I can."

Her eyes shifted from him to the flying snake. Slowly she bent to recover the knife, placed it on the antique dresser nearby, and laughed nervously.

"That doesn't make any sense, but neither does anything else that's happened to me in the past few weeks. Besides, if half of what I've heard is true, a knife's pretty useless against a minidrag."

"Not half," Flinx corrected her. "It's all true." He kept his distance. "Would you like to sit down? You've been unconscious for several days."

She put a hand to her forehead. "I thought I was dead.

Out there." She indicated the window that looked over the town. "I was never so certain of anything in my life. Now I'm not sure of anything anymore." She blinked and tried to smile at him. "Thank you. I will sit down."

There was a lounge chair made of epoxied lianas. Under the epoxy, the wood flashed a rainbow of colors. It was the only brightly colored piece of furniture in the room. Flinx sat down on the edge of the bed while Pip curled herself around one of the short bedposts, looking like a carved decoration. Scrap settled in his lap. He stroked the back of the small flying snake's head absently.

"How old are you, anyway?" the woman asked him as she slumped into the chair.

Why do they always ask that? he wondered. Not "Thank you for saving me" or "Where do you come from?" or "What's your business?" His reply was the same one he had been using for years.

"Old enough. Old enough not to be the one who was lying out in the Ingre making a meal for the millimite bugs and dying of exposure. How'd you end up like that?"

"I escaped." She inhaled deeply, as if the cool air in the room was an unexpectedly rich dessert. "Got away."

"I didn't think you ended up there by choice. You weren't dressed right. Alaspin's not a forgiving place."

"Neither were the people I was with. What did you say your name was?"

"Didn't, but it's Flinx."

"Just Flinx?" When he did not respond, she smiled slightly. It was beautiful to see. "All right. I know there are limits to questions in a place like this." She was trying to act tough. At any moment she might start cursing him—or burst out crying. He sat quietly, stroking the lethal creature snuggled in his lap.

"You said you escaped. I thought maybe your vehicle had broken down. Who'd you escape from? I'd assume whoever beat you up."

Her hand moved instinctively to the half-healed bruises beneath her left shoulder. "Yes. It doesn't hurt as bad now."

"I've been giving you first aid," he explained. "I've been in situations where I've had to take care of others as well as myself. My resources were as limited as my knowledge, I'm afraid. You were lucky. No broken bones, no internal injuries."

"That's funny, because it feels like everything inside me is busted."

"Whoever worked you over didn't want to kill you. What did they want?"

"Information. Answers to questions. I told them as little as I could, but I had to tell them something . . . So they'd stop for a while." Her voice had grown small. "I didn't tell them everything they wanted to know. So they kept at me. I feigned unconsciousness—it wasn't hard, I'd had plenty of practice. Then I got away from them.

"They had me in a place out in that jungle somewhere. It was at night, and I made it to the river. I found a broken log and just started drifting downstream. I had no idea it was so far from anyplace."

"I found you high up on a beach. You'd dragged yourself out of the water."

She nodded. "I think I remember letting go of the log. I was losing my strength, and I knew I had to get to dry land or I'd drown."

"You'd be surprised how far you crawled."

She was looking down at her hands. "You said I've been out for several days." He nodded as she turned her palms up, inspecting the scoured skin. "I guess you've done a good job on me. Thanks. I can't say that I feel good, but I feel better."

"Several days' rest is good medicine for any injury."

"I woke up and saw you lying on the other bed, and I thought they'd found me. I thought you were one of them." This time she did not smile. "I had the little knife. It fits inside the middle of my boot. That's how I got loose. Not much use against a bunch of people, but against one sleeping man . . . I was going to cut your throat.''

"Pip would never have allowed it."

"So I found out." She eyed the flying snake wrapped around the bedpost. "When it came at me, I tried to get out the door. It's sealed both ways. That's when I started screaming, but nobody came to see what was happening."

"I sealed the door because I don't like interruptions when I'm sleeping." Reaching behind the headboard, he brought out a thin bracelet and touched a stud set flush with the polished surface. The door clicked softly. "I bring my own lock. Don't trust the ones they rent you. As for your screaming, this is a pretty wide-open town. Not a place where people interfere in their neighbors' business. Hard to tell sometimes why somebody's screaming." He slipped the bracelet on his wrist. "Ever seen a picture of a body ravaged by millimite bugs?"

She looked down at her legs, then ran her fingers along the almost vanished welts. "These?"

He nodded. "They feed subcutaneously. They're not very big, but they're voracious and persistent. The first thing they do is eat their way to where the muscles are attached to the bone. They cut through the legs first. Then, when their prey can't move anymore, they settle in for a leisurely month or so of eating."

She shuddered anew. "Here I am throwing questions at you right and left, and I haven't really thanked you."

"Yes you did. A moment ago."

"I did?" She blinked. "Sorry. My name. I haven't told you my name." She brushed at her short blond hair. He wondered what she would look like with a professional patina of cosmetics on that exquisitely sculpted face. "I'm Clarity. Clarity Held."

"Pleasure to meet you."

She laughed, a little less uneasily this time. "Is it?

You really don't know a thing about me. Maybe if you did, you wouldn't think it such a pleasure.''

"I found an injured human being lying exposed to the jungle. I'd have picked up anyone under those circumstances."

"I'll bet you would have. Come on," she chided him, "how old are you, really?"

He sighed. "Nineteen, but I've been around a lot. Listen, what's this all about? Who beat you up and why were they holding you against your will?"

Suddenly she was looking around the room, ignoring his questions. "Is there a bathroom in this place?"

Flinx put a damper on his curiosity and nodded at the holo of an icy fountain off to the left. "Behind there."

"Is there a bathtub?" There was an edge in her voice. He nodded, and she smiled gratefully. "About time things started evening out. From hell to heaven in one waking breath." She rose and started toward the holo.

"Wait a minute. You haven't answered any of *my* questions."

"I will. I'll tell you anything you want to know. After all, I owe you my life." She glanced back at the doorway. "You sure no one can get in here?"

"I'm sure. Even if they did . . ." He nodded in Pip's direction.

"All right. I should be working on getting out of here, on getting off this world. Because I'm sure they're looking for me right now. But I feel like something that just crawled out of a sludge pit. If I don't clean myself up, I won't be able to stand me long enough to answer your questions. Bath first." She smiled to herself. "There's always time for a bath."

He leaned back against his pillow. "If you say so. Nobody's after *me*."

"That's right," she murmured thoughtfully. "Nobody is after you. Do you think you can help me get away from here? Away from this town? What's the name of this place, anyway?"

"Mimmisompo. You didn't come through here?"

"No. I was on a big skimmer, for a long time." She frowned. "Alaspinport, I think. They brought me down drugged, and we got right in the skimmer. I was pretty much out of it except when they brought me around to answer questions. I'll explain everything I can, tell you all I can remember, but later. Right now a hot bath would be just about the most wonderful thing imaginable."

"Then go ahead and indulge. I'll keep an eye on the door."

She took a step toward him, then hesitated. "Nice to have a friend here." A quick turn and she was through the holo that closed off the bathroom from the rest of the apartment.

Her passage automatically turned off the image, and she did not bother to reset it, her mind on nothing but the bath. Moments later the sound of running water reached him. Hands behind his head, he lay back on the bed and contemplated the ceiling. Strange. One would have thought she had had enough of water in the river. The peculiar regard women held for hot water was something he did not understand.

By rolling over and stretching ever so slightly he could see her sitting on the edge of the diamond-shaped tub. She was lightly sponging herself. It was hard to estimate another's inhibitions without first knowing her world of origin, social status, and religious inclinations. She looked up suddenly and saw him watching her, and she smiled. Not invitingly but not mockingly, either. Simply a pleasant, relaxed smile.

Knowing that did not keep him from turning away in embarrassment. Then he was angry at himself for doing so. Pip looked up curiously while Scrap explored the pile of blankets where Clarity had slept. The flying snake reacted to his every emotion, not only those that were threatening.

Clarity Held rose from the bath and begin drying herself. This time it was not necessary for him to stretch to enjoy the view. This time he deliberately did not turn away.

"That was heavenly!" Apparently the society in which she had been raised did not recognize the nudity taboo, a historical development on an as yet unknown world for which he was very grateful. She sang to herself in a voice that was only slightly off key, then put the towel aside without a suggestion of shyness and began to remove her clothes from the room's autolaundry.

I have talked to the wise men of Commonwealth, Flinx mused. I have spoken with captains of industry and of alien warships. I have made contact when no one else was able with an artificial intelligence thousands of years old and kept my composure in the face of evils both human and otherwise. So why the hell can't I have a sensible conversation with a single member of the opposite sex of my own race without bumbling and stumbling over every word?

He had heard about verbal seduction but had not the slightest idea where to begin. He wanted more than anything else to ingratiate himself so powerfully that she would forget about his age and start thinking of him as a man. He wanted to persuade her, to reassure her, to dazzle her with his resourcefulness and brilliance, to defuse her fears and activate her senses.

What he said was, "Bath make you feel better?"

"Immensely, thanks." She was drying her hair now, fluffing out the blond brush, the single flanking pigtail bobbing like a cat's toy behind her ear. He wondered who had performed the spectrum shift that had given her turquoise eyes. Surely that color could not be natural.

"If you plan on doing any more traveling around here, we'll have to find you some more appropriate clothing."

"Don't worry. The only environments I want to experience between here and the shuttleport are humanx-made. I'm straightlining from here to orbit, if you'll help me." She nodded in the direction of the window. "They're out there right now, wondering how I got away.

Hopefully back along the river." Her hands paused, and her cheerful expression abruptly darkened. A little terror crept back into her voice.

"You said I left a long trail from the river onto the beach where I crawled out. They could find that. They'd know I was still alive."

"I didn't know you'd been kidnapped, so I saw no reason to take the time to obliterate it. But don't worry. Even if they find it and interpret it correctly, the next thing they'll do is start searching the immediate vicinity with a heat sensor and image processor."

"They'll see your crawler's tracks, too. They'll consider that I might've been picked up."

"They have to find the place first. You clean and relaxed?"

"More or less."

"Then how about some answers to my questions? Let's start with who you are and why these people find you so intriguing."

She started toward the window. Halfway there she thought better of exposing herself to the outside, privacy shield notwithstanding, and pivoted to head toward the dresser as she spoke.

"My name you know. I'm a division chief for an expanding enterprise. These fanatics picked me because I'm uniquely talented."

For an instant Flinx went cold, then realized she had to be speaking of some other kind of unique talent.

"It's a fantastic deal for somebody my age, just starting out. I supervise a dozen specialists, most of them older than me, and I own a piece of the profits. I mean, I knew I was better than anybody in my field when I was doing my dissertation, and I've proved it subsequently, but it was still an impressive offer. So naturally I jumped at it."

"You have a high opinion of yourself." He tried not to make it sound like a criticism.

It bothered her not at all. "Justified in the lab." She

was talking easily now that they were on a subject she was comfortable with. "It's exciting stuff. I wanted to be out front. I could be making even more money elsewhere. Doing cosmetic work on New Riviera or Earth. You know, I had a chance to go to Amropolous and work with the thranx. They're still better at micromanipulation than any human. Some of their work's more art than science. But I don't like heat and humidity.

"This bunch that grabbed me, they're extremists of the worst sort. I'd heard about them before—everybody reads the fax—but I didn't think they were any different from half a hundred groups with similar aims. Shows how little anybody knows. There was this young guy—" She looked away from Flinx. "—he was plated. I mean iridescent, like a tridee star."

"Good-looking." Flinx spoke emotionlessly. "Go on."

"We went out a few times together. Said he was with port authority, which is why I hadn't seen him around. Couldn't get through company security, so we met outside. I thought I was falling in love with him. He had that ability, you know, to make you fall in love with him. He asked me to take a stroll topside with him one night. It was pretty calm upstairs, so I said sure." She paused.

"You've got to understand that it was real exciting intellectually where I was working, but socially it was plasmodium. Just about everyone was a lot older than I, and frankly, none of them were much to look at. Physicality still plays an important role in interpersonal relationships, you know."

Tell me about it, he thought. He was not happy with the turn the conversation had taken, but he had nothing to add.

She gave a little shrug. "Anyway, I think he drugged me. He was one of *them*, you see. The next time I saw him, he didn't look so handsome anymore. Physically yes, but his expression was different. It matched his companions'."

"Species?" He was thinking of the AAnn's relentless assaults on advanced human technology.

"All human as near as I could tell. If they were alien, they had terrific disguises. They hauled me offworld. When I woke up, it was hot and sticky and somewhere out there, I guess." She waved absently in the direction of the Ingre. "That's when the questions started. About my work, how advanced it was, what the company's plans were for future expansion and development, and a lot of basics like our lab layout and security setup and so on.

"I told them I couldn't answer because everything they were asking me was covered by the Interworld Commerce Secrets Act. They didn't say anything. They just turned me over to this one tall woman who started beating the crap out of me. I'm not a real brave person. So I started telling them what they wanted to know, as little as possible about each subject.

"I knew I'd keep telling them until I'd told them everything, and I had a pretty good idea what would happen to me when I'd finally answered their last question. So I made it clear one night and ran like hell. It was pitch-black, and things kept biting me and stabbing at me, so I went into the river and found my log and started downstream. I didn't know where I was or where I was going. I just wanted to get away."

"You're lucky you made it as far as the river," Flinx said somberly. "Alaspin has its share of nocturnal carnivores. The insects you know about."

She scratched reflexively at one leg. "I woke up here, jumped to conclusions, and thought about killing you. Now I've had a bath, I feel two thousand percent better than I did the last time I was conscious, and you're going to help me get off this world and back to my people. I'm sure they're searching for me, too, but not around here. In addition to being well liked personally, I'm irreplaceable. I'm sure there'll be a reward for my return. I imagine there always is in a situation like this."

"I'm not interested in any reward."

"No? You're that prosperous, at your age?" He chose to ignore her slip.

"I have an inheritance. Enough for my needs. What about you? What makes you so popular?"

She grinned ruefully. "I'm a gengineer. In fact, I'm the best gengineer."

His expression didn't change. It didn't have to for Pip to react to his emotional surge. The flying snake leapt from its position on the bedpost, flew once around the startled Clarity, and then settled abruptly back on the bed.

He turned away, unsure how well he had concealed his reaction. Not perfectly, it seemed.

"What's wrong with your pet? What's the matter? Did I say something to upset you?"

"No, nothing." Even as he spoke he sensed the transparency of the lie. "It's just that someone very near to me had trouble with some gengineers a long time ago." Hastily he donned the innocent-child smile that had served him so well in his childhood days of thieving. "It's nothing now. Just old history."

She was either more perceptive or more mature than he thought, because there was genuine concern on her face as she came toward him.

"You're sure it's okay? I can't change what I am."

"It had nothing to do with you. What occurred all took place before you were born." Now he smiled again, a crooked smile, confident she would not know the reason behind it. "Before I was born, in fact."

No, neither of us was born when the Society began their experiments. You were already several years old when the experiment coded "Philip Lynx" came into the world with his DNA tossed like salad in a bowl. I can't tell you that, of course. I can't tell anyone. But I do wonder what you'd make of me if you knew what I was. Would you have any idea if I'm a good result or a bad one?

It would have helped had he grown up a scientist. Instead he had spent his childhood as a thief. It was difficult to tell which would have revealed his origin to him sooner.

Her fingers touched his shoulder. He stiffened, then relaxed, and she dug in gently, massaging. The hurt is deeper than you can reach, he thought, eyeing her.

"Flinx, you aren't afraid of me, are you?"

"Afraid of you? That's funny. I'm the one who dragged you out of the jungle half-dead, remember?"

"Yes, and I'm as grateful as anyone who owes her life to someone else can be for what you did for me. You will help me leave Alaspin before they find me again, won't you? They're mad but resourceful. Crazy smart. I'm not so sure they're smarter than you. There's something about you—I'm usually pretty good at slotting people, but you're a total blank to me. You look like a gangly, overgrown kid, but you seem to know your way around."

Around? He smiled inwardly. Yes, you might say that I've been around, little gengineer. I've traveled to the Blight and the fringes of the Commonwealth. I've done such things as most men only dream of, and others that cannot be imagined. Oh, I've been around, all right.

He had turned away from her again. Now he felt her pressing up against him, her front tight against his back, her arms sliding around his waist in a graceful serpentine flanking movement as she nonverbally began to make it clear exactly how grateful she was to him and how grateful she might be.

Without really knowing why, he found himself slipping free of her grasp and turning to face her. There was hurt on her face and real concern in her voice. That made it harder.

"Now what's wrong?"

"I haven't known you long enough to like you that way. Not consciously, anyhow."

"You liked me better unconscious?"

"That's not what I mean, and you know it." Time for

a subject change. "If you still feel threatened, you ought to report what happened to you to the authorities."

"I told you, they have spies everywhere. That's how they got to me in the first place. We'd only have to talk to one wrong person, and then they'd have me again. You they'd probably kill, just to keep from talking."

"That would upset you?"

"You're damn right it would." She was looking straight at him. "You're a curious savior, Flinx." She cocked her head to give him a coquettish sideways stare. "I'd like to find out just how curious. Don't you find me attractive?"

He swallowed. As usual he intended to be in complete control of the situation, and as usual he was not.

"Extraordinarily attractive," he finally managed to mumble.

"That clears that up, anyway. Oh!" Scrap startled her as the adolescent minidrag landed on her shoulder. Unable to coil around her shoulder, he settled for wrapping his tail tightly around her thick, short blond sidetail.

"His name's Scrap. I think he likes you."

"How do you do?" She bent her head to eye the tiny instrument of death snuggling cozily against her neck. "How do you know he likes me?"

"Because you're still alive."

"I see." She pursed her lips. "You said his name was Scrap?" At the mention of his name, the young flying snake's head rose slightly.

"They tend to bond, you know? Form close emotional attachments with human beings they're attracted to. Do snakes bother you?"

"I'm a gengineer. Nothing living bothers me except a few creatures I can't see with the naked eye."

I wonder what you'd think of me if you knew my history, he mused. "They're telepathic on the emotional level. Scrap knows what you're feeling. If he chooses to bond with you, you'll never have a more devoted companion or effective bodyguard. Pip and I have been together my whole life. I've never had more than a moment or two to regret the relationship.''

"How long do they live?" She was stroking the back of the flying snake's head the way she had seen Flinx caress Pip.

"Nobody knows. They're uncommon on Alaspin, practically unknown offworld. This is a tough place to do studies in the wild, much less on anything as dangerous as a minidrag." He thought a moment. "Pip was mature when I found her, so she must be around seventeen. That'd be old for a reptile, but the minidrags aren't reptiles."

"No. I can feel the warmth." She smiled at her new friend. "Well, you're welcome to stay there if that's what you want."

It was. Flinx could feel it. After considering taking her in his arms and kissing her firmly, he sighed and sat down on his bed. He was an expert at such scenarios but utterly inept at putting them into practice. His fingers worked nervously against each other.

"I said I'd help you. How do you want to proceed?"

"I have to get back to my people. I'm sure they're worried sick by now. As far as I know, not a soul knows what's happened to me. They'll be frantic."

"Because they miss you personally or because you're such an important part of their research machinery?"

"Both," she assured him without batting an eye. "But it's bigger than just me now. From their questions, I gather that these fanatics want to shut down our whole project. Kidnapping me was one way to slow everything down as well as acquire the information they wanted for the rest."

"Pardon me, but you don't look old enough to be that important to any company."

Her expression started to twist. Then she saw he was teasing her. "Your point. I won't make any more comments about your age if you'll do the same for me."

"Much better."

"I have to get back quickly. My absence slows every-thing up. I'm kind of the insightful hub of the project. They come to me for breakthroughs, for new ways of looking at things. Not for everyday design work. I'm in-tuitive where practically everyone else is deductive." She spoke so matter-of-factly that he knew she was not boast-ing, just stating the facts.

"It's all going to come to a grinding halt without me there, if it hasn't already. Just get me to Alaspinport. Then we'll decide what to do next. I guess I'll have to disguise myself somehow. Besides looking for me out here, you can be sure they'll be swarming all over the one shuttle area like lice, or whatever it was you called those things that scarred my legs."

"Millimite bugs, mostly." He stared at her thighs.

When he looked back up, he saw her grinning at him. "Like what you see?"

He struggled to appear blasé. "Nice legs, bad bites."

"Maybe I shouldn't try to get out on the first ship. I'll bet not too many call at Alaspin." She was arguing with herself, he saw. "But if I don't try for the next one, I might be stuck here for weeks until another liner orbits, and that'll give them that much more time to close in on me. So I suppose I'll have to try slipping onto the first one no matter how many people they have watching the port." As if suddenly remembering she was not alone, she glanced back at him. "I don't suppose you have any friends in the planetary government?"

"There is no planetary government. This is an H Class Eight frontier world. There's a Commonwealth-ap-pointed administrator and peaceforcers on call. That's about it. Pretty wide-open place."

"Well, it doesn't matter," she said firmly. "I have to try to make it clear on the first available ship not only to save myself but to warn my people."

"Alaspin has a deepspace beam. Paid for by the pro-tectors, I understand. You could try contacting them that way."

She shook her head. "No receiver station where I come from."

"How about beaming a message to the nearest receiver world and sending it along by courier?"

"I don't know. They might be watching the message depot here as well. And it's easy to intercept a courier packet. Then I wouldn't know if they received my message or not. Don't underestimate these people, Flinx. I wouldn't be surprised if they're screening everything that goes through Alaspinport. They knew enough to smuggle me in. They'll make it hard to smuggle anything out."

"Sounds to me like you don't have a lot of options."

"No." Her voice fell. "No, I guess I don't." She stared at him. "You said you'd help me. I asked you for suggestions. I'm asking you again. Maybe we could bribe someone to let us skip departure procedures."

"Not enough of a crowd to get lost in." He coughed silently into a closed fist. "There is one other possibility. I could take you back."

She made a face. "I don't follow you. Are you talking about something like me traveling along as your wife under an assumed name? Maybe in some kind of disguise?"

"Not exactly. I mean I could literally take you back. See, I have my own ship."

A long silence followed. He found himself fidgeting uncomfortably under her stare. "You have your own ship? You mean that you come from a ship in orbit and are waiting to rejoin the rest of the crew? That's what you mean, isn't it? An unscheduled freighter or something like that?"

He was shaking his head. "No. I mean that I have my own ship, registered in my name. I'm the owner. It's called the *Teacher*."

"You're teasing me, making a joke. It isn't funny, Flinx. Not after what I've been through."

"It's no joke. The *Teacher*'s not very big, but it's more

than spacious enough for my needs. One more human being won't crowd my space.''

She gaped at him. ''You aren't kidding, are you?'' She slumped in the chair next to the still unrestored bathroom-door holo. ''A nineteen-year-old b—a nineteen-year-old who owns his own ship. By himself? It's not sublight?''

''Oh, no,'' he said quickly. ''It'll go anywhere in the Commonwealth you want. Full KK-drive, very narrow projection field, custom dish lining, the full complement of automatics. I just tell it where we want to go, and she goes there.''

''Who are you, Flinx, that at your age you can own an interstellar vessel? I've heard that the heads of the great trading families have their own private crafts, and that others have access to special company ships. I know that the government maintains ships for diplomatic service, and that the Counselors First of the United Church have small fast vessels for their needs. Who are you to treat equally with them? The inheritor of one of the Great Trading Houses?''

Mother Mastiff would have found that amusing, Flinx knew. ''Hardly. I've never had much interest in commerce in the conventional sense.'' *I used to relieve the wealthy of their excess without their knowledge, but that hardly qualifies as trade,* he thought.

''Then what are you? What is it that you do?''

He considered the question carefully, wanting to give her an answer she could believe without stretching the truth overmuch.

''I guess you could say I'm a student doing advanced work.''

''Studying what?''

''Mostly myself and my immediate environment.''

''And what is your 'immediate environment'?''

''For someone whose life was just saved, you ask a lot of questions. Wherever I happen to be at the moment, I guess. Look,'' he told her with some firmness, ''I've offered to take you anywhere you want to go, to help you get safely off this world and away from these mysterious crazies you keep talking about. Isn't that enough?''

''More than enough.''

There was no reason for him to go on, but something within him compelled him to answer the rest of her question. ''If you're so interested in how I came by ownership of the *Teacher*, it was a gift.''

''*Some* gift! For what even the smallest class of interstellar vessels cost, I could live in comfort for the rest of my life. So could you.''

''Living in comfort doesn't especially interest me,'' he told her honestly. ''Traveling, finding things out, meeting interesting people, that interests me a great deal. I did a favor once for some friends, and their gift to me in return was the *Teacher*.''

''Whatever you say.'' Clearly she did not believe a word he had told her but was sensible enough not to probe further. ''Your personal life's none of my business.''

''You don't have to accept if it makes you nervous.''

He was surprised how badly he was hoping she would accept. True, she was a gengineer, a member of a profession he had come to regard with both awe and fear. But she was also attractive. No, he corrected himself, that was not quite right. What she was, was extraordinarily beautiful. That was not a quality often found in tandem with great intelligence.

Put simply, he did not want to see the last of her. Not even if much of her story was a carefully crafted fabrication designed solely to gain his help. If that was the case, she had certainly achieved her aim.

''Of course I accept. What else am I going to do? I'm ready to go right now, this minute. It's not like I have to pack. Nor do you strike me as the sort of man who carries around a lot of excess baggage.''

Rather than probe possible double meanings, he replied simply, "You're right; I don't. But we're not leaving just yet."

"Why not?" She was obviously puzzled.

"Because after ferrying you halfway across the Ingre jungle only to wake up and find you with a knife in your hand and self-confessed intentions of slitting my throat, I need one decent night's rest in a real bed."

She had the grace to blush. "That won't happen again. I told you, I was confused."

"Doesn't matter. It's been a long couple of weeks for me, and now I have to consider you and your troubles. We'll leave first thing tomorrow morning, when it's less hot. Remember, we should be rested. You've been sleeping for days. I haven't.

"Besides, if these people are trying to track you, delaying here will cause them to spread their search wider and wider afield. Be that much simpler for us to avoid detection when we leave."

"You know best," she said reluctantly. "Look, I know it's a lot to ask considering everything you've done for me already, but my stomach feels like the inside of Cascade Cavern."

"Where's that?"

"On the world where I'm working."

"I'm not surprised. You've been surviving on intravenous and ampoules since I found you."

"Any kind of solid food would be wonderful."

He considered. "I suppose your system's ready. I guess since I'm going to take you an unknown number of parsecs, I can afford to spring for a couple of meals as well."

"Oh, I'll see that you're paid," she said quickly. "When I'm returned, my company will pay you for the trip and your trouble."

"No need. It's been a long time since I've bought supper for a beautiful woman."

My God, he thought sharply. *I actually said that, didn't I!*

The softening of her expression was proof that he had indeed.

"Just don't overdo it. Otherwise it'll kick back on you, and you'll be sick for the whole journey."

"Don't worry about me. I have an iron gut. I can eat anything. Or doesn't that square with your image of the beautiful woman?" She was disappointed when he did not comment. "You say you're a student, but that still doesn't tell me what you're about."

He checked the hallway carefully, Pip riding well back on his shoulders, Scrap clinging with his tail to Clarity's sidetail. Only when he was sure it was quiet and empty did he proceed in the direction of the small hotel dining room.

"That's all," he told her. "Just a student."

"Null and void. You're more than that. I'm no emotional telepath like your flying snakes, but I can tell there's more to you than studying, Flinx. More than learning. Don't tell me if you don't want to. Damn; there I go, prying again." He sensed rather than saw her smile. "You've got to excuse me. It's the nature of my mind, not to mention my work. If you're half the student you claim to be, you'll understand my curiosity."

Curiosity? Yes, he was curious. Also frustrated and angry and frightened and exhilarated. Wasn't that true of any young human being?

As to what he was really about, no one, not even the people who had played God with his mind and body prior to his birth, knew the answer to that.

I am, he thought suddenly, a drum in a vacuum.

Chapter Five

There weren't many people in the dining room, for which he was grateful. For the first time in memory he found himself enjoying a conversation that touched on nothing of importance. It was relaxing and reassuring. Wasting time, he found, could be fun as well as therapeutic.

He had heard of half sleep. It was the time called waking by others, when one was not quite conscious yet no longer asleep. He had never experienced it. One moment he was sound asleep, the next he was fully awake and alert. There was never anything like a transition stage as there seemed to be with other people. Whether it was a function of his peculiar mind or simply his street upbringing in the back alleys of Drallar, he had no way of knowing. He had never spoken to anyone else about it.

So it was that he found himself staring into near darkness with only the light of one of Alaspin's two moons casting shadows through the room. Pip was lying close to his face, her tongue flicking rapidly against his left eye until it opened. Realizing that she had awakened him and knowing she would never do so arbitrarily, he was instantly alert.

He kept his eyes half-closed as he studied the room. A long low outline was visible beneath the covers on the other bed. He could hear Clarity's soft breathing as she slept comfortably and undisturbed. What reason, then, for rousing him? Someone else might have risen then to have a look around. Flinx did not. Whatever had upset Pip would make itself known to him as well.

Only after a while did he see the shapes moving against the far wall. He tilted his head imperceptibly until he could see the door. At first glance it appeared closed. Only by concentrating hard was he able to make out the light mask that had been unrolled in front of it. Half-open at least. Probably a noise mask behind it. The treated Mylar foam would give the impression to any casual onlooker inside or out that the door was still tightly shut.

He made out a pair but knew there might be more. On the floor, perhaps, or behind the screen. One advanced into the light from the window. Instead of trying to avoid the moonglow, the figure continued blithely on, taking on the slightly mottled color of the light and shadows, blending perfectly into floor and walls.

Chameleon suit, Flinx mused. Fits like a second skin and adapts instantly to any background and lighting. As a boy he had often wished for one. Not the kind of toy children normally wish for, but then, there had been little that was normal about his childhood.

The only things the chameleon suit could not camouflage were the slits for eyes, nose, and mouth. Three more sets of eerily disembodied organs were advancing along the other wall in the direction of the two beds. It would not be necessary to ask the wearers their intentions. One did not enter a private room in the middle of the night in a chameleon suit, breaking a lock in the process, to hand someone winnings from a lottery.

In such a situation a number of options were available.

You could sit up and demand to know what the intruders wanted. You could pull a gun and start shooting, leaving questions for the police. Or you could do as Flinx did: lie quietly, imitating normal sleep breathing, watching out of half-closed eyes to see what the intruders planned to do next.

Three of them paused close together. They did not converse but merely exchanged looks, having obviously planned their moves well in advance. He dared not raise up or move his head for a better view.

The leader took something from a pocket attached to his right leg. It gleamed dully in the moonlight, a small canister with a flexible cuplike scoop over one end. Gas, Flinx thought automatically. Probably odorless, colorless, and fast-acting. Certainly not lethal. If the intruders had intended to kill the room's occupants, they could easily have done so from the door.

The figure bent low and moved to the foot of Clarity's bed, extending the canister before it. Abruptly it halted as something appeared between it and the sleeping woman. Something small, superfast, and hissing.

The intruders had rehearsed certain possibilities, but small superfast hissing creatures had evidently not been figured into their various scenarios. The sudden appearance of a small flying snake half a meter from one's face would be enough to unsettle the most professional assassin.

The man let out a startled oath and stumbled backward. It was enough to stir Clarity. Rolling onto her back, she drew a hand across her forehead and moaned softly. Flinx saw her eyelids flutter.

One of the canister carrier's companions spoke quickly and intently. "Stun the animal and then her. Now!"

The figure holding the canister raised it and moved a thumb over the recessed stud, which he never had time to press. From the tubular ridge tucked beneath its palate, the minidrag ejected less than half a cc of venom under high pressure. The poison hit the intruder in the eyes.

It was the end of pretense, of stealth, of careful movements in the dark. The man flung the canister across the room in a single convulsive movement as both hands went to his face. Screaming in pain as the highly caustic toxin ate at his eyes, he began ripping at his suit, tearing it from his head. Dissolving flesh bubbled audibly in the no longer quiet room.

Flinx dropped out of bed. Not on the far side, which was where anyone would expect him to go, but into the narrow cleft between his bed and Clarity's. As he did so, a previously unobserved intruder rose from the other side of his bed and fired a needle beam, which penetrated pillow, mattress, and probably the floor beneath the bed where Flinx had been sleeping moments earlier. The beam was bright blue in the darkness, and it crackled nastily.

Realizing he had seared nothing but linen, the gunman started to rise for another shot at the bed's unexpectedly absent occupant, only to find Pip hovering shockingly within wingbeat of his face. His eyes widened, visible even in the bad light, and he jerked his head to one side.

To give him credit, he was fast. The venom struck him at the hairline instead of in the eyes.

The man Scrap had struck lay motionless on the floor, already dead. Minidrag neurotoxin killed in less than a minute once it entered the bloodstream, freezing the human nervous system as easily as one would stop an appliance by touching a button. The intruder Pip had hit had escaped this instant death. Instead, he had to deal with the poison that was entering his head via the auditory canal. He was staggering about and screaming as he fired wildly with the needler.

Pip and Scrap darted effortlessly about the room, avoiding clumsy shots and creating enormous chaos. There were more than three intruders, Flinx saw. More than five. That was when he noticed Clarity starting to sit up. Her mouth opened, and she inhaled preparatory to screaming.

Clamping his right hand over her mouth, he used his left to drag her out of the bed and down to the floor. She fell on top of him, which under different circumstances would have been delightful but at that moment did not intrigue him in the slightest.

"Quiet," he whispered intensely as the battle raged around them. "Just shut up and be quiet. You're in the safest place in the room right now."

She stared dazedly into his eyes, then nodded slowly. He removed his hand from her face.

All around them was the noise of pounding feet, screams, the metallic hiss of needlers and the hum of hand beamers as the small army of kidnappers fired madly at the swooping, spitting minidrags. More often than not they ended up hitting one another.

It seemed to strike them simultaneously that they could do no good here, the way an invading army suddenly realizes it has been outflanked by the enemy it intended to crush. A silken rip sounded as one man plunged head-first through the light mask and out into the hall. Brighter light from the hallway fixtures flooded into the room. He was followed by his companions. There were too many for Flinx to count in the confusion. They must have been infiltrating the room for thirty minutes or more before Pip woke him.

Some continued to howl as they tried to cope with the effects of minidrag toxin while they retreated. Other shouts were beginning to be heard, confused and angry voices. Doors opened onto other rooms, and tenants peered out to see what had disturbed their sleep. As they caught sight of the chameleon suits and the weapons, they retreated in haste.

"Pip?" Flinx straightened cautiously. "Pip, get back in here! That's enough."

It was several minutes before the big flying snake re-turned to the room, having pursued the last of the intruders to the bottom of the first flight of stairs. If Flinx had not called her back, she would have emptied her store of poison and might well have killed every last one of their assailants. Flinx did not want that. He planned flight, not mass murder. And in better light there was always the chance one of the attackers might get off an accurate shot.

Scrap hovered behind her, straying aloft while his mother landed at the foot of Flinx's bed. She did not fold her wings and relax, Flinx noted, a suggestion of more trouble to come.

Only then did he notice how tightly Clarity was clinging to him. "It's them," she mumbled, the fear sharp-edged in her voice.

"Of course it was them. Unless there's someone else who wants you badly enough to kill." He looked toward the still open door. "There were a lot of them. More than I would've expected."

She turned her face toward him. She was only centimeters away. "I told you how badly they want me." He could feel her trembling against him. No false bravado now. She was scared out of her wits.

"It's okay." He wanted to be clever and fearless and nonchalant but only ended up being himself. "They're gone."

"The snakes," she murmured. "The minidrags." She glanced at Pip and her still hovering offspring. Scrap kept pivoting in midair, spoiling for more fight, searching for fresh enemies.

She stood, and he rose with her. Half a dozen bodies littered the floor. Several lay facedown. Others did not. The latter were not nice to look upon. Flying snake venom and nitric acid had similar effects on human flesh. No wonder people who were familiar with the minidrag's abilities hurried to cross the street when they saw Flinx coming.

"Pip woke me," he told her. "She sensed the threat. There was no need for me to move first. If I had, someone would've shot me. I always try to avoid that sort of thing because minidrags don't have half-reactions. You can't tell Pip just to wound somebody. There's no such thing as a limited flying snake strike.''

They stepped over the body of a very large man who had fallen at the base of both beds. Clarity's eyes rose from the body to the doorway.

''I wonder if they'll come back?''

''Not immediately. Would you?''

She shook her head sharply. Scrap darted toward her, and she moved to duck. Flinx hastened to reassure her.

''Relax. I think you've made a friend, though there's no way of telling if he acted to protect me, his mother, or you. Remember that he can tell what you're feeling, so he knows you mean me no harm. As long as that's true, there's no reason for you to be afraid of him.''

''You told me,'' she said, straightening. ''You told me, but I still couldn't imagine how lethal they are.''

''Many people know that they're deadly. What they don't realize is how fast and agile they are or how rapidly their toxin acts on the human body. Short of military-class armor or an atmosphere suit, there's no protection against them.''

He could feel as well as see the tension in her when Scrap decided to settle anew on her shoulder. Though the young minidrag relaxed, he kept his wings unfurled and ready for instant flight.

''They must still be out there or Pip would be falling asleep after exerting herself like that. Must be trying to formulate some new strategy.''

Clarity turned nervously to the window. ''Surely they won't try to rush the room.''

''Not now they won't. Pip and Scrap aside, too many guests saw them fleeing. But if they want you as badly as they seem to, they might not act rationally.

''When they first broke in, the intention was to gas you. Probably me as well, as a safety measure. If they really want you and they have access to a decent volume of the stuff, there's nothing to keep them from gassing the whole hotel, particularly if it's strictly morphic in nature.''

''The police?''

He grinned slightly. ''Mimmisompo's a small, open frontier town. If the hotel manager lives in, he might, just might, try contacting the cops. The hotel automatics will talk to police automatics. In either event, the police will take their time getting here. If the shooting was reported, they'll take a lot more time in the hopes that all the shooters will be dead by the time they arrive.''

He was already at the dresser, throwing his few belongings into the simple carryall pack. ''That means we have to move fast, because if your friends intend trying for you again, they'll want to do so before any police happen to wake up and take an interest in the night's goings-on.''

She took a hesitant step toward the door. ''How can we leave if they're still out there?''

''We have to leave because we can't stay here. They came in when the door was locked. They won't stop because a few people happened to see them leaving.'' He took her by the hand. ''They might be on their way back up already. We don't want to hang around and find out.''

She let him pull her along. ''Where are you going?'' He did not reply.

Pip rose from Flinx's shoulder to scan both ends of the hall, whizzing in seconds from one end to the other and back again to her master. Night-lights glowed from their recesses, giving everything an eery olive-hued cast.

Only one door stood ajar, framing a large older man with a protruding paunch. His whole head had been shaved down to the ears. Hair trailed a dozen centimeters over them, surrounding his head. The effect in the dim light was as if someone had yanked a fringed cap down below his eyes.

''Hey, what's happening? What's going on?'' He

leaned out into the hall as they approached. "Party's too loud for me. I'm gonna look for another hotel."

"Us, too," Flinx told him, his eyes working the corridor.

Pip spread her wings and zoomed ahead. The big man, who looked like he did not fear anything in this or any other world, caught sight of the oncoming minidrag and let out a shocked oath. He ducked back into his room, and Flinx heard the emergency latch click shut electronically.

"Everyone here knows what a minidrag can do." Flinx started down the fire stairs. "As long as Pip stays in front of us, no one else will."

She was going to need a huge meal, he knew. Hovering and flying so much burned a tremendous amount of energy. It seemed impossible they could maintain flight for so long, but as little was known about the flying snakes' internal makeup as was known about the rest of their nature.

They descended carefully, Flinx grateful that the hotel was only three stories high. No one challenged them in the stairwell, where the night-lights were even dimmer than those lining the hallways.

There were two doors at the bottom, one to either side of the lower landing. One probably led back into the hotel, to the kitchen or warehousing area. The other led . . .

Into a service alley that ran between commercial structures, which they entered after Flinx had disarmed the fire alarm on the door. A narrow, charged rail ran down the center of the alley, providing power and lift for robotic delivery vehicles. Flinx cautioned Clarity to avoid the rail as they hurried down the damp corridor. It would not kill, but it could badly shock a full-grown man.

"Where are we going? To get a vehicle, right? We're going to get transportation and head for Alaspinport. Will there be a rental agency open this late?"

"In a town like Mimmisompo you can get anything you want at any hour, if you have enough money. But we aren't going to rent. Rentals can be noted, and traced.''

He anxiously scanned the route ahead. Not for the first time in his life he wondered if he should be carrying a weapon. The only problem with a gun was that it was a provocation as much as a defense. Besides, Pip would deal much more effectively with any serious threat. Her reactions were a hundred times faster than his. As a child he had found himself in situations where possession of a weapon would have been more of a hindrance than a help, so he had learned to get along without them. That did not keep him from occasionally wishing for the comforting weight of one at his belt or in a shoulder holster.

Scrap rode high on Clarity's shoulder, a good indication that the danger, while not ended, was not immediate. He could not count on her pursuers delaying for very long, he knew. They might be in the bedroom already, might have discovered their quarry missing. The next thing they would do would be to thoroughly search the hotel and its immediate environs, checking other rooms to see if Flinx and Clarity had sought refuge with another guest. Certainly the front entrance would be covered from the start.

It would take them a while to figure out that the alarm on the back stairs had been disconnected long enough to let someone out into the service alley. Despite his caution, he knew they were leaving all kinds of trails behind them. Body scent heightened by fear, pheromones, heat signatures—all could be isolated and followed if one had the right kind of equipment. It could not be helped. Whether their pursuers were equipped with such sophisticated tracking devices depended on whether they had anticipated possible failure. It did not seem likely, but he could not count on convenient oversights to shield them.

''This way.'' He all but wrenched her arm loose pulling her around a sharp corner. Now that Alaspin's second moon had joined its companion in the night sky, the light was better for trying to find a new route through the city.

Already they were passing residences, the service alley far behind as they kept to back streets. Lights made owls' eyes of oval and round windows while the echo of tridee and music drifted out to the otherwise empty streets. There were no bugs to worry about. Industrial electronic repellers kept even the persistent millimite bugs a hundred meters from the nearest structure. Unfortunately, Mimmisompo was not wealthy enough to afford climate control, so it was still hot and humid. Sweat trickled from both refugees as they ran.

"Where are we going?" Clarity gasped. "I don't know how much longer I can keep this up." She was breathing with difficulty in the midnight heat.

"You'll keep it up as long as necessary, because I'm not going to carry you."

They had left the private homes behind and found themselves surrounded by air pressure domes and fabric warehousing. "I'm looking for the right transportation."

She frowned as she searched the vicinity. "Here? I don't see any cars."

"I'm not looking for an aircar or slinkem," he told her tersely. "That's the first type of vehicle they'd watch for. I want something difficult to trace." He paused. "This'll do."

It didn't look like much of a fence, only a succession of posts set in the ground five meters apart. Each was six meters high and pulsed with faint yellow light.

"That's a photic barrier," she said. "You can't climb it because there's nothing to climb, you can't walk through it, and you can't tip over any of the posts. Do anything to disrupt the alignment and you'll probably set off a dozen distinct alarms."

Once again he ignored her as he studied the half dozen machines parked beneath a rain shield on the far side of the service yard. All were battered and heavily used and unlikely to draw attention to themselves. It was exactly what he wanted for himself and his companion. He settled on a large lumbering skimmer whose back end consisted of compartmentalized cubes for storing prepackaged cargo. It could have been anything from a hazardous-waste dumper to a dairy delivery vehicle. Clarity paid no attention to him. She was scanning the dark buildings they had skirted, looking for silent shapes afoot in the night. She didn't turn around until she heard the barely audible soft clicking.

From a back pocket Flinx had extracted something the size and shape of a pack of plastic cards. Taking a couple of steps away from the wall, he drew back his arm and flipped the object in a sweeping underhand motion. Instead of sailing in all directions across the damp street, the plastic strips snapped together to form a straight line five meters in length. Using his hands, he bent it in two places to create a rigid U shape taller and considerably wider than his body.

Clarity eyed it dubiously. "What's that for? It's not tall or strong enough to use as a ladder."

"It's not a ladder. It's a portable gate." Pressing one hand against each side of the U's interior, he lifted the entire frame. Holding it around him like a levitating headdress, he walked right through the photic wall. The glowing sensors didn't flicker as he intercepted their beams. No alarms flared to life. Pip rode through on his shoulder.

Now he turned on the other side and repositioned the gate for her. "Come on. Unless you'd rather stand out in the street."

Unable to concoct a reason for hesitating, she did as he instructed, bending to slip under his arm as he held the gate for her.

Safely inside the barrier, he gave the gate a magician's twist and she gaped as it collapsed back into his hand. He slipped the packet back into his pocket.

"Doppler deck," he explained. "Bends light around you. It can't make you invisible, but under the right con-

ditions you can fake it pretty well. Bent the sensors
around both of us. We didn't interrupt them. Just made
them avoid us.''

"Fascinating.'' She followed him as he strode rapidly
across the lightly paved yard. "Expensive?''

He nodded. "It's not the sort of toy you'd find at a
special sale. It's a precision instrument designed to look
like junk, which is costly. When I was younger, I used
something like it that was a lot cruder. Sometimes it did
what it was supposed to. A lot of the time it didn't. That
was inconvenient at best, embarrassing at worst. I determined that if I could ever afford it, I'd have the best
analog equipment made. So I had this built for me.''

"Is that because you have to frequently override private security procedures?''

"Not really. I just like to have good tools handy.''

"You said you used something like it when you were
younger. What did you do as a child that required the
use of something like that?''

"I was a thief,'' he told her simply. "It was the only
way I could survive.''

"Are you still a thief?''

"No. Now I pay for everything I need, sooner or
later.''

"More sooner or later?''

"Depends on my mood.''

They hurried past the line of vehicles until he halted
before the bulky cargo skimmer. Another pocket yielded
a folded leatherine wallet that when opened revealed a
host of tiny tools. Each was as perfect and beautiful as a
jewel. In point of fact, the thranx who had fashioned the
wallet and its contents for him was renowned as a jew-
eler. Such projects as Flinx's wallet were a hobby for
him, a hobby that Flinx knew was more lucrative than
the thranx's admitted profession.

Choosing one particular instrument, he commenced
working on the trisealed secure lock that held the skimmer's door closed. Though still fearful of immediate at-

tack, Clarity was so absorbed in watching him work that she no longer stared past the photic barrier at the street beyond.

"You must've been a good thief."

"I was always considered advanced for my age. I don't think I've improved since, but I have better tools to work with now."

The door did not even click when he popped it open. He climbed up and slid in behind the drive controls.

The ignition was unlocked. It was easier to secure the doors than the engine and power plant. Under his skilled touch the readouts came to life. He glanced approvingly out at Clarity and nodded. Scrap released her hair to flutter into the cab, taking up a resting position on the back of the passenger's seat.

Elsewhere skimmers had open cabs, but not on Alaspin. Here all were enclosed, air-conditioned, and bug-resistant. Which would be especially nice as they were going to be traveling at night, he knew.

Clarity grabbed a handle and pulled herself up beside him. She closed her door and turned to regard him in amazement. "You know, I'm beginning to believe you actually have a chance of getting us offworld. You sure you're only—" She caught herself. "Sorry. I promised not to mention that again, didn't I?"

"You did."

The skimmer made more of a racket on low lift than he had hoped it would, but since the service yard he had penetrated was presumed secure, there was no need for a human guard to be kept on duty. The security monitor would report anything unusual to a central facility as well as to the district police.

Since there was no dome or solid roof, he assumed the presence of a short-range security blanket, close cousin to the photic wall he had already sidestepped. That would be necessary to prevent any would-be thieves or vandals from simply flying in over the wall. He also expected vehicles inside the wall to be appropriately equipped with the means for negating it. A couple of minutes' work with the skimmer's onboard 'pute produced the requisite broadcast code. He punched it in and waited patiently for it to notify the company's central security facility.

Hopefully no one would read the evening's report until morning. By then the absence of the big skimmer would probably have been noted visually. It would take time to determine that no night deliveries or pickups had been scheduled, more time to make certain the skimmer had not been borrowed by an authorized driver or executive. By the time Alaspinport authorities could be informed of its presumed theft and provided with a description, its nocturnal riders would have abandoned it none the worse for wear except for run-down batteries. For the use of which, he unnecessarily mentioned to Clarity, he intended to pay.

They had one bad moment as the skimmer lifted eighty meters above the yard and turned left out of the city. Out in the commercial district, away from the bars and simulated strip joints and stimclubs, few lights showed below—until a smaller, much faster skimmer shot by hard aport. Clarity yelped and tried to duck between the seats while Scrap rose and darted in all directions at once, getting in Flinx's way and causing minor havoc with his steering.

Flinx had a brief, appalling glimpse of the other vehicle as it veered sharply to the left without banking. Laughing, probably drunk young faces given ghostly life by the skimmer's internal lights leered at him for an instant and were gone.

"Kids." He looked down and to his right. "Get up. Your friends haven't found us. It was just kids out joyriding. Not much else to do in a place like Mimmisompo. Even scientists and prospectors have kids."

They were out over raw jungle now, heading for the immense savanna that bordered both sides of the Aranoupa River. Following the river southwest would take them to the granite outcropping occupied by Alaspinport, a crooked finger of land extending out into the sea.

She rose slowly, fright fading from her face like a temporary tan. She looked small, vulnerable, and afraid.

"I'm sorry. It was just so unexpected. Everything was going so well. You were handling everything so smoothly."

"I'm still handling things smoothly." His attention wandered from the night sky to the readout that showed their position relative to Mimmisompo and Alaspinport. Their transportation might be a well-used antique, but the internal electronics were reassuringly up-to-date.

Sitting back in her seat, she rubbed at her eyes with the backs of both hands, then looked over at him. "You're sure it was just a bunch of kids?"

He nodded. "Seventeen, eighteen. Mimmisompo's not a bad place for someone without education or training to try for a fortune."

"Like you, maybe? Except you aren't a kid."

Feeling it appropriate under the circumstances, he tried to smile and discovered that he could not. "I was born old. I was never a kid. No, that's not quite it; I was born tired."

"I don't believe you. I think you just like to pretend that you're slow and tired to keep others from trying to find out more about you."

"Can't you just accept the fact that I'm a quiet loner who likes his peace and quiet and privacy?"

"No, I can't."

"Why not?"

"Because I think I know you better than that already, if you'll excuse my presumption. You are also the strangest young man I've ever met in my life. I guess you'll be upset if I add that I find you particularly attractive, too."

"No. You can tell me that all you want." He was afraid she would do just that, but she did not. Apparently his reply was all she had wanted to hear.

It was the last question, for a while, anyway. She nestled back into her seat and gazed silently out at the empty Alaspinian night. Meanwhile he worried about the absence of a decent scanner. The skimmer was equipped with standard delivery system electronics, which meant you could always tell where you were but had no idea where anyone else was. It would help when they reached Alaspinport and he sought to abandon the vehicle in a safe place, but it was useless for trying to find out if you were being paralleled, followed, or otherwise tracked.

Pip could detect hostile intent, but only over a short distance. The minidrag was sound asleep, exhausted by her earlier exertions in his defense. Even Scrap rested, a gleaming scaly bracelet lit by the glow of the skimmer's instrumentation.

He preferred to assume their departure had gone undetected than to think of Clarity's assailants trailing them just out of sight. By now they must be combing the alleys and buildings around the hotel. The likelihood of their discovering the missing cargo skimmer and connecting it to their quarry was small. He reminded himself that he had no idea how extensive or advanced their tracking equipment might be.

He would have preferred company in the sky. The lone cargo skimmer would stand out on any plotting screen. Few people chose to travel across the treetops at night.

There he went, borrowing trouble again. Tiring himself out mentally dealing with a nonexistent threat. Better to conserve himself for real danger.

A glance showed his companion still alert and staring out the window. "Try to get some sleep. The sun'll be up soon."

"I'll sleep when I'm off Alaspin and in space-plus. The last time I tried to sleep, I had a rude awakening." She indicated the instruments. "Can't this hulk go any faster?"

"It's not built for speed. I picked it because I thought it would be the most inconspicuous on a screen and the most likely to be parked on full charge. I could have chosen something smaller, more maneuverable, and quicker. We could also have run out of power in the middle of the savanna. You don't want to try walking out of the Aranoupa savanna. The surface has a nasty habit of turning to sludge underfoot, and its full of unpleasant things that don't react kindly to having their habitat disturbed. Better we get to Alaspinport slowly but surely.

"Besides, anyone hunting you would first go after an obvious passenger craft, not a clunker like this."

"You've worked it out very carefully. And I thought you just grabbed the first machine you thought you could break into."

"I could have broken into any of them. And I'm sure I've still overlooked something important."

"You know," she said admiringly, "I think I'll be better off if I just shut up and let you take care of me instead of asking stupid questions."

"That's the first thing you've said since I met you that justifies your name."

She shook her head but could not repress a smile. "Awfully young to be so sarcastic." She turned back to the window and the dark view outside.

The skimmer was moving right at a hundred and fifty kph, clearing the tops of the tallest grasses by a good fifty meters. Occasionally Flinx would angle left or right simply to vary their course and confuse any plotting computer that might be tracking them. Significant variations would waste too much power. He wanted to keep enough of a charge in the skimmer's cells to approach Alaspinport in a wide curve, from the ocean side instead of from the savanna. That would further confuse anyone trying to tail them.

"How much longer?"

He checked the dash cartographic readout. "Straight line from Mimmisompo to Alaspinport is about fourteen hundred kilometers. We'll be there in time for lunch. You don't mind if we skip eating, do you? Not that I wouldn't mind something, but I don't want to waste time in a restaurant."

"I'm hungry right now."

He sighed. "Have a look around. This is a working machine. I don't see a protein synthesizer, but I'll bet there's an internal still for condensing drinking water out of the air. There might be flavorings or concentrates somewhere. A heavy-duty cloud banger like this might come equipped with emergency rations in case the driver is forced down somewhere."

"I'll have a look."

It took her half an hour to produce fruit-flavored ration bars and juice concentrates to add to the water the skimmer drew from the sky. The result was a nutritious if pedestrian meal. Human fuel.

Once back on the *Teacher* he could offer her a real repast. It had elaborate synthesizing facilities. A candlelight dinner simulated by electronics. Repair robots rapidly reprogrammed to serve as butlers and waiters. He grinned to himself. He could make a real production out of it, impress her with his resources and skills. And did he want to impress her? He tried not to glance furtively in her direction.

She had offered to help drive, and he had turned her down. The long flight relaxed him. He was much more comfortable with electronics than with people.

Sure, why not impress her? Maybe on board the *Teacher*, back in familiar surroundings, he would be able to relax in her presence. Get to know her and find out if she was half as brilliant as she thought she was. Certainly whoever was chasing her had a high opinion of her abilities.

She was not the only one torn with curiosity, he reflected as he smoothly guided the skimmer into a slow turn westward.

Chapter Six

Since no ship rose to intercept them or question their presence, he felt reasonably safe in approaching Alaspin on a narrower path than he had originally planned, coming in from the north instead of the east. When he was fifty kilometers out, he swerved sharply onto a straight heading for the shuttleport, saving a half hour's flight time.

They passed over the broad northern bay with its deserted white sand beaches, shadowing half a dozen low-flying sea skimmers that were working the shellfish beds off the inner reef. Alaspin's extensive, shallow oceans were ideal breeding grounds for shellfish, both native and introduced varieties, but the industry was just getting started. Most of what was gathered was for local consumption. Not that he cared about making money, it was just that all his life he had been around people for whom commerce was the raison d'être, and he could not avoid picking up a little of their way of thinking. Mother Mastiff, for example, preferred to talk about different ways of making money above all else.

90

He had acquired, however, greater concerns than building a fortune. Money was, after all, nothing more than a means for securing freedom, and freedom was the precursor to learning. And learning? What was learning for? He had not quite decided that one yet.

Hell, I'm only nineteen. Think about Clarity Held instead, he told himself. Better still, think about her legs and—he clamped down ruthlessly on that line of thought. Not yet. Don't think about that yet. For now, concentrate on making it safely back to the *Teacher*.

Alaspinport's underside was single-story gritty, bubbling with temporary storage domes whose sole purpose was to separate goods within from fauna and climate without. The few tall structures tended to cluster along the high ridge of land that formed a bluff overlooking the ocean at the end of the port peninsula.

The shuttleport itself occupied a section of cleared Savanna south of the main city. Though it slowed them down, Flinx inserted the skimmer in the automatic traffic guide pattern above town. It offered anonymity and convenience. Clarity was delighted to be back among crowds, sensing false safety in civilization.

Instead of requesting formal landing permission at the port, he set down among a cluster of other commercial vehicles near a recharging station. From there it was a short walk to a public tram that let them off inside the port itself.

There were several private shuttles parked off in their own area. Since no commercial ships hung in orbit that day, the only traffic was atmospheric, aircraft traveling between Crapinia and Mooscoop, frontier towns farther from Alaspinport than even Mimmisompo. The absence of a commercial shuttle lowered Clarity's spirits.

"If they're here, and you can bet they're all over the port, all they have to do is close in on anything prepping for launch."

"Why should they? What business is it of theirs if a

corporation or family shuttle makes ready to depart? There's no reason to assume you'd be traveling on one.''

"But they'll see me. They'll be watching all the departure lounges, and they'll see me.''

He tried to mute his exasperation. "First of all, while I don't know what kind of contacts these people have on Alaspin, no one's allowed in the private shuttle departure lounge without proper clearance.''

"Then they'll be watching from just outside.''

He considered. "Then we'll just have to get you through without being seen.''

"How? Disguise?''

"No. I think there's a simpler and more effective way.''

Overhead luminescent broadband displays directed them to the part of the port he was looking for, where a small man sat in a small office behind a flat LCD screen. He looked up expectantly as they entered.

"Can I be of service?''

Flinx pushed toward the narrow barrier that separated work from waiting area. "I want to use the facilities.''

The man's welcoming smile faded. "I'm sorry. I'll be happy to do any work you require, but we're not a self-service concern. Insurance regulations and all that, you know.''

Flinx extracted a thin plastic card from his pants, the lock on the card reading his thumbprint and heat signature and obediently detaching it from the securestrip that kept it fastened to the inside of the pocket. It was an ordinary-looking bright blue card.

"Run this through your show and tell.''

The man hesitated, then shrugged and complied. Clarity noted that he never did look up from the screen once the card had been decoded.

"Fix me a price,'' Flinx finally told him when the man failed to respond.

"What?''

"I said, fix me a price for the use of your equipment.''

"Price. Sure.'' He nodded rapidly, started to rise, then

slumped. "I told you that we're not self-service. I just can't possibly . . ."

Without asking permission, Flinx came around the barrier and ran his fingers over the screen's secureboard. The man looked up at him.

"You can't mean that."

By way of reply Flinx pressed SCREEN RUN. The machine beeped as it recorded the transaction. The man let out a long breath.

"What now? What do you want me to do?"

"Go have something to eat, or go to the bathroom, or go call your wife."

"I'm not married," the clerk mumbled dazedly.

"Then go call a friend."

"Yeah. Right."

He left the office quickly. Flinx locked the door behind him.

"What did you do?" Clarity asked, watching him closely.

"Rented the facilities. Come with me."

She followed. "What kind of place is this?" Piles of crates and boxes filled platforms and shelves in the long chamber behind the office.

"You'll see. Stand here." He positioned her on a circular platform.

"What are you going to do?" She eyed the platform and the nearby machinery warily. "Build me a disguise?"

"Not exactly." He sat down opposite another large LCD screen and keyboard, studying it thoughtfully.

"What if they find us here?" He had been examining the screen and board for five minutes, and she was starting to fidget.

"They won't find us here," he said absently. "Hold still." His fingers rose to the keys.

She looked down, startled. "Hey, what—"

"I said, don't move."

She froze, puzzled but trusting. She had no choice but to trust him.

It was a very elegant box. Normally it was used for transporting live, exotic tropical vegetation. The two-meter-tall cylinder was tinted green and brown to match its usual contents and came lightly scented. It occurred to Flinx that he had neglected to ask if she was claustrophobic, but it was too late now.

The packaging equipment wove the custom container out of a special fibrous material produced on Alaspin. The strong celluloid base would allow the free flow of air while simultaneously shielding the container's contents from radiation, which meant it would also foil any casually applied detection scanners. Internal noise would be muted. As befitted the transportation of expensive tropical vegetation, it was heavily padded on the inside. It moved on its own built-in, yttrilithium battery-powered repulsion kit. Gyroscopic programming kept it perfectly upright to protect the delicate petals of the plant inside. As a final touch he had stenciled on the exterior, PRODUCT OF ALASPIN—SENSITIVE FLORA—DO NOT OPEN, SCREEN, OR HANDLE.

"I hope that's comfortable," he said aloud when he had finished. There was no answer, of course. She couldn't hear him, nor he, her. The air inside the cylinder would be a little on the warm side, but while temporarily uncomfortable, she was in no danger of suffocation.

He kept a surreptitious eye out for suspicious types as he convoyed his personal baggage through port Security. No one intercepted him in the lounge, and no one confronted him as he guided the cylinder through the boarding corridor toward his shuttle. Then he was loading the little craft's cargo bay, a touch on the throwaway repulsor's control sending it rising by itself into the belly of the ship.

"Almost clear," he said aloud, though she still could not hear him.

He instructed the shuttle's computer verbally, giving

simple lift-off and docking instructions, then settled back
into the pilot's seat and waited. Upon receiving departure
clearance from port authority, the shuttle taxied itself
into position. A moment later it was roaring down the
runway, gathering speed, its wheels folding up into the
delta wings and nose as they cleared the first marsh grass.
Thin purple blossoms vibrated in the wake of its passing.

Clarity had worried needlessly. Whoever had kidnapped her might be resourceful, but they were not om-
nipotent. He rose. Using interior handholds as gravity
left him, he pulled himself back toward the cargo hold.
It was time to unpackage his passenger.

The woman standing over him was very tall and extremely pretty, much too beautiful for the vapid-faced
young man who had come in with her. An oddly matched
couple, but very polite. Almost deferential.

"You said he had a woman with him? A young
woman?" The towering blonde wore the uniform of a
port authority guard.

"Yes." This excited both of them tremendously,
though they took obvious pains to hide it. He still could
not decide which one was in charge. "Why? Is there a
problem?" The size of the bribe he had received from
his earlier visitor was weighing heavily on his mind.

"No, no problem," the young man said softly. 'We
just want to ask the young lady a couple of questions."

"Excuse me." A matronly woman in a bright pink and
yellow dress came through the door, a plant basket slung
under one arm. "I have some fresh-cured maniga root
I'd like shipped today to Tasc—"

The tall blonde stepped in front of her. "Sorry. This
office is closed."

The clerk behind the narrow counter blinked.
"Closed? No, we're open here until six."

"It's closed," the blonde reiterated without looking
back at him.

"But he just said . . ." the matron began.

The tall woman reached down, put a hand in the center of the older woman's chest, and shoved. The matron stumbled backward, barely keeping her balance, and gaped.

"Well, if you're closed, you're closed!" She spun and hurried out of the office.

"Hey, wait a minute!" the clerk shouted, rising from his chair. "Official port business is one thing, but—"

"It won't take long." The young man moved nearer as his tall female companion gently shut and locked the door. "And it will go much faster if you cooperate."

"Of course I'll cooperate," the clerk told him irritably, "but that's no reason to close us down."

"Questions are understood much better when they're not interrupted in the asking," the blonde said.

What a lovely speaking voice, the clerk thought, staring at her. Everything about her was gorgeous—except her attitude. And the port guards were noted for their politeness.

"Maybe," he said suddenly, "I'd better make a call and check with some people before I answer any more questions." He reached down for the com unit slung beneath his terminal.

The blonde reached it in two strides and locked her fingers around his wrist. "Maybe," she said softly, "you'd better not."

He tried to break her grip, but it was as if his wrist had been lassoed with wire. He forced himself to calm down. All these people wanted was some information, and who was he to deny them? There was the back door, but as she released his wrist he had the idea that making a run for it would not be a good idea. Why ruin his day and maybe more than that to shield some stranger's privacy?

"All right." He sat carefully back in his chair. "Go ahead and ask your questions."

"Thanks," the young man said. His left eyelid was jumping noticeably. "The people we're after are trying to ruin an entire world. You wouldn't want that to happen, would you?''

"Of course not. What right-thinking citizen wants that for any world?''

The twitching went away, though it did not stop completely. "See?" He looked back up at the overpowering blonde. "I told you it would be okay."

"I still think we should do it the other way, but—" She shrugged. "—get on with it."

The clerk found that he was trembling slightly inside, even though he had made the right decision.

Chapter Seven

Although she relaxed completely for the first time since he had met her once the shuttle cleared ionosphere, Flinx did not. He had been around too much and seen too much to know that mere vacuum offered no assurances of safety. He watched and listened intently, but nothing came near them. Traffic around Alaspin was nonexistent. The com unit was silent. They were alone.

Clarity Held had been impressed by his description of the *Teacher*. She was overwhelmed when the long, sleek mass of the starship hove into view beyond the shuttle's viewports. When she finally set foot inside after transferring through the personnel lock, the only reaction remaining to her was awe.

They were in the area that on a commercial vessel would have been designated a commons but that Flinx domestically called his den. In the center stood a raised pond filled with tropical fish from several worlds. It was surrounded by bushes and well-tended plants. The ceiling was dressed in a type of vine that grew extremely well in artificial light and did not shed.

Flinx was very fond of green. The world on which he had been raised was thick with evergreen forest. Pip's home world was all jungle and savanna. He had seen enough of both desert and ice to care for neither.

Artificial gravity made it all possible, even the bubbling fountain in the center of the pool that spouted both normal and light water. Heavy water behaved normally on board, but light water could be stained different colors. It was a blend of glycerine and gases encased in incredibly thin polymer membranes. It burst into the air in the form of multihued bubbles that were sucked up to vanish into a cone concealed by the ceiling vines. The cone condensed and recycled the bubbles through the water below.

The furniture was real, rough-hewn wood layered with thickly stuffed cushions that responded musically to whoever sat on them, adjusting their melodies to the movements and emotions of the sitters. Purple and deep blue forms chased each other seemingly at random around the circular walls, like so many bugs at a racetrack. The randomness of the chase was part of the art. The den was a remarkable mix of angular geometric shapes and glowing lights, of green growing things and sparkling water, of nature and science.

Clarity wandered around the room inspecting flora and art. Each element of the decor stood out bright as a child's eyes, as carefully crafted and arranged as if by a professional. Flinx had simply thrown it all together.

When she was finished, she found her breath again. "You actually do own all this?"

"People tend to give me things." Flinx smiled in embarrassment. "I don't know why. A few I've picked up on my travels." He gestured. "The fountain and the plants are there because I enjoy looking at both. There are robots, but I prefer working with growing things myself. I seem to have a way with plants."

He did not tell her he thought his success with plants had something to do with his empathic telepathy, nor did he mention the theories that stated that plants were capable of emotion and feeling. She already thought of him as weird, even if he had saved her life.

Maybe I should've been a farmer, he thought. Not that there was much room for farmers on Moth. If he had asked for help, the kind of plants Mother Mastiff would probably have encouraged him to grow would have been illegal.

"We ought to leave," she said abruptly, as if remembering what they were doing on his ship.

"We're already on our way."

"Where?" She looked around in surprise, but there were no ports in the common room.

"Outsystem, away from Alaspin orbit." He checked his wrist chronometer. "It's an easy command to give. The ship takes verbal direction. Much easier than trying to enter it via keyboard. If you hear a third voice speaking, cool, feminine-neutral, that's the *Teacher*. It's not capable of reasoning, so don't try arguing with it. I prefer it that way. I wanted something that would respond immediately to my wishes and not debate possibilities with me."

"Unlike me?" She walked over to the rock rimwall that enclosed the pool and sat down on the edge, trailing one hand in the water. A flash of crimson steel drifted over on turquoise wings to inspect her fingers. She reached lazily in its direction, and it darted away with a flick of trifinned tail.

"People give you things. Like this ship, you said."

"I have a number of interesting friends. They built it for me, actually." He shook his head with the remembrance of it. "I still don't know how they did it. Somehow it didn't strike me as the kind of thing they'd be good at, but then, they didn't seem good at anything. Surprising friends."

"Oh, how lovely!" She rose and stepped away from the pool. "What's this?"

She ran her hand over what looked like a dozen Möbius strips orbiting a common center. Where they met and intersected they appeared to vanish into nothingness. When she touched one, a deep bass rumbling filled the common room. Touching another generated a crude whistling. There was nothing holding the arrangement in place a meter and a half above the deck.

"Some kind of gravity projection?"

"I don't know." He shrugged. "I acquired it without instructions or explanation, I'm afraid." He nodded forward. "Put your hand in the middle, where the strips converge."

"Why? Will it disappear?"

He smiled. "No."

"All right."

Eyeing him challenging, she slowly moved her hand into the intersecting space. Her fingers were slightly parted. Instantly, her eyes shut tight and a look of pure bliss passed over her face. Her mouth parted slightly to reveal teeth tightly clenched. Slowly her head arched backward, then rolled forward, taking her whole upper body with it like a ribbon caught in a sudden breeze. He had to run to catch her.

He half carried, half dragged her to the nearest lounge and gently placed her on the responsive upholstery. The back of her left hand rested against her forehead, and beads of sweat were collecting on her skin like Burmese pearls. She wore the expression for two minutes. Then she blinked, wiped away the sweat, and turned to face him.

"That wasn't fair," she said huskily. "I didn't expect—anything like that."

"Neither did I the first time I put my hand inside. It's a little overwhelming."

"A *little*?" She was gazing longingly at the floating confluence of Möbius strips. "I've never felt anything like that in my life, and my hand was only in there for a moment. But it wasn't just my hand, was it?" She looked back up at him. "It was my whole body."

"It was your entire being, your self plugged into a high-voltage socket without the danger. At least, I think there's no danger. Just that wondrous surge of pleasure."

"That," she said firmly as she sat up straight on the lounge, "ought to be illegal."

He turned away from her. "It is."

"I never heard of such a device. Where's it built?"

"On an illegal world by illegal people. There are no restrictions on it because, insofar as I know, it's the only one of its kind. Nobody else knows it exists. The people who made this ship for me—" He looked around the commons room. "—made that as well. Another gift. They wanted to make sure I felt happy all the time, so they provided me with the means to do so."

"You could die from that much happiness."

"I know. Its designers have greater tolerances for everything, including happiness. You have to watch the dose. I only use it when I'm seriously depressed."

"And do you find yourself seriously depressed often, Flinx?"

"I'm afraid I do. I was always kind of moody, and it's worse now than when I was a child."

"I see. It's none of my business and you don't have to tell me, but is there anyone else on this ship?"

"Only you and I, unless you count Pip and Scrap."

She shrugged. "I couldn't expect you to tell me about your illegal suppliers."

"I don't mind. They're really fine folks. Special. I sometimes find myself thinking that they're the universe's chosen ones. They're innocents. Utter innocents, though I've taken some basic steps to remedy that. The Church knows about them, and the government, and they're afraid of that kind of innocence. My friends are also incomprehensible."

"Would I know of them?"

"Possibly, but I doubt it." Moving to a tall blue-green fern, he pushed aside one of the thick fronds to reveal a tiny keyboard. He let his fingers play over the keys. It would have been easier to have entered the command verbally, but he had a childish desire to impress her further.

To anyone unschooled in galographics, the star clusters that materialized in midair between Flinx and the fountain would have appeared haphazardly aligned. Only on closer inspection could a viewer make out the tiny bright green letters that floated above each sun. A very small proportion of the imaged stars were labeled with yellow pinpoint letters instead of green.

"The Commonwealth," he explained unnecessarily.

The AAnn Empire was not shown, though she did not doubt he could call it up with the flick of a finger. Nor was the Sagittarius Arm visible. The holo displayed only Commonwealth vectors and schematics. While she looked on, the entire complex configuration oriented itself to the position of the *Teacher*.

"It's a long ways out." He was peering deeply into the slowly rotating holo. "Maybe within Commonwealth boundaries, maybe not. Up near the Rosette nebula, out toward the galactic edge. Not a big world. Not impressive." He brushed the controls inside the fern, and she saw a green blip brighten to emerald.

His hand moved anew, and the holo shifted drastically. When it halted, a completely different world blazed brighter than any other. "Alaspin." His hand moved yet a third time, highlighting a world on the very fringes of the Commonwealth.

"Existing world, different perspective. The first holo was legal. A mask. The positions are falsified. These are correct, and proscribed."

She stared. The new world he had brought to brilliance moved perceptibly, enough to throw off anyone trying to locate it. This time it was not green but an intense red.

"I don't have much use for a floating map," she murmured, "but I've seen worlds marked green and blue and pink and yellow, but never that color before."

"It means the world in question is under full Church

Edict. No one's supposed to know it's there. There are automated weapons stations in multiple orbit stationed six planetary diameters out to prevent unauthorized approaches, much less landings.'' He waved his hand, and the entire holo vanished, an evaporative cosmos. "If people knew it was there and Under Edict, someone would try to go there simply because it's forbidden. The result would be dead adventurers and a discomfited bureaucracy."

She looked at him steadily. "But you've been there. You said the people who lived there built this ship."

"Yes. My friends, the Ujurrians.'' His eyes flicked beyond her as if expecting to see something else. Perhaps something three meters tall and furry. But he saw only plants and fountain.

"Why is it Under Edict?"

"If I told you, I'd be in violation of the Edict itself."

"I won't tell. I owe you my life. I can keep your secrets."

He considered, then looked away and sighed. "I'm getting to the point where I don't care who knows what anymore. The Ujurrians are a physically large ursinoid race, paragons of ingenuousness by our standards. At least they were when I met them. They are also potentially the most advanced people ever encountered."

Clarity frowned. "That's no reason to put them Under Edict."

"They are natural telepaths,'' Flinx told her. "Mind readers. Not empathic telepaths like the flying snakes." And myself, he added, but not aloud.

She whistled meaningfully. "You mean true mind-to-mind communicators? Like the people in the tridee plays and in books?"

He nodded. "The one thing we've always feared more than anything else in an alien race. People who could read our minds when we couldn't read theirs. And not just our minds. There was an AAnn installation on Ulru-Ujurr. The Ujurrians could read them as well. They chased the AAnn away. I think they can even read Pip's mind, as much of a mind as she has.'' The flying snake looked up briefly from his shoulder before lying back down. ''And that isn't all.''

''Isn't that enough?''

''They learn on an exponential curve. When I met them, it was almost level. They were living in caves. Now it's heading upward, and fast. By the time I left they'd learned enough from the files at the AAnn station to start an impressive little city. Also to build the *Teacher*, though I still haven't figured out how they put the necessary infrastructure together so fast. They also have other abilities.'' He smiled slightly. ''They like to make jokes, play games, and dig tunnels.''

''Tunnels? That's funny.''

''Why is that funny?''

''You'll find out soon. But they're not hostile?''

''On the contrary. They're fluffy and rather amusing-looking and roly-poly—if you can conceive of something three meters tall massing out around eleven or twelve hundred kilos as roly-poly. We got along real well.''

''I would think so.'' She was trailing her fingers in the water again. ''If they built a ship as a gift for you. How many ships do they have?''

''As far as I know, the *Teacher* is the only ship they've ever built.'' That reminded him of a certain Ujurrian who was so peculiar that even his fellow Ujurrians found him strange. ''There was a male named Maybeso who didn't need one, though I suppose I shouldn't say that because I don't know what his range was.''

Her eyes widened. ''Teleportation, too?''

''I don't know. They call it something else. I think they can do other things as well, but I didn't know enough to ask the right questions. It's been a long time, and I need to go back.'' He blinked. ''You can understand why the Church would put a world like that Under Edict. The Ujurrians are a race of telepathic, possibly teleportational innocents with limitless mental potential. You know how the Outreach Bureau thinks. Just because they're friendly now doesn't mean they'll be friendly tomorrow. 'Pananoia is survival,' and that sort of nonsense.''

She nodded slowly, and he turned from her to gaze moodily at the pond. ''You don't have to worry about any pursuit now. The *Teacher*'s very fast, and we're armed, though I've no idea if the armament is functional. I've never had to use it.''

''Unlike the people who took me,'' she said quietly.

He checked the readout strapped to his left wrist. ''We'll be far enough out to engage the drive pretty soon. Once we're in space-plus, nobody can touch us.''

He did not tell her that the *Teacher* was the only ship in the Commonwealth capable of taking off and landing directly from a planetary surface. Those innocent geniuses, the Ujurrians, had solved in a week a problem that had tormented the Commonwealth's best physicists since the development of the KK-drive. There were still a number of secrets he intended to keep from his guest. One would be the fiction that his ship was no different from similar vessels.

''If it was Under Edict, how did you come to be on this world and ingratiate yourself tightly enough with its inhabitants to make them want to build you a ship?''

He was examining the ceiling. Amazingly, there were bugs up there, establishing themselves in the vines. He could not imagine how and when they had come on board. They were the real dominants in this universe, he thought. Not humans, not thranx, not the AAnn. It was always the little ones who ruled. Insects had managed to colonize everything but vacuum. Now they had taken the *Teacher* for their own. They added to the common room's homey feel—except when one of them dropped off a vine onto his head. Thus far nothing dangerous had hitched a ride in his hair. Anyway, insects rarely bit him. Perhaps he was not as tasty as other people.

He remembered her question and replied absently. ''I

was looking for someone, and I visited a lot of peculiar places.''

"Can I ask who you were looking for?"

"My father and my mother."

"Oh." That was not the reply she had been expecting. "Did you find them?"

"I found out that my mother was dead. I still don't know what happened to my father, or even who he was."

"Are you still searching?"

He shook his head violently, surprised at how tense he was. "I've crossed a lot of void, touched many worlds trying to come up with an answer. The searching sapped a lot of the passion for it. Now my interests are changing. What was critical to me a few years ago isn't critical to me anymore. While I'd still like to know, I don't see the point in devoting all my attention to finding out."

"So you grew up an orphan?"

That made him smile, as memories of his childhood always did. "I had an adoptive mother. Mother Mastiff. A lying, cheating, foul-mouthed, filthy, unattractive old lady whom I love very much."

"I can see that," she said softly.

"You know," he told her suddenly, "all I ever wanted was to be left alone. I didn't ask to be given this ship, just as I haven't asked for all the problems I've had to deal with. Deity, I'm not even twenty yet!"

"You're a lot more mature, Flinx, than most of the older men I've known." So deep was he in contemplation of himself that the implications of her comment flashed right past him.

"I'm just beginning to have a glimpse of the forces that move the universe, Clarity. The sentient portion of it, anyway. Nothing is exactly as it appears. There are barely perceptible undercurrents swirling about our affairs, and for some damned reason a lot of them seem to be swirling around me. The more I try to run from them, the more they wash up against me."

It was her turn to smile. "Now you're talking nonsense."

"I wish I were. Maybe I am. Maybe you're right." After all, he thought, as messed up as his nervous system was, his imaginings might seem as solid as reality without his being able to tell the difference.

"So you think the universe is out to get you?"

"It's not out to get me. It just won't leave me alone. All I ever wanted from it were the identities of my mother and father. While trying to find that out, a number of people have died around me. Yes, died," he said emphatically in response to her skeptical look. "It's a burden I can't off-load. Violence follows me. Look at you. You're a perfect example."

"Meeting you was sheer coincidence," she argued. "A lucky one on my part. Surely you can't think there's some grand cosmic scheme devoted to making your life miserable?"

"I know it sounds insane. Sometimes I don't know what to believe. There are times when I think I should just stay aboard the *Teacher*, choose a vector at random along the galactic plane, and rush off at top speed until the drive gives out. At least then I'd have peace."

She let the resulting silence linger for a long time before speaking again. "It seems to me you're going to have to choose between peace and answers to all your questions."

He turned back to her. Gradually the tension drained out of him. "That's a very perceptive observation, Clarity."

"Hell, I'm a very perceptive kind of person. Besides being a biological genius. Self-damnation's no more a solution to anything than self-pity."

"What can you know of either? Still, it's nice of you to try to make me feel better. Considering your own situation, it's nice of you to think of me at all."

"Yes, you're really in sad shape, aren't you, Flinx? You're independent, wealthy enough to operate your own private starship, and you're all of nineteen. It's pretty difficult to feel sorry for someone who moans and groans about a setup like that.''

She only analyzes what she sees, Flinx thought. She doesn't consider the internal variables. But it was thoughtful of her nonetheless.

''Whether you believe it or not, I'm sick of all this. I just want to be left to myself, to do my thinking and my studying. The Ujurrians called this vessel the *Teacher* in my honor. They should have named it the *Student* because that's what I am. My primary subject is myself. I want to know who and what I am. Maybe I already know and I'm either too stupid or too scared to recognize it.''

At that she rose and walked over to him. Her hands moved. ''I think you're just fine, if you'll put aside some of this silliness you've gone and burdened yourself with.'' He retreated a step, and she actually pouted.

''Where do you want to go?'' he muttered uneasily.

She took a deep breath. ''Ever hear of a world called Longtunnel?'' He shook his head. ''Call it up on your holo map. You think Alaspin's a frontier world? There's only one outpost on Longtunnel, and it's understaffed. With good reason, as you'll see for yourself when we get there. That's where I need to go.''

''If I take you back to where you were, won't your kidnappers be looking for you there?''

''I'm sure they will, but I need to tell my colleagues what happened so they can take steps to protect themselves.'' She smiled. ''You'll understand immediately why I reacted so sharply to your reference to your Ujurrian friends being fond of tunnel digging. I don't think they're responsible for any of the excavations on Longtunnel.''

''Probably not. Though it's hard sometimes to understand them clearly, mind-to-mind communication notwithstanding. Extreme guilelessness and extreme sophistication are a tough combination to handle.''

They might not be so guileless now, he told himself.

Not after he had introduced them to the game of civilization. Though knowing them as he did, they might by now have moved on to another game entirely. He ought to find out—once he had handed this young woman back to the safe custody of her friends.

He murmured into the concealed pickup, disdaining the time-consuming use of the keyboard this time. He might be ignorant of Longtunnel's location, but not the *Teacher*. Stored within its memory were the whereabouts of every known world in the Commonwealth.

Flinx jumped slightly as Clarity came up behind him. Pip left his shoulder in favor of a decorative sculpture on the far side of the pool. Scrap was playing with the fish in the water, darting and striking harmlessly when they neared the surface. A scaly, misplaced kingfisher, Flinx mused.

Her arms slipped around him and gently drew him against her body. He could have disengaged himself but this time felt no compulsion to do so.

"So we're on our way to Longtunnel?"

"On our way, yes. What are you doing?"

"It's better to show," she whispered into his ear, "than to tell."

What she showed him was a means for shrinking parsecs. For once he was not bored during the long journey through space-plus, nor was he forced to retire regularly to the ship's library for surcease. The library had been limited to what the Ujurrians had had access to when they had built the ship. During his visits to other worlds Flinx had expanded it substantially. He introduced Clarity to it when they had time.

He did not fall in love with her, though he easily could have. There was too much still buried inside him for that. It was not a worrisome concern since she showed no signs of falling in love with him. All she was doing was making the jump from Alaspin to Longtunnel the most enjoyable journey he had yet taken on the *Teacher*.

There was a great deal to be said for not traveling

alone, for not shutting oneself off from the rest of humanity. Particularly when humanity took the form of someone as lively, vivacious, intelligent, and attractive as Clarity.

Even from orbit Longtunnel looked abnormal. There was a lone beacon on the surface. Linking with it, the *Teacher* estimated average wind speed in the temperate zone at a hundred fifty kph.

"Comparatively calm day." Clarity was reading over Flinx's shoulder. "It blows much stronger than that."

They stood on a traditional anachronism: the ship's bridge. Since Flinx could address the ship's computer from anywhere, including the bathroom, the existence of a bridge was nothing more than a sop to archaic design. But it felt good to sit before a control console and inspect the line of manual instrumentation. He understood some of the functions, but nowhere near enough to enable him to fly the ship in an emergency. Piloting an interstellar vessel was so complicated that humanx pilots rarely had anything to do and were glad of it. They were little more than a backup for a supposedly fail-safe system.

The controls and the view through the broad sweep of plexalloy were at least attractive, and it was a good place to watch incomprehensible information come in. The screens on the bridge were larger than those in the staterooms and commons.

"How windy does it get down there?" he asked.

"Three, four hundred kph. Maybe more. Nobody pays much attention unless there's a supply shuttle due in."

"I'd think if you were living in it you'd notice it all the time."

"That's just it. We don't live in it. The surface of Longtunnel's uninhabitable."

"You live in underground structures?"

"You'll see." She nodded toward a readout. "Just follow the navbeacon down."

"All right." He did not move.

She waited a while longer. "Aren't we going to the shuttle?" she asked finally.

"Of course." He rose smoothly. "Just checking a few last things."

As much as he enjoyed seeing new worlds and meeting new people, he always felt a pang of regret whenever it came time to leave the *Teacher*. In a universe of insanity it was his one refuge: always compliant, always comforting.

They made a clean drop and cut a tight curve around the northern hemisphere, homing in on the single landing beacon. Since there were no other vessels in orbit, there was no need to request clearance, and Clarity assured him there were no aircraft based at the outpost.

"That means our arrival will be noted not only by your friends and port Security but also by any local contacts your kidnappers may have established."

"You could always repackage me again for delivery," she said with a grin.

"True. Ribbons and bows this time." He studied the shuttle readouts. "They may have given up on you by now, or they may be concentrating all their energies on Alaspin."

"The latter's possible, but not the first." Her expression was somber. "I don't think these people give up on anything."

The little vessel shuddered as it sank through angry atmosphere. High-altitude winds buffeted them from side to side. Despite its compensators, they found reason to be grateful for their landing harnesses. Jetstreams warred with one another, treating the intruder with rude indifference. Pip and Scrap wrapped themselves around the two empty seats and held on tightly.

Lightning troubled him more than the wind. It was thunderous, continual, and struck sideways between the clouds as often as from cloud to surface. The shuttle was hit twice, but the only damage was a scorched wing.

"Is it always like this?" The steady roar and rumble

reached them even through the shuttle's superb sound-proofing.

"So the climatologists say. I wouldn't have their job for anything. They have to stay near the surface and go outside every so often to monitor their instruments."

Locally it was midday, but when the shuttle finally broke through the bottom layer of clouds it was as dark as early evening. Lightning continued to flash all around. Flinx was grateful that all they had to do was sit back and hang on while the ship's brain conversed at high speed with the mind of the landing computer below. The two machines calmly sorted out angle of approach and descent, landing speed, wind direction and shear, and the thousand other vital details that had to be determined and agreed upon in order to get two fragile humans down intact. Despite the best efforts of both mechanicals, the little craft bucked and heaved.

There was just enough light to enable Flinx to see through the front viewpoint. The terrain was worse than unpromising: tall pillars of pale stone, a jagged network of broken spires and crags, unhealthy-looking vegetation clinging grimly to exposed rock or hiding in the few sheltered places as it tried to avoid being mugged by the unrelenting gale. It was raining lightly.

As they dropped lower and closer to the menacing outcrops, Flinx strained for sight of a light, a building, anything to indicate they were coming down in the right place.

The shuttle's engines roared unexpectedly, slamming him back in the pilot's chair, the harness pressing tight against chest and legs. As they rose and banked, he had a brief glimpse of blue lights lined up in the darkness. That was all: no field, no hangars or blast pits or any of the other numerous appurtenances of a regular shuttle-port.

"Coming around on approach." The shuttle's voice sounded tinny in the rocking, swaying cabin.

"Why again?" Flinx asked sharply.

"Too much wind. Landing Command voided our initial descent. I am circling."

"And if there's too much wind again this time?"

"We will continue to circle until Landing Command authorizes touchdown. In the event fuel becomes critical, we shall return automatically to base for refueling."

That meant they had enough for maybe two more tries, Flinx knew. The *Teacher* did not carry a lot of reserve fuel for the shuttle. He always fueled up wherever he touched down. Now it was too late to wish for extra tanks.

They came around in a curve so tight that it threatened to rip the wings right off the sleek delta-shaped craft. This time the approach went much more smoothly; the wind's speed actually dropped below a hundred kph for a few precious moments.

Clarity was talking to cover her nervousness. "Are you on a familiar basis with all your computers?"

"I try to be friends with as many intelligences as possible. There are plenty of humans who don't deserve the label. This flying bothers you, too, doesn't it?"

"Of course it bothers me!" she replied tightly. "But it's the only way to get on or off Longtunnel. I've done it half a dozen times, and I'm still doing it."

"Another way of saying that the odds haven't caught up with you yet."

"You know, for a charming young man you can be very depressing at times."

"Sorry."

He could see the line of blue lights directly ahead and below now as the shuttle pointed her nose at the first light. They were flying below the tallest peaks. The outpost and port had been situated in a deep valley surrounded by high peaks. To cut down on the wind, he told himself. What were the surface winds like beyond the protection offered by the mountains?

When they finally touched down, he let out a sigh of relief. The shuttle rose once in the grasp of the relentless

wind, then set down once and for all as the computer
back-thrust the engines to cut their forward motion. They
felt the wind and heard the thunder more clearly when
the engines fell to idle.

A green light appeared on their left, blinking insis-
tently. The shuttle turned on its landing gear to track
another beacon, one they could not see.

"A good landing." Clarity was already loosening her
flight harness.

"Good?" Flinx was more shaken than he wanted to
admit. "This is a hell of a place."

"Full of possibilities, or none of us would be here."

"What's the air like?"

"Breathable—if it doesn't knock you off your feet. Just
keep in mind that any landing on Longtunnel is a good
landing. We might not have been able to touch down at
all."

"Why not?"

"Landslides." She was staring out the nearest sweep
of plexalloy.

At least out in space you could see the stars, he
thought. Here there was only bare rock dimly visible
through the dust and dark. A light mist was falling sideways, the wind howled, and the outside temperature was
unbearable thanks to the greenhouse effect engendered
by the dense cloud cover. He had been on less hospitable
worlds but never before on one quite so sheerly miserable.

"I'd rather live on Freeflo," he told her.

"Yes. But nobody's here to live. We're here to study
and work and produce."

The barrier that rolled up to admit them was set in
stelacrete walls framing a natural opening in the side of
a sheer cliff. As if to remind him of the landslides Clarity
had mentioned, a few large boulders came tumbling down
to smash into the badly pitted landing strip off to their
right.

Then they were inside, the wind a baleful memory, the

shuttle bathed in the rich sterile glow of artificial illumination. The barrier door rumbled down behind them,
shutting out wind, mist, and heat.

"What do you use for power here?" The amount of
light filling every corner of the hangar seemed extrava-
gant for an outpost port. He ought to have guessed.

"Wind turbines on the top of this mountain," Clarity
replied. "Heavy-duty blades and tiedowns. We have fusion for backup, but as I understand it they've never had
to bring it on line. Anyone wants a few more kilowatts
for their operation, all they have to do is struggle up
topside and set up another turbine. They're built to handle winds like these. It's helped make development here
practical. You pay for the turbine and its installation and
for tying it into the system. After that the power's free.
And at these wind speeds, plentiful."

He could see figures approaching the shuttle. They
moved slowly, cautiously. "Doesn't look like they're used
to unscheduled arrivals."

"For all I know you may be the first. This isn't exactly
a well-known vacation world."

"What do I tell Landing Authority?"

She laughed. "There isn't much authority of any kind
here. You're with me, so there's no problem. I'm with
Coldstripe, and everyone knows us." She watched as Pip
uncurled herself from a chair. "What about your pets?"

"Pip comes with me. Scrap can come or go as he
pleases. They're used to Moth's climate, so they should
be able to tolerate anything in here, so long as it doesn't
freeze."

"Never."

Flinx followed her out of the shuttle as it shut itself
down under instructions from Landing Command. A few
workers in beige overalls glanced in their direction before continuing on their way. Flinx suspected their stares
were intended for Pip and Scrap more than for the two
humans.

Clarity had been tense emerging from the shuttle. Now

she looked better. "Nothing out of the ordinary, looks like. I wonder how many knew that I was missing. They live in their own little worlds here."

"I'd think in a place this small, news of a kidnapping would travel quickly."

"Only if allowed to roam free, unrestrained. The company would try to keep it as quiet as possible so as not to alarm anyone else. And there's not much interfirm socializing here. Everyone tends to keep to their work and to themselves. Some are physically isolated, and the rest, well, they're the competition, aren't they?"

She led him across the smooth surface. Distant thunder echoed from beyond the massive hangar gate as they walked away from it.

A few quick glances sufficed to show that they were crossing the floor of an enormous cavern that had been modified to serve as a hangar. It was commodious enough to hold several dozen shuttles.

"The space was here," she replied in response to his query about the cavern's origins. "That's one thing Longtunnel has plenty of."

"What about native life, flora and fauna?"

"Ah," she said with a smile, "that's why we're here in the first place. It's incredibly diverse and adaptable. A unique and challenging ecosystem. As you'll find out for yourself in a little while."

Flinx glanced back at the hangar barrier. "I didn't see much when we came down, and I wouldn't think you'd get any diversity out in that kind of weather."

"You don't." She was still smiling. "Low scrub growth and a few hard-pressed insects and lower mammals. Nature isn't stupid, Flinx. When Longtunnel's discoverers landed here, the first thing they did was get out of the weather. The native lifeforms have had billions of years to do that. Don't you think they'd do the same themselves? If it's storming outside, you move inside. That's just what Longtunnel's inhabitants have done."

They entered the port receiving facilities, which were

simple and sparse. Flinx was fascinated by the amount
of bare rock visible in the ceiling, floor, and walls. We've
reverted here, he thought. Strung it with fiber-optic cables and AI terminals and contact switches, but it's still
the ancestral cave. Only the wall paintings have changed.
Stalactites and stalagmites remained in place where they
did not interfere with routine functions.

Few glances came their way. They were far enough
from Alaspin that Pip would be regarded simply as an
exotic pet by people unfamiliar with her lethal reputa-
tion.

The port was busy but understaffed, though the excess
space would have given it an underpopulated appearance
anyway. It was an easy matter to separate the long-timers
from recent arrivals. The skin of the former was pale
beyond pallid.

"Everyone here takes tanning treatments," Clarity explained. "Some are more diligent about it than others.
Artificial lighting can only compensate so much."

"Then why do they stay on here?" Flinx knew it was
a stupid question even as he asked it.

"For the money. Why else would anyone come to this
place? For money, and maybe for fame."

"And do they find it?"

"Some do. The fame, anyway—the money is just starting to come in. In my case, a share of royalties on a
newly approved biopatent. I have others pending, more
than you might think for someone my age. The work I've
been involved in here is just starting to bear fruit."

"What kind of work is that?"

"That's right," she said teasingly, "I haven't told you
yet, have I?"

"Only that you're an gengineer. You haven't told me
what it is you're engineering."

"You'll see. You'll see everything and to hell with
company security. I owe you that much, if that's what
you want. If not, I guess you're free to leave. You've
done everything I asked you and more."

He remembered the jump from Alaspin to Longtunnel and said dryly, "It wasn't exactly an arduous task on my part. I'm intrigued by what you're doing as well as by this place. I would like to see what you're up to."

"I was hoping you'd say that," she said warmly. "I'll get you clearance.

"Longtunnel is one big karstic formation, or so the geologists claim. The whole place was covered by shallow ocean for billions of years."

Flinx nodded, studying the exposed walls. "This is all limestone."

"Most, not all. Limestone, gypsum, calcite—soft minerals. As the oceans receded while Longtunnel cooled, the three continents were exposed to this wind and, more importantly, to constant rain. It's been chewing away at the limestone for millennia. The results are caves like the one we're in now and the bigger one we just left that's used as a hangar.

"Exploration is still in its infancy here, but some think Longtunnel is home to the largest, longest cavern systems anywhere in the Commonwealth. You can't walk through undertown without tripping over a starry-eyed speleologist. The whole contingent's been stumbling around in a collective daze since the nature of the planetary surface was first deduced. They're always posting revised lists as they discover a new biggest this or more wondrous that. Do you like caves?"

"Not as a general rule, no. I'm not afraid of them, but I prefer the feel of sunshine and the smell of growing things."

"You'll find half of that here, though maybe not the kind of smells you enjoy. The air's always cool, but the surface heat seeps down and moderates it. You can work in a short-sleeved shirt. Nobody knows about the lower levels. The speleologists have been so busy up here in what we call the temperate zone that they haven't had a chance or the inclination to take their lights any deeper. The water, by the way, is about as pure and refreshing as you can find anywhere, naturally filtered. There's talk of starting up a local brewery and exporting. If nothing else, it would have novelty value.

"There are four underground rivers located so far." They were strolling past a cafeteria. A few people were removing food from service bays. "They expect to find more. There's even talk of underground oceans."

Flinx frowned. "Surely a cavern large enough to hold something that size would have fallen in on itself by now."

"Who knows? Longtunnel is rewriting a number of long-held geological rules. Biological, too."

Ever since they had left the hangar behind, he had been conscious of a constant hum in the air, a soft whine like a tenor choir murmuring the same tune over and over.

"Pumps," she explained when he asked about the sound. "There's a lot of water in Longtunnel. Caverns are still growing, still being formed. It's always raining topside, and the water has to go somewhere. Most of it drains away naturally, but there are places we want to move into where the water also wants to be. So we run pumps. Like I told you, energy's no problem down here."

"Somebody still has to pay for it, for all this."

"The port infrastructure and support facilities are jointly supported by the government and the private concerns operating here under license. Everything else is privately run."

"Healthy. Are all the firms located in the same cavern?"

"No, they're scattered all over the place, connected by communications fibers. Short-range wireless doesn't work too well through multiple walls and solid rock, no matter which technology you employ. Cheaper and cleaner to run fibers. Internal walls are only for privacy, since every outfit can have its own cavern. You pick out an unclaimed space, scrape off the formations, and set up your desks and files and beds and cooking facilities and lab equipment. There's more office space on Long-tunnel than a dozen worlds could ever use.''

"It all seems very efficient and well run. Why would anyone want to interfere with your operation here?''

Her expression turned dark. "I'm not really sure. They didn't actually come out and tell me. But then, I only respond to logic and reason.''

He almost said, "You're too pretty to be so sarcastic,'' but then thought better of it. First, he did not think she would appreciate it, and, second, he was never sure exactly what to say around attractive women. Somehow, when he tried to talk to them, he always drew a frown instead of a smile. He did much better when he did not talk at all.

"Whoops, careful.'' She put a hand on his arm to lead him to the right.

He didn't see them at first because he was looking straight ahead. It took a moment for his eyes to detect the motion.

Chapter Eight

There were three of them traveling parallel as they crossed the left half of the poured plastic flooring Flinx and Clarity were following. Each was mostly mouth a dozen centimeters wide with a body that was broad and flat, like a pale yellow flounder striped with blue. Bright pink lips outlined each wide mouth.

At first he thought they were large insects advancing on tiny legs or cilia. As they moved closer, he saw rippling fur. Each was half a meter in length. Except for the gaping, flattened mouths that quivered as the creatures advanced, they had no visible external features except two black pinpoints located just above and behind the jaws. They might once have been eyes. Each of the two dozen or so limbs they walked on was articulated in the middle and ended in a flat, round pad. A hairless tail several centimeters long protruded from the back end. They looked like a trio of faceless, mutated platypuses that had been given the legs of an oversized millipede. Flinx stood gaping at them as they trundled silently past like so many miniature reapers.

"Floats." Clarity gestured as she explained. "We screen all the work and living areas. There are dangerous predators on Longtunnel, and there may well be others not yet encountered. The floats are useful as they are. We've semidomesticated them."

"They don't 'float' very high," he observed.

"I didn't name them; somebody else is responsible for that. They're trisexual, which is why you'll always see them traveling in trios. We let them roam where they please."

"What are they doing—vacuuming the floor?"

"No." She laughed. "They don't consume dirt and dust, if that's what you mean. But this world is alive, Flinx. The floors and walls, the very air in the caverns, is full of rusts and yeasts and fungi. Half the research scientists working here are mycologists. Most of what they've classified is benign, but not all, and some is downright dangerous. The cartographic spleologists take masks with them on the chance they might run into something lethal.

"Between the benign and the fatal there's a large group of small organisms that will give you an instant cold or otherwise interfere with your breathing or excretory systems if you inhale any of them. They spend most of their time on the ground, but walking stirs them up. The floats love them. So they are vacuumers, but not of dirt. They filter out the organics they suck up. Like baleen whales, only on a much smaller scale. Of course they eat the benign organisms as readily as the harmful ones, but that's no loss to us."

She was heading toward a familiar-looking shuttlecar-system terminal, familiar except for the fact that they were the first of their kind Flinx had ever seen without canopies. The settlers of Longtunnel did not need to protect themselves against the weather.

"It's not far to Coldstripe's complex," she was saying.

"Aren't you going to call ahead to let them know we're coming, that you're back?"

She grinned wickedly. "No. They're a pretty staid bunch. Let's shake them up with a surprise."

She climbed into one of the four passenger cars, and he followed. Her fingers thumbed in the destination setting. Instantly the compact car rose half a centimeter above its magnetic repulsion rail and began accelerating forward.

Flinx noted the smooth walls and the narrow service walkway as they sped through an irregular tunnel. The lighting along the route was pleasantly bright, and except for the solid stone walls there was nothing to indicate they were underground. They might have been in any transportation corridor on Earth or any of the other industrialized worlds.

Other cars raced past above the paralleling rail, heading for the port. Some were small passenger cars like the one they rode, others miniature trains carrying cargo. There were branch rails leading into side tunnels, but they continued to speed along the main line.

"Did you notice that they were heavily pigmented?"

"What?" Flinx was staring up the tunnel. It reminded him of an amusement ride Mother Mastiff had taken him on when he was a child. Less active, no holos, but in its own fashion just as fascinating.

"The floats. Yellow and blue. That's because many lifeforms here are still dependent on food drifting in from above. The wind and rain and heat make it almost impossible for anything like higher fauna to survive, but some plants have done well and spread out. There's nothing on the surface to feed on them. So the organic matter they produce finds its way into cave openings and sinkholes. There's a whole ecosystem dependent on the transition zone between inside and outside. The floats are part of that. So they have coloration, while most of the creatures that thrive in the deep cave system have lost all pigment entirely. It's quite an experience to see something like a goralact, which is a pretty good-size animal, about the mass of a cow. But it has six legs and is almost transparent. You can watch the blood coursing through it like a diagram in a junior physiology program. Almost everything we've encountered has eyes of some sort, but they're mostly vestigial. The best of them can distinguish shape. The majority do well to react to bright light. There's even one, the photomorph, that uses it to its advantage.''

"What the hell's a photomorph?" Pip fluttered her wings as the car banked sharply around a curve, then relaxed on his shoulder.

"You'll see." She was grinning at him. "When one attacks."

He was mildly alarmed. "Attacks? Should I be ready for something?" He viewed the tunnel ahead in a different light.

"Oh, no. Photomorphs and their relatives are harmless to humans. They don't know that, the poor things, so they keep trying. If you let one get on you, it could be dangerous, but they're easy enough to avoid. They don't rely on speed when they attack."

He pondered the photomorph until the car halted. Clarity led him through a succession of caverns and passageways where the cave formations had been leveled. He could hear other voices clearly. It was not surprising, since sound traveled well inside a cavern. There were brief glimpses inside large rooms separated from others by spray-fiber walls. If one put up a mesh frame, sprayed a color over it, and waited until it hardened, one had a solid partition—the cheapest kind of construction.

She stopped outside a door set in a wall painted a garish shade of blue. The door admitted them to a room occupied by a man not much older than Clarity. He was tall, and black hair worked at covering his face.

"Clarity!" He brushed nervously at the hair. "Christ, where have you been? Everyone's been worried sick, and the brass all have sealed mouths on the subject."

"Never mind that now, Jase. I've a lot to say, and I have to say it to Vandervort first so she can take appropriate steps." She indicated Flinx. "This is my friend. So's the flying snake lounging on his neck. So's the one on *my* neck—it's under my hair, so don't go hunting for it."

The tall young man's eyes traveled from Flinx to Pip and back to Clarity. His expression radiated delight. "Hell, I've got to tell everyone you're back." He started to turn, then hesitated. "But you said you wanted to tell Vandervort first."

"Just details. You can slip the news to Tangerine and Jimmy and the rest."

"Good—sure. Hey, you want to come in?" He stepped aside to make a path.

Flinx followed Clarity into the extensive lab as Jase dashed for the nearest wall comm to spread the news. "Sounds like you've been missed, like you said you would be."

"One or two projects probably came to a complete stop in my absence. I'm not boasting. That's just how it is."

Flinx admired the state-of-the-art equipment lining tables and walls, the gleaming surfaces, the spotless plexalloyware. There were four technicians at work in the chamber, two robotic, two human. All looked over at the visitors, waved, and returned to their work.

"Thranx work for Coldstripe also?"

"A couple. It's pretty chilly down here for them. If not for the wind, they'd prefer it topside. They do most of the maintenance work on the turbines. The constant humidity helps, and they enjoy underground work naturally. So they wear heat suits. Their own living areas are roofed over and steamed up all the time inside. Good way to get sick: Go from any cavern into Marlacyno's quarters. An instant twenty-degree jump."

They walked through a subdividing door, then a second, and Flinx found himself in a room alive with hisses, squeals, and whines, none of which were being generated electronically.

"Specimen storage," Clarity informed him unnecessarily.

Flinx didn't recognize any of the creatures cavorting in the holding cages. Thin wire of varying grades kept them restrained. All of it was translucent.

"Carbfiber base." Clarity touched a nearly invisible wire. "Keeps them in but relaxed. There isn't the feeling of being caged. Here's the one I wanted you to see."

He looked in the indicated direction and was momentarily blinded when an intense light lit his face. Stars danced on his retinas as his vision cleared. Clarity was chuckling at him, and he realized that she must have shut her eyes at the critical moment.

"That's the photomorph I was telling you about. I said you'd see it when it attacked. You'd think they'd realize it's too bright in here for their own light to have much effect, but since they can hardly see, they probably don't realize how diluted their weapons are."

As his sight returned, Flinx could see several of the creatures slowly moving from the back of their cage toward the front. Each was about half a meter in length, the same as the floats, and was covered with a fine gray fur that formed something not unlike a long handlebar mustache below the double nostrils. The snout was short, blunt, and filled with sharp triangular teeth. The nostrils sat on the tip of a four-centimeter-long trunk. Each of the four legs ended in a clawed three-toed foot. The claws were hooked and looked extremely sharp. The translucent bars of the cage appeared far too fragile to hold such squat, muscular creatures in check, but he was confident they were stronger than they looked.

The photomorphs were advancing in slow motion, like sloths.

"They'll stop when they reach the front of the cage and realize they can't get at us. They have hardly any eyes at all. In their case that's an offensive adjustment. I told you there were carnivores here."

"If they can't see us, how do they know we're here? Smell?"

She nodded. "Other carnivores have lines of electric sensors along their faces and bodies so they can detect the presence of prey by the faint pulses every body generates. Still others have sensors to detect the movement of a prey animal, by analyzing air currents and pressures. Look at the top of the head, where you'd expect to find ears."

Flinx stood on tiptoes to do so and found a double line of slightly glassy beads.

"You might mistake them for eyes, but there are no pupils or irises. They're photogenerators. They build up the light in their bodies until they let loose with that single bright flare to stun their prey. Remember that most of the higher animals we've classified have the ability to detect light in darkness. So the photomorph puts out an impressive number of lumens and overwhelms the prey's photosensors. It's a real brain jolt and usually stuns for several minutes. Call it a phototoxin. While the animal is sitting there stunned, the photomorph and his companions wander over leisurely and start making a meal of it."

Flinx was duly impressed. "I've heard of creatures that use light to lure their prey, but not to actually attack it with."

"You'd be shocked at the kind of offensive and defensive weaponry animals can develop in the absence of light. The xenologists here are surprised by something new every time they make another field expedition. Longtunnel's lifeforms are unique, and that's why we're here. To study potentially useful varieties."

Flinx nodded in the direction of the caged photomorphs. "How might something like that be useful?"

"Other biophotics like fireflies and deep-sea fish generate their light chemically; the photomorph employs an electronic process that's never been seen before. No matter how efficient we get, there's always a market for still another way of generating light and power. Our people don't have a clue to what makes the photomorph tick, but they're working on it.''

"And you don't have a clue either?''

"Not one of my projects. I'm busy enough. It's good to be busy down here. There's not much else to do except for recreational spelunking and forming casual assignations.'' She led him out of the zoo. "Given a little more food and a little less competition, just about everything down here will breed like mad. If you can find a useful job for something that multiplies like crazy and lives on fungi or slime, you have a marketable bioproduct. Ever hear of Verdidion Weave?''

Flinx shook his head, then hesitated. "Wait a minute. Some kind of living carpet, right?''

She nodded. "Our first real success. The one that's financed all our subsequent work here. I'm at least half responsible for its development. That was several years ago. Since then we've come up with a few additional products. Small stuff. Nothing on the order of Verdidion Weave. But we're close to some major breakthroughs. Or we were, before my work was interrupted. I'll show you some of them when I get a chance.''

"I'd be very interested in seeing them.''

They were back in the main lab. The tall man was waiting for them, eyes shining. "Vandervort wants to see you immediately.''

"Damn. I wanted to break the surprise myself.''

"You were seen coming through Security. Everyone wants to talk to you, but I imagine you'll want to talk to Vandervort first.''

"I don't have much choice now, anyway, do I, Jase?''

"I expect not.'' He looked concerned. "Was there some kind of trouble? There were rumors—the company tried to keep news of your disappearance quiet, but you can't keep secrets down here.''

"I'm not going to go into the details now, but if it hadn't been for my friend, I wouldn't be here.''

Jase studied the slim young man standing quietly next to the gengineer, sizing him up and dismissing him quickly. That was fine with Flinx.

"I was in a position to offer assistance," he explained, "so I did."

"Yeah, nice of you." Jase's gaze switched back to Clarity.

Flinx saw that the other man was hopelessly in love with Clarity Held. He wondered if Jase had any idea how obvious he was being. From his new height and greater maturity, Flinx was able to regard the other man with tolerance.

"Everything went crazy when you up and vanished." Jase chose to ignore Flinx, having cataloged and filed him like one of the inhabitants of the specimen zoo.

"I figured it would. Don't worry. I'll be back on station by tomorrow." She reached out, and for a moment Flinx thought she was going to take the other scientist's hand. But she was only gesturing at the door.

"Let's go. It's time we check in with Vandervort. You'll like her. Everyone likes her."

"Then I'm sure I will, too."

They walked instead of using the ARV system. As they did so, they passed people clad in attire that screamed Security. Most of them wore sidearms.

"Looks like someone's taken a few precautions in the wake of your disappearance."

"Amee isn't dumb. Any outfit would get suspicious if one of their top people suddenly vanished without leaving behind a message of resignation or notice of intent to terminate. I didn't go as quietly as the people who grabbed me thought I would. I'll bet there are missing persons bulletins out across half the Commonwealth by now."

They were walking down a corridor open to the ceiling. The floor was polished limestone and travertine. Plastic sheeting hung in several places, and he could hear the dripping of water against the impermeable Mylar.

She noticed the direction of his glance. "I think I mentioned that the majority of the cavern system explored so far is alive."

"What do you mean, alive?"

"A cavern with water running through it is still creating and adding to formations. It's a live cave. One that's dried up is considered dead."

"I see. I should've known that, but most of my studies have been directed outward on the worlds I've visited."

She eyed him curiously. "How many worlds have you been to? I've only been on three. My home world of Thalia Major, Thalia Minor of course, and now Longtunnel. I guess I should call it four, counting Alaspin."

"I've been to more than four." He did not want to go into specifics. She probably would not believe him, anyway. Instead, he changed the subject, a skill he had mastered years ago. "Clearly everyone here's on alert. Yet you look more relaxed than I've ever seen you."

"They don't know it's over. I was anxious right up until we landed. But everything's okay now, especially since Security's been called out. You've seen what landing on Longtunnel can be like. There's only the one port and landing strip. There are no facilities anywhere else. All they have to do is keep the port under guard and nobody can get in or out without having to run Security first. You ought to relax, yourself."

I'd like to do that, he said to himself, but I think I forgot how about five years ago.

They turned another corner and stopped before a door set in a yellow spray-wall. Clarity didn't buzz or identify herself. She simply walked in. No scanner bade them pause; no autosec announced their arrival.

Now that he was here, he understood why. There was no need for internal security on Longtunnel. All you had to do to prevent unauthorized entry was monitor port facilities and watch the front door because there were no back ones to sneak in through. It also explained how Clarity's abductors had been able to slip her out. Once you were inside, you had only a single checkpoint to clear to get out again. There must be individual company security, but that was a different matter, especially if you were trying to break out and not in.

The office they entered was spacious, and why not, when it was simply a matter of subdividing another cavern to your liking? What made it interesting was the presence of dozens of ceiling growths. In this chamber they had been left undisturbed. Glistening stalactites, helectites, soda straws, and gypsum twists sparkled above the artificial lighting. Limestone and water had decorated the office far more beautifully than any professional could have.

There was no need for climate control. The temperature was the same in the office as it had been in the hall outside: cool and slightly damp. Off to the left, near the back of the chamber, cave water tumbled musically from a crack in the rock wall and was drawn away by a floor drain.

Storage files, a couch, office furniture, and cojoined desks stood out starkly against the gemlike natural formations. The woman who rose from behind one desk was much shorter than Clarity. Her long red hair had been pulled back and bound in a neat bun—knife-edged gold crystals pierced the bun in three places. Her smile of greeting was warm and inviting, her voice was deep and throaty, and a narcostick dangled precariously from one corner of her mouth. It in no way impeded her speech. Her stride and handshake were equally vigorous.

Flinx figured her to be in her midfifties and was genuinely surprised when he learned later that she was seventy. Late middle age. Instead of shaking hands with Clarity, she embraced the younger woman, patting her affectionately on the back.

"Maxim and the gang down in Development have been spinning their wheels ever since you vanished."

That made Clarity frown. "They went into my cubicle?"

"My dear, everyone went into your cubicle. What did you expect? There was a lot of moaning and wringing of hands when Security ventured their opinion that your departure had not been voluntary. I suppose I am due some of the responsibility. I should have insisted on tighter security right from the beginning. But who imagined something like that happening? An abduction, from Longtunnel? I am correct, am I not, in assuming it was something like that?"

"That's it."

Vandervort nodded knowingly. "The signs were clear to the forensics people. Not to the rest of us, but to them the message was clear enough. Well, it won't happen again, I can promise you that."

"We saw the new Security on our way down."

"Good." She turned to examine Flinx, not neglecting the minidrag relaxing on his shoulder. "Interesting pet you have, young man. I notice that Clarity has acquired one for herself."

"Pip isn't a pet. Our relationship is mutually beneficial."

"As you will. That's part of what our work here is about, you know. Or are you aware of that already?" She glanced back at Clarity. "How much have you told him about us?"

"Everything that isn't classified. He saved my life. Maybe yours as well. I couldn't shut him out."

"I can't wait for the details," the woman replied sardonically. "By the way," she said as she extended a hand to Flinx, "I'm Alynasmolia Vandervort. Everyone calls me Amee. Or Momma. I'm Coldstripe's supervisor-in-charge here."

He returned the firm grip. "I assumed something of the kind."

"It appears we all owe you a debt of gratitude for returning our Clarity to us. You're not claustrophobic by any chance, are you? We have pills for those who display the symptoms."

"I'm fine," he told her. "If anything, it's more spacious than I would have imagined."

Vandervort looked pleased, resumed her seat behind the desk, and directed her visitors to chairs. "Who was it?" she asked Clarity.

Flinx feigned indifference while listening closely to Clarity's story. The supervisor sat motionless and intent. She did not touch the narcostick, but by the time Clarity had finished, it had somehow migrated from one corner of her mouth to the other. She leaned back in her chair and let out a soft grunt.

"Could be any of several dozen radical groups. There are plenty of 'em out there, but usually they confine themselves to making speeches nobody listens to, or taking up free space between entertainment programming on the newsfax." She had a peculiar, jerky manner of speech that was matched by the ceaseless movement of her eyes from one person to the next.

"Our debt to you, young man, is real. You know that Clarity here is irreplaceable."

"I know. She told me—several times."

Vandervort laughed at that, a hard but in no way masculine chuckle. "Oh, she's not shy, our Clarity. With all she's accomplished already, she has no need for false modesty. Whoever carried out this execrable act did their research well. Clarity's the one member of our scientific staff we can't afford to lose. Now that you're back among us," she added grimly, "we won't lose track of you again."

"I'm not worried. It looks like you've shut everything down tight, Amee."

"That we have." She hesitated. "Would you feel more comfortable with a full-time bodyguard?"

"I already have one." Clarity reached up to pet Scrap, secure in his place beneath her sidetail.

Vandervort issued another of her soft grunts and turned to Flinx. "Clarity's told you what we're doing here?"

"You're working with malleable local lifeforms to produce commercially viable offshoots."

She nodded. "Genetically, Longtunnel is a mine whose shafts have already been dug for us. We haven't been set up here very long. Barely begun to classify, much less extensively select, breed, and gengineer. Even so we've managed to come up with several successful products."

"Clarity mentioned your Verdidion Weave."

"That's been our big success thus far, but not the only one." She reached behind her and opened a drawer in a metal cabinet. Sweet smells filled the room as she withdrew something and placed it on the desk in front of her.

The shallow pan of blue metallic glass was filled with cubes of jelly: red, yellow, and purple. They did not shimmer when she slid the pan across the desk top.

"Have a bite." Flinx studied the jelly uncertainly. "Oh, go on, dear." Vandervort selected a purple cube, popped it in her mouth, and chewed enthusiastically.

"Go on, Flinx." Clarity helped herself to a pink-hued square. "They're wonderful."

Hardly able to sit and cower in terror while the two women munched away, Flinx chose a bright green cube and cautiously put it in his mouth. Anticipating a lime or gooseberry taste, he was startled by the explosion of flavors that shocked his taste buds. The cube's density was another surprise. It was tougher than gelatin, closer to rubber in consistency. Yet once he broke it down, it dissolved readily in his mouth. The multiple flavors lingered powerfully long after he had swallowed the last bite.

He helped himself to another green cube, then a purple one. The flavor burst was as different and exciting the third time as it had been with the first two. It occurred to him as he was chewing the fourth cube that he might be consuming some extremely valuable products, though Vandervort hadn't withdrawn the tray. On the contrary, she appeared to delight in his enjoyment.

"Remarkable stuff, isn't it, young man? When people

have exhausted their purchasing power on electronic gadgets and labor-saving devices and art, there isn't much left to dally over except food. A new taste sensation is worth more than the most powerful new personal computing device. Whether intended for mind or stomach, entertainment is always more valuable than anything the gengineers can invent.''

"What is it?" a sated Flinx asked, licking his fingers.

"Almost as nutritious as it is tasty, for one thing." Clarity was wearing her prideful smile again. "It tastes like it's packed with sugars, but it's a sham. In reality it's almost solid protein."

Vandervort took obvious delight in identifying it for him. "It's a pseudoplasmodium slug."

Flinx stopped licking his fingers. Vandervort's smile grew wider. "A slime mold, young man."

Flavors began to fade rapidly. "I don't follow you."

"A pseudoplasmodium is an amoebeic aggregate. Strange lifeform, slime molds. When grouped together they behave as a single entity, but if you take them apart, shake them around in water or something, they break down into individual clusters quite capable of sustaining life." She gestured at the half-empty tray. "We don't know what we're going to call it yet. I don't deal with advertising and publicity."

"I'm sure they'll call it something like Flavor Cubes," Clarity said.

"Yes, dear. 'Flavor Cubes from the taste mines of Longtunnel.' Or some such drivel to appeal to the popular taste." Vandervort sounded almost bitter. "They certainly will not market it as slime mold."

"I take it the stuff is reasonable to produce," Flinx murmured.

"More than reasonable. It's a saprobe. It lives by decaying other organic matter. Some are parasites. These—" She indicated the tray again. "—are easily managed. The organism thrives on garbage and waste. How's that for a practical food resource? A new food that tastes good, is visually appealing, and is good for you. And all it needs for growth is a little dampness and garbage.''

"It grows naturally here?" Flinx asked.

"No, dear, but something very like it does. We intensified the colors, the rate of growth, and greatly manipulated the natural flavors. We'll be ready to commence production on a limited basis in a couple of months. Not right here: This will always be a research facility. A pair of large virgin caverns are being developed off to the west. It'll be sold as a luxury item at first, like the Verdidion Weave. We'll expand gradually into the mass market.''

What's in a name? he mused as he gazed at the tray of slime mold. The Commonwealth was rife with foodstuffs no one would touch if he or she had an inkling of their origins. That was what advertising existed for: to make the impractical and unappetizing irresistible. If Vandervort had allowed it, he would gladly have emptied the entire tray.

"Clarity mentioned someone named Maxim. Is he a gengineer, too?"

"No. Max is our head mycologist. Not everything we're working with down here is fungi, though. Longtunnel's subterranean world is alive with astonishing lifeforms. You wouldn't think to find so much variety thriving in darkness. Plenty of mammals or close relations.''

"I've seen the floats and the photomorphs.''

Vandervort nodded approvingly. "There are a few creatures the taxonomists haven't figured out how to classify. Distant relations of deep-sea dwellers on Earth and Cachalot. Their ancestors lived next to sulfurous vents. The sulfides were metabolized by bacteria that lived in the creature's gills, or by special organs; microbes broke down the sulfide compounds and used the resultant energy to make carboyhdrates, proteins, and liquids.

"When the oceans here on Longtunnel receded, exposing the limestone and creating the caverns, these ocean dwellers didn't die out. Instead they became air-breathing land creatures, and food for others. Many of them occupy the same ecological niche underground that chlorophyllous plants do topside. We expected to find a simple food chain here, and instead we stumbled into something wondrous and complex. To top it all, the entire ecosystem is particularly amenable to gengineering." She leaned back in her chair and regarded her guests speculatively.

"I'll see to arranging some sort of suitable reward for you, young man."

"That won't be necessary."

"It really isn't," Clarity told her supervisor. "He's not short of resources. He has his own ship."

Vandervort's expression was unreadable. Flinx noted that her eyebrows had been neatly and recently plucked, then dyed to match the rest of her hair.

"His own ship, you say? I am impressed. But we must give you something for returning our Clarity to us, young man. I suppose we could carpet a room or two on your vessel. You would be astonished to learn what our first rolls of Verdidion Weave sell for on places like Earth and New Riviera. It would be a suitable gift."

"Thanks, but I like the floors on my ship just the way they are. If you're going to insist, though, I wouldn't mind having a few trays of that." He nodded at the lustrous pseudoplasmodium.

Vandervort chuckled, picked up the tray, and returned it to the refrigeration unit concealed in the cabinet behind her desk. "As I mentioned, we're not at the production stage yet. But I'll talk to the lab and see what can be done. Feeding you doesn't seem like much of a reward, but if that's what interests you, we have a couple of other new ingestible bioproducts on the shelves that might tickle your taste buds. Clarity can show them to you. She's already breached most of our security regulations, anyway."

"He saved my life!" Clarity reminded her supervisor.

"Take it easy, dear. I was only teasing." She smiled ingratiatingly at Flinx. She was very good at what she did, he knew. The "harmless kindly aunt" act was excellent. The feelings he felt emanating from her suggested someone a good deal more calculating and professional. As a connoisseur of emotions, he always applauded a skilled performance. She took his smile for indifference.

"You aren't interested in our little industrial secrets, anyway. Are you, young man?"

"I'm a student, but not of those. Anything secret stays with me. I'm interested in knowledge for its own sake. Not for sale."

"What a quaint notion. Well, if you're good enough for our Clarity, you're good enough for me." She smiled and extracted the narcostick, which despite appearances was not permanently affixed to her lower lip.

"I leave it to Clarity to exercise proper judgment. Under her supervision you may have the run of our facility. It's the least we can do. Just promise me you're not wearing any concealed recording devices. How long do you plan to stay with us?"

"I don't know how long I'm going to stay, and I'm not wearing anything except what you can see," he replied, knowing full well he probably had been scanned for concealed instrumentation as soon as he'd emerged from the shuttle.

"Very well, then. Enjoy your visit." She was smiling an entirely different kind of smile as she glanced back at Clarity. "Do you think we can find suitable lodgings for our young man, my dear?"

"I think so," Clarity managed to reply with a straight face.

Vandervort rose as she spoke. It was a gesture of dismissal. "Just remember, young man, that she has an unbreakable long-term contract here, and now that we have her back, I have no intention of letting her leave, voluntarily or otherwise."

"I've no intention of interrupting my work here,
Amee."

"I'm glad to hear that, my dear. I am aware of other
incentives to travel besides wealth and fame, and I'm not
so old that I don't remember how powerful they can be."

Chapter Nine

The following day she formally checked in with her colleagues and fellow workers. When they heard her story, Flinx was battered by a barrage of friendly backslaps and congratulatory handshakes. Everyone was grateful to him for what he had done. He bore their gratitude patiently.

He tried to involve himself in their conversations, but the technical terms were outside his range of experience and study, though Clarity was obviously in her element. A short, swarthy, and perpetually nervous young man introduced himself as Maxim. He was not much older than Flinx. His lab was overflowing with an extraordinary array of chlorophyll-less growths. A few were quite mobile. Maxim clearly enjoyed the role of teacher and tour guide.

"We still aren't sure whether the fungi derived from the algae or the protozoans, but there are genotypes on this world that blow most of our traditional theories all to hell."

Flinx listened enthusiastically, as he did to every new

piece of information that came his way. Nor was the tour only of labs and libraries. There was time and the means to relax as well. Individual food service, undated entertainment on disk and chip, even occasional live performances that made the rounds of the various company facilities. Everything, Flinx thought, to make life underground as pleasant and endurable as possible.

"Small compensation," Clarity said, "when you realize we never get to see the sun or the sky. Coldstripe does its best, though. We're the biggest research outfit on Longtunnel. The others are small and just getting started. Most of them are just doing pure research. We're the only ones who've gone as far as developing a salable product. The House of Sometra is trying, but they have no real production facilities as yet. Once the Flavor Cubes join Verdidion Weave on the market, everyone will stop asking where Longtunnel is. The plan is to export directly through Thalia Major. But I don't imagine you're very interested in the economics of it."

"I'm interested in everything," he told her quietly.

It was fascinating to watch her in the lab. When working, she underwent a complete transformation. The smiles disappeared, laughter became muted, and she was all seriousness and attention to business when trying to analyze the genetic structure of some new fungus or sulfide eater.

She rarely worked with the actual lifeform. That was left to the surgeons and manipulators. Her career and work were bounded by the limits of a twenty-by-twenty infinite-screenfront Hydroden Custom Designer, with several billion megabytes of online storage in a superconduct Markite Cylinder Tap. Without touching a living cell, she could take entire complex organisms apart and reassemble them on demand, could run an entire evolutionary schematic in a few hours. Only after a possible recombinant had been simulated and overchecked would it finally be tried in vivo.

It was mesmerizing and disquieting to watch—because

it was too easy for him to empathize with the lowly creatures whose genetic codes were being played with like a child's blocks, even if they were lifeforms as simple as fungi and slime molds. Because it was all too easy for him to imagine a cluster of faceless strangers bent over similar devices, moving molecules of DNA around with electronic probes, inserting proteins and removing genes. Because it was all too easy to envision the end product of their dispassionate and emotionless work as himself.

Clarity disquieted him in another fashion entirely. For someone who had recently vowed not to involve himself any further in the problems of a frivolous and uncaring humanity, he was powerfully attracted to the young gengineer. She had already willingly demonstrated how attracted she was to him.

He delighted in observing her with her colleagues. When working, she was no longer the frightened, exhausted woman he had hauled out of the Ingre jungle—she added a decade in maturity and self-confidence.

Their relationship had begun to settle. It was not as if she had turned cool toward him. If anything, she was more relaxed in his company than ever before. But with the return of her self-assurance had come a slight and welcome distancing. If he pressed the issue, he did not doubt that she would respond readily. That was plain to see in her eyes, unmistakable in her voice. It was simply that she was no longer dependent on him for her continued survival. Better this way, he told himself.

Unfortunately, her increased confidence and self-assurance in their relationship were marked by a steady decline in his own. While he was the intellectual equal or superior of any of her male acquaintances, in matters of social interaction he had less experience than the average nineteen-year-old.

Well, he had always been a loner, probably always would be. He tagged along as she made the rounds and performed her work, content with the moments in between when they could talk of other things.

Clarity was deeply involved with something called a Sued mold. It looked like a cross between a mushroom and a jelly. The mold itself was useless, but its mature spores smelled like fresh-mown clover. More important, when properly applied, the powder had the ability to mask human body odor completely. The effect lasted only a few hours.

If Clarity and her colleagues could reengineer the mold to produce spores whose odor-killing ability would last for at least twenty hours, or two or three days, they would have a new cosmetic product that could readily compete in Commonwealth markets. Tests showed the spores were harmless and had no side effects, being a natural product, whereas many deodorants contained metals that were potentially dangerous when absorbed by the human body. Clarity had tried it on herself, with no ill effects.

She turned away from the designer. "Not very glamorous, is it? Bringing all the resources of modern gengineering to bear on the problem of body odor. Amee say sometimes the products that make the most profit are the ones that address the simplest problems.

"Derek and Hing are working on another slime mold that exists in semiliquid form. It can metabolize toxic chemicals and turn them into useful fertilizer. If its natural metabolic rate can be speeded up and it can be raised cheaply enough and in sufficient quantity, we can spread it over half the restricted dumps in the Commonwealth. Imagine being able to literally transform poison into peaches. Sludge and stinks—that's what we're about down here."

"Very money-oriented."

"Does that upset you?"

He turned away. "I don't know. I just have a lingering problem with altering the natural order of things purely for profit."

"Now you sound like my kidnappers," she said, chiding him gently. "Flinx, every business since the beginning of time has altered the natural order of things for profit. We just begin at the source. There's no pollution here because we're working within Longtunnel's established ecosystem. We aren't setting up smelly factories or dumping toxins down pristine tunnels. On the contrary, we're working on products like the kind you've seen that are designed to reduce and clean up pollution on other worlds. A whole new industry is starting up here. If our plans pan out, this formerly useless world is going to become the source of a host of new purifying products. We're working with one ecosystem to improve dozens of others.

"Until Vandervort and her backers decided to take a chance on Longtunnel, this world was nothing but a thin file in Commonwealth galographics. Now that we're actually established here, we're discovering dozens of new and exciting possibilities every day."

"And who benefits ultimately?"

She blinked. "You mean besides the people who buy our products?"

"That's right. Which big firm is going to be pulling money out of this world's DNA?"

"No big firm." She eyed him in surprise. "I thought you knew. Coldstripe is an independent self-contained setup. Amee has backers and runs the whole operation here. Maxim and Derek and myself and the others—we are Coldstripe. Each of us owns a piece of the company. Do you really think they could hire people of that quality to come and live in a place like this for just a salary? We're here because we have a chance to make our fortune. We're all dependent on each other's work. That's why I was missed so much."

She put a hand on the shoulder opposite Pip, and he felt it burn into him. She had beautiful hands, with long graceful fingers and neatly trimmed nails. He did not try to shrug it away.

"You warned Ms. Vandervort about your abductors?"

"She's taken steps. We were prepared to cope with industrial espionage, but ecofanatics don't play by any rules but their own. They talked to me a lot when they weren't asking questions. Trying to brainwash me, I guess. Their program, insofar as it could be called that, was to preserve the purity of all worlds 'untouched' by the Commonwealth. Whatever that means."

"To some people," Flinx murmured, "purity is an end in itself."

"A dead end," she said sharply. "Whether prodded by reasons of commerce or simply a desire to know, science always advances. If it stands still, then civilization dies. There's no such thing as ecological purity on any world. Something's always on top, socially and via the food chain. Oh, it's not all one-sided. I'd be the first to agree with that. There are always the unscrupulous, who'd exterminate an entire species for a few million credits. We're not like that here. Coldstripe is Church-certified. We're not interested in damaging the natural order, only in using it. But we're an easy target because we're new and small.

"Keep in mind we're not interfering with sentient or even semisentient creatures here on Longtunnel. We're dealing with fungi and slime molds and very basic organisms. We have a chance to use them to benefit all mankind. Developed under proper supervision, the lifeforms of Longtunnel have much to offer civilization, and I'm not just saying that because I have a chance to make a great deal of money while doing so. We're not just involved with the decorative arts. Coldstripe is much more than Verdidion Weave." Her expression wrinkled.

"I guess some people can't see that. They'd rather leave a world untouched, ravaged by an impossible climate, forever dark and unused. It's the old story about the tree falling in the forest. If there's no one around to hear it, does it make a sound? I say that if no one's here to study and learn from Longtunnel's beauty, then that beauty doesn't exist. The people who kidnapped me want all that beauty left locked up and unseen. I can't understand an attitude like that. Our work hurts no one and nothing. Those organisms we modify thrive in their altered states." She sighed sadly.

"The goal of these fanatics is to stop all research in our fields. They want to bring gengineering and its related disciplines to a dead halt. There are half a dozen branches of science they'd ban if they could. As for the ecological 'purity' they want to preserve, do they propose to ban evolution, too?

"If they can stop Coldstripe, they can stop development here. The private research groups will pull out fast. Universities don't want their people involved in a shooting match."

"What about requesting peaceforcer protection?"

She laughed, not at him but at the idea. "Longtunnel's so small that the outpost here doesn't even rate official recognition yet. There's just not enough people or development to warrant that kind of expenditure. We're trying. We're expanding as fast as we can, even trying to bring other, nondirectly competitive firms in so we can attract some attention. Until that happens we're on our own."

"I can see why they're so anxious to put a stop to your work here."

She nodded. "If they can shut Coldstripe down and drive us out, then the other outfits here will follow. The Commonwealth won't step in because there isn't enough property and personnel to justify intervention. The fanatics will seal up the whole place. No one will try to reestablish. Eventually it'll all be forgotten." She spread her hands in a gesture of helplessness.

"All this potential will be lost. No more Verdidion Weave. No Flavor Cubes, no toxin-eating fungi, nothing. The floats will drift back to the wild, only their population will fall off in this area because they'll no longer have easy, protected access to food." There was sadness and passion in her voice.

"Only a tiny portion of the caverns have been explored and charted. It takes so much time. This is the first world we've tried to settle where aerial surveys and mapping satellites are useless, because the only part of the planet we're interested in is buried. Like a treasure chest. Even Cachalot could be mapped from orbit. You can't do that with caverns. Some of the techniques the cartographers are having to use are thousands of years old. Longtunnel is Aladdin's cave, Flinx, overflowing with biogold instead of coins. The jewels here are alive and mobile and need studying. We can't let a bunch of madmen take that away from us. We won't."

"They got to you once before. They may try again."

"We'll be ready for them this time," she said confidently. "You heard Amee. Security is in place. They won't slip past port authority this time. Everyone coming in is to be triple-screened. Luggage is being hand searched. Now that the word's out about what happened to me, everyone's checking on everyone else. If the fanatics do have an operative working here, he or she won't be able to go to the bathroom without being observed. They're going to have to keep a low profile, or they'll be noticed and brought in for questioning." Her gaze rose to meet his.

"I just want to be sure you understand what it is we're trying to do here, Flinx. You sounded unsure, or at least questioning. It's not just a matter of making money; every week, every month we make a major discovery that adds to the general store of human knowledge. Not just in ecology or geology but in a whole range of sciences. Longtunnel is unique. There's nothing else like it anywhere in the Commonwealth.

"Take the airway sensors. Nobody's ever seen anything like them. The taxonomists are going crazy trying to decide if they need to create a whole new class to explain them. It's tremendously exciting. Lifeforms living in ways we never suspected existed. That's reason enough to fight to keep this installation functioning.

We're adding daily to humanx knowledge and humanx comfort. The thranx who are working here, they think they may have a line on a sulfide eater that can be gengineered to rebuild broken exoskeleton. You can't regenerate chiton, but this stuff secretes it as a by-product. You plant the wound, wait, and it grows together like new.

"Do you realize what that means to a thranx? You know how afraid they are of damaged exoskeleton. It's about the severest kind of external injury they can suffer. They haven't cracked the problem yet, but we're trying to help. We'd split the profits from such a discovery. It would be a major medical advance in the treatment of thranx trauma and would save many lives. Isn't that worth fighting for?"

"I wouldn't know." He turned away from her and studied the wall. "I'm a little young to be debating the great ethical issues. I have enough trouble sorting out my own sense of ethics, let alone humanxkind's."

She was obviously disappointed. "Then you don't agree that what we're doing here is worth the slight alterations to the ecosystem?"

"Certainly they're worth it to Coldstripe. All the rest— it's not for me to say."

"But we're not tampering with the ecology," she said in exasperation. "The fungi that became Verdidion Weave still exist in a 'natural' state. We're only growing the gengineered variety we developed. There's no impact on the subterranean environment whatsoever."

He turned so sharply that it startled her. "I'm only here because of you. I have no right to an opinion on the matter either way." He took a step toward her, halted abruptly, and eyed the floor. "Also, it's about time I was on my way."

"Leaving?" She looked puzzled. "You just got here. You said you were a student. I thought you were enjoying your tour of the facilities, meeting the other workers and learning about their projects. If that's boring you, why not study Longtunnel itself? Check out an outfit and go spelunking.''

He glanced back at her. "What do you care? Why are you interested in what I do?"

"Because you saved my life, of course, and in doing so probably saved the whole installation. Because I like you." She frowned at her own words. "That's odd. I usually prefer older men. But there's definitely something about you, Flinx. I'm talking about more than what we shared on the journey here.''

"What?" He spoke more sharply than he had intended, but as always he suspected perception where there was only guilelessness.

"You're just—different." She moved close to him. Pip fluttered her wings but remained on his shoulder as she slipped both arms around him from behind, not trying to pin his arms to his sides, just holding him. The contact made him shiver.

"I guess I'm not making myself clear," she whispered. "I'm better at making myself understood on the Hydroden. What I'm saying, Flinx, is that I more than just like you. I want you to stay here. Not to study. To be with me. We haven't had much time to talk about that, about us. I've been so busy since I got back. All I've talked about is Longtunnel and its importance and my work. It's time to talk about you and me.''

"There's nothing to talk about." He wanted to sound utterly calm, cool, uninvolved, but the proximity of her body made that impossible.

She sensed it, hugged him tighter, and pressed herself against him. "Isn't there? You've become special to me. I like to think I've become a little special to you. I think ours is a relationship that, if nurtured, could grow into something really spe—"

"*Stop it!*"

The violence of his reaction shocked her into letting him go. "I thought. . . ."

"You 'thought.' There's nothing to think about, Clarity. You don't understand. You don't understand anything about me.''

Alarmed by her master's emotional outburst, Pip took to the air in search of an unseen enemy. In this instance the enemy was not visible because it was Flinx himself.

Clarity's confession of almost-love shattered the emotional balance Flinx had carefully nurtured the past weeks. It had nothing to do with the fact that she was so obviously attracted to him. He had dealt with that previously. It was because he was so deeply drawn to her, mentally as well as physically. She was intelligent and beautiful and older, but she did not talk down to him. It was the first time in his life he had experienced that kind of all-enveloping emotional surge in a woman. More than anyone else could know, he knew it was genuine. So he coped the only way he knew how to cope with what he perceived to be an intrusion—by pushing back, pushing away, and trying to maintain objectivity. It was frightening to discover that he could not be half as cold as he wanted to be. The reality of love was infinitely more difficult to deal with than the philosophical concept.

''What's wrong, Flinx? Tell me.''

''You don't really know me. You only know what I've let you see.''

''Then let me see everything so I can understand,'' she implored him. ''Let me have that chance. I could get to know you well enough for us to be happy together.''

''We could never be happy together,'' he said decisively. ''I can never be happy with anyone.''

Hurt joined confusion in her voice. ''You're not making any sense.''

There was nothing to do but plunge on ahead. The small craft that tossed and flung him down the rapids of his life never seemed to put into shore.

'You're a gengineer and a good one. Surely you've heard of the Meliorare Society.''

''The—'' She hesitated. Clearly that was not what she had expected him to say. But she recovered quickly.

"Outlaws of the worst kind. Renegade eugenicists. They did genetic alteration of unborn human beings without consent or approval."

"That's right." Suddenly Flinx was very tired. "Their intentions were honorable, but their methodology blasphemous. They violated every law covering gene splicing and cosmetic DNA surgery that exists. I understand a few new ones were added to the code specifically to cope with their offenses."

"What about them? As I recall, the last of them was hunted down and hospitalized or mindwiped a long time ago."

"Not so very long ago. Not as long ago as the official records suggest. The last of them were active up until a few years back." He eyed her strangely. "As a legitimate gengineer I expect you disapprove of what they did far more than would the average citizen."

"Of course I do. The details of their work were never made public. The government kept it as quiet as possible, but being in the field I had access during my studies to bits and pieces of information that fell through the cracks in security. I know what the Meliorares did, or tried to do. They were replicating the barbarities of the twentieth-century B.A. on a much larger scale.

"Now they're history. The Meliorares were criminals with scientific training. None of their work will ever make it into the legitimate gengineering journals. The government ordered all of it sealed."

"True. The only problem they couldn't solve was that while they could lock up all Meliorare research, they couldn't account for the results of all their experiments. Oh, they caught up with most of them, cured those they could, put those who were damaged beyond hope of a normal life out of their misery. But they didn't find everyone. At least one of the Meliorare's experimental subjects reached adulthood without giving himself away or manifesting any serious illness. There may have been others. Nobody knows. Not even the Church."

"I wasn't aware of that. The final report on the matter, which is standard reading in gengineering histories, says that the last of the Society members was rounded up and dealt with years ago, and that all their work had been accounted for."

"Not all of it," Flinx corrected her. "They didn't get everyone." His eyes were fastened on hers. "They didn't get me."

Pip had finally settled down on a nearby railing. Scrap had moved away from Clarity to be close to his mother. He was confused and frightened by Flinx's outburst and allowed Pip to shelter him beneath one wing.

Clarity stared at the young man who had suddenly moved away from her. Finally she smiled—but it was a crooked, uncertain smile.

"What kind of talk is that? 'They didn't get me.' You aren't old enough to have been a member of the Society, not even in its final days."

It was his turn to smile humorlessly. "I told you you didn't understand anything. I wasn't a member of the Society. I'm one of the experiments. Funny, isn't it? I look normal."

"You *are* normal," she replied with conviction. "You're more normal than anyone I've ever met. Shy, yes, but that's just another sign of normality."

"I'm not shy; I'm careful. I wear shadows to hide myself, I keep to the darkness and try not to leave even memories behind."

"You've certainly failed in my case. Flinx, you can't be serious about this. There's no way you could know in any case."

"I was on Moth when the last Society members fought the authorities and both groups blew themselves to hell. They were fighting over me. But I didn't get blown up. I got away." He did not tell her how he had escaped, because he still had no idea how he had done so, and it troubled him to think about it.

Her eyes were searching. No doubt seeking the bulging

forehead, the extra fingers, any physical manifestation of the possible mutations he was alluding to, he thought sardonically. She would not find anything. The changes that had been wrought in his system had been made while he was still in the womb. Only he thought they were visible.

"I wasn't born, Clarity. I was built. Constructed, conceived in a design computer." He tapped the side of his head. "What's up here is a perversion of nature. I'm just a working hypothesis. The people who thought me up are dead or wiped, so there's no one left who knows what they were trying to make of me.

"Naturally I'm as illegal as the Society members. Guilt by birth instead of association. If the authorities find out what I am, they'll take me into custody and start poking and probing. If they determine that I'm harmless and certifiably normal, they *may* let me go free. If they find otherwise . . ."

"You can't be sure of this, Flinx. No matter what you've seen, or learned, or been told, there's no way to be sure."

But he saw that besides shocking her, his confession had made her uncertain. Her attitude toward him was still hopeful, still affectionate, but more considered now. The unrestrained emotions had faded beneath the weight of the questions he had planted in her mind. It was shaming to spy on her feelings like that, but he could not have stopped himself had he wanted to. No longer was she certain of the man standing across from her. The simplistic lens she had been seeing him through had been permanently shattered. With it had gone something he feared might be lost to him forever.

Not that any choice had been left to him. It was important for her to back off, to realize what a freak she was dealing with. Because he knew he had been on the verge of falling hopelessly and dangerously in love with her, and he was not yet in a position to permit that. He might never be.

"Flinx, I don't know what to make of what you've just told me. I don't know how I can believe any of it, even though you obviously do. All I know for certain is that you're good and kind and caring. That much I don't have to submit to inquiry. I've observed it, experienced it. I don't think any of that was . . ." She hesitated before hazarding the word. ". . . programmed into you before you were born. Those characteristics are functions of your personality, and they're what attracted me to you."

She meant every word of it, he knew. It was an honest, straightforward outpouring of affection. It made him tremble inside.

"Everyone has problems," she went on. "If any of what you say is true, then who's better equipped to understand them and sympathize with your troubles than me?"

"You have no idea what I might do," he warned her. "I don't know myself. As I get older, I can feel myself changing, and I'm not referring to the passing of adolescence. It's deeper than that. It's physical—here." He touched the side of his head again.

"Changing how?"

"I don't know. I can't say; it's impossible to tell. There's just the feeling that something major is happening to me. Something I can't control. Once I thought I knew what it was all about, that it was something I could study and learn to master. Now I'm not sure. I have this feeling that it's much more than I originally thought it was. Maybe a lot more than what my designers intended. The mutation is mutating, and whence it goes, nobody knows.

"As you get older, you're supposed to start finding answers to your questions. I only seem to come up with more questions. It's maddening sometimes." Seeing the look that came over her face, he hastened to reassure her. "I don't mean maddening in the sense of going insane, but maddening as in frustrating and puzzling."

She managed a small, wan smile. "I have moments

like that myself, Flinx. Everyone does. I just want for us
to be together. I think if we're together and you come to
feel for me the way I feel about you, there's nothing we
can't cope with. I have access to sealed records. My security clearance is very high. Coldstripe may be small,
but our contacts are excellent.''

He was shaking his head. ''You'll never get into the
Church records concerning the Society. There's a moral
imperative lock on them. I know, I've tried. You can
work your way through the government copies with bribes
and coercion, but you can't do that within the Church.''

''We'll manage. Anything's possible when you're in
love.''

''Are you so sure you're in love?''

''You don't give a centimeter, do you?''

''I can't afford to. Are you?''

''I'm not sure, now. I thought I was, but—is anyone
ever really sure?'' Her smile expanded. ''See, you aren't
the only one who can be badly upset by something happening inside them. What I don't understand is why you
keep pushing me away when all I want is to help and
comprehend. Why won't you let me help you?''

''Because I am dangerous. Isn't that obvious?''

''No, it isn't. Just because some misguided people tin-
kered with your genes before you were born, *if* any of
that is true, doesn't make you a threat. When I look at
you, all I see is a young man unsure of himself and his
future who went out of his way to help me when I was
in trouble, and who could just as easily have ignored me
and gone on his merry way. A young man who risked his
life to save that of a stranger. A man who is kind and
gentle and intelligent, if a bit cynical at times. Why
should I see a threat in that?''

''Because you don't know what I might do. Because *I*
don't know what I might do.'' He was almost pleading
with her now, wanting to keep the distance he had opened
between them but not wanting to frighten her.

''The Meliorares wanted to improve humanity, as I

recall it. If your mind reflects your ethics, then I've nothing to worry about.''

"Clarity, you're just not seeing it, are you?"

"You said I couldn't. Help me to understand, Flinx." She took a step toward him, then stopped. She wanted desperately to hold him, to embrace and comfort him and tell him that no matter what was wrong, it was all going to turn out all right. Yet at the same time she could not put aside his warning that it might be better for her if she did not.

Both were torn between what their hearts wanted and what their minds ordered, though for differing reasons. They might have settled everything then and there, might have changed their lives one way or the other, except that their conversation was not allowed to continue.

Chapter Ten

The explosion seemed to echo endlessly down the tunnels and corridors. The chemical fluorescents attached to the ceilings and walls did not flicker and go out since each was independent of its neighbor.

A second explosion followed close behind the first. It came from the entrance to Coldstripe's cavern, up past the laboratories and living spaces.

"Accident," Clarity shouted.

Flinx was shaking his head. "I don't think so." He recognized the report of a shaped demolition charge but did not want to alarm her until he was absolutely certain.

At the same time he damned himself for an overconfident fool. There were sidearms on board the *Teacher*. He had left them there, confident that he had time to deliver Clarity to her colleagues and then move on. He had expected persistence on the part of her kidnappers, but not speed. And her tour of the installation had subsequently engendered in him a false sense of security, now rudely shattered. No installation was impregnable. Tse-Mallory would have been disappointed in him. That old man had tried his best to stuff his young friend's skull as full of tactics and strategy as he had of humanities and science.

"Our civilization is founded on law and reason," he had once told Flinx, "but never forget that the forces of darkness are always roaming its fringes, testing its strength, always probing for a way in. Nor am I speaking solely of the AAnn. I fear them less than I fear internal corruption and a breakdown of morality, those for whom ethics is merely an inconvenient concept. You must always be on guard against them. They'll slip up on a civilization like a bad cold, and before you know it, the body politic is comatose with pneumonia. It can strike individuals as easily as institutions.

"That's why we have the United Church, to provide moral leadership and succor to those who need it. Perfect it's not, and the padres know it."

I need a gun right now, Flinx told himself as he and Clarity raced hand in hand up the corridor, not moral suasion.

Confused shouts and panicky yells mixed with the explosions' dying echoes. "Your friends have come back for you!" he shouted above the noise.

"Impossible! There's no way they could get past port Security."

Pip buzzed her master's head, constantly sweeping the corridor ahead with her eyes. "What if they came in someplace else?" he asked her.

"There is no place else," she insisted. "The best VTL shuttlecraft would have a fifty-fifty chance at best of setting down off the landing strip in one piece. The odds for a successful lift-off would go down. As for the outpost itself, there's only the single entrance, and you saw the barrier door we taxied under. It would take a direct hit from a warship to penetrate that. Everyone comes in that way."

"Since I've been here, all I've heard about are the extensive caverns of Longtunnel. If they could get down intact, isn't it possible they could find or enlarge another entrance? There must be other openings to the surface besides the one that's utilized for the formal port of entry."

"I suppose. Yes, I guess that would be possible. Anyone trying it would have to come in with full spelunking gear: ropes, lights, everything. There are some horrendous pits and sheer drops, but it's conceivable they could do that, if they were determined enough."

"Or fanatic enough." As they rounded a corner a third explosion, smaller than the others, boomed down the tunnel. Flinx came to a halt just in time.

The next charge went off ahead and slightly to their right, close enough for them to feel the heat and see the flash. The ceiling had been cleanly shorn or they might have been skewered by falling stalactites. The force of the blast was still powerful enough to dislodge rock from the roof and knock both of them to the ground.

"You all right?" As Flinx helped Clarity to her feet, he caught a brief glimpse of a tall blond woman in a chameleon suit running into a room up ahead whose door had been blown away. Several smaller people, similarly clad, followed her inside. Several of them looked too old to be engaged in such business, but then, fanaticism knows no age.

They had used the suits to help them infiltrate the facility; now that they had been discovered, they had thrown back the hoods in order to see and hear more freely.

Two bodies lay in the corridor. One was moaning and rolling on the floor, clutching his torn left arm. Clarity started toward them, and Flinx had to grab her from behind.

"That's Sarah! She's hurt."

"We can't do anything here. They're right in front of us. If they get you back, I won't be able to help you again. Someone else will take care of her."

He dragged her with him as he retreated. In addition

to being bigger than her, he was much stronger than his slight frame suggested. The legacy of hanging from his fingers to avoid the attentions of the police and of leaping from wall to window, he told himself.

A fresh explosion erupted in the room the attackers had assaulted. Yellow flame burst upward and spread out across the ceiling.

"Oh, God," Clarity moaned. "That was our microsurgery! It takes years to get delivery of some of the equipment that was in there."

"You'd better start worrying about the equipment between your hair and your boots. That takes even longer to replace," he warned her tightly.

The cavern was alive with the sound of small arms fire: the crackle of needlers, the soft hiss of lasers. Shots easily pierced spray-plastic walls. The corridor was beginning to fill with smoke as flammable materials reacted to the kiss of heat-generating weaponry.

They could hear the flames that ate at the cool cave air. Other rooms and laboratory facilities were being put to the figurative torch. The attackers were methodical in their destruction. However they had come in, Flinx surmised that they had first moved to seal off Coldstripe from the rest of the outpost. Then they had begun working their way backward, destroying everything they encountered as they advanced.

"Why?" Clarity was crying as Flinx half walked, half carried her down the tunnel. "Why, why?"

"Kidnapping you wasn't enough," he muttered, his eyes checking each door and passage before racing onward. "Your escape forced them to move openly. You as much as told me that they wanted to shut you down."

"Not like this! Not killing and burning."

"They're probably looking at it as some kind of twisted cleanup operation. I don't think they're really keen to murder. It's the facility here they want to destroy. That doesn't mean they're going to stop and reason with anyone who thinks differently or gets in their way."

She looked up suddenly. "Do you think they know I'm back here?"

"Maybe. Obviously their information's better than anybody thought."

It was becoming hard to see through the thickening smoke. Just then someone stepped out of the murk on his right. The sight was so unprepossessing that for an instant Flinx was not sure how to react.

The man was short and electively bald, with heavy white sideburns framing his jowly face and a potbelly protruding from his midsection. His suit was too big for his body and hung in wrinkles around his chest and thighs, which distorted its camouflaging ability. A breather clung to his face like some seagoing arachnid, its presence proof that the attackers expected to have to deal with smoke and bad air.

He had stepped out of a service corridor awash in acrid smoke. Though he looked less than dangerous, there was a madness burning in his eyes that belied his appearance, and there was nothing laughable about the high-powered needler he was gripping in both hands. The instant he caught sight of Flinx and Clarity, he began bringing it around to bear. He spoke in a high, maniacal voice that was anything but humorous.

"Over! All over for you now, damn you! You're done here; you're finished. We're putting an end to this blasphemy forever. This is only the first step, only the beginning." The gun was still moving. "Death to all destroyers of the environment!"

Flinx shoved Clarity hard and threw himself the other way. His arm jumped involuntarily as the near miss from the needler grazed his shoulder. He landed and rolled fast, then came up to see the muzzle of the gun swing toward him.

The second shot was never fired. The man ripped his lungs screaming as Pip's venom caught him square in the eyes. Probably he never saw the flying snake. Pip had been so involved in keeping herself positioned between her master and the greater threat far up the corridor that she had been late in getting back to deal with this unexpected one.

The little man fell backward, flung his weapon aside, and began clawing at his disintegrating face. Steam rose from his skin as venom ate into the flesh. Though he did not know it, he was already dead. By the time Flinx had helped Clarity back to her feet, their assailant lay motionless on his back.

Clarity was bleeding from shallow scratches on her arms and legs where she had struck the ground. Making sure she could stand by herself, Flinx went to remove the dead man's breather, not forgetting to pick up the needler he had thrown aside in his agony. A couple of power cells for the gun fit neatly in two empty pockets. A quick search of the man's suit and inner clothing turned up nothing that could be used to identify him or the organization to which he belonged.

Flinx was checking out the handgun as he rejoined Clarity. "Whoever they are, they're very thorough. No identification whatsoever. Nothing to lead the authorities to them or to their base of operations." When she continued to stare blankly past him, he raised a hand as if to strike her. "Clarity! Wake up!"

She instinctively raised both arms to protect herself. It was enough to shake her out of the daze into which she had lapsed.

"Sorry. I'm—I'm okay."

A laser hissed into the ceiling behind them, boring a hole through damp limestone. In one smooth swooping movement Flinx brought the heavy needler around and fired. No body appeared out of the swirling smoke, but his return fire was not answered, either.

"They aren't trained for this," he mumbled, as much for his own reassurance as for Clarity's. "They're not soldiers. They're relying on determination and surprise, both of which they've brought in quantity. It's not a real military operation. If they were professionals, we'd be dead or captured by now." He tried to see through the roiling smoke. "Some of the security people must be putting up a fight."

The upper reaches of Coldstripe's cavern were filled with smoke and flame. In such conditions it would be difficult for both attackers and defenders to tell friend from foe. The local ventilation system was still functioning or they would have already suffocated, but if vital fans or ducts were destroyed, the air could turn unbreathable rapidly. He tried not to think about the possible airborne toxins that might have been released into the enclosed atmosphere when the invaders had blown up the company labs.

The fanatics had come equipped with breathers. Coldstripe's people might not be similarly prepared. Having effectively eliminated the research station as a viable entity, he found himself wondering, would the invaders be content to stop there? Victory could be a powerful narcotic. They might well attempt a takeover of the entire colony.

Even now they might have a small army of fellow fanatics waiting in orbit, anxious to follow their shock troops down via cargo shuttle. If they could take control of the port, they could hold everyone hostage. Demands could be drawn up and presented to the government. The newsfax attention would be extraordinary.

"Is there another way around to the port and hangar facilities?"

Her eyes were watering from the smoke. She hacked and coughed out a reply. "No. Each concern has its own complex. The only way back to the port is the way I brought you—brought you in. Some of the university people share space to save money, but every private outfit like Coldstripe has its own cavern with its own access. That's to ensure company security. If they break out into the main port area. . . ."

"That's what's been bothering me. At least now we know there's more than one way out to the surface. They didn't blast their way in. If there's one natural passage in, there might be another leading from here to the port.''

"Then it hasn't been mapped," she insisted as they stumbled along, racing the smoke. "Not even a crawl space."

His eyes required constant attention. It seemed strange that ordinary smoke could sting so badly. Burning Mylar and spray-walls might have released irritating chemicals into the air.

"We've got to have a light we can carry with us." He longingly eyed the chemtubes that showed the path, but they were bolted down tight.

"Somehow we have to get clear of this complex. I don't think they're going to take the time to look for you specifically. At least not right away. Too many bodies around. First they're going to secure what they've taken and make plans for holding on to it. They they'll decide on follow-up measures."

"It doesn't matter, it doesn't matter anymore." She was sobbing, and not from the effects of the smoke. "They're destroying everything! All the work we've done, all our specimens, the records—all ruined!"

"Did you think they'd be selective in their destruction?" he said. It came out sounding harsher than he had intended. "Discrimination requires a system of values. Much simpler to condemn it all and engage in wholesale destruction than to waste time trying to decide if something might be beneficial. They're operating on their own private moral code, not civilization's. You saw the expression on that man's face." He gestured behind them, in the direction of the dead man who had tried to shoot them.

"There's something much more exciting about taking part in physical action instead of a debate. Instant gratification. Right now they must be thinking they won the world. All they hold is a little piece of this one, but you'd never convince them of that. Not now, not at this moment.''

Her sidetail swung up against her ear. "How come you know so much about mass psychology?"

"I had teachers who knew all about it. Pick up your feet."

She ran more easily now, letting him lead her deeper and deeper into Coldstripe's storage sector. In a little while they found themselves surrounded by cached supplies. The light tubes here were weak and in need of replacement. They were smaller and more manageable than the big ones up in research but still larger than he was looking for.

He questioned Clarity without much hope of learning anything useful. She was a gengineer, not a quartermaster. They started inspecting individual crates, reading the stamped labels while wishing for a code scanner.

They found plenty of concentrates and stuffed their pockets. Near the back of the big chamber they encountered several small side caves that had been sealed off to prevent unauthorized access. A number of the containers behind the restrictive barriers were marked as radioactive. Most were simply expensive. The barriers protecting them were not complex. They were designed to keep out only casual thieves. None had been erected with foiling professionals in mind.

Flinx fumbled for the tools he had used to such good effect on Alaspin. *Ironic how circumstances keep forcing me out of retirement,* he thought.

Clarity watched him defeat the locks and pop the gate in less than a minute. "You must have been very good at your trade when you were working at it."

"I was. Then I started growing, so I gave it up permanently. Tough for a tall thief to remain inconspicuous." He dragged the gate aside.

The high-priced electronics and scientific instruments did not interest him. What he wanted was the compact, high-intensity chemtubes that illuminated the storage cave itself. Each was half a meter long. It was not hard to pry a couple of the brightly glowing cylinders from their mountings. He passed one to Clarity and kept the other for himself.

He tried to choose the brightest pair. They were designed to operate for a long time without attention or maintenance and required no batteries, no power packs, no charged chips. As long as the tube's integrity remained inviolate, they should have illumination for as long as they were likely to need it.

"What about water?" He felt better now that they had food and light. "It's liable to be a while before the situation here is resolved."

"You don't need to carry water on Longtunnel. The caverns are awash in it. Keep in mind that there are whole rivers down here." She eyed him uncertainly. "What are you planning, Flinx?"

"We're going to wait. We'll find a deep, dark, quiet spot where nobody's shooting at anybody else and wait. In a couple of days we'll come back and see what's going on. If the port is still holding out, we'll try to work our way back there. After the initial fighting comes the negotiating. Maybe the destruction of Coldstripe's facilities will satisfy them. Maybe they'll bargain for safe, unopposed passage offplanet and leave. Maybe."

"If they manage to take over the entire port, we'll have to find some way to make it to my shuttle." He was staring past her. "Do you know your way around the unoccupied caverns?"

"No. There was never any reason to go any farther than the farthest lab. Spelunking was a hobby for some of my friends but never for me."

"Damn. Well, never mind. We'll manage."

They reentered the main warehousing section, keeping low and staying behind concealing crates and packages as she led him toward the back of the chamber. Eventually they halted in front of a spray-wall. It was a theoretical partition more than a realistic one, cardboard thin: a bright blue boundary.

He felt it with his fingers. It was flexible to the touch.

"What's back here?" Without waiting for a reply he flicked the wafer-thin latch holding a spray-door shut. It opened inward, and he shoved the tube he was carrying into the darkness beyond. There was no other light on the far side of the partition, no adamantine overheads or biotubes lining the floor. The ground was rough and pebbly.

"Nothing," she told him. "Just empty cavern. More Longtunnel."

"How common are those dangerous lifeforms you mentioned? Are they all as harmless as the photomorph?"

"You wouldn't think a photomorph was harmless if it got hold of you. It's a good thing they're slow." She was trying to see past him. "Not much of anything comes this close to the installation. Too much light and noise."

"That's what we want." There was satisfaction in his voice. "Dark and empty." He stepped through the portal. "Come on, what are you waiting for?" He tried to see over the shelves and cylinders that filled the warehousing cavern. None of the invaders had penetrated this far, but eventually they would start hunting for possible pockets of resistance. Depending on what they had brought down with them, they might need to begin scavenging for supplies. The warehouse would be a logical place to start. For any of several reasons they might show up at any moment, and he didn't want to be around when they did.

The same thoughts must have occurred to Clarity, but she continued to hang back. "I can't," she said finally.

"Can't? What do you mean, you can't? Are you afraid of dangerous animals?"

"No, it's not that." Her voice had grown very small. "It's just that I—Flinx, I'm afraid of the dark."

He gaped at her. "And you came to work in a place like Longtunnel?"

"There's no permanent dark here." She spoke defiantly. "The biotubes burn around the clock, and some part of the installation is always on work shift. The only time it's dark is when you turn out the lights in your living quarters. It's not the same kind of dark as that.'' She nodded toward the emptiness that swallowed the light beyond Flinx's tube.

''There's all kinds of things down there, Flinx. For every one we've found there must be a hundred more we know nothing about.''

''Then it's a choice, isn't it? What you don't know about down there and what you do know about out that way.'' He gestured back the way they had come with the brightly glowing tube.

As she stood hesitating, someone screamed far up a branching corridor. It was a long, drawn-out scream, high-pitched but not necessarily female. Not the sort of scream a person would make if he had just been hit by a weapon. It decided her.

''I'm coming—but will you do one thing for me?''

''What's that?''

''Would you hold my hand?''

He glanced at her extended right hand and tried to hide his puzzlement. Clarity was a mature, intelligent human being. A scientist, for Deity's sake! The simple absence of light was not something to fear. It did not threaten, it was not a physical presence, it could not hurt you in and of itself. Yet otherwise-rational people were easily terrified of it. He could feel the fear within her and knew it was for real.

Now was not the time or the place to debate unreasonable psychological deficiencies. He just took her hand and gently brought her through the portal, carefully closing the millimeter-thick door behind them. The two tubes enveloped them in a circle of light half a dozen meters in diameter, keeping the blackness at a comfortable distance. He did not feel it pressing in on him at all. It simply was.

The first thing was to move deep enough into the next cavern so that anyone peering through the door they had used would not be able to detect their lights. He doubted anyone would bother to check, since the logical thing for anyone fleeing to do would be to try to sneak out to the safety of the port. But he was not taking any chances.

The floor was relatively smooth except for pebbles and gravel. In places, water had worn a flat but slick path. They crossed a running stream, and Flinx paused for a sip of pure, cold cave water. As he bent toward the rivulet, a host of tiny white legless creatures sped in all directions, fleeing his light.

At the *scritch-scritch* sound of something much larger hurrying away into the darkness he brought his light around fast. There was nothing to be seen, not a suggestion of movement between the glistening stalagmites, but he could feel the life all around, keeping to the hidden places.

As they traveled farther and deeper, he could see pinpoints of light flashing beyond the range of the tubes. Photomorphs perhaps, or some other extraordinary kind of bioluminescent creature, possibly new to science. Whatever they were, their lights winked out when the brighter illumination of the tubes came near them. When they had hiked past, he turned and looked back to see the pinpoints flashing brightly again.

The comparatively easy footing enabled them to cover a lot of ground in a short time. For a while they were able to hear voices and explosions. These faded with distance.

The fanatics must have already reached the warehouse, he surmised. He and Clarity had left just in time. He tried to put himself in the attackers' position. If they were smart, they would put a permanent guard or two on station at the warehouse cavern's entrance, but he did not know how much credit to give them. Certainly they were as fanatical as Clarity had described them. That they had gone so far as to openly assault a legitimate commercial enterprise, not to mention an entire Commonwealth outpost, was proof enough of their devotion to their cause and their willingness to risk everything in its service. But that was no indication they would act logically in all things.

They had come far enough from the installation to relax in safety, but he kept going, wanting to be certain. The next clear, running stream, he promised himself, and they would set up a camp to wait out the assault. By then it might all be over, the invaders gone, the port authorities recovering. It would behoove the attackers to act rapidly on the outside chance a peaceforcer might be in the area. But without a deepspace communications beam, he reminded himself, a warship would have to be extremely close indeed to pick up a distress signal.

He checked his chronometer. Technically it was nighttime, but within the caverns that was the only time it ever was. Though he had developed the ability to catnap whenever necessary, he did not think Clarity shared that talent. So for her sake they would try to keep to a normal twenty-four-hour day.

It would have been nice to have had enough time to gather proper equipment: ropes, hard hats, long-range penetrating-beam lamps, maybe even a tent and sleeping bags. Not that he was complaining. They were lucky to have escaped with food and lights. While not frightened of the darkness, he had no desire to go stumbling blindly about in it. It would be easy to become disoriented, lose one's way, and wander the endless caverns until food or hope ran out.

"We'll stay here a few days," he murmured, reasoning aloud. "If they haven't left and it looks like they're settling in for a while, provided the port is still holding out against them, then I'll try something else. I know you're not enjoying this."

"You're so perceptive," she said, but her heart was not in the sarcasm. "What could you try?"

"After things calm down, I'll sneak back with Pip. They'll have made a thorough search of the installation and won't be expecting any surprises. If I can locate a couple of them who are approximately our size, I'll try to put them down quietly. Those chameleon suits they're wearing have hoods. There's a chance we could pass ourselves off as part of their army and make a break for the port. I don't want to try it unless I have to. I'd rather take it easy here and wait for them to leave. Except you're not taking it easy."

"No, I'm not. Do you really think they'll negotiate and leave?"

"Depends on what their ultimate aims are. If it was just to destroy Coldstripe, then they've done that. If they're planning to settle in for a long stay . . ."

"Our food will run out." Her eyes were moving constantly, searching, as though she expected a patch of darkness to suddenly become animate and jump down on her. The determined, self-confident researcher was gradually giving way to a frightened little girl. He could see she would not last a week in the caverns. All because of nothing more than the potential absence of light.

"You shouldn't be afraid."

"I know that!" she shot back angrily. "It's stupid and childish and unreasonable to be afraid of the dark. I'm quite aware of that. I know the medical terms and I know the causes, and it doesn't matter a goddamn because if you weren't here I think I'd go catatonic. Or panic and run around until I ran into something. Or until something ran into me."

"Well, I am here." He spoke soothingly. "So take it easy. We'll rest, have something to eat, maybe get some sleep. If you're that afraid, then I'll reconnoiter the port tomorrow."

"All my friends." She was murmuring to herself now. "Maxim and Ling and Shorona and Amee . . ."

"We saw only a couple of bodies, and we aren't sure anyone's dead. Except the fanatic Pip put down. They don't have to kill people to stop your research and development here. They've obviously come equipped and planned for extensive demolition work. If they do a lot of killing, it'll be much harder for them to negotiate a way out. They might not be able to slip free by the same route they used to sneak in. They may have a use for hostages. Besides, your friends weren't the ones fighting back. Security was doing that.''

"How could my friends fight? They had nothing to fight with.''

"See? Then maybe they're safely out of it, waiting to see who takes control. Standing comfortably on the sidelines.''

"Yes.'' She looked up gratefully, brightening. "Yes, that's right, they might be.'' She sounded hopeful. "Maybe everyone else will be okay.''

"How many nonsecurity personnel did Coldstripe have?''

She thought a moment. "About sixty, including administration.''

"That's a lot of hostages. You can bargain efficiently with that many hostages. Sixty corpses do you no good at all.''

"And you're not even twenty yet,'' she said, marveling at him. "When did you ever have to think about hostage bargaining and assault tactics?''

"I had to grow up in a hurry. I kind of regret that now. I didn't have what anyone would call a normal childhood, which I suppose is appropriate since I'm not normal. But I regret it all the same.''

Another violent explosion echoed through the caverns. Scrap stirred on Clarity's shoulder. The emotional strain of the past hours had taken its toll on the young minidrag. He flew rarely now, preferring to cling to Clarity's shoulder and sidetail.

Flinx was surprised. "I thought they were finished with that, and it had to have been close for us to hear it all way back here.'' Ten minutes later a second explosion followed the first.

"Something's wrong. They should have concluded

their demolition work by now. Unless there was a part of your complex I never saw.''

Clarity shook her head. "You saw everything."

He chewed his lower lip. "I can't imagine what's left to blow up, unless they've gone completely mad and are destroying the supplies." He climbed to his feet, picking up a tube. "I'll go have a look. You can wait here."

"Not a chance." She rose nervously. "I'd rather be lying half-dead on that beach back on Alaspin than be left alone down here."

"All right. But when we get close, we're going to have to muffle the light from the tubes. We can use our shirts."

"Anything you say, but I'm not staying here alone."

They never did make it far enough to see what was happening. When they had retraced half their steps, Flinx noticed that the faint glow of distant biotubes through spray-wall was absent. Rumbles continued to reach them from progressively fainter explosions.

"We must have taken a wrong turn somewhere."

"No, this is right. This has to be right." She caressed an oddly bent stalagmite. "I tried to memorize landmarks, specific features. That's one of the first things they drill you in when you come here, in case you do stray from a lit path."

"Then we just haven't come far enough."

He thought they had walked the required distance when they found themselves standing opposite a solid wall of rock. Flinx played his tube over the broken surface while Pip and Scrap fluttered curiously nearby. The echo of another explosion reached them, very distant now. That was strange, because it should have been louder.

He bent to examine a place where broken stone was layered against a sparkling brown and white stalagmite. Clarity was kneeling and pushing aside fragments of rock.

"These look like unicorn horns. There's no fresh growth, and the stalactites are still damp where they've broken loose from the ceiling." Her gaze rose to the solid wall in front of them. "They must be destroying the back passageways."

"It's not enough for them to ruin your work here." Flinx rose, his expression grim. "They're trying to entomb it by demolishing the corridors and rooms."

A slight quaver crept into her voice. "If they're blowing up all the tunnels on their way out, then we're trapped back here."

"They found a new way in, we can find a new way out."

"But they had proper spelunking equipment, and the passage they found is somewhere in there." She indicated the immovable wall. "We only have a couple of light tubes, and when they run out—"

"Calm down!" Flinx ordered. It had the intended effect, which was to quickly dampen her rising hysteria. "There have to be other exits to the surface from here, otherwise there'd be no decent air for us to breathe."

"There are probably a hundred openings that go all the way up," she said tiredly, "and most of them less than a meter in diameter, and they twist and turn and curve on their way in. Nothing a human being could fit through—nothing a cat could fit through—but enough to allow air to circulate. Alternative entrances to the outpost were checked and rechecked before construction began. The only practical way into the complex is via the ancient river canyon which forms the shuttle landing strip." She ran her hands along the wall. It might have been in place for a million years for all the chance they had of forcing a passage through the tons of collapsed limestone.

"We'll have to find a way through this somehow," he told her. "Maybe a couple of large stones fell against one another and left a clearable space between."

They did locate one spot where an immense fallen stalactite three meters in diameter formed a low arch. A hopeful Flinx crawled through, only to find his way blocked by debris from a second wall less than half a dozen meters beyond. Unable to turn, he laboriously crawled backward until he was standing outside the archway.

"No good. They set off more than one charge in here." He brushed dust from his clothing, noticed the small flying snake peering at him from Clarity's shoulder, and smiled. "Pip and Scrap could probably get out through one of those air passages you spoke of, but they're not homing animals. They couldn't take a message through, and in any event, Pip wouldn't leave me in my current state of mind."

"Then we're trapped. We'll never get out. Even if there was another way, we'd never find it. We don't have any equipment."

"But we do have time. The food will last if we're careful with it, and water's not a concern."

"It's not that. It's not that." She held her light tube so tightly, he was afraid she'd crush it between her fingers. "What happens when these start to go out?"

"They're not going to go out until we've found a way out."

"How can you know that?"

"Because we have to find a way out first." He looked past her. "If they're slowly filling in the entire Coldstripe complex, then our best bet is to try to circle around to the port area. If they've taken over the entire outpost, then it doesn't matter where we go, but we can only proceed on the assumption that there's a safe haven waiting for us at the end of our search. We need to find a way into a developed section of cavern.

"They can't have brought enough people to keep watch over every room, every chamber. Most likely they've rounded everyone up and are keeping them under guard in one place. By the time we've found our way around to another part of the outpost, they won't be looking for strays." He took a determined step past her.

She didn't follow. "You think it's that easy? You don't know anything about caves and cave systems. Caverns big enough to shelter half a city are often connected by crawl spaces too low for an infant to pass. You tell yourself, just a little more, just a little farther and you'll be through, crawling on your belly, pushing with your feet, clawing with your hands while dust you can't brush aside falls in your eyes. You can get close enough to see the next cavern beyond, and then the roof dips another centimeter and you're stuck, and you can't back out and they can't pull you out and so you just lie there trying to shrink your skeleton enough to pull free and—''

''That's enough!''

She started crying, not caring if anyone overheard, wanting someone to hear because anything was preferable to being marooned forever in that awful darkness, alone in a cavern that had suddenly become a potential tomb. Better to be a prisoner, better to suffer any amount of abuse by captors than to be trapped here.

''F-Flinx, I don't want to die down here.''

''I'm not particular about the place,'' he replied coolly, ''but I am about the time, and it isn't now. Come on, we're wasting time. We have to work our way around, whether we have to climb or crawl or glide to do it. There *has* to be another way out.''

They started following the wall, traveling north by Flinx's illuminated compass, one of the hundred functions he could call up on his chronometer.

His hope was that they would quickly find a passage leading to the back of some other company's research installation. But Clarity was right. He knew more of the vastnesses above worlds than he did of the hollow places beneath their surfaces.

The first problem was that the ground did not stay level. Despite their constant efforts to remain at the same depth, they found themselves unwillingly working their way deeper. Nor did the wall they wanted to keep on their left curve gently around toward the port. It wandered and split, forming new passageways and small caves and tunnels until it was impossible to tell which was part of the original wall and which was entirely new.

The narrowest crawl space might lead to salvation, while spacious walkaways always seemed to end in rockfalls.

He thought they could find their way by following breezes coming from the west, but holes in the ceiling centimeters wide and hundreds of meters long all admitted fresh air from the planetary surface. The result was a constant swirl of air, directionless and unhelpful.

The bright flare from the chemtubes they carried did little to dispel their sense of disorientation. Flinx had no idea of the port's layout and knew only the direction in which they were traveling; Clarity, still terrified by the darkness, was completely lost. To her credit, she struggled to keep mind and soul together with as much hope as she could muster.

"Maybe heading down isn't so bad," she said, trying find the good in a bad situation. "There are levels below Coldstripe's. I think there's a big storage area located beneath the port. We just need to make sure we don't descend too far or we might walk right beneath it and out on the other side."

"We'll find it. Or something close to it," he told her with an assurance he did not feel.

Chapter Eleven

They walked, ate several meals, and marched on. It dawned on Flinx that one could go quietly mad trying to find one's way around Longtunnel. It did not help when Clarity informed him that several of the geologists believed the wondrous cavern system extended the length and breadth of the continent. The hoped-for back way into another company's chambers did not materialize. Even while paying constant attention to a compass, it was easy to get turned around.

Wild photomorphs fled from their lights. There was also an unseen creature that spun an intensely phosphorescent, bright pink web. They carefully avoided the sticky strands as they walked past, content to admire the web from a distance without feeling compelled to summon its owner forth.

Following a straight path was impossible. The farther they went, the more difficult it became to know if they were still anywhere near the colony. For Clarity's sake Flinx espoused a positive line, but after several days of climbing over fallen boulders and through forests of stalagmites, during which time they encountered not a single sign of humanx presence, he found he was becoming discouraged himself.

Pip's and Scrap's moods reflected those of their humans. They rarely flew, preferring instead to ride shoulders and arms while displaying none of their usual exuberance and curiosity. Flinx knew that Pip's lethargy was a true reflection of his own current state of mind. It was not a good sign.

The sheer enormousness of the caverns was putting a severe dent in his self-confidence. They might already have walked past half a dozen tunnels leading straight to the port complex. Instead, they had explored dozens of blind alleys and corridors that gradually narrowed to the width of a knife. As Clarity relentlessly pointed out, climbing higher might only lose them in different caverns.

If only they could get near enough to an installation to see a light, hear a noise. But there was only the trickling of water, the high-pitched squeals of cavern dwellers, and the strange unnerving noises produced by shadows in the darkness that scuttled out of sight whenever a tube was thrust in their direction.

On the third day Clarity said, "They might really want to destroy everything. Not just Coldstripe."

"How do you mean?" Flinx had to turn sideways to fit through a narrow passage between a row of stalagmites. She turned to follow him, carefully keeping her precious tube away from any projecting rocks.

During the past days the tubes had faded slightly. Hardly enough to be noticeable, but it did not take much to panic Clarity. She had not complained, had not pointed out the reduced level of illumination, but he knew she had noticed. It was an effort for her to stay calm from the time they began walking until they lay down to go to sleep.

"If they can wipe out the entire installation, bury every corridor and fill in every developed cavern, they might try concocting a story about some kind of natural disaster. They could claim they were headed here to carry out an experiment of their own, or to make a mild protest, only to have found that an earthquake or something had recently destroyed the colony. Make it look as if natural causes were responsible. If they can invent a plausible enough story, the Commonwealth office for this sector might not think it necessary to send out their own inspectors to check it out.

"They could then convince the authorities that Longtunnel is unsuitable for further exploration. It wouldn't take much. All you'd have to do is show a layman's jury tridees of the surface. They could shut down the whole world, bar it to further research. But that would mean," she finished in a small voice, "that they'd have to kill everybody. Not just the scientists and administrators. Everybody."

They walked in silence for a while. "Sometimes," Flinx finally said softly as he raised his tube for a better look ahead, "those who speak of preserving life aren't above taking it to further what they perceive to be their ultimate aims. Often the only life they're not interested in preserving is that of their fellow man." As he lowered the tube, he studied it thoughtfully. "It's a shame we can't switch one of these off and preserve it."

She shook her head. "It's a steady-state chemical reaction. Once it's activated, you can't turn it off unless you break the tube and release the mixture. It's fading."

"Only slightly."

"They don't last forever. When one becomes too dim to be useful, it's just replaced. Most of them are reliable, predictable, but a few last much longer than the rest, and a few . . . a few go out rapidly. You never know which is going to do what. That's a consequence of the chemical imbalance inherent in every batch of luminescent liquid. No matter how much attention is paid to the mixing, there are always a few that are slightly off one way or the other. I've seen some tubes wink out hours after they

were installed and others that have been glowing steadily
since the first corridors were cut on Longtunnel.''

"I hope these are two of the long burners. Look, is
there anything in particular we should be watching out
for down here? I keep hearing noises."

"I told you there were carnivores. So far we haven't
run into anything except some photomorphs and that web
spinner. One thing I've been trying to keep an eye out
for is straw worms. They look a lot like those soda straws
we passed yesterday."

"Soda straws?"

"The long, thin, almost pure calcite stalactites we
passed yesterday. The ones that look like needles hanging from the ceiling. Straw worms hide themselves among
the formations. They hang from a sucker at the tail end.
If something edible passes underneath, they let go and
drop straight down on it. None of the four species that
have been studied thus far are toxic, but they all have
three concentric rings of teeth in their jaws. They're like
leeches, only much harder to get off. They lock on, dig
in, and secrete a fluid which liquefies flesh and bone.

"Fortunately they aren't very strong biters. As long as
they don't land on exposed flesh and get a grip on you,
it's simple to grab them behind the head and throw them
aside. The critical thing is not to give them enough time
to chew through your clothes. There've never been any
fatalities from straw worm bites, but then, nobody's ever
been lost down here without light, either. You said you've
heard noises. Was a lot of that like a ringing in your
ears?"

He nodded. "Yesterday particularly."

"There are small mammals that have huge ears and
cone-shaped mouths. They're kind of cute, actually, once
you forget that they have no eyes. We call them coners.
All ears and mouth on oversized feet. They range their
prey with ultrasound. The biggest is maybe a third of a
meter tall. All they eat are blind insects.

"After they home in on a bug, they turn up the frequency and knock it off its perch, or out of the air, or stun it on the ground. Sometimes we can feel the vibrations. Nothing dangerous. They'd eat us, too, if they could, but they have no teeth. Only that funnel-like mouth. So they just scramble out of our way.

"The coners aren't the only animals that hunt with sound. We've one specimen only of something that looks like a cross between a tiger and a hippo. If it can generate sound in proportion to its size and on the wrong frequencies, it could conceivably be dangerous to us, but with only a dead specimen to study, we can't tell. It has teeth big enough to do the job."

"Earplugs probably wouldn't help."

"No, they wouldn't. But we shouldn't be worried about sound generators. The poison carriers are the ones that concern me. There's one that lives only on top of certain stalagmites. You can't tell by looking at the stalagmite. The differences are apparent only to the darters, except for the absence of water.

"They have a dozen legs that help them cling to the drier limestone. The proboscis is ten centimeters long and uses air pressure to fire a little dart, an organic hypodermic if you will, that's attached to the inner nostril by a thread-sized length of tendon. The dart contains a particularly powerful hementin-based toxin that attacks fibrinogen. If it's not countered, you bleed to death through the wound the dart makes because the hementin prevents the blood from clotting. Then the little bastards climb down off their safe, high perches and suck up the remains. But if we don't blunder into any, we won't have any trouble.

"That's why I'm glad this is a live cave system. The darters only perch on dead stalagmites. So try to stay close to the growing ones. They don't like the water that drips from the ceiling."

"And I was thinking how peaceful and calm it was down here."

"Don't let the darkness fool you. We're walking

through a treeless jungle. In its own way, this subterranean ecosystem is as vibrant and competitive as Alaspin's. It's just that we're bigger than the majority of inhabitants. And if they have any photorecepting capability at all, they instinctively shy away from our lights.

"There is at least one big something, though. It's never been observed, but we have measured tracks. Eight legs and pad prints a meter wide. It keeps to the largest caverns. It's been named vexfoot.

"Then there are the creatures that inhabit the underground lakes and streams. I won't go into them since I don't expect we'll have to do any swimming." Her tube suddenly faded sharply. She shook it vigorously, stirring the contents like a luminescent cocktail, and was rewarded when the light returned to normal. He could sense her relief.

"So these tubes are a defense as well as our guides. If they went out, I don't know what would happen, except that you'd quickly meet a lot more of the local fauna than you have thus far."

"There's no reason for them to go out." He tried to reassure her. "No reason according to all you've told me why they shouldn't last for weeks or months."

"No. No reason at all."

"Even if we were to be attacked by something, Pip and Scrap would act to stop it."

"I know, but flying snakes need light as much as we do. Unless they have some kind of echolocation mechanism."

"None that I know of. But by nature they're nocturnal. They can see quite well in very low light."

"That doesn't do any good down here. When these tubes go out, there'll be no light at all. No moonlight, no stars. It's the blackest black imaginable, much worse than empty space."

"Except for the bioluminescents," he reminded her. "I guess we could always capture a couple of wild photomorphs and put leashes on them. A pet that lights its own way at night.''

His attempt at humor failed. She was clearly worrying about how she would react when the tubes started to fade permanently. No matter, he told himself firmly. By that time they would have found a way out. He wished they had a way of knowing how the battle against the ecofanatics was going. They could have sealed themselves up in Coldstripe's station or taken over the entire port. Or port Security might be driving them out, back the way they had come, while he and Clarity wandered needlessly through Longtunnel's unmapped depths. That thought was harder to deal with than the others. Not knowing what was happening was as frustrating as not knowing where they were.

She halted abruptly, almost stumbling, and looked back sharply. ''There's something over there.'' Scrap's head rose from behind her sidetail, the adolescent minidrag looking more like a bejeweled shoulder ornament than a living creature. His stance wàs alert, the pleated wings half-unfolded. He had definitely taken a liking to Clarity, Flinx thought.

''I heard it, too.''

He unlimbered the needler he had taken from the man who had tried to kill them and checked the setting. Half power remaining. That should be sufficient to deal with anything they ran into. A needler was not his weapon of choice. You had to be careful with them. Sometimes they leaked and could give the wielder a nasty, unexpected jolt. But he was glad to have the firepower.

''We could backtrack a little,'' she suggested.

''Backtrack to where? Let's just stand here a minute. Maybe it'll go away.''

The rustling noise was moving around. They followed its progress through another part of the cavern as it came parallel to their position, then moved on ahead. Intervening formations played tricks with echoes as sounds bounced off soda straws and draperies and flowstone.

Something moving far away could sound quite near, while a cautious stalker could use stone and water to muffle the noise of its approach.

It was ahead of them now and closer, a rough mewing. Flinx whispered to his companion.

"Recognize it?" She shook her head tensely. "Well, I'm not standing around until our light goes out." Taking a determined step forward, he passed beyond a sheet of rippling travertine and came face-to-face with a mouth.

It was a round, impressive mouth. Apparently, round jaws were common on Longtunnel. This one was lined with three concentric rings of inward-pointing, serrated teeth. As he gaped at it, the rubbery lip ring flexed and his nostrils were filled with the smell of decaying matter. The jaw did not so much close as iris-shut. If someone's head happened to be inside during the process, he thought wildly, it would be snipped off at the neck as cleanly as if by a surgical cutter.

The mouth was the face, and the face was the mouth. Any vestigial eyes were hidden beneath the pure white, long, silken fur against which the black lip lining the mouth stood out starkly. Atop the massive skull, a fan-shaped single ear flexed freely. Flinx wondered if it had evolved that way or if two ears had eventually grown together to form one.

He did not wonder about it long as he threw himself sharply to one side. The irising mouth opened with astonishing speed and snapped at him, the short neck extending slightly. Teeth clashed as the snout-jaw was sucked shut.

Clarity screamed as the monster lunged in her direction, advancing on four heavy legs. Flinx glimpsed the nostrils set just behind the top of the mouth. Jaws, nose, and ear were all set in line, like a multiple sight on a gun, all positioned for maximum hunting ability.

Then he could not see Clarity anymore because her tube went out. Frantically, he tried to set his own safely aside and aim the needler.

Pip and Scrap had both flown into action, but the flying snakes were confused by the sight of a creature with no eyes. While they puzzled over what to attack in the absence of their natural target, the monster was trying to decide which of two potential prey to strike at next. Clarity was moaning and trying to keep a large stalagmite between herself and that singular mouth.

Maddened by the panic she felt in her master's mind, Pip let loose a stream of venom at the creature's face. The dense fur absorbed most of the caustic liquid, but a few drops struck the ear membrane. While not as sensitive as an eye, it was certainly delicate.

Instead of roaring or bellowing, the white monstrosity let out a loud, pain-racked moan as it rose on its hind legs and snapped with that slightly extensible mouth in the direction of the minidrag. It was extremely quick for so massive an animal, but not anywhere near as agile as the flying snake. Pip simply backed air and hunted for another opening.

By this time Flinx had the heavy needler aimed. There was no time to fool with the setting. The important thing was to distract the carnivore from Clarity. The gun whined softly as the narrow beam struck its target just behind the head. It uttered another of its oddly muted moans and turned toward him. As it did so he fired again, aiming for the open mouth.

It shuddered and moaned, the circular jaw irising open and shut several times. As it came on, he fired a third time, heedless of the weapon's rapidly diminishing charge. When it was several meters away, it dropped to its knees and continued to advance in that manner despite having absorbed three shots that would have killed most creatures its size.

Flinx paused long enough to reset the needler. He took enough time to take more careful aim when he fired. This time the shot struck the monster's spine. It let out a heave and vibrated all over, then halted. The mouth slowly opened halfway and froze in that position. There were no eyes to close.

They were able to tell it was dead because it had stopped breathing. Shaken, Flinx recovered the light tube, listening intently in case the monster had not been alone. The cavern was still alive with noise, but there was no more dangerous mewing.

An agitated Pip was darting like an angry bee around the head of the fallen carnivore while Scrap fluttered anxiously nearby. But there was no need for her to spit again.

Clarity was leaning against her lifesaving stalagmite, breathing hard and staring at the dead mass of fur and flesh. "It's all right," she mumbled before he could say anything. "I'm okay. I'm sorry I screamed." Her anger was directed at herself.

"No matter. I would've screamed myself except I didn't have the time."

Her eyes met his. "No, you wouldn't. But thank you for saying so."

"What is it, anyway?"

"Not a vexfoot." She let go of the stalagmite and moved hesitantly toward the corpse. It might have been resting instead of stone dead. "Half the requisite number of legs. Maybe a related form. I've never seen anything like it, and I don't think anyone else has, either."

"I must have surprised it. Otherwise I don't think it would've let me get that close before attacking. Of course, without any eyes it couldn't be that certain of my position."

"Don't bet on it. We've been talking for hours. It must've heard us."

"Unless it was listening on a different frequency or tracking something else. If it was stalking us from the beginning, why didn't it attack from behind?" Suddenly something else came to mind, and he looked back at the stalagmite. "Where's your light?"

She swallowed hard, turned, and pointed. "Over there."

He raised his tube and saw where she had flung hers. It had shattered against a cluster of small stalagmites. Like a phosphorescent worm, the liquid light that had been contained within was running away in several directions, disappearing into cracks and holes in the floor.

"Never mind. We still have mine." He did not offer to let her carry it.

"It startled me. I panicked, and I'm sorry. It was a dumb thing to do."

"You're right. It was a dumb thing to do. I've been known to do one or two dumb things in my life, too. Well, it can't be helped and it probably doesn't matter. Chances are both tubes would have gone out at the same time. We'll have light for as long as we would have, anyway. We just won't have as much of it." He frowned suddenly. "Where's Pip?"

She looked past him. "Scrap's gone, too. They were here just a minute ago."

"Pip?" He raised his voice and the light tube. Brown and white flashed back at him from the ceiling, but there was no familiar darting pink and blue diamondback pattern.

"She's over there." Clarity pointed to where the flying snake was hovering, staring back at them out of slitted eyes.

"Let's go." Flinx gestured with his chin. "We have to keep moving."

Instead of complying with her master's command, the minidrag whirled and sped off into the darkness, returning briefly only to vanish a second time.

"She's found something."

"Not another of those round-mouthed carnivores?"

"Think straight. If she had, would she be trying to lead us toward it?"

"No, but what else would make her act this way?"

"Strong emotional reaction, but that doesn't make any sense since you and I are the only ones down here." He hesitated, watching his anxious pet. "Or are we?"

* * *

The thranx lay on his side, an unnatural and uncomfortable position for one of his race. A light harness was strapped to his thorax and was surmounted by an odd-looking double-barreled instrument slung crossways. As they drew near, Flinx saw that the device was a shoulder light. It was not working. Small picks and other duralloy instruments dangled from the pack and abdominal belt, the latter fashioned of yellow leather that was gouged and scratched from heavy use.

He held his light close. By the absence of ovipositors he knew the injured thranx was male. His chiton shone deep blue with only slight purpling on the dorsal plates. Middle-aged, then, and apparently otherwise healthy. Brilliant orange and yellow ommatidia formed the large compound eyes. The feathery antennae hung limp and collapsed on the thranx's face.

Flinx edged a little closer and then stopped, his expression changing to one of disgust. "Deity! What's that thing that has him?"

The thranx walked on four trulegs. The right front limb was shriveled and distorted by a dense growth of slimy glistening tendrils that extended from the middle part of the leg back to a huge wet mass that filled most of a hollow beneath a drapery of flowstone.

"Careful." Clarity put a hand on Flinx's arm and drew him back. He kept his eyes on the wounded thranx as he retreated, feeling the gorge rise in his throat. "It's a necromarium. A scavenging carnivorous fungus. It shoots those tendrils at its prey, though like the photomorphs it's not hard to avoid them."

"I doubt he'd agree with you." Flinx indicated the inert form of the thranx.

"Is he still alive?"

"Here." He passed her the light tube. "Bang your head against the wall if you want, but not that."

"Don't worry." She accepted the admonishment without comment. "I'll break an arm before I lose this one."

Dropping to hands and knees, he pressed his middle three fingers against the b-thorax. Because of the unyielding outer exoskeleton it was difficult to take a thranx's pulse. The b-thorax, which corresponded to the neck in humans, was the best place to try. Instead of the rhythmic pounding a human being would produce, he felt a warm pulsing, as if he had laid his fingertips against a concealed stream. The circulatory system was still functional, which meant the heart was still working, which meant . . .

Something brushed lightly against the back of his hand. One of the long antennae was stroking him. The head moved next, slowly and painfully, and the four opposing mandibles parted. Flinx leaned close, trying to make out broken words in low thranx. Not an easy language but simpler than high thranx. Thranx spoke Terranglo better than humans spoke their language, and there was always symbospeech, but in his pain and distress this one was understandably resorting to his native language.

Flinx kept his comforting hand on the b-thorax. "Just take it easy. We're friends." The antenna withdrew, and the mandibles relaxed. Though he was a mature adult, if the thranx had been standing on all four trulegs his head would not have come up to Clarity's. Flinx would have towered over him.

Something lightly stung the back of his other hand. Looking down, he was horrified to see a thin silvery tendril protruding from the skin. Instinctively he pulled away, but the stuff was stronger than spider silk.

Pip was there in a second, responding to his distress. But this time there was no enemy to spit at, nothing except a large mass of glistening brown and silver that looked like a disintegrating pillow.

Flinx rose to his knees. A second tendril exploded from the cushiony mass beneath the flowstone curtain and just missed his flailing fingers. It landed instead on the thranx's b-thorax and began spinning and convulsing. Flinx could see the tiny pinprick of a hook at the tip, spiraled like a drill point as it tried to work its way into the softer flesh underneath. It could not penetrate the tough exoskeleton. Flinx assumed the other tendrils must have infested the thranx through a leg joint.

He could feel the one that had hooked his hand worming its way deeper into the muscle. The pain was severe, barely tolerable. Forcing down the nausea he felt, he used his free hand to pull the needler, reduce the setting, and fire at the main body of the abomination, spraying the beam methodically back and forth across its surface.

It was almost too primitive to kill. It had to be slain one part at a time and absorbed more charge than they could afford to expend, but he was in no mood to be logical. He persisted until the entire organism had been reduced to a steaming, smoky mass. It smelled of ooze and carbonized corruption.

The tendril still clung to his hand. A minuscule burst from the needler severed it a dozen centimeters from his wrist.

Clarity carefully inspected the skin. The tendril was losing its healthy silvery sheen, turning a dull gray. "Not toxic or you'd be feeling the effects by now."

"It hurt real bad when it was digging in. Now that it's not moving anymore, it just stings."

Aiming the needler precisely, he sliced away the ankle-thick cables that clung to the thranx's shriveled truleg. "Can we do anything for him?"

She checked the pocket on her left pants leg and removed a small packet. "Omnifungicide," she explained. "You don't go anywhere on Longtunnel without it. Comes with the clothing."

He was staring at the thin tendril that hung limply from the back of his hand. "Do you know what this thing is?"

"No. The species is new to me. That's not surprising. I told you how little we know about Longtunnel."

She pressed the applicator to the back of his palm. Immediately the lingering burning sensation went away, replaced by a soothing coolness. Several minutes went by before the tendril fell to the floor, no more dangerous now than a cotton thread.

Bringing his hand up to his face, he inspected the tiny wound the drilling tendril had left. A single drop of blood had emerged and was already beginning to coagulate. He flexed his fingers.

"No pain. You're sure it's not poisonous?"

"I'm not sure of anything. I'm no mycologist, Flinx. But most of the venomous flora and fauna we've cataloged so far possess toxins that are fast-acting. You're still walking and talking, so if it is poisonous, it didn't have sufficient time to work on you." She nodded at the motionless thranx. "Unlike him."

He kicked the smoking ends of the tendrils that had enveloped the thranx's truleg. "What is this stuff, anyway?"

"Haustorium. A hyphae network. The fungus you fried puts them out, and they keep subdividing and subdividing until there's one to penetrate each cell of the host. That's how it eats. It started to eat you." She nodded at the unlucky thranx. "It looks like it's been eating him for a while."

"I couldn't break it with my hands," he murmured. "It's thinner than most wire, and I couldn't snap it." He indicated her pants. "Any wakearounds in those pockets?"

"Ought to be." She felt her pants. "Do you think they'll work on him?"

"They should work on any oxygen breather. We'll find out."

She found two of the thin tubes, one in each side pocket. Flinx bent over the thranx and snapped one above the nearest quartet of breathing spicules. The powerful chemical made the thorax jump.

The insectoid moaned, an eerie inhuman noise. With Flinx's help, he managed to roll onto his front, gathering his trulegs and foothands beneath him. The valentine-shaped skull looked up at Flinx, mandibles trembling. A sure sign of discomfort and pain. The inflexible face was capable of little in the way of expression, so the thranx relied on movements of the entire head, the antennae, and the delicate fingers of the uppermost set of limbs, the truhands. These were working tightly against each other.

"Try to relax."

The endless weaving of tiny stiff digits slowed. When he spoke this time, the words were soft but comprehensible.

"You aren't with them? The mad humans who attacked the outpost?"

"No. We're refugees ourselves."

Clarity moved nearer. "I'm Clarity Held. I was chief gengineer for Coldstripe. Who are you?"

"Sowelmanu. I am with the research team from Willowane studying geofood sources." The blue head swiveled to gaze at the smoking mass of tendrils beneath the flowstone curtain. "It would appear that is an interest which works both ways. A fair turnabout, though one I could have done without." He dropped his eyes to the remnant of truleg still encased in the severed haustorium.

"I have consumed my share of the local flora. I suppose it only fair that they enjoy their meal in turn." The trembling in his voice belied the humor he was struggling to put on the situation. "It hurts rather extensively."

"What's he saying now?" Clarity asked. "My low thranx is pretty bad."

"He's hurting," Flinx told her. "The thing's been eating his leg."

"Damn. I hope it hasn't worked its way up inside the abdomen."

Flinx put the question to their new friend and explained about Clarity's linguistic deficiencies.

"No," he replied in perfect Terranglo. "I think the infestation was confined to the leg." He gazed curiously at Flinx. "You speak the finest low thranx of any human I have ever met. Are you a linguist?"

"No." Flinx looked away. "I had an excellent thranx instructor. We can chat about my expertise another time. Right now we've got to do something about your leg."

"Ah, yes. My leg." He studied himself thoughtfully. "I fear that is a lost cause. Little appears to remain of the original limb. I am sure if you had not come along that thing would eventually have consumed all of me, leaving the head for last. An unpleasant way to die."

"We could try to carry you," Flinx suggested.

"That will not be necessary, as I think you well know, but I acknowledge your courtesy. Truly you understand the ways of the Hive. I could limp along on my three remaining trulegs, but I think I would prefer to suffer the indignity of utilizing my foothands and enjoy easier if less dignified locomotion. My posture will be servile, but I will be able to keep up quite well, thank you."

Flinx had suspected the thranx would choose that option, but Hive courtesy required that he make the offer to carry the thranx in a proper upright position. In addition to their four trulegs and two small truhands, the insectoids had a fourth set of limbs located at the base of the thorax between truhands and fore trulegs. These could be employed either as a second set of hands, as was usually the case, or as an extra set of legs with the individual walking with its body parallel to the ground. The thranx preferred not to walk in that manner since it reminded them of their primitive insect ancestry.

"I look for rock-borne food sources," he said. "You have told me what you are," he said to Clarity. He looked expectantly at Flinx.

"I study things," he said tersely. "Look, if you can move, I'd like to leave this place. There aren't many dangerous lifeforms that frighten me, but I have fears of creatures that parasitize."

"I comprehend. I can walk. You are a student?"

Clarity explained everything, including how Flinx had come to share their predicament because of the help he had given her.

"I am sorry for you to be involved," Sowelmanu told him, "but then, I am sorry to be involved myself. The problem is not my leg. If you worked here, you would realize that to leave an open wound unattended for very long is to invite the worst sort of certain death. That must be taken care of, somehow, before I can attempt to travel."

"What's he talking about?" Flinx asked Clarity.

"Spores, The caverns are thick with them. The air currents keep them aloft and moving around. Most of the fungi and molds reproduce through spores. They'll infect any open wound. Sooner or later a hyphae network will develop and spread through the host. That's why you don't see any corpses lying about, despite the extensive animal population. There are no vultures or ants or their analogs. The fungi take care of carrion disposal."

"We must find a way to close off the wound," the thranx muttered.

"Your 'wound' consists of what's left of your whole leg," Flinx pointed out.

"That is what I mean," Sowelmanu replied quietly. "I have observed the weapon you carry. From the destruction of the haustorium which infected me, I presume it is functional."

Flinx checked the readout. "There's still some charge left."

"Very well, then." The thranx sighed, a light whistling sound. "You are not be any chance a trained surgeon?" Flinx shook his head. "Pity. At least you know how to use a gun." With difficulty he rolled back onto his side. "Take your best aim and kindly relieve me of this useless limb."

Flinx stared at him. "I can't perform an amputation. If I do that, you won't have a chance at rehabilitation. It might be a long time before we reach medical facilities."

"I realize that. It could be worse. The creature could have struck my eyes, in which case you would be in the difficult position of having to amputate my head. I think my prospects for survival are better in this case. If you do not comply, then I will acquire an airborne fungal infection within a day, which will not be so easily excised. The weapon will cauterize the wound and seal it sufficiently until I can obtain proper treatment. That is," he added softly, "providing these mad humans have not destroyed the outpost infirmary along with everything else."

"I wouldn't put it past them," Clarity said.

"You speak as if you are familiar with their cause. I am naturally interested. What is it they want?"

Flinx was calibrating the needler as they talked. He wondered if the geologist was really curious or if he was simply rambling to keep his mind off what Flinx was about to do to him.

"They want to close down Longtunnel," Clarity told him. "Shut down all research here. They're the worst kind of ecopurists, the type who go berserk if they think you're gengineering a snail to change the color of its shell. We're all of us blasphemers against the True Religion: the religion of No Change."

"I see." The thranx whistled third-degree understanding layered with a suggestion of compassion. "That would explain why they went first for Coldstripe. They would naturally consider you the most serious 'offenders.' "

"Somehow I'm not flattered. How is the fighting going? We left in a rush."

"As did I, so I cannot tell you more than you probably already know. When they broke into our cavern, a couple of our study-team people began shooting back. They carry sidearms for defense against the larger carnivores. After that it was like a tunnel collapse: all dust and chaos. I was just coming in from concluding some fieldwork when I heard the shooting, saw it was going badly, and turned to flee." A foothand bent up and back to tap the thorax pack and its peculiar lighting bar.

"I had not gone out with a full charge, not expecting

to be gone long. Only when I stopped running did I notice how weak my light had become. I tried to retrace my steps before it died completely on me, but in my haste I had left behind all our marked trails.

"As you know, we can see quite well in poor light, but no one can see in the total absence of light. I tried to find my way back by feel, but in the blackness every formation feels like its neighbor. I became disoriented, and lost.

"Then I felt something sting my leg. I tried to pull away and could not. More stings followed. I could not see what was attacking me, and when I tried to pull away, I fell and struck my head." He glanced up at Flinx, who was almost ready. "That's the trouble with this place, you see. Nothing soft here, even in the oldest tunnels. On Hivehom we built a civilization out of soft earth. We didn't try to dig through rock. But I bore you with basic thranx history that every human learns in larva school."

"Bring the light over here," Flinx told Clarity. She approached and held herself poised like an ancient samurai warrior about to strike. "I wish we had some anesthetic."

"The general region is already numb from nerve damage."

Flinx considered the butt end of the needler. "I could hit you on the back of the head with this."

"Thank you," said Sowelmanu dryly, "but my skull is already tender where I struck the ground. One such blow is sufficient." He stiffened, the digits of the truhands interlocking tightly, then the foothands, lastly the back legs as he readied himself as best he could. "I would appreciate it greatly if you would not linger any longer. It would be disagreeable to go to all this trouble only to find out I had been infected by airborne spores in the interim."

"Go ahead and do it, Flinx. He's right."

"The female speaks truth."

Pip stirred in alarm as Flinx pulled the trigger. Two

quick, sharp bursts were all it took. What remained of the truleg fell aside, still encased in graying haustorium. The six-centimeter-long stump steamed slightly.

It was difficult to tell how the amputation had affected the geologist. There were no eyelids to close tightly shut, no lips to clench in pain. But the interlocking hands and feet did not relax for a long time.

Clarity was already down on her knees inspecting the stub, the scientist in her fighting off any discomfort. "It looks like a clean seal. I don't see any haustorium protruding." She looked up at the geologist. "You should be safe from redevelopment."

Sowelmanu had to speak slowly to make himself understood. "I am grateful. I am sorry you are trapped down here with me, but I am glad you came along. I would not have enjoyed a graceful death." He tried to sit up then. Flinx slipped an arm under his thorax, trying not to block any breathing spicules.

"The growth is more of a danger to you than to me. If I had not rendered myself unconscious, I would not have been infected, since it can only penetrate an exoskeleton at the joints or eyes, whereas you who wear your bodies outside your skeletons would be vulnerable all over."

"I'll keep that in mind." Flinx kept his arm behind the weakened thranx. "Do you want to try to stand yet?"

"No, but I do not want to lie here like a helpless larva, either."

He pulled his foothands up under his thorax, leaving the remaining trulegs beneath his abdomen, and pushed. His stride was shaky as he worked on compensating for the missing leg. Turning a small circle was a major chore.

"Disgusting to have to walk like this, with one's head so near the ground. This is the position our ancestral workers were forced to maintain even after we had evolved an upright posture."

"Don't complain," Flinx told him. "If I lost a leg,

I'd be almost immobile. You lose one and you still have five to walk on.''

"One still can't but view the loss of a limb with some regret.''

"Don't move.''

Sowelmanu peered back at Clarity, who was bending over him. "I assume you also are not a trained physician, madam?''

"No, but I am a gengineer, and I do know some basic medicine.'' She was using a tiny, thin spray can on the stump of the missing truleg.

"That is for sealing and repairing human flesh. It will not work on chiton.''

"True, but it will bond around the cauterization, and it's a good sterilizer. An extra precaution against spore intrusion.''

"There is the delicate matter of food. I have already eaten what little I took with me, expecting to be out less than a day.''

"We have concentrates,'' Flinx told him. Many thranx foods were safe for humans to eat and vice versa. Taste, however, was another matter. In his current state Sowelmanu was not likely to be overly fastidious.

Chapter Twelve

The thranx preferred soft food, but the geologist had no difficulty downing the protein cubes that constituted the bulk of their scavenged stock.

"I think that's going to have to be enough." Flinx passed the geologist a third cube and sealed the storage sack that had produced it. "We're going to have to measure out our rations since we don't have any idea how much longer we're going to be stuck down here."

"I beg apologies." Sowelmanu made a sound of second-degree sorrow. "I was starving."

"You ended up here by a different route." Clarity was trying to repress the excitement she felt. "Do you think you can find your way back? They were blowing up all our service corridors and storage chambers and walled us out."

"I ran long and hard, and too much of the time in total darkness. But I spent a lot of time in the main warehousing chamber beneath the shuttleport. My group has limited funds, so we had to store our bulkier equipment down there. Unless these people plan to demolish the

201

entire outpost, that area is too large and too critical for
them to destroy. It would also be a good place to hide.''

"Do you think the area will stay safe?"

"It's directly beneath all port facilities: Landing Control, Security, everything. If any place holds out against
these fanatics, it will be that sector. If Security can keep
control, they can send a message to the first ship that
makes orbit. So these people must move quickly no matter what their ultimate aims.''

"Unless the ship they arrived in is armed as well,"
Clarity pointed out glumly.

"Too many imponderables. Let us worry about our
situation here underground, not potential problems several planetary diameters out. The first thing is to find our
way back to civilization. The second is to hope a little
civilization remains to be found.''

"I'm open to suggestions." Flinx nodded to his right.
"We were heading in that general direction when Pip
found you." He displayed his multifunction chronometer. "I have a compass, and Clarity has apprised me of
this world's magnetic alignments, so we can't be too far
off line.''

"Excellent. To carry such an instrument you might
almost be prescient.''

Flinx was startled for an instant until he realized that
the geologist could have no idea of his particular abilities, much less his unique history. Sowelmanu was simply paying him a thranx compliment.

"We can follow this little creek upstream," he murmured.

"I find no reason to object." Sowelmanu tested his
legs a last time, his head unnervingly near the ground.
"Embarrassing.''

"Better degraded than dead," Clarity told him en-
couragingly.

"Two intelligent humans. I am fortunate indeed. One
moment." Reaching up and around with both truhands,
he unfastened the straps that held the double light ar-

rangement to his upper thorax. "I have no hope of recharging these down here. Therefore, I will travel better without the additional weight."

"What's in your pack?" Flinx inquired as they started up the creek. Having reslung the nearly empty needler, he had retaken the light tube from Clarity, who was glad to be rid of the responsibility of carrying it.

"Drilling equipment, sampler corers, field test chemical kit, sample cases—the same assortment I habitually carry with me on field trips. I dumped my specimens when I ran. A thorax burdened by rocks is a liability during flight."

"Assuming some of them are power tools, why couldn't you switch packs with your shoulder lights?"

"Different voltages, terminals, and no way to homogenize them." The geologist whistled a note of first-degree negativity coupled with common assurance.

"That's too bad," Clarity said.

"Yes, too bad."

Sowelmanu did not appear to mind the darkness that pressed close on all sides, but that was only natural. The thranx had evolved and matured in tunnels beneath Hivehom's surface. They preferred to be underground, though not in the dark. With technology had come a need for light as they had begun to rely on their eyes to the exclusion of other senses. It was gratifying to know that if their remaining tube faded to a strength of a few footcandles, Sowelmanu would still be able to see clearly enough by it to guide them.

Before that happened, Flinx promised himself, they would have found their way to the vast common storage room beneath the port and worked their way up to join its stalwart defenders—assuming any had managed to hold out against the attacking fanatics and provided that they did not encounter any more haustorium-firing fungi or pseudo-vexfoots along the way.

Thanks to Sowelmanu's superb night vision, they made better progress than ever. He was able to see much farther by the light of the tube than either of them could. This saved them from exploring a number of dead ends and enabled them to follow the most promising passages first.

But the geologist could only see farther; he could not divine what lay ahead. They still had to back down two tunnels for every one that led onward.

Two days of ups and downs, and discouragement had set in as deeply as before.

"If we watch our intake, we have enough food for another week," Flinx informed his companions.

"Never mind food. What about the light?" Clarity's voice was a dull monotone. The climbing and hiking had exhausted her, and she was utterly disoriented.

So was Flinx. If they could just get close enough to the base, he would try to pick up an emotional scent. At least it would give them a direction. But days of straining to detect a single feeling had produced nothing. He knew his talent was functioning because he could easily sense Clarity's despair and Sowelmanu's typical thranx stoicism. Beyond that was only an emotional void and the cool, dark emptiness of the caverns. That meant either that his perception was operating at a low level or that they were farther from the port than they believed. And all it would take would be a single localized magnetic anomaly to render his compass useless.

In trying to find the major storage area beneath the port, had they descended too deeply? The geologist did not think so but could not be certain. Flinx was not about to argue with him. When underground it was always better to trust a thranx's sense of direction, even one suffering from the aftereffects of a serious injury, than that of the healthiest human.

"I think we have circled around far enough," he told them, studying dark shadows and shapes among the formations. "Now we need to start working our way back to the west."

"What makes you think we can find a way into the

warehouse area? Surely when the place was excavated, the contractor would have sealed off any entrances large enough for dangerous animals to slip through."

"They may have missed some." Sowelmanu did not dispute Flinx's point. "Remember that we need find only one. If we encounter a place that has been heat sealed, we may be able to break through, and we will at least know that we have reached our objective." He nodded at the needler Flinx carried.

"The weapon you took from our assailants will cut through any spray-wall."

"*If* there's enough charge remaining, and provided we don't have to use it to defend ourselves again." He glanced at his wrist. "All right. We're going this way."

"No." Sowelmanu uttered clicking sounds of high negativity. "That is a dead end. We must go around it—that way."

Flinx squinted but could see only darkness ahead. He shrugged and followed the geologist.

"It really is a shame," Sowelmanu said the following day.

"What is?" Clarity asked him.

"As a geologist I should be living on the uppermost level of delight. We have observed unique formations and growths these past days, yet I have not felt the urge to take a single note."

"When this is over and done with, you can return and observe to your heart's content," Flinx told him. "Personally I marvel you can think about work at all at a time like this."

"A good scientist," the thranx replied evenly in a tone suggestive of complete assurance tinged with second-degree insight, "is always working no matter what his personal circumstances happen to be."

"That's fine and philosophical," Clarity argued, "but in my case I—"

Her comment became a scream. She had been walking on Flinx's right. He threw himself aside as the hole

opened under her. Sowelmanu scampered clear on his
five legs.

Both of them were cautiously leaning over the edge of
the gap before the dust had settled.

"Clarity!" He was poised to retreat. The stone beneath his feet felt solid, but so had the floor that had
given way under his companion. He had felt her fear as
she had fallen. The fact that he could still feel it was
ample evidence that she was alive and conscious somewhere below.

A small winged shape joined them. Scrap was coated
with limestone dust but otherwise unhurt. Flinx thrust
the light tube into the opening.

"Clarity, can you hear us?"

Her reply was faint but audible, full of fear and confusion. The red-hot sting of pain was absent.

"She does not appear to be seriously damaged," Sowelmanu observed. "See there, to your left."

Flinx moved the tube. The pit into which Clarity had
tumbled was steeply banked and slick-sided. Water trickled from an underground passage and limed the bottom
of the tunnel. There were no stalactites or stalagmites
visible.

"A rain drain," the geologist declared confidently. "It
has other names, but that is what this kind of formation
is usually called. It carries excess precipitation from
above to lower levels. That is why there are no formations within the tunnel. Fast-moving water has kept them
from growing."

"Very interesting, but what do we do? We have all the
supplies up here."

"We could leave her some food and come back with
help. I am sure she is within reach of water."

"We might not be able to find this place again no
matter how carefully we mark it. Besides, she has no
light. She's afraid of the dark, Sowel. I know that's difficult for a thranx to understand."

"Humans are heir to many incomprehensible phobias.

I sympathize, but what else can we do?'' His mandibles clicked disapprovingly. "I suppose we could slide down and join her and then attempt to find our way back to this level together. There should be a number of passages we can climb. But I dislike the idea.''

"So do I. You can stay here if you want to.''

Flinx tossed Pip into the air. Then he sat on the edge of the rain drain, his legs dangling. Scrap hovered close to his mother. The minidrags watched as Pip's master took a deep breath and pushed off, carefully resting the light tube against stomach and chest.

The descent was wild, fast, and mercifully brief, ending in a shallow pond of icy water. Nearby, a two-meter-high waterfall tumbled into a pool that was the birthplace of a fast-moving underground stream.

Clarity let out a shriek at his unexpected arrival, then relaxed gratefully when she was able to identify the intruder.

"I'm sorry. I'm sorry, I'm sorry!'' She rushed into his arms, and he had to juggle the tube to keep from dropping it. She was sobbing, and her clothing had been battered by the rapid drop through the drain. He reminded himself that she had ridden the water-slicked chute in total darkness, not knowing when or how it would end. The darkness had magnified her panic and her fear.

"It's all right,'' he murmured, trying to relax her. "It's all right.''

A second splash made him wince as cold water splashed him anew. They turned to see Sowelmanu rising carefully. The geologist began preening his antennae as soon as he realized that the water barely came up to the underside of his abdomen.

"Are you intact, Clarity Held?''

"Yes, thank you.'' She released Flinx and stepped out of the pool, terror having given way to embarrassment. "It's just that I didn't know what lay at the bottom of the drop, or even if it had a bottom.''

"There is no need to apologize for your fear and concern. My reactions would doubtless have been similar had I been the one to tumble through first.''

"No, they wouldn't." She managed a small smile. "You would have been busy studying on the way down."

"Well, perhaps just a little," The geologist let out a whistle of midlevel laughter. "In any event it is I who should apologize, for not noticing the weakness of the floor which hardly covered the drain."

"It looked the same as everywhere else," Flinx chided him. "Clarity doesn't need to apologize, and you don't need to make excuses. What we need is to find our way back up."

"That should be possible. We may emerge farther west or north than we were originally. I do not think I need to add that we should watch our footing more carefully lest we encounter a succession of these drains. They often cluster together in the same areas." He indicated the end of the tunnel that had dumped them in the pool. Water dripped from the travertine lip. "This drain was short compared to some which have been measured. We do not want to find ourselves deposited on a level from which it will be difficult to ascend."

They resumed their advance, this time letting Sowelmanu take the lead. Not only was he much more likely to spot a possible drain before either of them, but with five legs and two truhands, he stood a much better chance of avoiding a fall.

So intent was he on tracking the geologist's progress as they began to climb back to their earlier level that Flinx neglected to watch his own footing. They were leaving an especially damp cavern, and the entire floor was slick, not only with water but because it supported a profusion of mossy growths, molds, and fungi. There were sulfide eaters as well, trailing tendrils in the water.

After surviving the pseudo-vexfoot's assault, the haustorium-firing fungus, and the rain drain that had swallowed Clarity, it was almost ironic that he should stumble on a dry, smooth chunk of rock. He felt his ankle twist-

ing, fought to compensate, went over backward, and was
rewarded with a loud *crack*. A rich trill of horrified realization raced through him.

Clarity scrambled over to the broken light tube and
clutched at it as though she could heal the break by sheer
strength of will.

"Get some tape, some skin spray, anything!"

"The spray seal you used on me," Sowelmanu murmured. He and Flinx tore through the supplies.

Flinx finally located the svelte cylinder and emptied
the contents on the crack in the plastic. Clarity and Sowelmanu tried to hold the tube together as liquid light
leaked out around their fingers.

The spray seal worked wonderfully on human flesh and
adequately on thranx chiton, but it simply refused to ad-
here to the clear plexalloy tube. Despite their frantic efforts, the chemical light continued to trickle from the
broken tube. It was not simply a matter of plugging a
hole. The crack ran half the length of the illuminator.

Finally Flinx sat back against a smooth chunk of fallen
flowstone. "It doesn't matter, anyway," he muttered
morosely. "Once that stuff is exposed to air, it begins to
decompose."

"Yes, that's right." Clarity moved across the floor to
sit close to him, drawing her knees up to her chest and
clasping them with both arms.

Thereafter no one said anything. The magnitude of the
disaster was sinking in. Sowelmanu joined the two humans as they watched the luminescent liquid run across
the floor, forming a small glowing river. It was already
beginning to fade, the chemicals debonding under contact with oxygen.

Clarity let go of her legs to lean against Flinx. "Whatever else happens, when the lights go out, don't let go of
me. I couldn't stand not having some kind of contact."

He did not reply. This would be a strange place to die,
he thought. There was plenty of air, food, and water, but
no way out. Trying to find a path would result only in a

faster death, not in freedom. There was no way they could negotiate a route in the darkness. They had stumbled and fallen into a region Longtunnel's cartographers had yet to explore. There were no guideposts, no landmarks, nothing to indicate direction.

In any case, they would not perish at the touch of a vexfoot or carnivorous fungus. He found himself coldly fondling the needler, wondering if enough of a charge remained to do the job he had in mind for it.

Clarity inhaled sharply as the last of the luminescent liquid that had been their guide and hope gave way to utter, total darkness. It was darker, Flinx mused, than the inside of one's eyelids when one closed them tight in sleep, darker than dreaming, darker than any space above a rotating world.

Silent it was not. There was the constant gurgle of running water all around. When the light finally went out, photosensitives began to emerge from their hiding places and the cavern was filled with strange whines and clicks and mewlings as the troglodyte inhabitants called uncertainly to each other.

"We have no other source of illumination?" Sowel-manu whispered.

"None." In the pitch black their whispering sounded like normal conversation. He could feel Clarity pressed tightly against him and was suddenly grateful for her presence and warmth, even if it was motivated by fear more than by affection.

"I am wondering, though it is too late to do so, if we might have modified the power cell in your needler for use in my shoulder lights."

"I doubt it. Weapons cells are a lot different from those in commercial batteries. If it had worked at all, it would have been only for a short time. That's if it hadn't blown the elements on contact."

"Ah, I understand. Perversely, that makes me feel a little better. There is always the chance that our security force has driven off the invaders and that our absence has been noted. Searchers may yet find us.''

"First they'd have to determine that we're not among the dead,'' Flinx reminded him. "Then they'd have to surmise some of us got trapped outside the demolished corridors, in unlighted areas. And then they'd have to find us. Too much surmising and too much time. They'll be busy with more pressing concerns.''

"I had forgotten,'' the crestfallen geologist said. "So much wanton destruction.''

Flinx blinked in the darkness. His mind never rested except when he slept, and not always then. "What about natural bioluminescents like the photomorphs? Could we do something with them? Try to capture and restrain a photomorph or something like it? Even a little infrequent light would be better than none at all.''

"I suppose we could try.'' Clarity didn't sound very enthusiastic. "The photomorphs put out more light than any other lifeform we've studied, and that's not a great deal, except in brief bursts. There's also something like a long millipede that has a blue light which runs its whole length.''

"Perhaps if we can capture several such creatures, we could fasten them together and at least use them to see the floor. Remember that I can make better use of light than you,'' Sowelmanu told her hopefully. "If you can see several centimeters by their light, then I can probably see twice as far with the identical output of lumens. Enough to find a slow way upward, perhaps, and to avoid dangerous drop-offs.''

"Then let's keep our eyes peeled,'' Flinx said, grinning at his own mocking joke, "for anything moving that's producing any kind of light.''

As they sat motionless, listening and watching, their eyes grew accustomed to the blackness. Otherwise they would never have seen the faint light emitters that were starting to appear. Unfortunately they were all sliders, an airborne mammal that lived in the larger caverns. They were impossible to catch but did give the trapped trio something to focus on. The quarter-meter-long fliers soared back and forth among the stalactites drooping from the ceiling.

Pink triangular patterns flashed beneath their wings, identifying individuals to others of their kind.

It was almost noisy now. More photofauna gradually emerged.

"They fled from our lights and voices and footsteps," Clarity whispered. "Now they're reclaiming the darkness. They were around us all the time, watching and waiting."

While she was talking, one of the sliders dropped like a stone. It flapped spasmodically across the floor, the lights on its wings shining brightly. Then it rose without moving its wings and came straight toward them.

Clarity and Sowelmanu were puzzled and confused, but Flinx only smiled. "Pip's been hunting. No matter what happens to us, the minidrags won't starve. She can't see any better than us, but she can hunt the light sources."

They could hear the two flying snakes tearing into the body of the dead slider. Biting and swallowing was an unfamiliar process for creatures used to downing their food whole, but the minidrags were not true snakes. They had small teeth capable of rudimentary chewing. Oversized food was better than no food at all.

Flinx felt better knowing that his lifelong pet would survive him as long as there were sliders to hunt. "If there was enough light or another emotional presence nearby, Pip could lead us out. We're not completely paralyzed here. Sometimes I forget she can be more than just a companion." Suddenly he tensed.

Clarity felt him stiffen. "What's wrong, what's the matter?"

"There's something else here. Not sliders or little things. Something a lot bigger."

"Vexfoot," Clarity hissed fearfully. It would have no trouble finding them in the dark.

"No. Something else. Not a vexfoot. Different."

"I can't hear a thing."

"Nor can I," said Sowelmanu, straining with his great compound eyes. "How do you know, my young human friend, that there is anything out there at all?"

Flinx hesitated, then gave a mental shrug. They were probably all going to die together, anyway, so what did it matter what they learned about him?

"Because I can feel their presence."

"I don't understand," Clarity said. "There's nothing around to feel."

"I don't mean with my hands."

"There is something you are not telling us, young man."

Flinx turned toward the thranx's voice in the darkness. "My pet is an Alaspinian minidrag. They're telepathic on the emotional level, and they occasionally bond that way with human beings. But in my case it's not all one-way. You see, I'm telepathic on the emotional level myself."

Clarity twitched, but the darkness kept her from pulling away. "You're saying you can read others emotionally, just like the flying snakes?"

He nodded, then realized she could not see the gesture and replied aloud.

"So you know what I've been—feeling ever since we've been together," she said.

"Not all the time. It's an erratic ability, it comes and goes without rhyme or reason, and it always works better when Pip is close by. I think she acts as some kind of amplifier or lens for me."

"I have heard of the empathic telepaths of Alaspin." He could sense Sowelmanu brooding intently in the darkness. "I have never heard of them 'focusing' such a talent in another creature."

"That's because insofar as I know, there's no one else

like me,'' Flinx told him tightly. ''I'm sorry, Clarity. I
thought it was better to keep it a secret.'' He hesitated.
''I told you I wasn't normal. Now you know why.''

''It's all right,'' she said in a small voice. ''If you
really know what I'm feeling, you'll know that it's all
right.''

''Absolutely fascinating,'' Sowelmanu murmured.
''Heretofore telepathy was considered nothing but material for superstition and fiction.''

''It's not true telepathy,'' Flinx corrected him. ''It's
only operative on the emotional level.''

''You read emotions.'' Clarity's tone was flat. ''Can
you sense the presence of a vexfoot or photomorph?''

''No. I'm only stimulated by an intelligent presence.''

''Then your talent is playing you false in the darkness,'' Sowelmanu told him with conviction. ''There are
no intelligences on Longtunnel.''

''Well, *something* is out there, and it's much more
emotionally sophisticated than a flying snake.''

''We would know.'' Clarity spoke patiently. ''There
are no sentients here. Intelligencewise, this is an empty
world.''

Flinx was having difficulty searching and speaking simultaneously. ''What if they didn't want you to know
they were here? You've admitted the outpost is a small
one, that exploration has been limited to the area around
the port.''

''You can't have a sentient race existing in complete
darkness.''

''I'm sure they'll find your observation interesting,
Clarity.''

''What do your 'sentients' look like?'' the geologist
inquired skeptically.

''I've no idea. I can't see them. There are no mental
images, only feelings.''

''Then what is it you feel?''

''Curiosity. Peacefulness. A particular intensity of a

kind I've never felt before. What I'm not feeling is more important."

"I don't understand," Clarity said.

"No anger, no hate, no animosity."

"That's a lot to tell from sensing a few emotions."

"I've had years of practice. Emotions don't have to be blunt. The subtle ones can be equally revealing. There are a lot of them around us right now."

"Perhaps we should try moving toward them," Sowelmanu suggested.

"No. No sudden movements or gestures. They're curious. Let's keep them that way."

So they sat silently in the darkness, two humans and one thranx. For all his companions knew, the mysterious creatures Flinx had spoken of were standing only centimeters away.

Clarity listened for a sound: breathing, feet or claws scraping against stone, anything. The complete silence was not surprising since the ability to move silently in this underground world would be a necessary survival trait. Only Flinx knew they were moving, inspecting, because only he could feel the individual emotional centers shifting around him. If they conversed, it was via emotional surges and not words.

"They're very close now."

Clarity let out a yelp. "Something touched me!"

"Relax. I said they're not hostile."

"We have only your word for that," Sowelmanu murmured. Then he let out a soft click as he, too, was touched.

The quick, hesitant contact turned into caresses, careful fingering designed to inform. They were accompanied by a surge of emotion too vast for Flinx to handle. Pip was curled tightly around the back of his neck, and he knew she was sensing the same flood of feeling. Unlike her master, she had insufficient mental equipment with which to interpret that powerful rush. It was enough that she felt no hostility.

Finally Flinx extended a questing hand. His fingers made contact with something soft, furry, and warm. Alien digits responded. The touch was so light and delicate, he could not tell if it involved fingers or tendrils until one of the creatures let him run his hand along its arm. They were true fingers, thin and fragile as the helectites Sowelmanu had delighted in pointing out earlier in their flight. Tactile sensitivity would also be a useful trait in a world of permanent night.

They let him run his fingers over their faces, or where faces ought to have been. Even vestigial eyes seemed to be absent, though they might have been concealed beneath the thick fur. There was a smaller than expected set of nostrils; small ears that flared from the sides of the head; and two arms, two legs, and a tail whose tip seemed as sensitive as any finger.

During the entire extended physical exploration he was overwhelmed with feelings of awe and amazement.

The fur was short and dense and covered the entire body except for the ears and the tip of the tail. There was no clothing, which made sense. They were insulated and warmed by their fur, and there could be no nudity taboos in a world of blindness. Throughout it all they kept projecting one particular emotion with regard to themselves. Though it was a feeling and not a sound, he ascribed a series of syllables to it.

Sumacrea.

A voice neither human nor thranx said suddenly in the darkness, "Sumacrea!"

"They can talk!" Clarity said in astonishment.

"I'm not certain they can. They have a rich emotional language. They may make sounds to call attention to themselves or to warn of danger, but I'm not sure they communicate other than by reading and broadcasting feelings."

"Then they are not intelligent," Sowelmanu said.

"I disagree." He tried to prod the Sumacrea next to him into making additional noises. They responded with

a succession of chitterings and phonetic intonations that
if part of a language, suggested a very primitive one indeed.

This was in contrast to their highly evolved emotional
discourses, full of sensitivity and understanding. After
trying to make sense of humanx feelings, it was like discovering a long-lost cluster of friends. He understood
easily, without recourse to clarification, and he felt that
they understood him, though his feelings must have
seemed crude and coarse by comparison.

Except for their unique method of communication,
however, they were no more sentient than a tribe of apes.

How perfectly suited to their environment! he thought.
Why try to construct a word to describe something one
could not see or show to a companion when one could
instantly convey everything about it to another by ascrib-
ing an emotional resonance to it? One could explain
whether it was good or bad, hard or soft. What he at first
took to be color shadings he realized soon had nothing
to do with colors but with feelings. These people, he
mused, really could feel blue. It was an entirely new
means of communication, one that cut readily across in-
terspecies barriers in a way verbal description of abstract
concepts could not.

The average Sumacrea stood a little over a meter high.
All those he examined fell within that limit. Either there
were no infants in the area or they were being kept out
of touching range. A hunting or exploration party, perhaps.

"I think they've been aware of the humanx presence
here for some time," he told his companions, who were
about to go crazy with pent-up curiosity. "They've just
been cautious. One let me feel its teeth. I'd bet they're
vegetarians. Both humans and thranx are omnivorous, so
they might have sensed you eating meat. That would
make them understandably reluctant to initiate any kind
of contact."

"It's still incredible we never ran into any of them."

As she touched and was touched, Clarity momentarily forgot her terror of the blackness surrounding them. The presence of warm, friendly creatures helped keep the childhood fear at bay.

"Not when you consider that they could feel you coming before any mere instruments could detect their presence."

"If they can understand our emotions, then they must know we intend them no harm," Sowelmanu said.

"Possibly." At that moment the individual he was caressing suddenly jerked away from him. Flinx tried to ease his mind as much as possible. After a couple of minutes the Sumacrea returned and let the human resume his touching. This time Flinx was more careful when he reached the area that had produced the sharp reaction.

"They do have eyes. Very small."

"I haven't felt any," Clarity said.

"They're on the backs of their heads." He almost laughed. It had a salutary effect on the Sumacrea nearby, and they moved nearer. "I don't know if they evolved that way or if earlier eyes migrated around the back the way a halibut's move to the top of its head. If they're only light sensors, it's a way of detecting what's behind you. Nose in front, eyes behind. You can watch your enemy while running away from him." The thought came quick and unbidden.

"That explains it. Anyone mapping or studying the caverns would come equipped with the brightest light they could carry."

He tried to conjure up the image of an exploding brightness. It was not really an emotional concept, but he put the feeling across. The Sumacrea recoiled, returning only when he had shunted the sensation aside.

"Light-sensitive. The photomorphs would threaten them, too. Their concept of light is akin to a tremendous flame going off inside one's head. There must be natural heat sources down here somewhere, hot springs or thermal pools. They have distinct, variegated emotions to describe differing degrees of temperature. Light comes near the top of the list even though to us it's something quite cool. If someone had come down here without light, they would probably have made contact by now.''

"How fortunate we are," Sowelmanu muttered. "Disaster enables us to make the most important discovery in the brief scientific history of Longtunnel. A grand revelation no one else will ever hear about.''

At the moment Flinx could not have cared less about their future. He was utterly immersed in the wondrous, extraordinary world he had uncovered. His impatient companions would simply have to wait until he tired of exploring it.

Chapter Thirteen

The Sumacrea had developed an infinitely more intricate emotional language than humans had ever dreamed of, and they were not averse to sharing it with him. In fact, their delight at encountering one so similar to themselves among the strangers who had come from the roof of the world was exceeded only by their desire to learn more about him and where he had come from. Sowelmanu and Clarity were forced to sit silently, occasionally conversing with each other, while Flinx sat motionlessly, his eyes closed, touching the natives on a level they could barely imagine.

From time to time he would speak and try to explain what he was feeling, what he was learning. Words were a poor substitute for the actuality of soul-to-soul emotional communication.

At the same time, he was trying to sort out Clarity's feelings toward him. His confession, coupled with what he had told her of his history, would justify a certain animosity and even fear toward him on her part, but he could detect none of that. Her attitude was still friendly, affectionate even, but colored now by a definite ambiguity that she took pains to conceal in her speech.

It did not bother him. Nothing could bother him now, enveloped as he was in the swirling, complex rush of emotions generated by the Sumacrea.

It was astonishing how much could be communicated by emotion alone if one was subtle and precise, if one knew how to convey as well as sense. Hunger and thirst, fear of the fanatics above, admiration for the Sumacrea and for how they had coped with their lightless world— he had no trouble explaining himself or understanding their replies.

Under their tutelage his ability was rapidly refined, his talent honed. They knew Pip for a friend as well as they did his master, and Scrap also, but they were sorrowed and puzzled by the blindness that afflicted his other companions. He tried to explain that he could understand them clearly but that while they could crudely convey their own emotions, they could not sense those of others at all. They were shocked when he told them that of all his kind, he was the only one he knew who could communicate readily with them via feelings and emotions.

He decided that blindness was a relative term, the lack of sight a matter of history. Vision was a broad term encompassing all manner of perception. In the case of sight by light, it could be enhanced or brought to life by any number of medical techniques. Transplants, inserts, miniature video cameras connected directly to the optic nerves—all were feasible if one had access to enough money.

But despite the Commonwealth's technical skills, he knew of no method for improving the emotional sensitivity of man or thranx, no way to make audible the deeply felt and stirring dialogue of the Sumacrea.

"You're sure," Clarity asked him the following day, "that you're not just exchanging feelings with these people? That you're actually communicating with them? Without words?"

"I'm sure, and it's becoming easier. You just have to learn how to manipulate your emotions the way you would sentences. Like ancient Chinese writing, you exchange entire concepts at once instead of using words to form sentences. For example, instead of saying, 'I want to go to the other side of the cavern,' you have to express your longing to be in a certain place. If you do that to the exclusion of all else, I guarantee one of the Sumacrea will come over and take you by the hand. It won't do for science or mathematics, but it serves better than you think for putting across simple ideas."

"Since you are becoming so skilled at this unique method of communication . . ." Sowelmanu began.

"I didn't say I was getting skilled. Just meandering along."

"Isn't it about time you tried to project our intense desire to return to the vicinity of the outpost? By a roundabout route, should they be familiar with one."

"If it exists, I'd bet the Sumacrea know of it. We have time. Shouldn't we wait a while longer? Our food is holding out well, and if they do show us the way, it shouldn't take long to climb back to the level we left."

The geologist's mandibles made a sound indicative of mild derision mixed with second-degree impatience. "While I confess I am becoming used to this darkness, that does not mean I am growing fond of it."

"The longer we stay, the better attuned I become to the Sumacrea's method of communication."

"Are you sure that's the real reason you aren't in a hurry to leave?" Clarity was sitting close to him in the darkness. He knew she was near because during the past few lightless days, their respective senses of smell and hearing had grown acute. "It's obvious you share something unique with these people. Something which Sowel and myself cannot share with you. As far as this kind of communication is concerned, he and I are effectively blind, as you've put it. It's no fun being blind in the land of the locally sighted, Flinx.

"Maybe you aren't in a rush to get back to the port. Maybe this kind of emotional intercourse is all you want right now. But Sowel and I need light and speech. And all of us need to find out what's happening."

"Just a little while longer. That's all I'm asking for." Flinx was not aware of the intensity of his plea, though of course the Sumacrea were. "You don't understand. I'm completely comfortable here. These are the first people I've ever encountered that I could be totally myself with. I don't have to watch what I say or how I react. I'm not constantly on guard. I can't hide anything from them, and I don't want to, nor can they hide how they feel from me. That's the truth. I can tell."

"You can," she replied, "but Sowel and I can't. Flinx, we have to make our way back to port. We need to find out if the rest of the installation has managed to hold out against the fanatics or if we can help in some way. That should be our first priority. If everything's settled down and they've left or been driven off, then you can scramble back down here and . . ." She hunted briefly for the right word. ". . . meditate all you want.

"The discovery of native sentients will naturally change the way exploration and research are carried out on Longtunnel. But it won't stop. Our work will continue and will enable us to help the Sumacrea. They must suffer dreadfully from the depredations of creatures like the vexfoot and the dart shooters." A different note crept into her voice as she argued with him.

"Flinx, Sowelmanu and I are going a little crazy down here while you sit like a statue swapping emotions with your native friends. If my feelings mean anything to you, and I know you can sense them, then please, please help us find the way back to the port, where we can do some good. We have a responsibility to our friends and co-workers."

"I don't," he told her simply.

The mass emotions of the Sumacrea washed over him like a warm wave, highly refined, precise, as complex as

any spoken language: feelings of love, of mild hunger or
thirst, of family bonding and affection. Curiosity and
confusion, amusement and sadness, admiration and disappointment needed no explanation or elaboration to be
understood. He could listen to them simultaneously or
tune out the background and concentrate on a single individual who would respond in kind. There was no hesitation or artifice, no lying when it could instantly be
detected. No theft when a thief's guilt would mark him
as brilliantly as a signpost in the darkness. No envy of
appearance when there was nothing to see. In the world
of the Sumacrea, no one looked good. All that mattered
was how one felt.

Odd that a blind society should be more peaceful and
content than a sighted one. The Sumacrea were calm and
relaxed among themselves. There was much to learn from
studying them, from living among them, and of all humanxkind, only he was properly equipped to do so. A
number of ancient human philosophers had imagined so-
cieties whose members existed in perfect harmony with
the natural world, but as far as Flinx could remember,
not one of them had postulated blindness as a precondi-
tion for the success of such a social organization. And of
course none of them had ever envisioned anything like
empathic telepathy.

If not for Clarity and Sowelmanu, he would have remained without hesitation, working and studying in the
darkness, exchanging ideas and whole concepts without
ever uttering a word. He would have Pip for additional
companionship. But his friends would go mad here, unable to share in the Sumacrean discourse, wondering what
was happening to their associates and colleagues back at
the outpost. His own revelations and conversation would
not substitute for that.

Dammit! he thought to himself. The one resolution he
had vowed to keep—not to involve himself in the affairs
of others and to keep aloof—was the one resolution he
was constantly breaking. By saving Clarity, he had in-

volved himself in her life. By helping Sowelmanu, he had done the same with the thranx. He now had a responsibility to both of them. No matter how hard he tried, no matter how diligently he worked at it, he always seemed to find himself tied to the destinies of people he had never met before.

Perhaps the port's defenders had managed to subdue the unmilitary fanatics. Or possibly they had reached a truce allowing them to depart. Clarity was right. It might be perfectly safe to return to the outpost complex. If not, they could conceal themselves in the main warehouse, as they had originally intended. And if the attackers still held sway, the Sumacrea would be here to welcome them back. In that event, he told himself, neither Sowelmanu nor Clarity would argue with a decision to return.

Right now his companions' desire to have light again, to speak to other humans and thranx, far outweighed their fear of being captured. Clarity had reason enough to stay clear of the fanatics, but if she was so desperate to return, then he owed it to her to at least find out what was happening. She had held up remarkably well since their last light tube had been lost, but he could sense the constant edginess and terror in her. She was uncomfortable at best. Unable to perceive as he could, she drew no benefit or reassurance from the Sumacrea's presence. To her they were not a soothing repository of friendship. They were only whistling, grunting, unseen shapes.

Dammit again. I can't even bury myself literally. He sucked cool air. "I'll talk to them about leading us back. No, that's not right. I guess you could say I'll feel them out on the subject. I'll try to explain what's happening at the outpost, what our position is in the situation, and why we have to go back.

"They're not ignorant of the surface, by the way. They have legends that speak of it, tales of brave individuals who reached the great fiery cave that lies above the real world. They wore masks to shield them from the light, dim as it is after it's been filtered through that perpetual cloud cover.''

A hand fumbled at his shoulder. Fingers trailed down his arm until Clarity had hers locked in his. Her relief at his decision was apparent in her voice as well as her emotions.

''Thank you, Flinx. I really couldn't take this much longer. I tried so hard not to say anything.''

''You didn't have to say anything,'' he told her, and was immediately embarrassed at having reminded her of her lack of emotional privacy. ''I'll converse with them right now, tell them what we want to do. What we have to do.''

There were no Sumacrea close by, but it was easy enough to call some. All he had to do was project a desire for company, for companionship, and add his own emotional signature. Clarity and Sowelmanu had them as well, though they could use them only involuntarily and without conscious control. A moment later several of the natives could be heard shuffling toward them in the darkness.

He felt his companions turning toward the new arrivals and smiled to himself. They might not have his abilities, but smell and hearing compensated somewhat. They were not as blind and helpless as they thought.

''Keep in mind,'' he reminded his friends, ''that first of all they may not consent to help guide us, and second, there may not be a way open to the outpost.'' There were plenty of additional reasons for pessimism, but he kept them to himself. Clarity's feelings of hope were too strong for him to want to dampen them with reality.

Emotion traveled well in the caverns. He wondered if a Sumacrea would be as overwhelmed and disturbed as he was whenever his Talent was functioning at full capacity in a major city, surrounded by thousands of feeling, emoting people. Here it was easy to identify individuals, to project precisely.

Strange to be having an in-depth emotional exchange

with people you had never set eyes on and might never actually see. He had learned to think of them, at least the ones with whom he conversed on a frequent basis, by name. The names were suggested by their emotional signatures. There was Weeper, who oddly enough was the least emotional of the tribe, and his friend Heavy, and Thoughtful-grave. They absorbed the feelings he projected toward them and pondered.

As expected, the exchange did not proceed smoothly. The Sumacrea were convinced that if they went too close to the Outer Cave, they would not be able to find their way back. It was a region devoid of all feeling, and it frightened them. Flinx argued with them patiently, Pip sitting supine on his shoulders, knowing that his emotions were going out pure and clean and unmistakable. It calmed them, and they agreed to help.

Thoughtful-grave and Heavy knew the way up to the Outer Cave, from which they had lately detected strange emotions and sensations, feelings they now understood after having encountered Flinx and his friends. Clearly there were more like them above, thinking, intelligent creatures in spite of their blindness.

There was nothing to pack. Food they would find along the way. The route they would take was not far but complex.

When the time came to leave, there was much touching and exchange of strong emotions. For the first time the Sumacrea revealed the depth of their trust by bringing forth their offspring, small, furry things on short legs that whistled and hooted frequently as they carefully caressed the huge bodies of the visitors from the Outer Cave.

When the last farewell had been emoted, Heavy assumed the front position, with Thoughtful-grave in the rear. They would progress by touch, Heavy feeling for the right way with Sowelmanu behind, then Clarity and Flinx.

Scrap fluttered nervously against Clarity's sidetail, reflecting her fear as they left behind the now familiar section of the Sumacrean cavern. Flinx sensed it also and let his hand slip frequently from her shoulder to her hip. It confused her emotions and thus helped submerge her fear in other thoughts and feelings. She could not turn to slap away his hand since she could not see him and would lose contact with Sowelmanu, so she had to content herself with comments. It took her mind off their difficult situation.

"I hope these people can feel their way as efficiently as they can their emotions," Sowelmanu said conversationally. "I would dislike stepping in another of the rain drains which swallowed us all, or into a less friendly hole."

"This is their world, Sowel," Flinx reminded the geologist. "They know where they are and where they're going. We couldn't lose ourselves if we wanted to. They'd simply trace our emotional projections through the darkness."

"We're ascending." There was a hopeful note in Clarity's voice for the first time in days. "They really do know the way."

"We are not there yet, young woman." It was thranx nature to be cautious. "Restrain your enthusiasm."

"The less noise we make, the better." Flinx kept his own voice to a whisper. "There might be other ears listening that are as sensitive as the Sumacrea's but whose intentions toward us are less benign."

Clarity lowered her voice but was unable to repress her excitement. The higher they climbed, the nearer they were to light and to being able to see once again.

Mindful of Sowelmanu's description of the main warehousing location, Flinx tried to explain to their guides that it was necessary to enter the world of the Outer Cave dwellers at a specific place. When he was through, he could not be certain he had gotten the concept across. It was one thing to express how one felt about something, quite another to try to communicate specifics. A location, after all, is not a feeling. One could feel better about being somewhere or unhappy about being some-place else, but to project a feeling of one particular spot was difficult no matter how sophisticated the emotional language.

After climbing steadily for some time, the path they were following finally leveled off. They kept on until the injured Sowelmanu complained of exhaustion. Five legs or not, he was still not comfortable with his awkward gait.

They rested for several hours, then resumed climbing. Eventually it was the turn of Heavy to call a halt. Sowelmanu and Clarity, unable to detect his intentions, piled up against him and each other.

"What now?" she asked Flinx.

He was straining to feel clearly. "Warning. Uncertainty. Confusion and pain."

"You mean he's hurt himself?"

"No. It's an emotional pain. Something nearby is upsetting him. You and Sowel stay put. I'm going up to see what it is."

Feeling his way past his companions, he advanced by placing one foot carefully in front of the other. If they were in any immediate danger, Heavy would have warned him to stay back. That did not mean there could not be a sheer thousand-meter drop immediately to his left or right. Sometimes the absence of light could be a blessing instead of a curse. The danger one could not see did not exist.

He touched Heavy, who stepped aside. Flinx cautiously felt his way forward until his right foot bumped something soft. He halted immediately.

Using his feet, he felt his way around the body until he had circled it completely. At first he thought it was one very large form. Closer tactile inspection revealed the truth: There were two.

"What is it?" Clarity inquired from the darkness behind him. Though she was standing less than two meters away, she had no idea what was happening.

"Humans. Both of them dead. They've been cold for a while. Both male, both armed."

"The fanatics? Or port Security personnel?"

"I don't know." He bent and continued to use his hands in the absence of vision. "I think one's wearing a headlight. The other has some kind of lens arrangement strapped across his chest. It might be a light, too."

"Well, try them, see if they work!"

"What do you think I'm doing?" he replied irritably. Moments later he straightened. "No luck. Both unresponsive."

"If they perished here," Sowelmanu said thoughtfully, "they may have done so with their lights on. Perhaps they carried spare cells. I will help you look."

"Me, too." Clarity bumped into Sowelmanu, who muttered a typically gentle thranx curse. Thereafter they forced themselves to work slowly through the pockets of the two corpses.

"I've found something—I think." Clarity passed the small cylinder across to Flinx.

"Might be. Might be an old dead cell, too."

"Just now I prefer optimism to realism, my friend." Sowelmanu's tone was thick with first-degree anticipation. "Try it."

"I'll see if I can fit it in the chest unit. It should be easier to open. And don't rush me. Be a fine irony if somebody makes me drop it and it rolls into a crevice."

It took nearly an hour to accomplish the switch, a task that in normal light would have required a few seconds. He wanted to be sure of position and contact. Only when he was positive that it was securely in place did he take the additional time to unstrap the chest unit from the faceless body.

"What are you waiting for?" Clarity prompted him. "Try the contact."

"I can't just yet. One more thing I have to do."

Concentrating the way he had been instructed to, he imagined a tremendous burst of heat. It produced an image many times the brightness of a photomorph. Excessive, but better not to take any chances. Something as intense as a high-powered incandescent beam might do permanent damage to the feeble light-sensing organs of the Sumacrea. Heavy and Thoughtful-grave understood and made sure they were facing him, their eyes pointed away and well shielded beneath protective fur.

So concerned was he with protecting their guides that he neglected to warn his companions. He also forgot to prepare himself. The result was that all three of them let out varying screeches of discomfort when the light came on. They had spent so many days in total darkness that the refulgent beam stung them as severely as it might have the Sumacrea. Pip and Scrap were similarly affected.

Heavy and Thoughtful-grave retreated behind a drape of opaque flowstone, bending their hands up and back to cover their eyes. Enough light still managed to penetrate hands, hair, and stone to cause them pain. Flinx felt the emotional cries as deeply as any scream and quickly shut off the beam.

"Why did you do that?" Clarity asked loudly. "Why'd you turn it back out? What if it doesn't come back on? What if . . ."

"Calm down. There's nothing wrong with the unit. It just needed the new cell. The light was hurting our friends. It hurts them even when they hide from it. We still need them to lead us to the back side of the warehouse. Just because we can light our way doesn't mean we're any closer to finding the right route. When we had the two tubes before, we just went around in circles."

"We have to have *some* light." Clarity was adamant. "I'm not stumbling around in pitch darkness when we have a perfectly good high-L beam."

"A suggestion." They both turned in the blackness to face Sowelmanu. "Utilize the clothing of these unfortunate humans to muffle and dim the light to a degree the Sumacrea find tolerable. They have observed sliders and photomorphs and their cousins, so they can stand certain minimal illumination. We do not need light to follow them, but it would, as Clarity implies, be refreshing to be able to see where we are placing our own feet.''

Flinx considered. ''Not a bad idea. I'll try to explain it to Heavy and Thoughtful-grave. Then we'll give it a try.''

It was while removing the shirt from the first body that he thought he felt something moving slightly beneath the underlying layer of flexible body armor. The special plastic would stop a needler blast but not a laser. Evidently it had failed to stop something less advanced but more sinister. It reminded him of something . . .

''Back!'' he shouted as he rose hastily. ''Everybody back!''

''What's wrong?'' He could hear Clarity and Sowelmanu retreat with gratifying speed.

''I felt something moving.'' Pip was coiled tightly around his neck, and he had to physically loosen her coils so that he could speak clearly. ''Under the shirt. Under the armor. It felt familiar.''

''I do not understand,'' the worried geologist said.

''Give me a minute to think.''

Once more he warned Heavy and Thoughtful-grave to take cover. This time they would do a more thorough job of it since they had some idea of what to expect. Only when he was certain of their safety and of his companions' preparedness did he switch the high-lumen beam back on.

Gradually, painfully, their eyes grew accustomed to what was really a very low level of illumination but one that to their light-starved optic nerves seemed like a dozen suns all blazing simultaneously. When they could finally see without crying, Flinx shone the beam on the first dead man.

His uniform indicated that he was a member of port Security. The other body wore an ill-fitting chameleon suit. None of this had meant anything to the organism that had killed them.

Both bodies showed signs of hand-to-hand combat. In battling one another they had fallen too near—something. Thin but unbreakable loops of fungal matter were locked tightly around the first man's arms and the other man's neck. The second man had been lucky: He had perished of suffocation.

What Flinx had felt moving slightly beneath the first man's body armor were bunched strands of haustorium.

Clarity moved up beside him to study the half-eaten corpses. With the light it was easy to trace the hyphae network to a nearby crevice. It was ten meters long, and half of it was full of glistening fungus.

"It's ignoring us because it already has all the food it needs for a while." She spoke with the enforced calm of a lab technician readying a new tray of samples for inspection.

"I recognize the haustorium," Flinx muttered, "but where did those damn loops come from?" He could not take his eyes from the bloated face of the second victim. The man's hands were still locked around one loop as if trying to tear it free.

"From the same place as the rest of those filthy tendrils, I would venture to say." Sowelmanu looked to Clarity for confirmation.

"*Dactyella* and *Arthobotrys*, only on a larger scale. A mycologist could tell us more. They lasso their food. This looks like a giant relative."

"We should burn them or something," Flinx said disgustedly.

She shrugged. For a change, she was more at home with the local flora than he, able to distance herself from its effects. "In a few days there'll be nothing left. Not even bones."

Flinx stared at the two bodies a moment longer, then remuffled the light. When it was almost too dark to see one's feet, Heavy and Thoughtful-grave emerged from their hiding place. Their emotions were still unsettled.

As were Flinx's own.

If possible, everyone trod more cautiously than before as they resumed their march. The security man and the fanatic had engaged in a long-running battle through Longtunnel's upper reaches, because it took another day for the refugees to draw near enough to the port to enable Flinx to detect the first glimmerings of human emotion. Without Pip he would not have been able to sense anything, but when she was near and his Talent was operative, his range was considerable. Painful in a city street, useful here.

His ability to control and manipulate his Talent was increasing. Some of that he attributed to instruction from the Sumacrea, but his skill had been rising before that encounter had taken place. Maybe it had something to do with him maturing physically as well as mentally.

"We're getting close," he informed his friends.

"I don't hear any fighting," Clarity said as she strained for the slightest sound. "No shouts, no guns going off."

"We're not near enough to overhear verbal shouts, but weapons discharging ought to be audible."

"Either there is a lull in the fighting in this vicinity," Sowelmanu commented, "or we may presume that one side has prevailed and taken control."

Clarity suddenly sprinted ahead, heedless of rocks and growths underfoot. "Light! I can see light!"

Flinx and Sowelmanu followed at a more controlled pace until an emotional burst brought him to a halt. "Heavy and Thoughtful-grave can go no farther. We must make our farewells here. But I will have them wait a while."

"What for?" the geologist asked him.

"In the event the fanatics have won. We may want to retreat this way again."

Sowelmanu nodded, a human gesture acquired by the

thranx soon after Amalgamation. Together they turned to follow Clarity.

The light burst through a narrow slit in the wall on their left. Clarity was already peering through.

"If we don't come back soon, the Sumacrea will know to return to their home below," Flinx told the geologist. "I want to come back here someday. There wasn't nearly enough time to converse, to learn. I may be the only apt human pupil, human companion they'll ever know. It's hard to explain, but I feel at home among them. Like being with family."

"Have you been dwelling long in darkness, my young friend?"

Flinx looked startled, then realized the thranx was just employing a comfortable figure of speech. All the bugs fancied themselves philosophers.

They redistributed what little remained of their supplies. Clarity held the chest light they had salvaged while Flinx hefted the weakly charged needler. Even on low setting it was still capable of incapacitating two or three opponents before it died completely.

As he turned sideways to face the cleft, Flinx felt Heavy and Thoughtful-grave. Though he could no longer see them, the regret and sorrow they were feeling at his passing was as lucid as any verbal deposition. It was mixed with the sensation of leaving behind a part of himself. They understood him, shared his difficulties and troubles as easily as his friendship, and all without a word having to be spoken.

A different sort of illumination lay ahead. He inhaled and edged through the limestone slit.

Beyond lay a vast cavern roofed with low-intensity light tubes. They shone dully on neat rows and shelves of brightly hued plastic crates and cylinders. It was the main warehouse beneath the port facilities that Sowelmanu had described to them earlier.

"Still no signs of fighting," the thranx whispered hopefully. "Perhaps Security has at least retained control of this portion of the installation. It would be among the most heavily defended and the last to surrender.''

"I don't see any guards." Clarity followed Flinx through the crack in the limestone wall.

Nothing moved in the spacious chamber, not even shipping and sorting robots. Except for the heavy whisper of air pushed along by ventilator fans and pumps, there was no noise save what little they made themselves.

"They would be mounting a successful defense some-where above," Sowelmanu speculated. "If they had been driven back this far, the battle would be as good as lost. I believe we can ascend in confidence."

"I'd rather ascend in caution," Flinx muttered as he studied the deserted stairway that flanked the service elevators.

They kept to the shadows of the largest crates, huge containers full of drilling and excavating equipment. Each package was color coded as to eventual destination. A few were clad in the crimson of the United Church or the aquamarine of the Commonwealth.

Sowelmanu led the way. Though Clarity had been on Longtunnel longer than the thranx, she had never had occasion to visit the main warehousing facility. Every-thing was unwrapped, acknowledged, accounted for, and delivered by the time it reached her lab.

The armed man whirled but lowered his rifle as soon as he recognized Sowelmanu. "You're with the Hivehom geofoods team, aren't you?"

"I am indeed. Are the authorities still in control of this portion of the installation?"

The guard relaxed and slung his weapon over his shoulder. "Sorry about this. Thought you might've been some of those veginodes left behind. We're in control of a lot more than just this portion," he declaimed with grim satisfaction.

"You said 'left behind'?" Flinx was trying to see past him. "What happened? We've been in hiding and out of touch."

"Then I'll start from the start, right? The slip-suited bastards came at us out of the walls, like rats. They made a lot of noise and set off a lot of demo charges before we could organize and regroup, but they were lousy shots. Unprofessional, you know?

"As soon as he realized the outpost was under full-scale attack, Lieutenant Kikoisa pulled a bunch of us together and organized a counterattack. They must've had a shuttle some idiot actually managed to set down beyond the strip. As soon as we plowed back into 'em, they broke and took off for it. That's the rumor, anyways. Haven't seen any of 'em for a couple of days."

"Then everything's all right?" Clarity asked. "You drove them away?"

"Not all of 'em. There's plenty scattered around the corridors they didn't cave in. But they're a problem for the burial squad, not me. Who the hell do you suppose they were?"

"I think I know," Clarity said.

"No shit?" The sentry's eyes widened. "Hell, you better get yourself to the lieutenant or somebody, because everybody's been asking themselves that ever since they came at us. They didn't leave any wounded behind, and the dead don't have any identification on 'em. Not even labels on the chameleon suits they were wearing. Kikoisa's definitely gonna want to talk to you, Ms. . . . ."

"Clarity Held. I'm with Coldstripe."

The guard made a face and looked elsewhere. "Coldstripe, huh? That's tough. They really powdered your whole setup. Got there first and did it down right. Nobody's gonna be doing any work over there for a long time, and I'm afraid some of your buddies ain't gonna ever be doing it again, either.

"We all thought they'd go for Communications and the hangar first, but they didn't. They hit Coldstripe, then started in on your neighbors. Damnedest thing. Like they didn't care about anything except morbidizing the labs." He looked up at Sowelmanu.

"Yours, too, though I think I heard that your friends got out in time."

"Blessings upon the Hive."

"Some of the labs are just rooms full of rock. You'd never know to look at 'em that there was ever anything in there."

Clarity's throat was tight. "Where—where do I go to find out about survivors?"

"I dunno. I'm just walking sentry here. Try the dispensary staff. I'll bet they're set up for inquiries by now. Everything's been a lot more organized since we shot the last of the bastards."

Flinx put a comforting arm around Clarity's shoulders, forcing Scrap to squirm out of the way. "Maybe the loss of life doesn't match up with the physical destruction. If they had mass murder on their minds, they wouldn't have taken so much time and care with the demolition charges."

"You hope," she muttered.

"We all hope," he told her. "Let's go and see."

Chapter Fourteen

Her depression did not lift until they found Amee Vandervort lying in bed in a private alcove, curtained off from the rest of the wounded. The head of Coldstripe had one arm encased in spray-plastic and locked at her side. Her face was bruised and battered, but she sat up promptly when the three of them entered.

Sowelmanu paused outside. "Now I must find out if my good fortune equals your own." He extended both antennae, and they touched fingers to feathery tips in the thranx manner of parting. "Perhaps we shall see each other again. This is a small place. In that event I would be honored to buy you both the best human meal remaining on Longtunnel."

"Only if you let me pay for the drinks," Flinx told him.

They watched as their injured companion of many lightless days hobbled off toward the thranx wing of the dispensary, an enclosed compartment of higher humidity and temperature. Only after he was out of earshot did it occur to Flinx that he had gone to check on his comrades' welfare before seeking medical attention for his amputation. That was the thranx for you. Quiet, unassuming to a fault, desperately polite, and always concerned about the fate of others. It was partly their personalities and partly the lingering hive mentality, where everyone looked out for everyone else.

Alynasmolia Vandervort extended her one functional hand. "Clarity, dear!" She embraced the younger woman, then turned her probing gaze on Flinx. "I see you still have your charming and precocious young man with you. When you were not brought in with the other wounded, you were listed among the missing. That was days ago. We'd all long since resigned ourselves. This is the second time you've surprised us. I am so pleased, so very pleased you are alive and well. How did you escape the fighting?"

"We went out another way," Clarity said tersely. "Down instead of up. And we found," she added after a quick glance in Flinx's direction, "some interesting things."

Vandervort's eyebrows rose. "You were running for your lives and you made time for research?"

"I'm not sure that we weren't the ones being researched. Our assumptions about Longtunnel are going to have to be revised, along with everything else. There's a sentient race living here. In the lower caverns."

"I'd say that was impossible. But I said that about your Verdidion Weave until I saw it with my own eyes."

"You'll see these, too, if we can find a way to look at each other that won't harm them. They're as phototonic as you'd expect. I don't know about their sensitivity to infrared. They call themselves Sumacrea. I'll prepare a formal report later. Probably several reports. The important thing is for you to rest and get better."

"Heavens, girl, I'd be out of here now if it wasn't for the damn doctors."

"What happened at Coldstripe?"

They listened intently as the older woman told the story

of the battle for Longtunnel. How some of them heard or saw the attackers coming and managed to flee in time. How the crazed assailants ignored retreating people in favor of destroying labs and records and demolishing rooms and connecting corridors.

Several of their colleagues had shown more bravery than common sense by trying to intervene and stop the destruction. For their trouble they were shot. Most survived. Others perished accidentally when they were caught in the collapse of ceilings and walls obliterated by the invaders. They might never know exactly who lay buried beneath the tons and tons of limestone.

Eventually port Security had collected its men, arms, and wits and struck back. None of the invaders had been seen alive for several days. It was assumed they had all been killed or had fled by a hitherto unsuspected exit to other caverns or to the surface. The fight had ended as abruptly and mysteriously as it had begun.

"I'm pretty sure I know who they were," Clarity said.

"The same bunch that abducted you? Yes, my dear, we know now. They inquired among their temporary captives about certain personnel. Fortunate you had gone to ground elsewhere. Equally lucky, Jase had escaped to a secured sector early on in the battle. Maxim was not so fortunate. According to witnesses they brought him in wounded, made a rambling, barely coherent speech about meting out justice to the most serious offenders, and shot him on the spot. None of our other people thought they were going to get out of this alive. But when they fled, they simply left everyone they'd rounded up behind. They asked for me, too, you see. They were only interested in making object lessons of key personnel. In some ways we were very lucky."

"They want to shut us down. Like I told you. But I never thought . . ."

"Nobody ever thought, my dear. We don't build SCAAM projectiles here. Coldstripe isn't involved with munitions. There are no war industries on Longtunnel.

Who would have expected a military-style assault? Fanatics, the lot of them. A previously unknown group, well organized if not militarily efficient. For which we can all be eternally grateful. The first supply ship that goes into orbit will carry news of their outrage to the rest of the Commonwealth. The peaceforcers will round them up in short order, hopefully before they can wreak this kind of damage on some other unsuspecting, innocent colony.

"If as you said their aim was to stop our work here, then in that they certainly succeeded. It's going to take a very long time to reconstruct even a shadow of what we had here. But they didn't think things through. True, they destroyed all our equipment, all our specimens, but as a matter of routine we put all our records out in duplicate. We should be able to access most of what they think they obliterated. As for a facility, we will simply develop a new, untouched cavern. It's not as if they destroyed a structure. It's simply a matter of ordering in new instrumentation and setting up in a new location. We'll be back in business sooner than they believe possible, though I don't mean to demean the severity of our loss. Reconstruction will be limited by our existing capitalization until we can go outside for new funds." She turned her attention back to Flinx.

"The fact that there is a sentient race living here will change many things. I believe our research will be allowed to continue. The interest of the Church and sector government will be piqued. We may be able to tap into Commonwealth development funds."

"I know I'm being premature, but you don't have any ideas about doing gengineering on the Sumacrea, do you?"

Vandervort frowned at him, obviously puzzled by such a question. "Why would we want to do anything like that? They're people, if your observations of them are accurate. They're not fungi. If we were to even attempt something like what you infer, anyone involved would be an instant candidate for mindwipe. You don't turn intelligent beings into products. Usually the simpler the animal, the greater its potential for gengineering. Complex creatures generally make poor subjects.''

"Glad to hear it. Now, if you'll both excuse me, I know you have a lot to talk about, and I have to get Pip something to eat.'' He extended his arm toward Clarity, and Scrap fluttered across to join him. "They've been surviving on concentrates and what they were able to catch below. Their diet requires certain minerals. I'd prefer to take care of dietary problems before they occur. See how pale Pip is?''

The flying snake looked the same to Clarity, but who was she to argue with its master?

"The port commissary wasn't touched. I'm sure they'll be able to accommodate the needs of your pets.''

Both women watched Flinx depart. It was Vandervort who spoke first.

"What an extraordinary young man. A pity he has no interest in biomechanics. I think he'd train well for any field.''

"That's just the beginning,'' Clarity told her. "You've heard about the emotional bond that can form between humans and Alaspinian flying snakes?''

"No, but I take it from what you say now that such is the case with our friend and his animals.''

"There's more to it than that. These Sumacrea we discovered are also empathic telepaths. That's how they communicate. They also use a rudimentary kind of speech, but their emotional language is much more highly developed.''

The older woman considered thoughtfully. "If what you say is true, dear, the budget for research on Longtunnel will be quadrupled by every organization with the slightest interest in its future. It's not a commercially exploitable discovery, but the fallout will be of benefit because there will be a multifold expansion of government facilities that can only aid in Coldstripe's growth.

As a fellow scientist I applaud your industry. There are no proven telepathic races of any kind anywhere in the Commonwealth, the Empire, or our contiguous borders. But you say they are not telepaths in the accepted sense?''

"That's right. They're only telepathic on the emotional level. Like the flying snake and our remarkable Flinx.''

Vandervort smiled indulgently. "Now, child, just because he has a bond of affection with a primitive flying creature doesn't mean there is anything more to him than that.''

"No, no, it's much more than that. Amee, he communicated *with* the Sumacrea. That's how we found our way back to the outpost. He spoke with them, engaged in some kind of intricate emotional discourse, made friends, and had them lead us back to safety.''

"Sheer nonsense! You're simply misinterpreting the available data. Instead of communicating, he was only broadcasting his emotions, much as you and your thranx companion were doing. These Sumacrea, as you call them—''

"That's their name for themselves.''

"Whatever. They latched on to what you were feeling, your longing to return to your home, and thoughtfully escorted you back to us.''

"I'm sorry, Amee, but it wasn't like that at all. Flinx is a true emotional telepath, just like the Sumacrea. He can do it with people, too. He can tell what I'm feeling at any given moment, or you, or anyone else.''

Vandervort's expression darkened. "That cannot be, my dear. Mankind has been studying the concept of telepathy for well over a thousand years, and there simply are no such things as telepaths, not even on the empathic level. It may be that he can project his feelings more strongly than others, but read them? No, you must have it wrong.'' She had sat up straight in the bed and then leaned back, shaking her head and carefully favoring her injured arm. "He is simply a very perceptive, and perhaps persuasive, young man.''

Perhaps it was the excitement of the moment, perhaps only a desire to convince. For whatever reason, Clarity rushed on. "He's been altered. Did you ever hear of a banned organization called the Meliorare Society?" If anyone would understand that reference and make the right connections, it ought to be Amee Vandervort, a woman with forty years of experience in gengineering, biomechanics and related fields, and administration.

She was not disappointed. Vandervort reacted as if she had been stung, sitting up straight and staring at her cleverest employee hard for a long moment before slowly lying back against the cushion rest. She started to steeple her fingers, then stopped in irritation when she realized her injured arm would not be able to participate. Her tone was cool, polite, unemotional.

"What makes you think this?" No "dear" or "my girl" now. She was all business.

"Because he told me so." She smiled, reminiscing. "We've become close. I think he wanted to confide in someone. No, I think he *needed* to confide in someone. Each year it gets harder and harder for him to hold it all in."

"So my best gengineer has a little of the amateur psychologist in her, eh? You know he could be making all this up to impress you, not to mention to give false substance to his story."

Clarity shook her head. "He didn't say it to try to impress me, and he has better evidence to back up his claims than clever words. I think he actually did it because he felt we were growing too close, to try to put some distance between us."

"A fine young man." Vandervort spoke thoughtfully. "He's right, of course. You do need to distance yourself from him. Don't get too close to him, my dear. Don't get involved with him personally."

It was the younger woman's turn to be confused. "Why not? What could be wrong with that? Just because some renegade bunch of neeks fiddled a little with his DNA before he was born doesn't make him a monster. You've said yourself how extraordinary he is: quiet, polite, thoughtful, and good-looking in the bargain, though he doesn't think so. Brave and courageous—he put himself in danger to help me. I don't find anything in that to be afraid of. True, it's a little disconcerting to think that the man you're with always knows what you're feeling, but it's not as if he can read minds. If he is what he claims to be, an emotional telepath, I don't see why I should fear that.''

''You make a good case for him, Clarity. And you're right. If all he is is an emotional telepath, there is no reason to fear. But we don't know that. We don't know, can't imagine what else he might be. Something he'd prefer not to admit to being. Something he's chosen not to reveal to you. Or even something he's not aware of himself. Just as importantly, no one including himself knows what he might become—besides admirable.''

''You're saying that you think he might—change? Into someone dangerous?''

''I'm saying that where the products of the Meliorares' work is concerned, nothing is certain, nothing is predictable. They were among the most brilliant gengineers who ever lived. Also the most unbalanced. They tried things nobody else thought of trying, without much of an idea of what the results would be. The majority of their results were unpleasant to contemplate. A few were salvageable as human beings. A very, very few went unaccounted for.

''This young man's mind and body are a genetic time bomb that could go off at any time. He may be almost normal now, depending on how much of this empathic talent he lays claim to having he actually possesses. He may remain normal for many years. Then,'' she added ominously, ''unexpected changes in mind, body, personality may abruptly manifest themselves. Why do you think the work of the Meliorares has been so efficiently suppressed?''

"Because the practice of human eugenics is proscribed by the Church."

Vandervort smiled knowingly. "There's much more to it, my dear, than that. The Meliorares were reaching beyond their own limits, were tinkering with the very foundations of humanity. They were trying to improve on nature by eliminating serious diseases right in the genes, reducing the effects of aging, increasing physical strength, and raising intelligence levels. All well and good.

"But they also tried new things. Frightening things. They tried to goad the human body into achieving gains it had never been designed or intended to cope with. They were trying to stimulate evolutionary leaps, not merely cosmetic ones." She stared down at her left arm and its plastic sheath.

"A great many, too many, of their experiments ended in grotesque failure. There was a lot of mercy killing. I remember some of it from when I was young and just getting interested in gengineering and its related disciplines. As I matured, I developed the usual perverse interest in the Society and its work. Every gengineering student does, sooner or later. You dig up everything you can, which is very little. You learn enough to figure out that the Meliorares were as mad as they were brilliant. Skill and intelligence gone amok."

"You remember a lot," Clarity said shrewdly. "What finally happened to them? I did my own reading as a student. I'd like to see how it matches up with yours."

"The Society members? Most of them were killed in fights with arresting peaceforcers. A few chose to surrender and endure mindwipe. One of them," she added with no change of inflection, "was my mother's youngest brother. Not a member of the inner circle, but a supporter of their cause."

Clarity gaped at the older woman. "I didn't have any idea, Amee . . ."

"How could you?" Vandervort smiled gently. "I don't

walk about with the information emblazoned on my shirt. It wasn't something the family was proud of. Fine bio-mechanic, my uncle. Not blazingly intelligent or innovative, but more than just moderately competent in his field. Only the fact that he was a peripheral supporter and not intimately involved in the most outlawed work the Society did enabled him to escape.

"When I was little and we were alone, he used to tell me stories. I thought at the time they were amusing. You spoke of our Flinx feeling the need to unburden himself. I think my uncle had the same need. So he delivered himself to a young girl who had only the vaguest comprehension of what he was talking about. I'm sure he had no idea that I'd some day enter the same field or that I'd remember anything of his tales, but I did.

"He rambled on about ancient Terran philosophies and made up stories about creating a superhuman, someone who'd be immune to disease and doubt, full of confidence and vitality and physical strength, able to cope with any difficulties and solve any problem."

Clarity laughed with relief. "That certainly isn't Flinx. He's strong but not abnormally so. I've known plenty of stronger men. He's talked about his illnesses, so he's hardly disease-resistant. As far as intelligence goes, he's obviously much smarter than the average nineteen-year-old man, but there are dozens of other factors which could account for that. I've spent a lot of time with him, and he never propounded any new subatomic theories or tried to explain the true nature of space-minus to me. All the Society's work did was give him the ability to read another person's emotions, and we can't be sure that's the result of a Society operation. He may be a natural emotional mutant."

"All of what you say may be perfectly true, my dear. That was the sad thing about the Meliorares and my uncle. They had grand goals and vaulting dreams, worked so hard to achieve them, and in the end created nothing but misery and despair among their subjects. Flinx is at least not miserable or visibly deformed.

"What the Church and government have fought so hard to suppress is any information about those experimental subjects who were neither destroyed, deformed, nor surgically made human again. Those extreme few, perhaps only two or three, who might just possibly have become something else. Something the Meliorares with their scattershot approach to eugenics did not themselves foresee. Something new."

"Like empathic telepathy?"

Vandervort forced herself to sit straight and slide close to the spellbound Clarity. "Because I had a personal interest in their work and history, I spent more time researching it during my early studies than any of my colleagues. I never completely lost interest in what is after all a most fascinating subject. As an accepted scientist and scientific administrator, I eventually gained access to certain records that are kept sealed from the public and lower-level researchers." She glanced at something over Clarity's shoulder, then dropped her gaze again.

"I never suspected, no one imagined, that any of those special people might still survive, although it's interesting to note that even after all these years the Meliorare files are still listed as active in the relevant records. Individuals the government salvaged have been fully rehabilitated and certified human. There shouldn't be any blank spaces, but there are."

"You think Flinx is a blank space?"

"If his claims are true, then anything is possible."

"Did your uncle ever speak about things like emotional telepathy?"

"No, never. But I'll tell you a story that might make you think." She adjusted her position on the dispensary bed.

"There are oblique references to an unnamed individual who was involved with the capture of the last group of die-hard Society members. This took place on a minor world, oh, some six or so years ago. The government thought they had him along with the others.'' She was watching Clarity carefully now.

''The records acknowledge the possibility that this individual spontaneously imploded, taking an entire warehouse complex and a group of peaceforcers and Society members with him.''

Clarity stared at her a long time before breaking the uncomfortable silence with nervous laughter. ''That's a crazy story, all right. Even if it's true, it has nothing to do with Flinx because he's right here. You saw him leave for the commissary. Did he look imploded?''

''Obviously not, my dear.''

''So the records and your story must be referring to someone else.''

''Yes, you must be right. It is self-evident that if he was involved, he did not implode.'' She added nothing, just sat on the bed and waited while implications quietly percolated inside her most skilled protégée.

''You're implying something that makes even less sense.''

''I am not implying much of anything.'' Vandervort was watching the movement of medical personnel beyond her privacy curtain. ''In any event, he is a free individual, and what he is or what he does is none of our business.''

''Right.'' Clarity wondered why she felt so relieved.

''Now, go and run after him. But keep your distance. Bear in mind what I've told you and don't get too friendly. It's for your own good, child. He may be nothing more than a pleasant young man who may or may not also be an empathic telepath, but if his claim is true, he might on any given day become something else.''

Clarity rose from her chair. ''I think you're dead wrong there. I think I know him that well.''

''My dear Clarity, you have as much as told me that he does not claim to know himself.''

"It couldn't have been him in that warehouse since he's here and unharmed. I hope your arm feels better."

"Thank you, dear. It's healing properly. I will talk to you later. Remember that you're still an employee in good standing with Coldstripe. Look on this little enforced hiatus as an overdue vacation. With pay. I've already determined to request that status for all surviving employees. I'm sure our backers will go along with it."

"Then I might as well enjoy myself for a while." Clarity turned and headed out of the dispensary.

Yes, child, Vandervort thought. Enjoy yourself and watch your step.

Their fascinating young man did not present the appearance of an imploded personality. He was all of one piece, whole and intact. Which meant that the supposition she had read years ago was in error. Or else someone was trying to cover up an impossibility with an implausibility.

That suggested that something inexplicable had taken place in that obliterated warehouse. If this Flinx was the individual referred to only by number in the records, and he had not imploded and destroyed himself while the warehouse and its other occupants had unarguably gone to their respective destinies, then what *had* happened on that day and time? That was all much more interesting than it would be if he had imploded. It suggested certain things.

Lying in bed watching her arm regenerate, Alynasmolia Vandervort had plenty of time to think.

Flinx was eating at an empty table surrounded by empty tables. The reason for his isolation was clear to Clarity as soon as she entered the commissary.

Pip lay sprawled full-length in front of him in all her iridescent glory while Scrap squirmed nearby. The two flying snakes had raised off the table on their belly scales, looking like Terran cobras, their wings half-spread. They were begging for food.

While Flinx idly fed them, he sipped from a tall glass of dark liquid. Some kind of protein drink, Clarity decided. Quick and nourishing and that was about all. It struck her that he never discussed food. Perhaps he was one of those people who considered it nothing more than necessary fuel. It would help explain his wiry slimness.

"Amee sends her regards."

He looked up at her. "I'm glad she's feeling better. Just like I'm glad the trouble here has been resolved. It means we'll be able to leave as soon as we're ready. I have business that needs to be taken care of before I can return to make a proper study of the Sumacrea."

She sat down next to him, making sure there was some space between. "That's something we need to talk about, Flinx."

"How do you mean?" he said, frowning.

"I'm back where I belong. I don't need to go anywhere else."

"You want to stay here? After everything that's happened?" He flipped a small salty object in Scrap's direction, watching as the young minidrag darted sideways to pluck it from the air.

"This is where my work and my friends are. Those who've survived. There's a great deal that needs to be done. Tracking records, rebuilding . . ."

"None of which is your responsibility. You're a gengineer, not a construction specialist. I've been thinking about everything you said on our way here, about all we talked about, and I thought you might like to take some time off and go somewhere different. How about New Riviera? I've never been there myself, but I've heard about it."

"Everyone's heard about New Riviera. It's just not possible, Flinx. I'd like to go someplace like that, I really would. I've dreamed about that kind of traveling."

"Then why not go there? The *Teacher* can make it easily." He smiled at her then, and it was open and innocent enough to break her heart. "Didn't we get along well on the journey here from Alaspin?"

She turned away, pretending to be watching the flying snakes but unable to meet his gaze. "We had a wonderful time, but now it's time for me to work."

"I don't understand. Surely after all you've been through your firm will grant you a leave. If it's a question of money, if you're embarrassed to let me pay for everything . . ." He reached out for her, and she flinched. She tried not to but could not help it. It was a very small movement, but he noticed immediately.

"That's not it, is it? Nothing I've said has anything to do with what we're talking about. You pulled away from me just then. Jerked away."

"I'm just nervous, that's all. Still jumpy after all those days we spent in the darkness, after the kidnapping and escape and all the shooting. Being shot at doesn't go away as fast for everybody as it seems to for you."

He bent to peer into her face. Amber eyes seemed to see right through her. "What's really the matter, Clarity?"

"I've told you." She rose. It had been a mistake to confront him like this. She had thought she would be able to handle it easily, and she had been badly mistaken. "I have to get back. There are records I have to—"

As she turned to leave, he reached out and grabbed her by the arm. Initiating contact with another human being was something he did only rarely. He heard her sudden intake of breath and felt the fear race through her. Not fear of the blackness, not this time. Fear of a different sort of dark.

"All of a sudden you're frightened of me. Deity knows I tried to keep you at a distance when I thought we were getting too close, but I thought all that had changed. In spite of what I told you. Now everything's changed again. What happened? Don't try to tell me I'm wrong."

"I can't." Her reply was a feeble whisper. "How can

I? Could I hide my feelings from you even if I wanted to?''

He let go of her arm. "No. I can feel your fear. But it's not straightforward, not simple. You're confused; you don't know what you're really feeling."

"Please," she pleaded with him, "don't." She unexpectedly found herself starting to cry. "Maybe that's all it is. Maybe I'm just uneasy about being around someone who knows what I'm feeling all the time."

"But it isn't all the time. My—ability—waxes and wanes."

"How can I believe that?" She turned and ran out of the commissary.

A few fellow diners watched her retreat, then turned to glance in Flinx's direction before returning to their meals. His gaze slowly came back to the table before him. Attuned to his mental distress, Pip watched him expectantly. After a while she resumed eating but kept a wary eye on her master. Though puzzled, Scrap continued to eat as before. Flinx occupied half his mind by hand feeding the little minidrag.

What had happened to change Clarity's attitude toward him so radically? It was one thing to decide she had work to do, another to feel the fear he had sensed in her mind when he had grabbed at her. On the trip out from Alaspin she had been the one always flirting and teasing. Now the brightness had gone out of her.

Nor did it have anything to do with their sightless journey through the lower caverns of Longtunnel. The aversion she projected was directed at him, not at their shared experience together. No doubt the Sumacrea would be able to interpret it, but he was not that skilled, that sensitive. He could only feel the reality of her fear, not understand the reasons behind it.

That was the moment when he realized he was in love with her. Having never fallen in love before, he was unfamiliar with the process and so had failed to recognize it until now. His love for Mother Mastiff had been of a different kind, as had his restrained affection for women like Atha Moon. This was different, very different.

She had been the one seeking a closer relationship. She was the one with her finger on his emotional trigger, and now she was pulling out. It was not fair. He was disconcerted to discover that years of studying the emotions of others had failed to prepare him for dealing with his own. She was manipulating him when he should be manipulating her.

What truly hurt was that he could see no reason for her sudden change of heart. Perhaps being back among her own kind, friends and colleagues, had made her realize how much she missed them and their companionship. Jase had survived the fanatics' assault. Did her relationship with him go deeper than they had revealed?

After all, what could she see in him, a young man just emerging from adolescence? Except that he had never really been an adolescent.

Had he been normal, unable to read her emotions, he might have handled her reaction better. It was bad enough to have your love spurned, far worse to know that someone you felt so strongly for feared you. How much nicer to be normal and ignorant. Then he would merely be baffled, not hurt. His Talent functioned when he wanted to be deaf and failed when he desperately needed it. What good was the damned thing?

All right. For some reason she's no longer interested in you. She's afraid of you. Why not? It's only sensible. You warned her yourself, you damn fool. You're a self-confessed freak. She's older than you—though not significantly—and a respected scientist. You saved her life, and for a while she couldn't do enough to express her gratitude. Now that she's back among her own kind, her own people, safe and secure, she doesn't need your protection anymore. It's easy for her to see you for what you are. Nothing has really changed.

His eyes and throat were burning. That was the way it

was. That was the way it would probably always be for him, so he'd damn well better get used to it.

You're going to have to adapt to what you are, he told himself. You're going to have to be like Truzenzuzex and Bran Tse-Mallory—calm, logical, analytical in all things. Much easier to absorb and retain new knowledge that way, with no petty emotional distractions. You're the one who can feel what others are feeling. You're the last one who should let himself be overpowered by his own. Finish your meal and get out, get away from this place.

He took a long draught of his carotene-flavored protein drink. It slid down cold and undemanding. No, nothing had changed. There was still a whole Commonwealth to explore, to study. He would go and study as he had originally planned, and someday he would look back on this encounter as just another in a long list of learning experiences. Knowledge in and of itself. Knowledge of how another could feel about him. A valuable lesson. Wonderful how simple it was if you just put your mind to it, this ability to rationalize away extreme disappointment.

Go somewhere else. Find another intriguing world and punch it up on the holo projector. A world chosen at random. Not one where you would become lazy and vulnerable like New Riviera or a dangerous one like Alaspin. Something in between. A place stinking of normality. An ordinary, happy, content, developing world like Colophon or Kansastan where no one would know anything about him or his abilities. Where he would not have to confess to being the owner of a starship. Where he could lose himself among the masses of humanxkind and be free to observe while he matured. Blandness was what he needed now most of all. He needed not to be bothered, to be alone among his own kind.

Except that that was not ever really possible.

He was sitting there, content that he had come to terms with himself, when the shadow fell over him. Resolutions and hard decisions vanished as he turned quickly, heart leaping because he thought it was Clarity come back to tell him how sorry she was and say that she had not meant a word of it.

Instead he found himself eyeing a tall man wearing the uniform of port Security. His cap was cocked to the right, and the right sleeve of his shirt was shredded. Transparent skin-seal glistened through the rips where a doctor had performed some hasty but effective skin grafting.

"You the visitor who calls himself Flinx?"

Pip caught a last crumb and swallowed it whole. The officer's gaze took in the flying snake's movements, and Flinx felt his admirably brief flash of fear.

"Since everybody seems to know who I am by now, I don't see much point in trying to deny it." Realizing how belligerent he must sound to a polite stranger, he added, "I'm sorry. My friends and I just had a very trying experience. Amazing how fast word travels."

"Isn't it? I'm Feng Kikoisa, head of Security here. What's left of it." He looked to be in his early fifties, taut as duralloy, the kind of professional who could cope with a world like Longtunnel.

"We've got one ship in geosynchronous orbit. Next scheduled arrival isn't due for a month yet. I'm told that maybe it's your ship."

Flinx wiggled a finger in front of Pip and watched as the flying snake toyed with the movement. "I guess I'm not denying anything today. Am I in violation of some regulation?"

"Wouldn't matter if you were. Nobody's in any position to object. I'm just glad you're here."

Flinx turned his head sideways to squint up at the officer. "It's nice to be popular. So why do I think there's more to it than that?" He had a pretty good idea where the older man's conversation was headed.

"You strike me as an observant young man. I'm sure you've noticed how limited our facilities here are. We never expected to have to deal with anything like this. We don't have enough supplies, the right kind of—"

"I'll take them," Flinx said tiredly.

The officer was taken aback by Flinx's abruptness and perhaps also because he would not be able to deliver all of his carefully rehearsed speech. "There aren't that many." He spoke as if he were still reluctant to believe his request had already been approved.

"I said I'd take them." What else could he do? Leave and create a wake of notoriety behind him? "It won't be very comfortable. I'm not running a liner. There are only three staterooms."

"Wherever you put the seriously wounded, they'll be more comfortable than anywhere down here. Our medical people suggest Thalia Major or Minor as a destination."

Flinx considered. "I'd prefer to take them to Gorisa. It's about the same distance."

"Gorisa? I've never been there myself, but of course I know of it. Everyone in this sector knows Gorisa. I don't see any objection to that. Not that we're in a position to argue with you or order you about. Yours is a private vessel."

"That's right. It is."

"I'll convey your generous offer to my colleagues. I'm informed that for some of the injured, time is of the essence. When can you leave?"

"Immediately. Now."

"Very generous of you, yes." The Security chief had come prepared to rage and to beg. Instead he found himself overwhelmed by the young visitor's ready generosity. Actually, it had nothing to do with generosity. Not overtly, anyway. It was partly a matter of maintaining protective coloration and partly that Flinx wanted off Longtunnel as quickly as possible.

"You could also carry the official report of the incident here to the appropriate authorities. A pity we have no description, no knowledge of the ship our assailants employed."

"I'll send it down by high-speed transmission the moment we break out of space-plus," he assured the officer.

"How many shuttle trips do you think I'll have to make to get everyone up?"

"I've taken the liberty of inspecting your craft. I'd say two would do it. Most of the wounded we can care for here. You'll be taking people who've lost limbs or organs. We don't have organ banks or regeneration facilities here. We'll send along a couple of medtechs to look after the injured for the duration of the voyage." Kikoisa hesitated, then glanced away. "I really don't know how to express my—"

"It's not necessary to thank me. Anyone else in my situation would do the same." That was not necessarily true, but he was not used to taking credit for a good deed even when it was due him.

"All the more reason to do so." The lieutenant turned and headed out of the commissary at a brisk pace, no doubt to spread the good news to the rest of the outpost authorities.

Flinx methodically drained the rest of his drink and thought.

Chapter Fifteen

The last person he expected to see boarding the shuttle for the second and final run up to the *Teacher* was Clarity. The little vessel was already crammed full despite the lieutenant's insistence that the seriously wounded were small in number. No matter. They would find room for everyone. The common area was filling up with special beds and oxy-cocoons, but there was still space around the fountain.

"You injured?" She winced at his tone, and he was instantly sorry.

"No, but another ranking officer of the company has to come along to deliver our damage report so we can begin ordering new equipment. Amee may not be in any condition to do so. As chief of gengineering, I was elected." Coldstripe's director had been brought aboard the *Teacher* on the previous shuttle flight. "Besides, with everything ruined, there's nothing for me to do here."

"I understand." He turned to go forward.

"I'm sorry," she said hurriedly. "I'll try to stay out of your way. I'm sorry if—I hurt you."

"Hurt me? Funny. I'm not listed among the wounded."

"Flinx . . ."

"Save it. I know I frighten you. Told you too much, I guess. Let you see too much also, but I had no choice there. We needed the Sumacrea to find our way back." A small, brightly colored shape dashed from his shoulder to the back of her neck and began playing with her sidetail. She had bronze thread woven into it this morning, he noted.

"Somebody's happy to see you." He was unable to repress a slight smile as he watched Scrap toy with her blond hair.

She giggled as she tried to stroke the small flying snake. "Sometimes he tickles when he moves around like that."

"He'll settle down soon. Just glad to see you. Might as well let him keep you company. He knows his way around the ship."

She gazed back at him. For the moment there was no fear in her. "Thank you," she said simply.

He had to leave. "Yeah, sure. Forget it."

Though a long journey through space-minus lay ahead of them, he had no intention of talking to her. But the *Teacher*'s living area was not large, and the ship was very crowded, and since his presence was not actually required on the bridge, he found himself with a great deal of free time and nowhere to spend it except in his private stateroom. Since he was not by nature quite as solitary a person as he liked to believe he was, it was inevitable their paths should cross on more than one occasion.

The result was that eventually they did start talking again, but now without the playful intimacy that had characterized their earlier relationship. Both were nervous at first. The second meeting was easier, the third almost relaxed. He was glad. Better they should part as friends.

Several times she seemed on the verge of unburdening

herself to him, of trying to explain her fear and uncertainty. Each time she caught herself and changed the subject to something inconsequential. He never pressed for an explanation. If she wanted to tell him something, she would do it in her own time. Besides, he was not sure he wanted to hear what she might have to say.

Thalia Major and Minor were more mature worlds than Gorisa. Their populace was sophisticated and bored. Reports of an attack on an isolated scientific outpost would draw a lot of newsfax attention. Arriving wounded and other survivors would be subject to penetrating, thoughtful interviews and debriefing.

In contrast, Gorisa generated more than enough news of its own to keep several fax feeds occupied around the clock. It was the epitome of the fast-growing colony world. Bountifully endowed with heavy metals, productive oceans, and rich alluvial soil for farming, it lay on the fringe of the Commonwealth flanking a bulge of the AAnn Empire and the impossibly distant galactic edge.

Gorisa was already home to a frenetic, bustling population of over a hundred million. They were concentrated on the second largest continent, but a dozen satellite cities were under development on the four other major land masses. The climate was temperate and oxygen-rich, the gravity a shade less than Earth-normal, and each day offered incoming immigrants new ways to make their fortune.

A hundred sixty newsfax and entertainment channels competed for audiences on a world destined one day—its promoters insisted—to become the wealthiest in the Commonwealth. The arrival of a group of injured scientists and workers from a distant outpost scarcely rated a mention by the biggest newsfax combines. Only a single young and persistent faxer was more interested in how a nineteen-year-old without a famous name managed to run his own private starship than in the incident that had brought him to Gorisa. Flinx finally lost him in the crush and confusion of arrival and customs.

Owngrit was a city of eight million, with three major shuttleports and all the related facilities one would expect to find on a world where competition was fierce and credit flowed freely. The wounded from Longtunnel might have received slightly better care on Thalia Major or Minor, but Gorisa provided it immediately and without question, since there was heavy competition for business among the major medical facilities. Half a dozen deepspace beams offered Amee Vandervort the opportunity to transmit the detailed report Clarity had composed. Plans for rebuilding their installation on Longtunnel were under way before the last of the injured had been off-loaded from the *Teacher*.

Coldstripe was not the only organization to have suffered grievously at the hands of the fanatics. Research institutes and universities had lost material and personnel to the attack. The Counselor First of the United Church for Gorisa's sector had to be notified, as did Commonwealth authorities. Everyone became very busy very quickly.

As she watched him operate quietly and confidently in Gorisa's complex and combative society, Clarity was more impressed than ever with the young man who had saved her. He acted as if he had been dealing with wealthy merchants and self-important bureaucrats all his life. His attitude never became demanding or imperious, nor did he kowtow to government functionaries. At all times he was courteous, even deferential. He could also be immovable on issues important to him.

All this he did while maintaining his basic anonymity, a skill he had spent ten years developing. His increased height made it slightly more difficult to hide in the background. He had also considered dying his distinctive red hair, though the electric colors currently popular on Gorisa made that unnecessary for now.

Clarity thought she was beginning to understand him: how his mind worked, why he acted the way he did in public, what he might really want. His age and youthful appearance led others to underestimate him, and she believed he preferred it that way. She knew that behind those guileless green eyes a mind of extreme complexity and unique ability was always busy.

He had spoken to her of a difficult childhood. How much more to his personality was there than that? Or was he, after all, nothing more than an unusually intelligent, pleasant young man with a special talent?

Of one thing she was utterly convinced, despite anything Vandervort or anyone else might say: There was not a milligram of malignance in his whole body. If he was half-afraid of himself, what was more natural than that she or any other possible friends should share that fear?

She watched as he quietly helped care for and reassure the seriously wounded. The longer he was left alone, the more attention he devoted to others. It was as if he were afraid of being thought compassionate. Clarity was sure that Amee's suspicions were unfounded, her warnings misdirected. There was ample reason to like and even pity this young man, not to fear him.

Vandervort finally had her damaged arm properly attended to. She and other ranking members of the outpost told their stories to the authorities, who subsequently contacted Thalia Major. A peaceforcer cruiser was dispatched to Longtunnel to help with the cleanup and to begin the search for her assailants. It was more an expensive gesture than a necessary or practical move, but expensive gestures were crucial to the survival of any popular government. So the cruiser carried a full complement of marines even though there was no one left on Longtunnel to fight.

Contact was made with Coldstripe's backers. They were not as upset as Clarity had expected, but then, her expertise lay in gengineering, not in finance. Insurance covered much of the loss. What could not be replaced was the loss of key personnel. Everyone was greatly relieved to learn that Vandervort, Held, Jase, and the majority of the research staff had survived.

"They value us greatly, my dear," Vandervort told her via tridee. "There will be hazard pay and large bonuses all around. We may lose some people, but I believe most will elect to retain their positions and return to resume their work. What about you?"

"I have no intention of quitting, Amee. I want to go back to Longtunnel as soon as possible, both to continue my earlier work and to help with the new developments."

Vandervort smiled out at her from the flat screen. "I thought you would be one to see possibilities, but I wasn't sure until now. I cannot tell you how gratified I am by your decision. You are going to be a very wealthy and famous young woman." She glanced at something beyond the pickup's range.

"I'd like you to see our temporary field headquarters. I'll be coordinating the acquisition of new equipment and instrumentation from there. We've already begun." She flashed a series of numbers giving a structural position in Owngrit's north commercial suburbs. Clarity's unit would store it for easy retrieval. "Come by tonight, why don't you."

"Actually, I'd planned to see Flinx tonight."

Vandervort's brows rose. "I thought you were going to take my advice and keep your distance from that young man."

"I've done that. I don't see any harm in occasionally visiting with him. He has to be lonely, though he handles it very well. I think you're all wrong about him, Amee. He's not dangerous to anyone except maybe himself."

The older woman let out a sigh. "I told you. Just because he isn't dangerous at the moment doesn't mean he never will be. Anyway, it doesn't matter because he's going to be here tonight, too. I've invited him, and he's already accepted. So if you want to see him, you can meet him here. Good for you, good for me."

Something in Vandervort's voice made Clarity want to probe further—but if Flinx had already agreed to visit the facility . . .

"I'll be there, too, then."

"Good! I think it will have a bearing on your future. That is important to me, my dear."

Clarity grinned. "You aren't going to spring some kind of promotion on me, are you?"

"How perceptive you are, my dear. Something like that, yes. I'll expect you around nineish, local time."

"See you then."

Clarity let Vandervort break the connection, wondering what kind of promotion her director had in mind. She was already chief of Coldstripe's gengineering division and too valuable in the lab to be boosted into an administrative position. But then, Amee had not actually said it was a promotion. "Something like that" was what she had said. Curiouser and curiouser. She had always liked surprises.

Supper in the apartel's restaurant was lovely if lonely. Coldstripe's expense account was generous, more a reflection of good corporate policy than of benign munificence. As Amee had told her, personnel were more important than machinery. They intended to keep her and Jase and the others in good working order.

She took an MLV to the main northsub station, switched to a local, and hired a robocab for the last run. Coldstripe's temporary facility was housed in a brand-new, beautifully landscaped industrial park where none of the buildings rose higher than the imported trees. Two rust-leaved boles shaded the structure's entrance. A temporary sign floating above the front door identified the new lessee as Dax Enterprises. She wondered only briefly at the name change, deciding it must be for competitive reasons. It hung slightly crooked. The sign's field needed tuning.

With night having fallen, the near outer office was unoccupied. Nearly all the adjacent concerns had shut down

until the following day. Those few which still displayed
lights were located at the far end of the complex. There
was no receptionist on duty, a luxury Coldstripe did not
require. Clarity's company ident card passed her through
several security checkpoints until she encountered Amee
outside an inner office.

"You're on time. That's good."

"On time for what? How's your arm?"

The older woman raised her rebandaged limb. "As
you see, it's no longer necessary to keep it immobilized.
The new skin-seal is inconvenient, but that's all. The
itching should stop soon."

"I want to see what we've been able to get so far. Did
the backers approve my request for the Sentegen model-
ing projector?"

"You and your toys." Vandervort led Clarity not into
the large storage area behind the office but to a side door.
"That hasn't come in yet, but I'm sure it will. I've been
given a free hand reordering. The firm wants us reestab-
lished on Longtunnel as quickly as possible, so they can
take advantage of the free security the government is providing. For one thing, I'm told it lowers insurance rates
considerably."

Clarity did not recognize the security card Vandervort
inserted into the appropriate slot next to the door. It was
of a type unfamiliar to her, and it glowed faintly. The
door opened promptly, and they walked down a single
flight of steps.

"More storage? I thought we had enough upstairs."

Vandervort smiled at a private joke. "This is for special equipment."

The stairs made a ninety-degree bend in the middle
and descended another half a flight before ending in a
well-lit chamber. Since they were below ground level,
there were no windows, only featureless walls. Pipes and
ductwork hung exposed and unshielded. The entire room
was an afterthought, added on after the main structure
above had been completed.

There were basic living facilities off at one end: a couple of folding beds, cold food storage, sanitary setup, and simple storage. There was also a very large man who was currently aiming an extremely impressive handgun in their direction. He lowered it as soon as he recognized Amee Vandervort.

"Evening, ma'am."

"Hello, Dabis."

Clarity noticed a second man watching a wall tridee from one of the folding beds. He did not turn around or sit up. From the sound, she guessed he was eyeing some sort of sporting event.

"Everything all right?" Vandervort inquired as she stepped off the last step and started across the floor.

"Quiet as a nursery," said the big man. As he replied to Vandervort, his gaze was fastened on Clarity. It was not a kind gaze, and she laughed nervously as she looked away from him.

"What is this? Some kind of secret laboratory? Or are we into drug running now?"

"Neither, my dear. This is no more than a temporary way station. A stop on the road to fame and extreme fortune of the kind Coldstripe could never give us."

Clarity turned a puzzled face to her superior. "I don't follow you. And where's Flinx? You said he'd be here."

"So he is, my dear."

She walked over to where a large curtain hung suspended from a supporting bar and pulled it aside. Resting on a table behind it was a large octagonal container molded of gray plasteel. It looked like an oversized coffin. The surface was lightly pebbled, smooth and cool to the touch. Attached to its base was a second plasteel container a meter and a half long. It matched the larger one perfectly but was dyed beige instead of gray.

Set into the side of gray container was a touch control pad composed of glowing contact squares. Vandervort played a short sequence on them. A motor hummed compliantly, and the top layer of gray plasteel retracted halfway. Without being told, Clarity moved forward and peered through the transparent inner shield. Her heart skipped a beat.

Flinx lay beneath the transparent plexalloy. His eyes were closed, and his hands were crossed over his chest like those of a primordial Egyptian relic. Pip formed a tight, brightly colored coil below the crossed hands while a smaller duplicate of herself lay nearby.

Clarity whirled on the older woman. "Dead?"

"No, not at all." Almost as shocking to Clarity as Flinx's appearance was her superior's ability to muster a laugh. "They're only sleeping." She walked the length of the table and rested a hand on the beige container. "This assures that they sleep."

"You'd better explain yourself." Clarity was astonished at the hostility in her own voice.

The other woman ignored her tone. "One thing I never forgot about my uncle's tales was his fear of the Meliorares's wild approach to manipulative eugenics, the possibility that one or more of their experimental subjects might develop unpredictable abilities. My actions merely reflect ordinary caution when confronted by such a possibility." She studied the gray plasteel coffin.

"There is also the fact that even if our young friend is as harmless as he claims to be and you seem to think he is, his pets are anything but and should be handled with the utmost care." She smiled at Clarity. "You told me as much when you related the story of your flight from Alaspin.

"Fortunately, our young friend's desire to maintain the lowest possible profile worked to our advantage. As a result it is unlikely anyone will miss him. He ate in average restaurants, traveled by ordinary transportation, and, best of all, stayed in a middle-level hotel. Not too expensive, not too cheap. A place where people may be bribed.

"Since my expertise lies in administration, I took the time to locate and employ reliable help. You've already been introduced to Dabis. The gentleman on the bed goes by the name of Monconqui.'' The latter never looked up from his sporting match. Dabis grinned unpleasantly at Clarity. ''They supplied advice, obtained necessary equipment, and provided muscle.

''The gas that was introduced through the hotel room's venting system was quite odorless and colorless. We also took the precaution of injecting it while our young friend was asleep. Your story made me additionally cautious, you see. At first we feared his scaly companions were immune, but eventually they, too, were overcome. Dabis was for needling both on the spot, so I had to explain to him that the bond between man and minidrag would be an important component of future research. Difficult to carry out if half your subjects are dead.''

''Future research? What are you talking about, future research?''

Vandervort ignored her as she continued. ''Once they had been anesthetized, it was a simple matter to place them in this specially designed container, which is used by zoos and related institutions to transport dangerous fauna. I think our young man and his friends fit in that category. I did not and do not want him conscious until he has been placed in a facility that will render his pets harmless.'' She patted the beige container.

''This holds the sleep gas as well as equipment for mixing it with breathable air. The supply is constantly monitored to ensure the health of the larger container's occupants. In reality the two containers comprise a complete life-support system. Ports on the other side permit intravenous feeding when necessary without compromising the system's integrity. Don't be so melodramatic. Flinx and his pets will enjoy the kind of deep rest and comfort the rest of us can only dream about. This system is designed to keep expensive specimens optimally healthy.''

''He's not a specimen!'' Clarity could not contain her anger or her anguish any longer.

Vandervort pursed her lips. "My dear, I don't think you're taking this in the proper spirit. Perhaps you've not yet glimpsed the opportunity that lies before us. This young man can make our fortune. If he cooperates, it will make his fortune as well."

"I don't think he's interested in fortunes. His or anybody else's," was the angry retort.

Vandervort shrugged. "People often choose to deny their interest in large sums of money until it's actually offered to them, until they are faced with the reality instead of the concept. Your lack of interest in this project puzzles me. Insofar as we know, this young man is the only surviving sane product of the Society's work. I'd think you'd find that fascinating."

"Of course I find it fascinating. That doesn't mean I'm going to go poking around inside his head and nervous system without his permission. He's an individual with rights and—"

"Yes, yes." Vandervort waved off her objections. "I'm familiar with all the pertinent regulations. But we have here an exception to all the rules. An exception worth bending regulations to study."

"He may not cooperate. Have you thought of that?"

Again the smile, which in its own way, Clarity saw for the first time, could be more sinister than that of Dabis. "My dear, I like to think that I've thought of everything. I believe he will cooperate—eventually. I sincerely hope that he will. If not, there are ways to induce him to do so that do not involve physical coercion. For example, he is very attached to his pet. I am speaking of genuine affection and not just the unique emotional bond that exists between them. While I would be reluctant to countenance probing him against his will, I do not think I would have the same compunctions where a flying snake is concerned."

Clarity managed to calm herself. "I liked you, Amee. I thought of you as a second mother."

"I'm flattered, but I would much prefer it, my dear, if

you would think of me as a fellow scientist striving to extend the reach of human knowledge.'' She nodded at the coffin. ''Our young friend is reluctant to explore himself because he doesn't understand himself. That's to be expected. The conflict within him is social, not biological. As soon as he can be made to realize that, I think he will be eager to seek our cooperation. We intend to see that he has everything he could possibly want, that he's given the best conceivable living environment, and that he'll be working with dedicated professionals who only want to help him understand himself.

''I think he'll be grateful to us. He won't have to hide anymore, won't have to run. We'll keep him hidden from the government functionaries who'll only want to 'normalize' him.''

A sudden realization struck Clarity like a window opening in her mind. ''My function in all this is to act as one of his teachers and observers?''

''I can't imagine what else you had in mind.''

''You wouldn't be trying to include me as part of that 'everything he could possibly want'?''

Vandervort stared evenly back at her. ''If your presence at the facility which is in the process of being established resulted in your performing a dual function, I'm sure the company would be correspondingly grateful.''

''I just wanted to make certain I understood my position in all this. But suppose you have him figured wrong, Amee? Suppose he doesn't want any part of your generous offer to help him learn to 'understand' himself? What if all he wants is to maintain his privacy? Suppose that's more important to him than helping you 'extend the reach of human knowledge'—for your profit?''

''He'll profit as well.'' Vandervort sounded hurt. ''This will benefit him more than anyone else. I truly believe that.''

''I don't. What I also can't believe is that Coldstripe's backers would countenance something like this. I had the opportunity to meet several of them when I was hired, and they didn't strike me as the type who'd go in for this kind of thing. Sure, they want to preside over historic breakthroughs and get their names on the newsfax. Sure, they want to make money. But I don't see any of the men and women I talked to approving kidnapping as part of the necessary methodology for achieving those ends."

"A harsh choice of words, my dear. I prefer to think of what we're doing as helping a mentally distraught young man to find himself. And I should add that Coldstripe has nothing to do with this. Your assessments are correct in that respect."

That brought Clarity up short. "Then who?"

"Scarpania House is paying all our expenses. I've kept in touch with friends there for a long time. A survival tactic in the world of business. Always keep lines of communication open to alternative employment. Scarpania is a hundred times bigger than Coldstripe. They can provide private spacecraft, unquestioning customs clearances, everything an operation like this requires. When I explained to them what was at stake here, they readily opened their hearts and minds to me. Also their line of credit.

"I still don't think you're seeing the potential here, my dear. Imagine watching this young man under controlled conditions as he matures and develops. Even if he manifests no other talent, the close study of his capacity for emotional telepathy will be sufficient to guarantee us comfortable employment for life. Having been emotionally involved with him, you are in a better position than anyone else to engage in such research."

"I see where you're going with this, Amee, and I can tell you right now I don't want any part of it. Understand?"

"Think carefully, my dear. Think clearly. Cultivate a proper scientific attitude."

"I'm not going to cozy up to him so you can measure and record and analyze his reactions," she said bitterly.

"I'm not some damn soporific you can inject into his life to make him feel a little better about what you're going to do to him."

Vandervort moved away from the beige container. "At least you know what is wanted of you. I'm sure you'll change your mind, if for no other reason than that he'll need you. I urge you not to commit yourself to a snap emotional decision but to give it time and consideration. If nothing else, he is a very handsome young man, for all the pains he takes to conceal it."

"I'm not one of your tools. You can't buy me."

This time the older woman was genuinely amused. "That remains to be seen, my dear. I haven't tendered you an offer yet, have I? Consider also that if you return to Coldstripe, and I say now I will not stop you from so doing, you will never find out what happens to our Flinx: how he develops, what unsuspected talents he may display, or who might be hired to take your place."

This could not be happening, Clarity told herself. This was not Momma Vandervort speaking to her, calmly laying out the details of a plan as nefarious as anything seen on the tridee. Flinx was not lying doped and still as the dead in a plasteel coffin on that table to her left.

She knew the truth of what Vandervort had told her. If she did not agree to participate, then they would find someone else to try to insinuate herself into Flinx's confidence. They would keep trying until they hit on the right combination of empathy, beauty, and intelligence. Someone with less understanding of Flinx and fewer scruples than herself. If she wanted to help him, then she had to accept the older woman's offer, work for her and Scarpania at least temporarily until she could think of a way out for both of them.

Think! Buy some time.

"Just for the sake of argument, what if I abjure everything you've proposed and take this straight to the Gorisan authorities?"

Vandervort's tone did not change. "I'd rather you

didn't do that, my dear. Regardless of what you may think of me at this moment, I've grown fond of you during the time we've worked together. I think you are a highly qualified, potentially brilliant gengineer who is also blessed with enthusiasm and the talent to inspire her co-workers beyond their natural abilities.''

That was all she said. No threats, direct or implied. Only admiration and a gentle request backed up by the presence of Dabis and the still supine Monconqui.

"I could go along," Clarity told her, "agree to all you ask, and then slip away and spill everything to the Church."

Vandervort considered briefly, nodding. "Yes, you could probably do that. You're resourceful, and not as naive as when you first came to work for me. You might even find a padre who'd believe your story. But by the time anyone came looking, we'd have moved our facility and our young man to a place of safety. You won't be able to trace us, and neither will the Church. And while I would simply shrug off the additional expense, Scarpania likely would not. Since you would not have the money to reimburse them for their trouble, I'm afraid they would find another method of obtaining satisfaction."

Having run out of arguments, Clarity slumped visibly. Realizing she had gained everything she wanted, Vandervort forced herself not to smile with satisfaction. The younger woman would only react emotionally, and Vandervort had had enough of emotional reactions for a while.

Flinx was used to strange dreams. This one was no exception. He was drifting, floating just below the surface of a lake of pure crystalline water. Pip bobbed beside him, and Scrap next to her. But none of them were swimming. None of them were breathing. They simply hung there below the glassine surface, adrift in cool peacefulness.

Though he knew he risked drowning by doing so, he tried to taste the water, only to find he was unable to inhale a drop through either his mouth or his nostrils. It was very peculiar water, almost like air. Maybe that was it. Maybe he was floating beneath the surface of a sea of methane or liquid nitrogen.

At times he thought he could see shapes moving above. They passed by infrequently. Faces with wings that gazed mournfully down at him before fluttering away. He tried to speak to them, tried to reach up to them, but could not do so. He was unable to move. Nor was his Talent functioning, since he could not sense their emotions. What pale impressions he did receive were tenuous and imprecise. He felt neither hostility nor affection, only bland indifference.

He was not alarmed. Contentment seeped through him. Hunger and thirst were abstract concepts. Very faintly, something deep inside his mind tried to insist that this was not right, that he needed to bestir himself, to move about, to stand.

Waste of time. Useless and unnecessary to try to analyze his situation or his environment. Enough to lie in the lake heedless of the world around him, whatever it might be like.

He sensed the minidrags' emotions and knew they paralleled his own. They dreamed of flying through an empty sky with no land below, no trees, no clouds above. It was an unsettling dream, and Pip and Scrap fluttered their wings.

No one in the room noticed the two minidrags twitching and trying to fly. It did not matter, anyway, because they remained sedated. While their tolerance for the morphogas was higher than Flinx's, neither had recovered enough to regain consciousness. They simply moved a little before growing still again, moved and lay still, dreaming of flight while trapped on the ground.

Chapter Sixteen

Clarity had agreed to everything her boss had requested. In the final analysis the young woman was as logical and sensible as herself, Vandervort knew. Possibly she still harbored thoughts of somehow freeing Flinx, but she had neither the experience nor the knowledge to do so. Vandervort was confident that as time passed she would be able to manipulate both young people as required.

She had a private transport service coming to help with the moving. Dabis and Monconqui would be available also. The plasteel coffin, its top now closed so as not to reveal its contents to casual observers, would present no problem.

It was an off-work day and she had to pay double for the moving service, but that was one of the nice things about having a virtually unlimited expense account. Scarpania's own research people were more than anxious to have a look at her prize.

Two weeks to get everything ready. A secure installation had been thrown together on an isolated island on a modest colony world clear across the Commonwealth. They would travel on a Scarpanian freighter devoid of cargo except for themselves and their precious sleeper. To any outsider it would seem a flagrant waste of money, but several members of her new employer's scientific staff had recognized the importance of her discovery and appreciated its potential fully as much as she did.

Clarity was there, too: packed, ready to depart, and downcast, having barely resigned herself to the situation. Plotting and planning, no doubt. That was fine, Vandervort thought. It would give her something to do during the long, dull journey through null-space.

Dabis called down to her from the top of the stairs. "They're here, ma'am."

"You checked their idents?"

"Yes'm."

"Then let them in and let's get on with it."

She made a last sweep of the room in which she had spent so many busy hours this past month. Monconqui was checking the morphogas tanks to make sure they were full and working properly. He did not talk as readily as Dabis, but the two men were cast from the same mental mold. They were much more than simply dumb assassins. If one was willing to pay, one could hire intelligent muscle as easily as stupid.

The moving crew wore light green jumpsuits and caps. She expected people Dabis's size, but apparently the company had opted for numbers instead of individual mass. Perhaps it had been difficult to bring in their regulars on short notice even for double pay. Not that size and strength were necessary, she reminded herself, in these days of labor-saving devices. With the levitating grapples they carried, the four of them could easily position a two-ton generator. One of the women, a tall blonde of icy mien, looked capable of lifting one end of the coffin all by herself, though her three companions did not appear nearly as capable. Even with the grapples taken into account, one man in particular looked too old to be engaged in this sort of work. Not that she knew anything about the particular expertise moving work required, she told herself.

She walked over to the curtain and pulled it aside for the last time. "Let's start with this."

"Right," said the young man who seemed to be in charge.

The four of them placed their grapples and switched them on. Wrist movement alone was sufficient to raise the coffin and its attached atmosphere unit several centimeters off the table. Carefully they turned its head toward the stairs.

"Remember, you're handling extremely fragile and valuable equipment," Vandervort told them. Somewhere behind her, Clarity made a disparaging noise. Vandervort almost frowned but resolutely kept her expression neutral.

On the other hand, the tall blond woman smiled.

Why should she smile? Come to think of it, why would she react to such a bland statement at all? The smile was already gone. No need to say anything. No reason to comment.

But something made Vandervort stride forward and confront the much taller woman. "Something funny about that?"

The blonde's beautiful face was blank. "No, ms." She hesitated. "It's just that we're proud of our work. I was amused that anyone would think we'd take less than the best care of anything we were moving."

"I see." Vandervort stepped aside. A perfectly plausible explanation for an innocent little grin. Too plausible? Or too pat. "One more thing." The four movers paused, each with a hand holding the trigger of a grapple. "Could I see your identification one more time, please?"

The young man in charge hesitated for just an instant, then reached for his chest patch. It was the very old man who made the fatal mistake. Perhaps he thought he was speaking in a lower voice than he actually was. Maybe he was just slightly hard of hearing. Whatever the reason, Vandervort heard him hiss quite distinctly.

"Don't show it to her."

The blond amazon's eyes flicked in his direction. Ignoring the advice, the young man removed his chest patch and passed it to Vandervort, who made a show of inspecting it closely. Whispers, eye movement, inexplicable smiles.

"No problem, ms," the young man was saying cheerfully. "Something the matter?"

"Just a routine check." Holding the ident patch, Vandervort turned so they couldn't see her face. Her lips moved silently when she caught Dabis's eye. His widened, he nodded slightly, and that was when she dived for the cover of some hastily packed crates.

Dabis crouched and pulled his needler. Not having been warned, Monconqui was slower on the uptake, but he, too, made a dash for cover as soon as he saw his partner in motion.

The movers reacted swiftly, but they were not fast enough. Despite their recent experiences they still did not possess the fighting skills of professionals. The trailing member of the quartet took the blast from Dabis's needler square in the chest. It penetrated his sternum to fry nerves, blood vessels, and his spine as it emerged from the back of his shirt to spend itself against the wall.

Screams and shouts filled the room. Clarity was an easy mark for the movers, but they had no time to concentrate on her, and she was able to find shelter. Dabis and Monconqui were the problem. Both had taken good cover behind heavy packing crates filled with electronics and monitoring instrumentation. They were outnumbered three to two but were better shots. While they commanded the only exit, the fanatics had to expose themselves on the stairway in order to take aim into the room.

Firing continued steadily. A burst from a neuronic pistol just missed Clarity, momentarily paralyzing her left side. Feeling returned rapidly following the near miss, leaving behind a tingling sensation.

Vandervort lay nearby, watching the battle. "Keep your head down, child! You and I have nothing to do with the outcome of this." She was peering between two huge crates, her observation made easier by the fact that the fanatics were concentrating their firepower on the two bodyguards.

The mover who had been shot lay crumpled at the foot of the stairs, eyes staring blankly upward, the hole in his chest still smoking. Having been released by the movers, the plasteel coffin had drifted to a halt against the wall nearby, still suspended in its four softly humming grapples.

"Your friends from Alaspin and Longtunnel," Vandervort murmured as she struggled to get a better view without exposing herself. She raised her voice. "Give it up! These two men here will pick you off sooner or later. They're professionals, and you are not. There is nothing more for you here, whatever you intended. You cannot have Clarity."

"We'll have her." Clarity thought she recognized the voice of the young man. He was keeping out of sight near the top of the stairs. "And we'll have you, and we'll have the mutant as well."

"How could they know about that?" Vandervort was shaking her head in disbelief. "How could they have found out?" Abruptly she looked at the younger woman crouched nearby. Clarity's eyes widened, and she shook her head violently. The administrator considered thoughtfully before speaking again.

"I don't know what you're talking about."

The tall blonde responded this time with a harsh, feminine laugh. "We broke the Coldstripe communications code a long time ago, so forget about lying to us. We know everything. We knew about the mutant before Scarpania did."

"God damn," Vandervort muttered. "I *told* our people they had to change keys at least every other day. Lazy sons of bitches!''

The blonde was not through. ''How do you think we knew where to find you on Longtunnel, knew where your records were stored and the labs were located? When she was our guest on Alaspin, your life meddler told us some of what we needed to know, but not all. The rest we obtained from monitoring your local transmissions and from our operative within your own organization.'' She laughed humorlessly. ''Didn't it ever occur to you that your friend Jase seemed to have nine lives?''

The color drained from Vandervort's expression. Clarity delighted in the older woman's distress. ''Thought of everything, did you?'' The administrator did not reply. The blonde was still talking.

''The life meddler comes with us, to ensure she won't tamper with nature any further.''

''What do you want with our young man? He's being well looked after. His name is Flinx, and you have no right to—''

This time it was the young man who interrupted her. ''You'd lecture us on the rights of the individual? Do you think we're fools, like your former employers? You're spitting air, Vandervort.''

Despite her superior's warning, Clarity raised her head so that she could be heard clearly over the packages shielding her. ''Let nobody have him, then! Why not just let him go?'' She ignored Vandervort's frantic gestures. ''He's done nothing to you.''

''It is what has been done to him that matters in this.'' It was the voice of another man, speaking for the first time. His tone was commanding. ''We will treat him kindly while we attempt to return him to normal, try to correct the damage done by the Meliorares. There are expert gengineers who are sympathetic to our aims.''

''The Meliorares worked with prenatal cells,'' Clarity argued. ''That was different. You can't tamper with the genetic code of a mature person. You'll end up ruining his mind or his personality or both.''

"We intend neither," the man replied. "Regardless of the result, it will be an improvement on what now exists because the individual in question will once again be truly human when we have finished with him."

A burst of neuronic fire passed just over her head, and she was forced to duck back down, her scalp tingling. Dabis and Monconqui were quick to return the shots.

"You want him? Come and get him!" Dabis's tone was deliberately taunting. "He's floating right there at the bottom of the stairs, where he bumped into the wall. Why don't you just stroll on down and pick up your grapples?"

"We'll do that soon enough," the blonde shouted. "We may not have your training, but we've practiced long and hard for moments like these. We aren't ignorant of tactics. Maybe we can't take you out or recover the mutant, but you're trapped down here. We've cut all communications to the outside and secure-blanketed the entire building. A stray electron couldn't find a way out. You can't talk to anyone on the outside, nor are you expected anywhere for some time, so nobody's going to come looking for you. Your obsession with privacy, Vandervort, works to our advantage as well. We cannot get in, and you can't get out. So we'll have to find another way to resolve our little impasse."

"We'll resolve it, all right," Vandervort snapped back. "The three of you will join your friend on the floor."

"I think not. What we'll do is sit here and relax while one of us goes for help. That's our advantage. One person could guard this exit."

"You can bring a hundred cephalos back with you, but you'll never get them down those stairs!" Dabis was earning his money.

"No need to. The morphogas you use to keep the mutant inert can just as easily be introduced into this room.

You'll all quietly go to sleep." Dabis had no ready answer for that.

Monconqui tried. "We have filter masks. Gas won't bother us."

"Maybe you do and maybe you don't. Let's find out. We've nothing to lose by trying. Unless you'd consider bargaining with us."

The young man took over. "You two with the guns—this is only a job for you. Why risk getting shot for a credit boost?"

"Because it *is* our job," Dabis replied simply.

"Whatever Vandervort's people are paying you, we'll double it. Triple it."

"Sorry," and Monconqui sounded genuinely so, "but if we break a contract we'll never get another job. Also, there are bonuses waiting when we deliver our people to their destination."

"Admirable ethics in the service of a lost cause," the second man declared.

"Maybe we *can* strike some sort of bargain," Vandervort suggested.

"What kind of bargain?" Suspicion tainted the young man's reply.

"You want the gengineer. The mutant's more important to us."

Clarity stared at the older woman, and began backing away until she was pressed up against the wall. Vandervort smiled apologetically. "I am sorry, my dear, but the situation is grave. Extreme measures are called for to resolve it."

Clarity's response was a horrified whisper. "I never should have listened to you. I should have listened to Flinx. He's not the dangerous one here. He's not responsible for the way he is. You're the one who's evil and dangerous."

"Since you feel that way, I consider myself under no obligation to apologize." Vandervort turned away and raised her voice anew. "What do you say? You've already destroyed the Longtunnel installation. I'm only an administrator who's about to enter a different line of work. You can have the gengineer.''

The amazon replied, ''We must have the mutant also. The way I see it, we have the upper hand strategically. You can try to cross an open floor and fight your way up these stairs if you like. I don't see any reason why we have to bargain with you for anything.''

''We might not make it, but some of you will die,'' said Dabis. ''Be better if all of us could get out of this without any more deaths.''

A long pause ensued before the blonde responded. ''We'll think about it,'' she said finally.

''Don't think too long,'' Vandervort warned her. ''We might decide to leave without your permission.'' Having said that, she slumped back down behind her protective crates, suddenly looking her age. Still favoring her injured arm, she brushed hair from her face and caught sight of Clarity glaring at her as if frozen.

''Oh, don't look at me like that, my dear,'' she muttered irritably. ''It is quite boorish and unbecoming to you and does not affect me in the slightest.''

''You know,'' Clarity said evenly, ''I used to want to be just like you. I admired you for the easy way you mixed business with science. Someone who'd done it all and on her own.''

''Indeed, I have done everything on my own. I intend keeping it that way. This would have been easier with you assisting me, but even though you're the best, I will manage by replacing you with the next best. It is our young man who is irreplaceable, not you.''

The lake blurred. Suddenly the water was not quite so clear, his floating not as peaceful. He sensed rather than saw Pip and Scrap drifting alongside and knew their tranquility had also been disturbed.

Shapes continued to float above the lake's surface, but they were no longer placid and dreamy. Now they were

*angry and demonic of expression, full of tension and ha-
tred. For the first time he sensed he was not alone in the
lake. Things were moving in the depths, far below his
range of vision, down where the water grew cold and
dark. There was one immense green shapelessness that
kept straining to reach him, impinging on his consciousness like a flint striking sparks from another rock. Forms
in the void at once familiar and unrecognizable.*

*Though he concentrated hard, the green shape and the
strangeness faded as the demonic faces hardened like glass.
He felt as if he were starting to rise toward the lake's surface,
acquiring a sort of mental as well as physical buoyancy. Even
so, he was not prepared when he broke through.*

*Nothing made any sense. When he had been drifting
underwater, his breathing had been relaxed and easy.
Now that he was back in atmosphere once more, he found
himself choking and gasping for air. His eyes bulged, and
his lungs pumped wildly. Next to him Pip and Scrap were
two bundles of contorting coils.*

When the coffin had been abandoned, it had drifted on
its levitating grapples until it banged against the subterranean wall. The beige plasteel adjunct containing the
morphogas cylinders and flowmix valves had been very
slightly jarred. The result was a crack in one of the feeder
lines. Monconqui would have noticed it during one of his
routine inspections, but that individual had been otherwise occupied for some time.

Room air was leaking into the line while gas was leaking out. The atmosphere inside the coffin was very slowly
returning to normal. While the container was airtight, it
was not soundproof. The noise of arguing voices and
unleashed weapons was audible within.

It was, however, black as Longtunnel's caverns inside
with the observation window shield shut.

Flinx tried to make his brain work. The last thing he
could remember was sitting on the bed in his hotel room,
watching the tridee with Pip curled up on a chair nearby

and Scrap racing his tail around the overhead lighting. Now he found himself lying on his back in a restricting container of some kind with Pip and Scrap next to him. The ghosts of gunshots and voices penetrated the material. They sounded human; therefore, it was likely if not guaranteed that a breathable atmosphere existed outside his prison.

He explored the interior as best he could, but found nothing in the way of a release button or latch. That meant that it was designed to be opened only from the outside. That much made sense. Three thick hinges yielded their identity to his questing fingers.

He recalled his restful sojourn in the lake of his thoughts. Whether by injection or by some other means, he had been tranquilized, and judging from his aching muscles he had been unconscious for some time. Despite that, he felt healthy and alert. The long sleep had swept cobwebs from his mind. He let his Talent loose and found he could perceive proximate emotions clearly. Perhaps the combination of extended enforced rest and whatever narcotizing agent had been used on him had resulted in a heightening of his perception. Perhaps something had happened to him while he had been locked in his prison, unable to use anything except his mind. He had vague memories of powerful unseen forms, and in particular a vast greenness. Echoes of an exhilarating dreamscape.

He touched a number of hostile minds and moved on like a butterfly sampling flower upon flower. Sounds and emotions told him people were shooting at each other. Adrift amid the ocean of unfamiliar feelings were two he knew well. One was Alynasmolia Vandervort, a remarkable combination of greed, lust, ambition, hope, and hatred.

Clarity was filled with disgust, worry, fear, and something he could not lock down. That was when he whispered to Pip. Not all their communication was empathic. The flying snake was intelligent enough to learn and respond to a few basic verbal commands.

Edging as far to his right as possible, he tapped the lowest hinge of his prison with a finger while uttering the word. Pip noted the placement of his finger from the sound it made striking the hinge, waiting until her master had withdrawn his hand, and spit.

The acrid stink of dissolving metal and plasteel filled the container and threatened to choke Flinx anew. Fighting for breath, he tapped two more times, uttered the command twice more, and waited while Pip's response ate into the hinges. No one came to see what was happening. Either the dissolving hinges were not noticeable from outside or, more likely, the combatants he sensed were busy trying to kill one another.

Choking out the fumes, trapped in the confining darkness, he began to get angry. Everything that had happened to him had come about because he had tried to help someone. His own emotions had been toyed with, and the more he tried to help, the more people seemed to want to do him harm. He was more than a little fed up and more than a little furious.

Lying contentedly in his private lake, he had learned a lot about himself. Enforced meditation had revealed things he had never acknowledged before. One was that in all the universe there seemed only two intelligences that truly understood him. The Sumacrea were one. The other was a gigantic weapon constructed by a long-dead race. The Sumacrea's main purpose in life was to understand. The weapon's was to destroy. So be it.

Except he was not a weapon. He was Philip Lynx, né Flinx: a nineteen-year-old orphan with an unusual history, an enigmatic lineage, and an erratic Talent of unknown promise.

Whatever he was, it was quite a shock to everyone else in the room when he shoved the ruined lid of his container off its rim and sat up. It took a moment for his eyes to adjust to the light. In that instant everyone else had a chance to react.

Vandervort rose halfway above her protective wall of

crates and screamed, "Get them!" Dabis and Monconqui started to move. The older man squatting at the top of the stairway stared at Flinx as if he were regarding a reptilian carnivore instead of a slim young man.

"Kill the thing!" he bellowed. "Kill it now!"

The young man seated on the top step hesitated, but not the tall amazon next to him. She started to raise the muzzle of the neuronic pistol she was holding. Without being touched by any visible weapon, she abruptly slumped forward, rolling down the stairs to fall in a heap atop the dead man already there.

Pip and Scrap were airborne and ready to attack, but for the first time in his life Flinx did not need them. Having fought to break free of the lake, he found he could now break through with little effort. Using Pip as an empathic lens, he was able to project emotions as well as receive them. Maybe more than the lake and his sleep was involved. Maybe it had something to do with the shapes and forms that had tried to touch him. Perhaps he had been touched. He did not know.

Time later to find out, if he lived.

What he had projected into the mind of the tall woman had been fear and overwhelming terror. Now he sent it into her companion, who let out a quavering moan, rose to turn and run, and then fainted on the steps. The older man managed a shot in Flinx's direction. The bolt just missed him, numbing his arm. Instinctively he responded with greater force.

The result was unintended. The elderly fanatic rose trembling, eyes bulging, and collapsed atop his younger colleague. Unlike his companion, he had not simply been rendered unconscious. Fear had stopped his heart.

Observing the collapse of their opposition, the two bodyguards had halted in the middle of the room, relieved that they would not have to try to dodge the pistols of the fanatics. At almost the same time they noticed that their prisoner was sitting up in his coffin facing them.

They did not connect his resurrection to the destruction of their opponents.

An uncertain Monconqui raised his pistol. Clarity saw him, stood up, and screamed.

The two bodyguards proved harder to put down. They were familiar with the kind of fear Flinx had used to eliminate the fanatics from the scene. Nonetheless, every man has his breaking point. Beneath the barrage of withering terror they both eventually keeled over.

Then he was alone in the room except for Clarity and Vandervort. The older woman came around from behind her little fortress of crates and started toward him, a broad smile on her face, hand extended.

"Well, my boy, I don't know how you did that, but I know you are responsible. I saw you stare them down, or whatever it was you did. First that slime on the stairs and then my own people, who didn't have the sense to lower their weapons before they could find out we were all on the same side."

Flinx was climbing out of the coffin. "Which side is that?"

"Don't listen to her, Flinx!" Clarity blurted out hastily. "She's the one who had you drugged and put in that thing!"

Vandervort whirled on her. "Just shut up, you little bitch. If you know what's good for you, you'd better keep your mouth shut." Still smiling, she looked back at Flinx. He studied her noncommittally.

"Dear Clarity is upset. She's confused by everything that's happened, and I must say I don't blame her." Vandervort laughed, a velvety, comfortable laugh. "I am somewhat confused myself."

"Me, too."

Vandervort seemed to stand a little taller. "I'm certain we can sort all this out."

"So you're not responsible for any of this?" His stare was level, his voice calm. Pip hovered close by while Scrap darted uncertainly toward Clarity, back to Flinx, and ended up spinning miserably in the air halfway between the two.

"I didn't exactly say that. What I said was that it's all been very confusing."

That was what she said. What emanated from her was a combination of fear and anger, not all aimed at the unconscious or dead fanatics piled on the stairway. Some of it was directed at Clarity. Some of it was directed at Flinx.

"If you want to help me so badly, why are you so afraid of me?"

"Afraid of you, young man? But I'm not." Suddenly realization struck, and she smiled, but this time the smile was uneasy. "You *can* tell what I'm feeling, can't you? Not what I'm thinking, but what I am feeling."

"That's it. What I'm feeling right now is that you're not as fond of me as you're trying to make out."

"You mustn't take emotions literally, young man. They can be confused, and confusing. You just knocked out five armed assailants without so much as lifting your hand. I believe I'm entitled to at least be intimidated."

"But you're not intimidated. You're afraid, and that's something else again. I think you're feeling that as soon as I turn my back on you, you're going to go for one of those guns that your henchmen dropped."

All the color drained from her face. "You can't feel that. It's not an emotion; it's a specific thought." She retreated a step. "You can't—"

"Absolutely right. I can't read thoughts. But if I suggest something and you react to it, I can sense your reactions and thereby tell the truth of it as clearly as if you'd answered honestly. If you'd responded any other way, then I might have hesitated. I might have been unsure. I might've been tempted to listen to you."

"You aren't going to kill me," she whispered hollowly. "It isn't in you."

"Hey, we don't know what's in me, remember? I'm the unpredictable mutant you keep warning everyone

against.'' He was sickened not by the look of sheer terror
on her face but by the fact that he was enjoying it. He
sighed. "Enough death." He indicated the stairs. "Two
of them are dead, the rest unconscious. One of the deaths
was an accident, and the other the result of a needle shot.
I'm not going to kill you, Vandervort.''

The older woman stopped. "What are you going to
do?'' She was looking past him. "What you did to
them?''

"Just made sure they wouldn't bother me for a while.
Tell me: Is there anything you're really afraid of? Anything that truly frightens you?''

"No. I'm a scientist. I look at everything analytically.
I have no fears.''

Suddenly her eyes bulged like those of a fish trapped
by a receding tide. Her head went way back, and she
turned a slow circle. Fingers dug into hair, and she uttered a single piercing shriek before folding over in a
dead faint.

Clarity came out from behind the other crates. "What
did you do to her?''

He gazed sadly at the crumpled figure. "The same
thing I did to the others. Projected fear into them until
their nervous systems were overwhelmed. I sensed crawling things in her mind. Bugs, something else, I don't
know." He shook his head. "Specifics weren't required.
So much for the analytical approach.''

"Flinx, I'm so glad that everything—''

He turned sharply. "I think you'd better stop right
there.''

She did so, puzzled and obviously hurt. "I can imagine what you're thinking. I had nothing to do with any
of this.''

"You knew about it. Tell me you knew nothing of it.''

"I can't. You'd be able to tell if I was lying. Flinx, I
didn't know what to do, what to think. She told me stories—'' She nodded toward the motionless form of her
former superior. "—stories about the Society and their

work and you. About what you might become. I didn't believe her. I didn't want to believe any of it. But she's so much more experienced than I. I didn't have any choice. If I'd refused, they would have found someone else to take my place, someone who cared nothing about you.''

"Everyone has a choice." He lowered his gaze, tired of staring. Tired, period. "It's just that most people don't have the guts to make the right one."

"I'm sorry, I'm so very sorry." She was crying now. "They had you here in that damn box before I knew anything. It was too late for me to stop them. I went along hoping to help you later, somehow, when they'd let down their guard. You've got to believe that! You heard me shout a warning, didn't you? You just heard me tell you that she was responsible for everything that's happened, that this is all her doing."

"Yes, I heard you. That's why you're still walking instead of lying on the floor with the rest. I know you're telling the truth, or else you're the most skillful liar I've ever encountered."

"If you know that, if you can sense that, then you must also know that I love you."

He turned away from her. "I don't know anything of the sort. Your feelings are strong, but no matter what you say, I can tell that they're still confused and uncertain. One moment you say you love me, the next you're afraid of me. Hot and cold. I don't want that kind of relationship."

"Give me a chance, Flinx," she pleaded. "I'm so terribly confused."

He whirled to face her again. "How do you think *I'm* feeling? That's the one set of emotions I can never get rid of. After all that's happened, how can you think I could ever trust you with anything, much less with my life? Not that it matters, anyway. You can't share my life. Nobody can. Because, ironically enough, Vandervort may have been right about that. I can't, I won't take the chance of endangering someone else in the event I do turn out to be dangerous.

"I was uncertain about that before. Now I'm not. I shouldn't have let myself get involved with you in the first place. That much of it's my fault."

"Flinx, I know what you are. It doesn't frighten me anymore. You need someone like me. Someone who can give you understanding and sympathy and affection—and love."

"Someone to help me be human. Is that it?"

"No, dammit!" Despite her best efforts to repress them, the tears began afresh. "That's not what I mean at all."

He wanted her to be lying, but she was not.

"While I was asleep, or unconscious, or drugged, or whatever, my mind roamed freely in a way it never has before. I feel better about myself than I ever have. It was more than a rejuvenating rest, Clarity. Something happened to me while I was in that box. I can't define it yet because I'm not sure what it was. But while I was in there I sensed things. Some of them were beautiful and some were frightening and others were inexplicable, and until I can figure them out, I need to be by myself.

"You go back to whipping out custom genes and designer biologicals, and I'll get back to my studying. That's the way it has to be."

"You're not being fair," she sobbed.

"Once I was told that the universe isn't a fair place. The more I see of it, the more convinced I am of the rightness of that observation."

The rumbling began as a hum in the ears and a subtle quivering underfoot. The two met somewhere in the vicinity of the stomach. Not an earthquake but something much more pervasive. Clarity rushed to the plastic crates for support while Flinx stood his ground as best he was able. Pip stayed aloft while Scrap finally came to a decision and landed cautiously on Clarity's shoulder. That was painful for Flinx to see, but he could not waste time worrying about it now.

Of more immediate concern was the fact that the center of the floor was crumbling beneath his feet. He scrambled to one side, staring as the stelacrete and duralloy mesh turned to powder and vanished into the gaping maw of a vast dark pit some three meters in diameter.

The huge creature that stuck its head out of the hole and gazed curiously around the room was as tall as the opening was wide. Its dense fur was mottled with splotches, and it must have weighed close to a ton. The flat muzzle ended in a tiny nose above which a pair of plate-sized yellow eyes hung like lanterns. The ears were comically undersized.

Placing two immense, seven-digited paws on the edge of the hole, it boosted itself into the room, the furry head barely clearing the ceiling. Clarity goggled at it in disbelief as if it were something coalesced whole from a fever dream. Flinx flinched, too, but for a different reason entirely. At that point the monster saw him—and smiled hugely.

"Hello again, Flinx-friend," it said.

Except its mouth did not move.

Chapter Seventeen

Clarity heard it, too. She was mumbling dazedly to herself. "There's no such thing as a true telepath. There's no such thing."

"I'm afraid there is," Flinx said with another sigh. He turned to the monster. "Hello, Fluff. It's been a long time."

"Long time, Flinx-friend!" It was a mental boom. The massive Ujurrian trundled over to the red-haired young man and rested both massive paws on his shoulders. "Flinx-friend is well?"

"Very well, thank you." He was somewhat surprised to find that the mind-to-mind, human-to-Ujurrian communication was easier this time than it had been years ago, when he had first encountered Fluff's species on their Church-proscribed world. It was no longer difficult to understand.

Fluff nodded approvingly as two more giant Ujurrians popped out of the hole like ursinoid jack-in-the-boxes. Flinx recognized Bluebright and Moam. They examined their surroundings with the boundless curiosity of their kind.

"Flinx-friend's mind is clearing out. Not as much mud inside as before." Fluff tapped the side of his head with a fat finger.

Flinx gestured to his right. "That's my friend, Clarity."

Fluff started toward her, overflowing with gruff good feelings. "Hello, Clarity-friend." She backed away from him until she was flush against the wall. The Ujurrian halted and looked back at Flinx. "Why your friend frightened of Fluff?"

"It's not you, Fluff. It's your size."

"Oh-ho!" The Ujurrian promptly dropped to all fours. "This better, Clarity-friend?"

She hesitantly stepped away from the cold wall. "It's better." Her gaze rose, and she found Flinx watching her amusedly. "These are friends of yours?"

"Can't you tell by now?"

"But how did they get here? What are they?"

"They're Ujurrians. I think I mentioned them before."

"The world Under Edict, yes. That means nobody can get in or out."

"Apparently someone neglected to inform the Ujurrians of that. As to how they got here, I'm as interested as you are."

"Heard you." Bluebright's mental voice was as distinct from Fluff's as it was from Flinx's. "Her mindlight is bright."

Clarity frowned uncertainly. "What does that mean?"

"It means you have a strong mental aura. To the Ujurrians everything is like a light, brighter or darker to a varying degree. Don't be intimidated by their size. Oh, they're quite capable of taking a human being apart like a wooden toy, but we're old allies. And if it makes you feel better, they're mostly vegetarians. They don't like to eat anything that generates 'light.' "

Scrap cowered against Clarity's neck. It was the first time Flinx had ever seen a minidrag show fear. To the young flying snake, the Ujurrians' emotional auras must have appeared overpowering. Pip did not fear because she remembered.

"Heard you calling," Moam explained as he examined the unconscious forms scattered about the room. "Came fast as we could to offer help."

"Calling?" For a moment Flinx forgot Clarity. "I wasn't calling. I wasn't even conscious." He tried to recall what it had been like floating beneath the surface of the lake. Little remained of that memory, that fading mystic melody of thoughts suspended in morphogas.

"How did you people get here?" Clarity forced herself not to gaze into the black pit. "Flinx told me you made him a ship."

"A ship, yes," Fluff said proudly. "A *Teacher* for the teacher. For us, we don't like ships. Noisy and confining. We only built his because it fits the game."

"Game?" She turned back to Flinx. "What game?"

"The game of civilization." He spoke absently, still trying to remember. "The Ujurrians love games, so before I left Ulru-Ujurr I started teaching them that one. By the time the *Teacher* was finished they were getting very good at it. I can't imagine what stage they've reached by now."

"Like some parts of the game," Bluebright said. "Don't like others. Keep the parts we like, throw out the ones we don't."

"Very sensible. How's the tunnel digging coming along?"

"You aren't making any sense." Clarity couldn't disguise her confusion.

"It doesn't have to make sense. Listen and you'll learn a few things."

"Going very well," Fluff told him. "Still have many more tunnels to dig. Heard you calling. Decided to dig a new tunnel. Fastest digging we've ever done, but teacher was in trouble. Got here too late anyways maybe?''

"I'm okay." It was Flinx's turn to frown. If he had not known from experience what the Ujurrians were capable of, he could never have asked the next question. "Are you telling us that you *tunneled* here from Ulru-Ujurr?''

Fluff made a face. "Where else we tunnel from?''

Smiling to show he meant no offense even though he knew they could read the same thing in his mind, he said, "Clarity-friend is right. That doesn't make any sense."

The huge Ujurrian chuckled, his voice full of mock puzzlement. "Then how we get here? Was hard work, Flinx-friend, but also fun."

"That's it. I'm lost," Clarity mumbled.

"Not lost," Moam said earnestly, misunderstanding her thoughts as well as her words. "You start tunnel. Make bend here, then twist, then wrap around like so and so, and lo! There you are."

"I wonder if they 'tunnel' through space-plus or null-space," Flinx murmured in awe. "Or someplace else the theoretical mathematicians haven't invented yet. How did you find *me*? Can you tap into my specific thought signature across all those parsecs?''

"Wasn't easy," said Moam. "So we had somebody come and look."

Flinx's brow wrinkled. "Come and look? But who—"

A voice from behind made him jump. "Who you think?''

It was Maybeso, looking dour and distressed as always. Even for an Ujurrian, Maybeso was unique. His fellows thought him quite mad. If the inhabitants of Ulru-Ujurr were an anomaly among intelligent races, then Maybeso was the anomaly of anomalies.

"Hello, Maybeso."

"Good-bye, Flinx-friend." The giant ursinoid vanished as silently and mysteriously as he had appeared. He was not a talker.

Flinx saw Clarity staring. She had convinced herself she was beyond shock, but Maybeso's brief appearance had proved otherwise. "He goes where he wants," Flinx explained apologetically, "and he doesn't have to use a tunnel. Nobody knows how he does it, not even the other Ujurrians, and he doesn't tell. They think he's a little strange."

"Not strange. Mad." A fourth Ujurrian emerged from the bottomless pit in the center of the room. Looking like a cross between a grizzly bear and a lemur, Softsmooth plopped down on the floor and began cleaning herself. That was when Flinx noted the softly glowing rings each of them wore.

"These?" Bluebright responded to his inquiry. "Toys that help with the digging. We built your ship. We made these. All part of the game, yes?"

"Wait a minute. The other one." Clarity was gesturing weakly. "The one that appeared behind you, Flinx. Where did he come from? And where did he go?"

"Nobody knows where he comes from," Moam said, "and nobody knows where Maybeso goes."

"I think I'm beginning to understand," she said slowly, "why Ulru-Ujurr is under Church Edict."

"You have to keep in mind," Flinx told her, "that the Ujurrians are complete innocents. The AAnn were beginning illegal exploitation of their world when I showed up there. At that time the Ujurrians had no concept of civilization or modern technology or anything related to either. They lived and ate and mated and dug their tunnels. Playing the game, they called it. So I introduced them to a new game, the game of 'civilization.' It didn't take them very long to learn how to build a starship. That was my *Teacher*. I can't imagine what they've learned by now. How to make rings, apparently."

"How to have more fun!" Fluff roared. "Got here too late to help Flinx-friend—but not too late to have more fun. Had to find you, anyway. New element has entered the game. Very intriguing. You would say, 'Involves inexplicable astrophysical and mathematical metastasis.' "

"Maybe I wouldn't," Flinx said carefully.

"We ought to get out of here." Clarity was studying the stairway. "More of those fanatics might come looking for their friends."

"It doesn't matter anymore. There are Ujurrians here." He spoke to her, but he was thinking at Fluff. "What do you mean when you speak of a 'new element' in the game? I thought the rules I set down for you were fairly straightforward."

"Were, yes. You remember you also taught us that not everyone plays the game by the rules. You explained cheating. This is a kind of cheating."

Softsmooth took up the refrain, her mental voice distinctly feminine compared with that of the three big males. "You know we have always dug the tunnels, Flinx-friend. Found some interesting ideas for new tunnels in the information the cold minds left behind. Started a tunnel that way." She smiled, revealing long fangs and bone-crushing teeth. "We can dig all kinds of tunnels; dig through rock, through sand, through what you call spacetime."

"Fun to dig to other worlds," Moam commented. "Same world gets boring." He was inspecting one of the laser pistols Vandervort's bodyguards had dropped. Flinx was not worried. All Moam was interested in was the pistol's construction.

Softsmooth carried on. "Been digging many tunnels to other worlds." She indicated the empty pit. Flinx was careful not to go too close to the edge. If one fell in, there was no telling where and when one might stop.

"Dug tunnel to place your people call Horseye, natives call Tslamaina. Found an interesting thing there."

"Big machine," Moam put in. "Biggest machine we've seen ever." The usual feeling of frivolity was absent from his thought.

"Did some studying," Softsmooth continued. "After

a while something really very strange detected us studying and came to chase us away, but we left before it got
there.'' She smiled again. ''We can move quickly when
we have to, you know. Found smaller similar things all
linked to this one big thing on the Horseye world. Links
go like our tunnels, only a lot smaller.''

''What is horse?'' Fluff asked suddenly.

''A Terran quadruped,'' Flinx told him. ''They're no
longer common.''

''Too bad. Image is nice.''

''Shut up, Fluff,'' Softsmooth admonished him. ''I was
talking.''

''Don't tell me to shut up.''

They exchanged blows, the lightest of which would
have killed a large man instantly, before settling back
down as though nothing had happened. Clarity had run
to Flinx's side at the start of the fight, and he reluctantly
allowed her to remain next to him. His mind was clear,
but his emotions were in turmoil.

''Before the really very strange something arrived to
chase us away, we found out what the machine was all
about.''

''It's an alarm,'' Moam muttered. Flinx saw that he
was busily taking the laser pistol apart, his huge fingers
picking delicately at the internal circuitry.

''What kind of alarm?''

''To warn against something. Against a big danger.
Except that the people it was supposed to warn have all
gone away a long time ago.'' In Flinx's mind the mental
picture of ''long ago'' that Softsmooth was projecting
stretched into infinity. That was impressive, because the
Ujurrians never exaggerated.

''You said you had to find me, anyway. Because of
this?'' All four ursinoids nodded in unison. ''Why come
to me? I know nothing of a world called Horseye, much
less any weird machines on it.''

''You are the teacher,'' Fluff said simply. And then,
shockingly, ''Also because you are involved somehow.''

"Me?" Pip did a little hop on her master's shoulder before settling back down. "How can I be involved when this is the first I've heard of it?"

"The feeling is there." Even Fluff was now communicating with great seriousness. "You are the key to something, whether the machine or the danger or something else we do not yet know. We would like to know. It would help in the game. This danger worries us."

If it was real and it worried the Ujurrians, Flinx knew, then everyone else ought to be properly terrified. "Is the danger imminent?"

"Imminent?" wide-eyed Bluebright echoed.

"Is it going to strike soon?" Flinx inquired tiredly. In their innocence, the Ujurrians could instantly comprehend the most complex mechanical and mathematical concepts while simultaneously misunderstanding much simpler terms.

"Do not know. You must help us to understand this thing," Softsmooth said. "You are the teacher."

"I'm not a teacher!" he replied angrily. "I'm just a student. By now any one of you has more accumulated knowledge stored in your minds than I ever will."

"But you know the game," Fluff reminded him. "The game of civilization. That we are still learning."

"This is somehow part of the game," Bluebright said.

All four were staring at him, and he was unable to look into those vast yellow eyes and lie. Here it was again. Just when he was certain he was through with someone else's problems, another set materialized to take their place. If he insisted, they would go away and leave him alone. If he insisted.

They were pleading silently. It did him no good to turn away because that meant he had to look at Clarity, which was just as bad. There was no escape for him from himself. Not in this room, at this time, in this place. Maybe not anywhere, ever.

"I can't do anything to help," he said finally, "be-

cause I don't know anything about this. Can't you understand that?''

"Understand ignorance, Flinx-friend," Softsmooth
said without hesitation. "Can fix that.''

Flinx was taken aback. "How? By taking me to Horse-
eye?'' He eyed the black pit uneasily.

"No. Can show you a little, maybe. We cannot see it
ourselves but can help you to see. Will not be dangerous—hopefully.'' Fluff had come over to put a paw on
Flinx's shoulder. "We must know, Flinx-friend. Is important to us, too. It might be serious enough to stop the
game. To stop all games.''

Was there really anything to think about? Did he really
have any choice? Did he ever?

"How are you going to show me? Is this threat
nearby?''

"It is very, very far away. We can only guess where.
You will have to trust us. Teacher must trust his pupils.''

"If it's so far away, how can you show it to me?''

"The same way we found you here.'' A huge finger
pointed at his neck. Sensing the emotions directed her
way, Pip lifted her head curiously.

"Pip?''

"She is,'' Fluff struggled to frame a difficult concept,
"an amplifier for something deep inside you, inside your
mind. Something even we cannot see. Whatever it is that
lets you tell how others are feeling and may let you do
other things someday. We can help like that, a little. Your
small companion is an amplifier. We can be a preampli-
fier. A very, very big one.'' He tilted his head back to
regard the ceiling.

"Your body will stay here, but we can send your mind
elsewhere.''

"Elsewhere? Can't you be a little more specific?''

"Toward the threat, the danger. To observe and learn.
We cannot do it with ourselves, but we can do it with
you. Because you are different from us. Because you are
different from anyone else.''

The proportions of the Ujurrians' little problem were expanding far faster than he could keep pace with. "Why not just dig one of your tunnels in that direction?"

"Because it is too far. Unimaginably far."

"If it's unimaginably far, then how can it be dangerous to us?"

"It can move. It does not seem to be moving this way now, but we are not sure. We need to be sure." Fluff gazed fondly down at Flinx. "We would not force you, teacher."

"Oh, hell, I know that. Does it make a difference? Just make sure you don't lose track of me after you shoot me out to wherever it is I'm going." He took a long breath. "What do I have to do?"

"It might be a good thing for you to lie down, Flinx-friend, so you don't fall over and hurt yourself."

"Makes sense. If I'm going to engage in some kind of Ujurrian astral projection, or whatever, I wouldn't want to come out of it with a sprained wrist." As always, his sarcasm was lost on his hirsute friends, but it helped to mask a little of the fear that was beginning to surge within him.

He took a step toward the coffin, then quickly changed his mind. He was not going back in that thing. There were a couple of folding beds at the back of the room, and he chose the nearest, lying down after making sure Pip's coils were clear. He kept his arms at his sides, hoping he was not as stiff and uncomfortable as he must have looked.

"All right. What do I do now? Do you pick me up and throw me toward the ceiling?" He laughed nervously. Each of the Ujurrians stood at a corner of the bed. He could see Clarity between Fluff and Bluebright, eyeing him anxiously.

"Flinx? Maybe you shouldn't do this."

"Probably you're right. But I never have been able to do what was good for me. I always seem to end up doing what's best for others." He closed his eyes, wondering if it would make a difference. "Go ahead and do what you have to do, Fluff."

There was no transition, no delay. He was back in the lake, Pip alongside him. It was not what he had expected. Only this time he was not floating aimlessly. He was capable of movement. Experimentally he swam a few circles, Pip following. The transparent liquid did not pour down his nostrils and lungs to choke him.

By the time he had turned the fourth circle, the lake began to grow dark. He continued to swim and had the feeling he was traveling at great speed, yet his body hardly seemed to be moving at all. Hands and feet moved lazily while the cosmos rushed past.

Transparency and sunlight gave way to streaks of crimson and purple, as if his surroundings were Doppler-shifted to the extreme. Stars and nebulas exploded toward him, only to fade rapidly beneath his feet. An interesting illusion, but no more.

Is this what it feels like to be a quasar? he thought idly.

He would have liked to have lingered to study individual stars and planets. Like electric sparks, images of powerful races and immense galaxy-spanning civilizations impinged briefly on his consciousness and were gone. All were new and unknown, alien and unsuspected. His mind touched on theirs and then broke away, like a wave rising and falling on the shore.

Past the last sapient thought and still racing outward, now little more than a concept himself, a blemish on the precepts of conventional physics. Not a particle to his name, no more than an afterthought cast loose from the prison of the mind.

The stars were all gone by then, and the last of the sapience, and he found himself in a region that should not have existed. A place where vacuum was stained only by forgotten wisps of interstellar hydrogen and the oc-

*casional burning star core gleamed like a candle in a
bottle set afloat on an ocean of nothingness.*

And something else.

*Too big to be alive, and yet it lived. A roiling redefi-
nition of life and death, good and evil.*

*Even as the force that propelled him onward tried to
thrust him into its midst, he found himself slowing, re-
coiling. Whole civilizations he had touched, whole gal-
axies he had comprehended, but this was too vast and
too terrible for his disembodied self to understand. He
glimpsed its shadow and turned away, turned inward and
ran, fighting his way back along the path he had taken.*

*Even as he fled, it became aware of him. He tried to
accelerate, the universe a flat wash of laser-bright color
around him. Sluggish but immense, it reached for the
intruder—and missed. By a kilometer, a light-year, a galactic diameter—he would never know. All that mattered
was that it missed and left him untouched and unsullied
by what it was.*

*Back in upon himself he fled, at the last instant racing
past a great but confused mind that was more innocent
and ignorant even than the Ujurrians, an executor of still
greater potential. It was an expanding greenness, a pale
lime glazed on glass in which he saw himself and Clarity
and other humanity reflected. An emerald glue held it all
together. Then it was gone.*

*Replaced by still another, as different from its prede-
cessor as he was from it. Swimming in another part of
the same lake. When it raced by and touched him briefly,
he felt a great sense of peace. This second sapience was
warm and friendly and even apologetic. It was there, and
then it was gone the way of the greenness.*

*Third and lightest touch of all from a consciousness he
finally recognized. A lonely calling. Not at all what one
would expect from an artificial intelligence. Far out past
the edge of the Commonwealth, in the Blight. A weapon
and an instrument all at once, waiting for him to return*

*and direct it, blend with it, give purpose to its existence
even though all the old enemies were gone.*

*What now of enemies new? What of those who had
built the great warning network centered on Horseye?
Whence had they gone and why? None knew. The Ujurrians wanted to know. So did Flinx.*

*It hit him hard then. He was needed. Because he was
an offshoot, a sport, a freak. One those who had built
the alarm could not have foreseen. Just as they could not
have foreseen the evolution of the greenness, the warmth,
and the Tar-Aiym engine of destruction that cried in its
loneliness. They had built the alarm to warn them of an
inconceivable threat on the farthest fringes of existence
and had probably fled because they had not been able to
find a way to deal with it.*

*But the unforeseen had followed them. Life had
emerged and evolved beyond what they might have anticipated. Or had they anticipated it, anticipated everything, and left the alarm to warn whatever, whoever might
come in after them? The green, the warm, and the
weapon.*

*Only one thing they could not possibly have antici-
pated: a nineteen-year-old named Flinx.*

*It was possible that the Ujurrians had sensed this. How,
he could not imagine, but the ursinoids were capable of
much they themselves did not understand. Like Maybeso,
who could teleport when and wherever he wanted to but
would not do anything on request and was probably insane to boot.*

*So much happening all at once, and himself in the mid-
dle of it all. There was responsibility here he could not
evade. Whatever threatened him threatened sapience everywhere. The great civilizations he had sensed in passing, the intelligences still fighting to emerge from the
primordial ooze, the greenness, the warmth, and the
weapon that sang. And the Commonwealth, his Commonwealth. Mankind, thranx, everyone and everything.*

The vastness he had scraped with his sanity was be-

stirring itself. Preparing to move, though not for a long while. Long in his time or galactic time? He found he did not know. It was something he was going to have to find out.

Which made a great deal of sense. Was he not a student? He would have the help of the Ujurrians, and of his old mentors if he could find them. And he would go out again, beyond normal space, for additional looks. He would go because he was the only one who could. Something would have to be done about what he had detected, if not in this lifetime, then in another. Those who had constructed the warning system had thought so, too.

When he woke up, he was swimming in his own sweat. Pip lay spraddled across his chest, wings spread and limp, utterly exhausted. Four tired Ujurrians were staring concernedly down at him, along with one haggard human.

Clarity took his hand and pressed it to her chest, blinking away tears. Scrap still clung to her shoulder and neck.

As near as he could tell, he had not moved. But when he tried to sit up, nothing happened. Every muscle, every bone in his body ached.

"That was," he whispered, "exhilarating. Also frightening and informative."

Clarity put down his hand to wipe at her eyes and nose. "I thought you were dying. You lay there all peaceful-like, this wonderful contented expression on your face, and suddenly you started screaming."

He frowned. "I don't remember screaming."

"You screamed," she assured him, "and you arched and twisted until I thought you were going to break your arms. Your friends had to hold you down."

"Not so easy," Bluebright murmured. "Wouldn't think so much strength in teacher's little body."

"I was close to it," Flinx said suddenly, remembering. "Too close." He did not have to explain himself to the Ujurrians, who could see it in his mind, but Clarity possessed no such perception. "There's something out there," he told her calmly.

"Out where? Near Gorisa?"

"No. Out—there. Beyond the Commonwealth. Beyond our galaxy. Beyond the beyond, I guess. I don't know how, but they"—He indicated the silently watching Ujurrians.—"and Pip combined to send part of me out past the range of the best visual telescopes. But not the radioscopes. I think they've seen it, though the people reading the data have no idea what they're looking at. I'm not sure what it was, either. Only that it's dangerous. And big. Beyond beyond, and beyond big."

Fluff was somber. "No fun this. Serious game."

"Yes, serious game," Flinx agreed.

"What we do now, Flinx-friend-teacher?" Moam wondered.

"We try to learn more. There are others involved. Not just me and you, but others none of us have suspected. I have to find out about them, too. It's going to take work and time. I don't mind the work. I hope we have the time. I'm going to need your help."

"Always, Flinx-friend." The four spoke with a single mental voice.

"I wish you'd talk out loud."

He turned to Clarity, aware he had been engaging in purely telepathic exchange with the Ujurrians. "I've found out what I'm going to do with my life. I thought I was destined to wander aimlessly, acquiring knowledge without purpose. Now I have a purpose. Out there is an empty place. By the laws that regulate the distribution of matter in the universe, it shouldn't exist. But it does, and there's something in the middle of it. Something evil. I'm going to try to find a way to deal with it if it starts moving in this direction. In the process maybe I'll become a complete human being."

"You *are* a complete human being, dammit!"

He smiled gently. "Clarity, I'm nineteen. No nineteen-year-old is a complete human being."

"Are you making fun of me?"

"No, I'm not." Softsmooth gave him a hand up from the bed. Pip had barely enough strength to cling to his shoulder. Her pointed tongue hung limply from her mouth.

"I need a drink. Something cold." For the first time, he noticed the empty room. "Where is everyone?"

"They woke up one at a time," Clarity explained. She nodded at the place on the floor where Dabis had been lying. "That one came around before any of the others. The first thing he saw was Bluebright holding his disassembled pistol."

"They all left in a hurry," Moam said. "We would have talked with them, but their minds were confused and full of fear."

"I bet they left in a hurry." Flinx turned to Fluff. "What will you do now?"

"Go back to learning the civilization game."

"Good. I'll try to learn some of the new rules. Then I'll get in touch with you."

Fluff clapped his paws together, filling the room with a dull boom. "Wonderful! We make a new game of it. Maybe not so serious then."

"We'll try," Flinx told him. "I have studying to do. I have to learn, and to grow."

"We'll find you again when it's time." Softsmooth put an arm around his shoulders that nearly hid him from view and gave him an affectionate hug. The vertebrae in his neck cracked softly. "Never lose track of Flinx-friend-teacher. Can always ask Maybeso to find you."

"Yes. I wish Maybeso was here."

As if on command, the fifth Ujurrian popped into view. His perpetually sour expression had not changed. "Here," he grunted.

"Anything to add to all this?" Flinx asked him. He knew he did not have to explain what he meant by 'all this.' With Maybeso nothing needed to be explained.

"Later," Maybeso said brusquely, and vanished.

"That is one strange being," Flinx murmured admiringly.

"Very strange," Softsmooth agreed. "I think he like you, but who can tell?"

Flinx glanced at the stairs. "I don't think any of the people who were here will be coming back."

Clarity had to smile. "You wouldn't think men that big could move that fast."

"We'll talk later, then."

The four Ujurrians formed a circle around him and put their paws lightly on his hands. "Later," they said in unison.

They turned and jumped into the hole in the middle of the floor. He heard their minds bidding him farewell, listened until the last had faded from his consciousness.

Several minutes passed. Then the ground heaved as if the building had been kicked from below. Rock and dirt oozed up into the pit. Flinx and Clarity raced for the stairs and stayed there until the dust began to settle.

"Filled in the tunnel behind them," he observed thoughtfully. "Good idea. You don't want to leave something like that standing open for someone to fall into." He turned to Clarity. "Now you're going to ask me to take you with me wherever I'm going because you think you love me."

"I don't think it," she told him. "I know that I love you."

He shook his head slowly. "Sorry, but I think I've got it right. You think you love me. You're intrigued by me, and you might even find me attractive. But you must see that you can't come with me."

His rejection made her flinch. "You still don't trust me. That's it, isn't it? After what I did, I can't blame you. But that's all over and behind us now. I see you the way I first saw you, for what you really are."

"Do you? That's very interesting, because *I* don't see me for what I really am. I spent a long time trying to find out who my parents were. That didn't turn out so well. Maybe I'll have better luck finding out who I am. But that's not the reason you can't come with me. I can't take you along because I don't know what's going to happen to me. Isn't it strange, but I find myself siding with old Vandervort, after all.

"There are things at stake here that make individual relationships pale into insignificance. I'm going to have to devote all my time to understanding them. That wouldn't be fair to another person. Especially someone like you. I guarantee that after spending a few years moving incognito from world to world, studying obscure references in files, and accumulating arcane knowledge, you'd become deathly bored. I may myself, but I have no choice. I have to do it. You don't.

"There are other worlds to visit, other challenging jobs in your own profession."

"I don't care about that anymore." She was trying very hard not to cry, he saw.

"Maybe not right now you don't, but you will. There are other men out there, most of them more mature than I. Probably better-looking, certainly less mentally burdened. You can be happy with one of them, or two, or three, or however many men you eventually choose to sample. Happier than you could ever be with me. I'm not prescient, but I think I can promise you that much." He carefully wiped away the beginning tears.

"I think Scrap's taken a permanent liking to you. He'll be a good companion, and he'll certainly help you weed out the better men from the rest." He grinned. "The independent woman's ideal accessory. Protection and affection all rolled up in one scaly little package. Goodbye, Scrap."

He extended a finger toward the minidrag. Scrap could not understand the gesture, but he could feel the emotion of the moment. His pointed tongue flicked out several times to touch the warm human skin.

"We're peculiar creatures, we humans. The builders of the alarm didn't predict us. There's a lot out there they didn't foresee. Some of it I saw. I can't tell you any more about it now because I don't know any more than that myself. Evolution has a way of defeating the most advanced methods of predicting the future. In this case that may be for the better.'' He turned to go up the stairs.

"Flinx, wait! You can't just leave me like this. You can't just leave me *here*."

He hesitated. "You're right. You have no place to go, do you? No telling what kind of lies your ex-supervisor is going to spread about you as she tries to save her own skin from the Scarpanians. Let's see—you know she sold out Coldstripe. I think the company's backers would be interested in that information. Might even have a job for you somewhere else. You contact them and explain things, and I'll bet they keep you safe from Vandervort. There are ways to check the truth of your statements— and hers.'' Suddenly he sounded wistful.

"It's all part of the game, isn't it? Civilization. We spend our lives playing at it. I think what's happened to me is that I've just graduated to the next level. Keep at your gengineering, Clarity, and maybe one day you'll even be able to help me understand me better.''

He reached down to her, and she took his hand. Together they ascended the stairs.

"I'll help in any way I can,'' she told him when they reached the deserted outer office. "I'll do whatever you recommend.''

"Whatever you do, do it for yourself, not for me.'' He stood there, thinking to himself. "This warning system has been in place for more than a few years, and I think we have a little time at least before the threat it's monitoring requires our undivided attention. In order to understand it properly, I first have to understand myself, and in order to understand myself, I need to learn about my own kind. I can't promise you any kind of permanent relationship, but now that I think about it, I don't see any reason why you can't assist in my studies.'' He hesitated. "That is, if you're interested.''

She stared at him for a long time before shaking her head slowly. "Just when I think I've got you figured out, I have to dump everything I think I've learned and start in all over again."

"If it's that complicated for you, consider how frightening it must be for me," he told her somberly.

Clarity was delighted by his change of heart and content to stay with him for as long as he would allow, but no matter how enjoyable their time together might be, she knew she would never be able to put that last thought out of her mind.

DON'T MISS THE PREVIOUS
ADVENTURES OF
FLINX OF THE COMMONWEALTH

Commonwealth Chronology

(NOTE: Where "c" is used, the date given is approximate.)

1 billion B.C.	The Xunca are at their height. They discover something connected with the Great Emptiness and begin setting up their transmitter network.
400,000,000	The Xunca create the Groalamason Ocean on Horseye and modify the orbits of the planet's moons. They set up a transmitting station in the polar ice cap. A minor relay station is set up on Terra, but is destroyed by continental drift. A Mutable is stationed on every planet set up with a component of the system.
950,000	Hur'rikku begin to explore from the Galactic Center.
501,000	The Vom arrives on the last world it will devour. It has destroyed all life on about a thousand worlds.
500,000	The Tar-Aiym Empire is at its height. The Vom, contacted by the Tar-Aiym,

panics and destroys the investigating fleet. The Tar-Aiym send a robot fleet to contain the Vom. Peot becomes the Guardian and is placed in orbit around the Vom's planet.

499,000   Tar-Aiym contact the Hur'rikku; war is begun.

480,000   After enduring several attempts to be forced into the Tar Aiym Empire, the Hur'rikku threaten to use their anti-collapsar weapon on Tar-Aiym worlds. The Tar-Aiym begin intensive weapons research. The Krang is built on Booster. The fleet guarding the Vom is called away to help in the war with the Hur'rikku, leaving only a few ships and the Guardian.

479,000   "Living" photonic storm, released by the Tar-Aiym as a plague, decimates all intelligent life in the area, including the Tar-Aiym and Hur'rikku. A dying race on the edge of the plague area broadcasts a warning, so an informal quarantine is created. This area becomes the Blight.

97,000   Alaspinian civilization is at its height. Alaspinians explore more space than that contained by the Commonwealth, but don't establish settlements.

75,000   Alaspinians die out, possibly by racial suicide.

27,000   Most recent warm cycle begins on Tran-ky-ky.

17,000   Warm cycle ends and present cold cycle begins on Tran-ky-ky.

10,950   Tunnelling begins on Ulru-Ujurr.
c8000   Thranx civilization is born on Hive-

	hom. The "Eternal City" of Daret is founded.
c6000	The last wars are fought on Hivehom.
c5700	Human civilization is born on Terra.
c2000	The Priory of the Brotherhood "Evonin-taban" on Tran-ky-ky is established.
A.D.	(Anno Domini), Christian religion calendar change occurs on Terra.
c500	Temple of Moraung Motau is founded on Horseye.
c1800	Thranx achieve space travel.
c1900	Thranx discover posigravity drive.
c2000	Terrans achieve space travel. All killing of Cetacea is outlawed.
c2075	Off-course Terran "sleeper" colony ship reaches Centaurus System. Planets III and V are colonized.
c2100	Thranx have first contact with AAnn.
c2200	Off-course Terran "sleeper" colony ship reaches MIDWORLD.
2243	AAnn attack Paszex on Willow-Wane for the first time.
2270	Brain-enhancement serum is discovered.
2280	Posigravity drive is discovered on Terra by Alex Kurita and Sumako Kinoshita. The Centaurus System colonies are rediscovered.
2290	Cachalot is discovered. Ryozenzuzex is born on Willow-Wane.
2300	Covenant of Peace enacted; Agreement of Transfer made. Transfer of Cetacea to Cachalot.
2310	The Terran exporation ship *Seeker* is attacked by the AAnn, rescued by the Thranx ship *Zinramm* and taken to Hivehom. A mysterious message from

	Capt. Brohwelporvot sends Ryozen-zuzex on a journey to Hivehom to see the aliens.
2311	The Humans escape captivity on Hivehom and return to CENTAURUS VII, taking Ryo with them.
2312	The Humans and Ryo set up the Project on Willow-Wane.
2316	The Project is revealed to the general populace.
2320	Transfer of Cetacea to Cachalot is completed.
2340	First treaties between Humans and Thranx are signed.
c2350	Moth is discovered.
2360	First contact is made with Pitar. Terran-norm planet in the Pitar System is colonized.
2365	Destruction of Treetrunk (Argus V) by Pitar occurs. The Humanx-Pitar War begins.
2367	Humanx teams invent the SCCAM Missile and make major breakthroughs in improving the posigravity drive. SCCAM missiles are used in breaking the blockade around the Pitar worlds.
2368	End of the War brings the destruction of the Pitar Homeworlds.
A.A.	A.A. (After Amalgamation) - (NOTE: 0 A.A. corresponds to 2400 A.D.)
0	The Articles of Amalgamation are signed and the Commonwealth is created.
1	Commonwealth Council meets for the first time on Terra.
2	Commonwealth Council meets for the first time on Hivehom.

c10	Commonwealth Science Headquarters is established in Mexico City.
c20	The Universal Church is created, with the Terran island of Bali becoming the Church Headquarters.
c88	Alaspin is discovered.
c95	Horseye is discovered by Terrans.
c99	The Thranx build and inhabit Steamer Station on Horseye.
c100	Krigsvird-ty-Kalstund founds the Castle of Wannome on the island of Sofold on Tran-ky-ky. First contact occurs between the Commonwealth and the Quillp.
106	Eitienne and Lyra Redowl arrive on Horseye, and after five months start their trip up the Skar River where they discover the City of the Dead.
c150	Brisbane, Australia, becomes the capitol of Terra.
c175	The first human settlers arrive on Cachalot. CunsnuC begins developing a mind-control polyp.
c300	The Blight is discovered as survey ships do preliminary mapping. RNGC 1632 (Cannachanna) is discovered by a Visarian probe.
c350	Dis is discovered.
c361	Surfing contest on Dis is established.
448	Mother Mastiff is born on Moth.
450	Truzenzuzex is born on Willow-Wane. The Horde begins taking tribute from Sofold on Tran-ky-ky.
470	Knigta Yakus is born.
474	Bran Tse-Mallory is born.
498	Commonwealth Probe discovers a collapsar near the Velvet Dam. Skua

	September is born. The Meliorare Society is founded on Terra.
c500	Repler System is discovered by Johannes Repler. The AAnn Empire contests the claim and is eventually granted a small concession on Repler III. AAnn attack on the Quillp colony planet of Goodhunting is foiled by a Commonwealth Task Force.
511	Anasage (Flinx's mother) is born on Terra.
515	Tran-ky-ky is discovered. Humanx outpost of Brass Monkey is founded on the island of Arsudun. Lord Estes Dominic Rose begins his first drug dealings. Lumpjaw is born on Cachalot.
518	Ethan Frome Fortune is born. Lauren Walder is born on Moth.
c525	Skua and Sawbill September break forever over Sawbill's becoming an emoman. Skua's lover is destroyed by Sawbill's drugs.
527	The Analava System War results in 120 million killed. Skua September may have been involved in the start of the war. Flinx's sister, Teleen, is born.
530	Meliorare Society is broken up: the most ''normal'' subjects are scattered across the Commonwealth.
532	Kitten Kai-sung is born.
533	Phillip Lynx (Flinx) is born. Joao Acorizal wins surfing contest on Dis.
537	Anasage dies. Truzenzuzex and Bran Tse-Mallory begin jointly researching the Tar-Aiym.
538	Skua September attempts to buy Flinx, but fails. Mother Mastiff does

buy him. Flinx finds his pet Minidrag, Pip.

540   Mahnahmi is born.

543   Rashalleila Nuaman finances the building of an illegal research station on Midworld.

545   Hyperion Trees on Annubis are destroyed. Station on Midworld is destroyed by natives.

546   Agreement between Nuaman Enterprises and the AAnn Empire results in the building of an illegal station on Ulru-Ujurr. First Janus Jewels are mined and put on the market.

548   Attempted kidnapping of the duKanes fails; lifeboat crashes near Sofold on Tran-ky-ky. Planet Booster and the Krang are found by a prospector in the Blight. Isili Hasboga begins prospecting in Mimmisompo on Alaspin; Habib and Pocomchi arrive on the planet. Sawbill September works as an emoman on Thalia Major. Mother Mastiff is kidnapped by the Meliorare Society. Cruachan dies and the final destruction of the Meliorares occurs.

549   Expedition to the Blight investigates the Krang. Flinx discovers its function. The nomadic Horde on Tran-ky-ky is destroyed.

550   Rashalleila Nuaman dies. Flinx meets Sylzenzuzex. He breaks a Church Edict by traveling to Ulru-Ujurr. He solves the mystery of the Janus Jewels, and discovers his parentage. Ujurrians begin "Game of Civilization." Teleen Rudanuaman is killed. The Slanderscree arrives in Brass

	Monkey. The duKanes leave Tran-ky-ky. Ethan Fortune, Skua September, and Milliken Williams leave Brass Monkey to form the Union of Ice.
551	Flinx travels to Alaspin. Habib and Pocomchi die. Expedition to the Cannachanna System in the Blight discovers the Anticollapsar Weapon.
552	Hur'rikku weapon creates a ''rainbow star'' from the collapsar near the Velvet Dam. Flinx returns to Moth. He meets Knigta Yakus, and accompanies him to a Hallowseye mine in Dead-Place-On-Map.
553	Flinx travels to Alaspin to release the young Minidrags. He rescues Clarity Held and accompanies her to Longtunnel. The Sumacrea are discovered. Flinx decides on his mission in life.
555	AAnn explorers in the Blight discover the Vom and transport it to Repler III. The Vom is destroyed by the Tar-Aiym Guardian and Flinx.
600	Five floating towns on Cachalot are destroyed by whales. An investigation leads to the discovery of the CunsnuC.
c1530	Light from the Rainbow Star reaches Midworld.
12,550	Tunnel digging ends on Ulru-Ujurr. The planet shifts to a closer orbit of its sun.
c13,000	Current cold cycle ends; new warm cycle begins on Tran-ky-ky.

About the Author

Born in New York City in 1946, Alan Dean Foster was raised in Los Angeles, California. After receiving a bachelor's degree in political science and a Master of Fine Arts in motion pictures from UCLA in 1968–69, he worked for two years as a public relations copywriter in a small Studio City, California, firm.

His writing career began in 1968 when August Derleth bought a long letter of Foster's and published it as a short story in his biannual *Arkham Collector Magazine*. Sales of short fiction to other magazines followed. His first try at a novel, *The Tar-Aiym Krang*, was published by Ballantine Books in 1972.

Foster has toured extensively around the world. Besides traveling, he enjoys classical and rock music, old films, basketball, body surfing, and weight-lifting. He has taught screenwriting, literature, and film history at UCLA and Los Angeles City College.

Currently, he resides in Arizona.

By
ALAN DEAN FOSTER